"Faith, 'tis my angel!"
he murmured in disbelief. For this lovely piquant face that looked up at him half-expectantly, half-arrogantly, was the face he thought he'd dreamed. Those wide Delft-blue eyes with their dark-rimmed irises, shadowed by long dark lashes, were those that had looked down into his own that night he'd lain half-drowned on a strange beach. Those softly curving lips that smiled provocatively at him now had then been a straight worried line, and those wings of brows now so slightly lifted, perhaps by disdain, had been lost in a curtain of long tumbled hair that had streamed down, fair and wet as a mermaid's.

Stephen Linnington, the rake who had held so many women lightly in his arms and had left them all, looked into those lovely blue eyes and was lost. He seized her hand in his strong fingers and swept her away without asking into the dance.

Looking up at the stranger, Imogene, too, remembered that moment on the beach and trembled partly from her intense response to him and partly from the memory of the terrifying dream she'd had the night of his rescue . . .

Novels by Valerie Sherwood

This Loving Torment
These Golden Pleasures
This Towering Passion
Her Shining Splendor
Bold Breathless Love

Published by
WARNER BOOKS

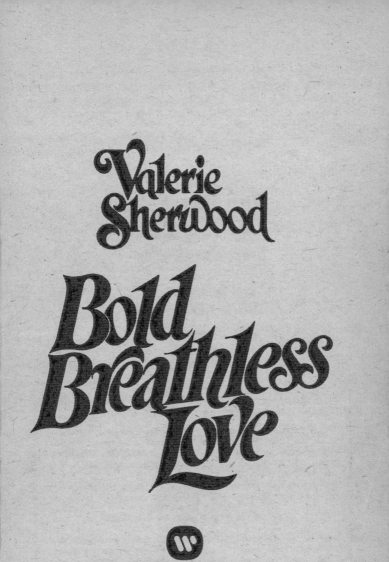

Valerie Sherwood

Bold Breathless Love

WARNER BOOKS

A Warner Communications Company

WARNING

Readers are hereby specifically warned not to use any medications or cosmetics or exotic food or drink mentioned herein without first consulting a doctor. For example, the cosmetic ceruse contains white lead, which is lethal—even so, it was a popular cosmetic of the day and widely used!

Valerie Sherwood

WARNER BOOKS EDITION

Copyright© 1981 by Valerie Sherwood
All rights reserved.

Cover Art by Elaine Duillo

Warner Books, Inc.. 75 Rockefeller Plaza, New York, N.Y. 10019

A Warner Communications Company

Printed in the United States of America

First Printing: August, 1981

10 9 8 7 6 5 4 3 2 1

DEDICATION

In loving memory of Silk, my lovely long-haired cat, big, gentle Silk with his thick shining black fur and clear green trusting eyes and great plumelike tail—Silk, who curled up and slept confidently by my typewriter no matter how it thundered.

Author's Note

Although this novel is entirely a work of fiction and all the characters and situations herein are of my own invention (save for obvious historical events, or personages such as Peter Stuyvesant), insofar as possible the places are either real or typical of their place and time. There really *is* a Star Castle in the Scilly Isles and a Castle of Ennor, there really are two tall standing stones there called Adam and Eve, New Amsterdam really had its Perel Straat and its windmill, and magnificent Wey Gat was suggested to me by a photograph of a multichimneyed stone house that to this day frowns down upon the Hudson.

And because this novel is a toast to a romantic world that is gone, it seemed appropriate to propose a toast to match each section. And as you join me for a little while in the turbulent, swashbuckling 1600s—a world where water spilled clean and sparkling down the brooks and the air was bracing as wine and whole continents waited to be explored and conquered—as you share with me the fabled Hudson Valley of the early Dutch settlers from quaint New Amsterdam to far Wey Gat, as you sail with me from the flower-filled Scillies to wealthy Holland and across the scented waters of the Spanish Main to Barbados and Tortuga and other sunny isles where fair women awaited their lean adventurers, let me propose another toast:

> A toast to the wayward, the jaded,
> The willful, the winsome, the lost,
> Whose memory ne'er will be faded,
> For they loved—and cared not for the cost!

Valerie Sherwood

Contents

Bold Breathless Love

A toast to the girl-turned-woman
Whose "great marriage" is a sham,
For she would be hardly human
If she did not desire a man

Prologue
The North River, 1658

Rising in the moonlight from the river's snow-covered eastern bank, the steep-roofed, high-chimneyed hulk of the half-completed great house frowned down the low bluff, silently warning all who plied the river that this was Wey Gat, the Wind Gate, stronghold of the great patroon Verhulst van Rappard, wealthiest man in all New Netherland.

No lights shone from the big stone structure, for even the kitchen servants had long since gone to bed. But behind the dark window of a second-floor bedchamber a thin young man, richly dressed in black and gold in the somber Dutch style, watched with narrowed eyes through the small frosted panes.

His lip curled as he thought of the maidservant Elise, whom he had personally bound and gagged and thrust into a tiny dressing room, hardly larger than a closet, down the hall. *She* at least would not be able to circumvent this night's work!

Now he leaned forward, straining to see through the wind-swept darkness. Did he see—? Yes! A figure had slipped from the house. There she was . . . Imogene, darkly cloaked and with a sable-lined blue velvet French hood obscuring her riotous golden curls. She had slipped out through a side door and was furtively making her way through the snow down the steep slope toward the sheet of gray ice that was the river.

His young wife, Imogene, on her way to meet her lover.

Van Rappard swallowed. God, how graceful she was, moving through the snow. How the rich cloak billowed about her as she swayed like a reed against the wind. Even at this distance her loveliness could still strike him like a physical blow; that this should be so made his thin elegant body tremble with fury. This night, *this night* he would teach his reckless English bride a terrible lesson.

Anger roiled in him as he watched her dainty progress down the slope. He had given Imogene everything—everything! Except one thing, of course. He had not pleasured her in *that* way. But jewels, lavish laces, imported silks, rich velvets, fine furs, servants—true, they all spoke Dutch, which Imogene did not, but they had all been hers to command. He had even imported a virginal from Holland for her to play (she had refused to do more than run her fingers listlessly across the keyboard) and one of the new blue and white tea sets from China (preferring coffee, she had not bothered to unpack it). And was he not building for her a great stone house finer than any on the river?

Yet here before his very eyes the faithless jade was slipping down through the snow to meet her lover and run away with him! She, the wife of a patroon! The black-and-gold-clad figure shook in a great burst of fury. Verhulst was totally unaware that he was cursing Imogene in a low bestial rumbling undertone that would have made a listener's hair stand on end.

Terrible visions were flitting through the young patroon's

dark head. In his imagination he could see Imogene strolling through a forest glade with Stephen Linnington—for all these months past he had known his rival's name. He could hear jays and bobolinks singing overhead and—so vivid was the vision— he could feel the heat of the sun as it struck down through a canopy of rustling green. Could hear Imogene's soft sigh and see her give the tall Englishman—for Verhulst's spies in New Amsterdam had reported the Englishman was tall and copper- haired and well favored and wore his hat at a jaunty angle—a long languorous look and sink down among the wild flowers and soft summer-grasses. There, in a pattern of light and shade that made her seem half witch, half woman, she unloosed her golden hair and then the hooks of her bodice, her fingers moving in a tantalizingly hesitant way, fluttering over each as if she could not make up her mind whether to undo that hook or no.

In the holocaust of his mind Verhulst could see Stephen Linnington's turquoise eyes light up as his gorgeous lady shrugged gracefully out of her tight bodice and then her fragile lacy chemise so that her fair white body rose up before him like Venus from the foam. Then she lounged back with another soft tantalizing sigh into the grasses, the gleaming mounds of her pink-tipped breasts rising up to taunt him.

She looked—*as she had looked through the keyhole when Verhulst had watched her disrobe nights here at Wey Gat! Watched and been afraid to enter, watched and felt a pain that caught and twisted in his groin but which he knew from bitter experience would come to naught. How many nights he had watched her standing there in her bedchamber in the candle- light, a magnificent woman, pale as the dawn, with her thick golden hair falling in a silky cloud down around her torso to caress her gleaming hips. He had watched, breathless, as she had strolled to the open casements on summer nights and stretched out her arms to the moon.* Was she making a wish? he had asked himself. And—the thought struck at him painfully—*was that wish for a lover?* And he who owned her, possessed her as a husband must his wife, he the patroon who ruled these broad river acres as any feudal lord—he had pressed his damp forehead against the door in the darkness, clenched his sweaty hands with their heavy rings, and admitted the truth to himself.

Whatever else he could be to this bewitching golden temptress, he could never be her lover. Since his early teens he had known he would never be a man as other men. That childhood accident with the iceboat had done for his manhood—yet left him eaten up with desire. He wanted the woman in that bedroom next door, wanted her with a passion and fury he would not admit even to himself, that woman who was his by right and law, and who was separated from him only by an oaken door to which he had the key.

Always his hand would tremble on the latch—and always it would withdraw.

For the young patroon was separated from his English bride by more than an oaken door. He was separated from her by a wall of fear and pride. Fear that she would learn his secret and despise him. Pride—desperate pride—that kept him from letting anyone understand him.

Now, cut off from human sympathy, alone in his aching world, a groan rose from deep within his tortured body. For the searing visions that rode his heart in gripping nightmarish fashion were with him again and he was seeing that imaginary woodland glade once more.

In Verhulst's burning imagination, Imogene was entirely stripped now. Her naked body lay invitingly relaxed, arms outflung, one knee bent. Verhulst's face contorted as his mind envisioned that silvered knee. She was looking up at the Englishman through dark, shadowed lashes. And now Stephen Linnington was naked too and he had fallen upon her. He was ravishing her! With inner agony the young patroon watched those demonically beautiful pictures flit by in his mind. There in that woodland Eden, Stephen's bright hair fell in a copper shower to mingle with the girl's tossing golden tresses. For a moment the ropy muscles of the man's back, the pale gleam of his naked buttocks obscured Verhulst's sight of the girl. Then he moved, luxuriously, and Verhulst could see that he was caressing her lovely naked body with strong, exploring hands, teasing, stroking—Verhulst in his agony could see her slight convulsive movements as the pressure within her built. Now . . . now he was nuzzling her trembling breasts with his lips. Now—oh, God, now he was entering her and she moaned as she received him. Verhulst could see the flash of her white legs, silvered by the rippling light, as they slipped alongside the Englishman's strongly muscled limbs, flailed weakly—and relaxed in abandonment. Her slender arms, wound around Stephen's neck, tightened as she surrendered herself completely, utterly. Through a red film Verhulst could see their bodies blending, arching, moving to some silent inner music that he would never know, moving to a beat that drummed and heightened to a frantic pace as the rapt pair strained and tumbled on the grass.

Verhulst, alone in the night at that window above the icy river, choked sobbingly. Heat like a fever surged through his blood and great beads of sweat stood out on his swarthy brow.

It had all happened! He was sure of it! All this time she had been deceiving him, laughing at him. And in the carved hickory cradle in a room down the hall was the living proof of Imogene's unfaith! The child had been christened Georgiana van Rappard, but she was not his—could not be his. Verhulst had never had a woman—any woman. God knew he had striven with chambermaids and dairymaids and strumpets from New Amsterdam's docks, but it had all come to nothing, he was unable. Those foolish wenches, with their sleek bare bodies, who had dared to laugh at him, he had struck with savage force across the face, splitting their scornful lips so that they spurted blood.

What Imogene had told him at first was a lie. The child was *not* premature. He had *not* come to her room drunk and taken her by force!

He had never taken anyone—by force or otherwise.

With his hands twisted cruelly in her hair, she had admitted the truth at last and named her lover. But she had insisted he was dead and no threat to Verhulst.

He had believed her. And now she was attempting to run away with that lover!

Sweat glazed the young patroon's forehead now as he returned from his searing private dreams to the stark winter of reality. He crouched forward, pressing his nose against the cold pane, the better to view the woman moving down the slope below. He could see that she had swept up skirts and cloak. Impeded by the snow, she was trying to run, and her slight figure, bent against the wind, cast a long blue shadow across the white moonlit expanse as she made her silent way toward the gray glimmer of the frozen river. The young patroon studied the cloak and hood of that flitting figure with bitter irony. He had ordered both for her from Paris as one of his marriage gifts to her. Lavishly embroidered, the cloak was lined with sable and had buttons of pure gold from neck to hemline. That rogue she had lain with—and whom she now slipped out furtively to meet—would give her no such cloaks, he told himself savagely.

His face contorted and then cleared, leaving it bleak. The rogue she had lain with would buy no cloaks for anyone after tonight. For Verhulst had spent those hours as he waited for

Imogene to make her move in devising a variety of horrible lingering deaths for Stephen Linnington. He would make Imogene watch. It would be a valuable lesson for the young wife he had brought from across the sea to Wey Gat. Those innocent-looking, snow-laden trees and dark clumps of bushes near the bank concealed his men, waiting patiently and half-frozen for him to give the signal to spread out and take the happy couple into custody. And then he, Verhulst, would part them—this time forever. Although there was a pistol stuck in his own broad belt, he had given orders that no firearms were to be carried by his men this night, for he wanted no quick death for the imprudent Englishman. He wanted to drag out his triumph, to savor it. He was the patroon; over these vast acres, stretching ever away, he held sole sway. At Wey Gat, he told himself, fingering the pistol lovingly, *he* was the law—he alone.

Now he frowned. Imogene's dark flitting shape, wind-whipped, had disappeared behind a tree, she had vanished temporarily from his view. Ah, there she was—he felt relief as the cloaked figure stepped out from behind the sheltering bole of a tree and cast a swift look back at the blank windows of the dark house on the bluff. She would see nothing, nothing, he told himself almost with delight, for his men lying in ambush well knew they would feel the patroon's wrath if they robbed him of his pleasure in tormenting her.

Imogene had reached the river's edge now. Suddenly she stiffened as she saw a movement on the ice. Verhulst saw it at the same moment—a dark shape, reddish in the moon's glow—a fox, crossing the frozen river by night. He wondered that the dogs—that fierce pack of hunting dogs trained to hunt men—did not see the fox and set up a baying. Then it came to him that Groot, who was Wey Gat's kennelmaster, would have the dogs well secreted in the brush along the bank so they would not warn the approaching Englishman. His orders had been to have the dogs waiting downriver to the south—in case the Englishman escaped him.

In case the Englishman escaped him! A thrill went through that black-and-gold-clad figure by the window as Verhulst envisioned a nightmarish chase across the ice with the tall, handsome Englishman running for his life, pursued by savage hounds. Verhulst and Imogene would watch from the shore. Like bands of steel, his arms would encircle her struggling figure, soft and female in its mantle of velvet and sable. But even through that he would feel the ripples of terror course through her shuddering frame and listen with satisfaction to her screams. White-faced, held fast, Imogene would be forced to watch this drama of life and death played out upon the ice. She would not be allowed to avert her face as Groot barked his orders and the men fanned out, pursuing the hounds and their desperate quarry. Trembling, she would watch her lover die.

Verhulst's eyes gleamed in anticipation. Imogene feared the dogs. She had lived in fear of them ever since the night when, half-drunk, he had sat at the table and—between toasts to her white shoulders—had told his shuddering wife in grisly detail how he had come back to Wey Gat from a skating party downriver to find his mother and father dead in their blood, scalped by a roving band of Iroquois. It had snowed that night and the Indians' tracks had been lost; Verhulst had never found them. His revenge had been wreaked on others. He had bought the fiercest hunting dogs he could find and had Groot train them to hunt men. They got their practice, he told her, raising his glass to toast her eyebrows, on thieving Indians. Woe be to any man, white or Indian, who pilfered the slightest thing at Wey Gat, for Groot, the kennelmaster, had standing orders to bring the culprit down—and it was never a whole man Groot delivered, but some torn and quivering flesh or, more mercifully, the broken remains of a dead man.

Imogene had stared at him that night with loathing in her wide, blue eyes—and fear too. It was, he told himself with a dark chuckle, the first time she had learned to fear him. There had been other times of course since then and he had reveled in them. Reveled in tormenting the young wife whose spirit he could not crush, and whose body he could not hold.

Tonight would be his crowning achievement. Tonight he would make Imogene watch the destruction of her lover!

On the river's east bank, Imogene's wind-whipped figure, recognizing the fox for what it was, lost its watchful rigidity. The fox, who had turned to regard the woman with luminous eyes, continued its moon-silvered path to the west bank.

Imogene watched him reach the safety of the opposite bank and merge into the snow-covered brush. From the second-floor window Verhulst could imagine her sobbing indrawn breath— *something* had escaped him, she would be thinking.

But you will not escape, he promised himself. *Tonight— even though I have to tie you to your chair—I will make you relive every moment. I will fill my glass with brandy and make you admit I am the better man—and if you are stubborn and will not, I will fling the brandy, goblet and all, into your lying face. No . . . not the goblet, for scars would dim your beauty and that must continue to delight me. You will continue to delight me, but this night's work will bring in upon you with force that here at Wey Gat you live but for my pleasure.*

He was all but intoxicated by his own thoughts.

The fox was gone now. Imogene, pulling her cloak tightly about her, bent down and slipped under the wooden pier that protruded on its pilings out into the frozen river. Doubtless she felt more secure there, Verhulst reasoned, for she was now out of view from the house. Her wide, beautiful eyes would be gazing to the south, he told himself grimly, for the note he had learned of had been sent downriver to New Amsterdam. He had not been able to lay hands on the note Imogene had penned but it had been delivered to one Stephen Linnington, fresh from England, and Stephen Linnington was the name he had wrung from her before the child was born.

"Linnington," she had sobbed at last, thrust to her knees at his feet, and with her head snapping back and forth from his rhythmic blows. "Stephen Linnington was my lover. But he is dead, Verhulst, he is no threat to you!"

Another lie—like her virginity.

For now that same Stephen Linnington had risen from the grave and come across the sea to reclaim his lost love.

And would die in the doing of it.

Still, Verhulst was puzzled by Imogene's choice of the wooden pier as a place to hide. Surely it would have been more like her to seek the cover of the trees that shadowed the river-bank?

As he puzzled over that, unbidden came the memory of the day he had met her.

He had been in Amsterdam five days. It was his first visit to the land of his forebears and the slender young patroon in his dark velvets and wide stylish boots was already finding himself a bit bored by museums and statues and parks and sightseeing. It had been very novel at first to look up at the dikes of Holland and see tall-masted ships floating by in stately grace above one's head as if they wafted along dry land, or to view the storks' huge nests perilously perched atop tall orange-brick chimneys, to browse in cellar shops or watch the goods of the world being loaded and unloaded into the upper reaches of the tall step-gabled houses. But on the fifth day it had come to Verhulst that he was after all a stranger in a strange land. America was *his* country and the wide, deep river that flowed from the Adirondacks to the sea was *his* river. His ships were not the tall-masted merchantmen that scraped sides in Amsterdam's busy harbor, but the fast, single-masted river sloops that sailed past his home at Wey Gat.

He was lonely.

Although he drank deep of metheglin in the inn's cozy common room, he slept but fitfully and on waking he had his first sight of Imogene.

She was never to know how much that meeting had shaken him.

Roused from his fitful sleep by a melody sung in a girl's fresh, light voice, Verhulst had stumbled from his bed and pushed open the wooden casements. As his dark head thrust itself out, the caroling notes died and he found himself looking into the startled face of a young girl in her night rail who had been leaning on her arms in the open casements of the room next to his, softly singing her heart out to the empty street below.

It was a magic moment. Verhulst would never forget it.

It was as if one of the great paintings from the museum's plastered walls had come to life and smiled at him. A swift, dazzling, beautiful smile flashed from a set of perfect white teeth surrounded by softly curving lips. She seemed completely unaware that she was wearing only her thin white night rail or that her golden hair tumbled uncombed down around her white shoulders. Her eyes were blue as delftware but her voice was English. "We are alone with the dawn, mynheer!"

Verhulst swallowed, for once at a loss for words. In the face of such earth-shaking beauty he felt tongue-tied. He could but gulp out some trivial answer before a scolding female voice called to her from within and her head disappeared from the casements.

Later that day, by dint of much clever maneuvering, Verhulst made the acquaintance of this vision—and that of her chaperon, Mistress Peale, and her ever-watchful maid, Elise Meggs, as well. Imogene was, Mistress Peale informed him vaguely, in Amsterdam "for her health" for an indefinite stay. But she did so hope, she added with a look that appraised the young patroon's handsome garments and priced the heavy gold chain that hung around his neck, that Imogene would be sufficiently recovered by fall that they might return to their home in the Scilly Isles at the southern tip of England, for a frozen winter in Amsterdam was not to be borne by ladies from the islands in the sun where ice and snow were almost unknown.

Verhulst had thought Imogene looked to be in excellent health and had said gallantly that she had brought the sun with her in the gold of her shining hair. Imogene had given a small perfunctory laugh to acknowledge the compliment, but the delft blue eyes had been looking elsewhere into the far distance . . . as far away as the sea or the Scilly Isles.

Verhulst should have been warned.

He was not.

In a chocolate shop on the fabled Kalverstraat he treated them to the expensive new "West Indian drink." As if he were a native—having arrived in Holland a few days before them—he took them on a round of sightseeing in this Venice of the north and marveled at the English girl's grace as she paused on an old stone bridge to look down at her reflection in the canal, or gave a small sigh as she looked up at the Schreierstoren, the Weeping Tower, as if she understood those legions of sailors' wives who had bade their seagoing men good-bye here—often for the last time.

Before the week was out Verhulst was madly in love with her. Imogene, preoccupied with her own thoughts, hardly knew he was alive.

Pressed by Mistress Peale, the attentive chaperon, Verhulst admitted expansively that he was in Amsterdam to collect paintings and fine fabrics to decorate the stone house his father had begun but a year before his death and that he, Verhulst, would complete, the house that was rising along the shore of the great river discovered by Henry Hudson, the Englishman, which the Dutch pleased to call the North River.

That much was true enough. What Verhulst van Rappard did not tell these fan-wafting ladies in their silk gowns was that, having come early into his patroonship at the untimely death of his parents, Verhulst had instantly chosen to woo the most beautiful daughter of all the river gentry. On graceful bended knee, during an intermission at a ball at her father's handsome house at Haerwyck, he had offered his fine old name to Rychie ten Haer—and been laughed at. Vivacious Rychie had heard the gossip about his youthful accident; she had no intention of tying herself to a eunuch. Callously, she had let Verhulst know as much.

Mortified beyond belief, Verhulst had plunged from the room and stumbled back to his waiting sloop, the *Danskammer*. Upriver the *Danskammer* had carried him, back to Wey Gat, where for three long months he had locked himself in his half-completed stone house, refused to receive friend or foe, and dined, word had it, on metheglin and brandy.

At the end of that time he had emerged, sober and apparently at peace with his world.

In that time Verhulst van Rappard, loftiest of New Netherland's proud patroons, had made a great decision: He had decided to remain a bachelor. Forever.

This serene intention flew apart when he encountered the earth-shaking golden beauty of Imogene Wells. He was incredulous that anyone could look like that. By God, she was stunning, she surpassed any girl on the North River. Indeed, Verhulst was secretly sure Imogene's feminine allure surpassed all the women in this world—and very possibly the next! What a decoration she would make for his handsome house. A living painting moving like a shaft of light from room to room. Damme, he would be the envy of every man who saw her.

The memory of Rychie's contemptuous turndown of his marriage offer made Verhulst's dark eyes gleam. *This* girl—even dressed simply and youthfully as she was in pastel silks and flowered calicos, and not in the queenly velvets and rich brocades in which *he* would outfit her—would put Rychie and all the rest of them in the shade!

The memory faded.

Out there in the snow was a faithless jade who had taken lying marriage vows and borne a child that he could not have fathered—indeed, he now knew the child had been conceived even before he met Imogene—and *that*, perhaps, he could have tolerated. He had been wild with rage at first, for the conviction that Imogene was pregnant—and not by him—had come to him suddenly at the dining table when, pale and wan, she had pushed aside all her food and in the same breath demanded a pickle.

Verhulst had laughed. "Did I not know better, I'd think ye were pregnant!"

He would always remember that proud white face, the way she straightened her slender shoulders and looked straight into his narrowed, dark eyes. "But I *am* pregnant, Verhulst," she had said quietly.

His world had spun, for what his head had told him his heart had not believed.

He had sent away the servants then and she had told him lies.

He had pretended to believe them.

But on another night, when the thickness of Imogene's waist had become a mockery to his lacerated spirit, he had confronted her again. He had locked the dining room doors and seized Imogene by her long, fair hair, wrenched her from her chair, and shaken her as a terrier shakes a rat. "His name!" he had shouted. "Tell me your lover's name!"

Her stubborn silence had maddened him. He had kept his left hand cruelly twined in her hair and struck her head back and forth brutally with his open palm.

Still she had defied him.

It was only when he had threatened to kill both her and her unborn child if she would not name her lover that Imogene had given him a name—the name of Stephen Linnington.

At that moment, borne on a gust of passion, Verhulst had reached out for the carving knife on the dining room table, thinking to kill his errant young wife. But the reaching hand had wavered, for hard on the heels of that thought had come another: Who along the river had ever heard of Stephen Linnington? And what was Imogene saying? The man was dead! A lover dead in England could not come back to haunt him. And when a child was born of this white-faced, half-fainting wench he held so savagely by the hair, all up and down the river that child would be considered *his*. Only he and Imogene would know, and neither of them was likely to tell. Indeed, when Imogene was delivered of her child, the fact that he would be accounted the father would be a further slap to Rychie and all her scornful ilk.

Thoughtfully, a man bemused, he had loosened his grip on Imogene's fair hair and she had slumped in a velvet heap to the floor.

His feelings toward her had swung widely after that. Like a pendulum, he was one day kind and another day cruel. And during those days she had learned to hate—and to fear him.

In time he might have forgiven Imogene and come to love the beautiful child she bore at Wey Gat.

But when he learned that the Englishman had arrived in New Amsterdam, that Imogene had been in communication with him, all the raging pent-up fires within him had burst and he had told himself fiercely that he hated Imogene, that he would yet bring the defiant wench to her knees in penitent submission.

Thrice before she had tried to escape him: he had stopped her each time.

The last time she had sat white and quiet before him until he had screamed at her to speak, to say something.

Looking at him with tired, defiant blue eyes—looking like a very queen, he had thought, in her incongruous diamonds despite her rumpled calico dress and windblown hair—she had said in a colorless voice, "I will find a way to escape you, Verhulst. You cannot hold me here forever at Wey Gat."

Now once again, she was attemping it.

And this time she had the Englishman to help her.

What had Linnington's note said, that note to Imogene that Verhulst had intercepted and then, craftily, had delivered to her? *I will be waiting for you when the moon is high. I have done all that you asked. Come swiftly, my darling, and we will be away on the wings of the wind!*

The wings of the wind indeed! Verhulst had snorted and stationed a sentry downriver to watch for Stephen Linnington and report his arrival. The sentry had not yet reported. Was Stephen coming by land, then? It hardly seemed likely with all this snow on the ground and roads that were scarcely more than Indian trails but . . . a man on snowshoes could make it, of course. Or a man on a strong, determined horse.

Not hearing of Stephen's whereabouts had fretted Verhulst. He wished he had been able to intercept that other note, the one Imogene had sent to Stephen in New Amsterdam. *I have done all that you asked*. What had Imogene asked of him? To take her away, most likely . . . no more than that. Verhulst snorted and took himself downstairs. He had wanted a wide view of the countryside as his wife left the house, to see if the Englishman would come from some unsuspected angle, but now he would go down and supervise operations.

Dawn, he promised himself as he clattered down the broad stairs, would find Imogene on her knees before him, tearfully offering to do anything—anything—to save her trussed-up lover.

Having reached the front hall, Verhulst reminded himself that he must not alert Imogene or he would spoil the hunt. Carefully he unlatched the heavy front door, opened it and stepped out into the snow. With his gaze never leaving the wooden pier beneath which Imogene crouched, he began to make his silent way down the white slope.

Away on the wings of the wind. . . . The wind, that wind that was whipping his dark hair into his eyes and trying to rip away the lace that spilled out over his dark velvet doublet . . . his father had named the estate Wey Gat, Wind Gate, because of the wild winds that swept downriver from the northern reaches, cold winds that screamed down from Canada, bringing ice and snow, and Verhulst had once heard himself referred to contemptuously at a ball in New Amsterdam as "van Rappard, the big wind upriver." He had turned sharply in an attempt to identify the speaker but had missed him amid the whirling bright-garbed dancers. *The wings of the wind* . . . it tore at his mind. Was there some secret hidden in the wind? He stared at the frozen expanse of gray ice before him.

Suddenly he stiffened. He had heard a familiar sound, a kind of crunching, grinding sound coming from upriver. And at that sound Imogene darted out from her hiding place beneath the pier, slipping and sliding as she ran across the ice out toward the center of the river.

Verhulst knew that sound! It was an iceboat, that was what Linnington had meant by *on the wings of the wind*—sails! The Englishman had tricked him, he was not working his way up from the south but flashing down from the frozen reaches upriver, driven by the almost gale-force winds that were even now sweeping down out of Canada. The note Verhulst had intercepted from the laconic Indian had come not from the south, as he had assumed, but from the north! In a moment a huge sail would appear out of nowhere and an iceboat on its greased iron runners would thunder down to sweep up Imogene and take her out of his reach forever!

And in his wild fear that she would escape him, Verhulst gave an order he would later regret, for it had never been in his mind to loose that savage pack of man-killing dogs while Imogene was running, frail and vulnerable, across the ice.

"The dogs!" he roared, stumbling down the slope. "Loose the dogs!"

BOOK I
Imogene

A toast to the fairest of maidens
That mortal eyes ever have seen,
A toast to her folly, her courage—
A toast to Imogene!

PART ONE
The Desperate Lovers

A toast to the desperate venture,
A toast to the lovers who dare,
Who—divided and lost and abandoned—
Never will cease to care!

The Scilly Isles, 1657
CHAPTER 1

It was a soft night in the Scillies, those sunny "Fortunate Isles" flung like a necklace of emeralds and gold westward into the Atlantic from England's southern tip, and behind the moon-washed stone battlements of Star Castle, despite all the edicts of the Puritans and the Lord Protector, a ball was in progress.

Two gentlemen, both resplendent in gold braid and sweeping plumed hats, clattered up the stone stairs to the rooftop festivities and were greeted by their satin-clad host and hostess. That formality accomplished, they betook themselves to a crenellated corner of this great eight-pointed edifice that surmounted Garrison Hill and there stood assessing the woman-flesh of this glittering assemblage.

"And who would that one be, Ambrose? The girl with the fine 'figger'?" wondered Stephen Linnington, the taller and older of the two newcomers. Not a woman in the room but had noticed the entrance of this tall stranger with the swinging gait and the shoulder-length copper hair, and now several soft glances were turned toward him. For above his lean body that bespoke the competent swordsman he was, gleamed a wickedly carefree smile that incited the innocent to lush forbidden thoughts and the experienced to infidelity. Stephen was not unaware of the effect he had upon women—indeed, seduction was his hobby, when he was not amusing himself with other things: dice and cards and dangerous adventures aimed at gain that usually came to naught. He had been reared in a luxury he could no longer afford. Even the ruffled white linen shirt on his broad back and the fine sweeping hat with orange plumes that seemed to highlight his own gleaming copper hair were not his own. Both borrowed—as was the appearance of respectability he was enjoying this night.

"Come, Ambrose, the lady's name. Ye must know her." Stephen's voice was lazy and jaded, but above the quizzical smile he flashed at Ambrose his hard turquoise gaze had come alert, for through the throng he had sighted a most wondrous torso clad in pastel pink silk. Now he stood assessing what he could see past three vaguely military-looking gentlemen who crowded about the girl, their heads bent over in their concentration as they talked to her. What Stephen Linnington could see delighted him: delicately molded breasts ornamenting a lithe torso that nipped to a tiny waist before the pointed silk bodice billowed out into wide rippling skirts and petticoat. Past an interested masculine back he could see that her slender white arm wafted a plumed fan. Those rosy plumes concealed the face that surmounted the "fine figger," but the hair that crowned the lady's head gleamed lustrously gold in the light of the torches that had been thrust into the stone merlons. She moved, gracefully, as if to elude the three men who pressed so close, and the pale pink silk of her gown rippled and was gilded by that same torchlight to tones of peach and gold like a tea rose. At the far side of the parapet the musicians would soon strike up, and the tall gentleman who had asked the question gave his young friend an impatient look.

"Who?" His stocky companion, young Ambrose Duveen, squinted short-sighted eyes across the torchlit throng.

"The lady in pink—the one waving the plumed fan," answered his copper-haired friend, wondering in his heart how he could have been thought to mean anyone else.

"Oh—her." Stocky Ambrose frowned. "That will be Mistress Imogene Wells. Ye're a stranger in these parts, Stephen, while I've lived here all my life, so I do feel I should warn you—well, she's not your dish, I'd say."

"And why would you say that?" Amusement in the lazy voice.

"Imogene's a rattlebrain. Two betrothals of marriage she's broken off at the last minute and both good matches who will not offer for her again, I can tell you!"

Light broke over his tall companion's hard visage. "Ambrose, did *you* offer for her by chance?"

Ambrose flushed to the roots of his brown hair. "No, of course I did not! 'Twas my brother Hal," he finished lamely.

"Ah," said Stephen, his mind contemplating big Hal Duveen: silent, steady, dull-eyed, a good sailor—and doubtless he'd one day make some girl a fine husband. But not this artful wench who wielded her fan so flirtatiously! "So she turned Hal down," he said softly.

" 'Twas not like that." Resentfully. "Hal did but reprove Imogene for her wild ways and *that's* when she told him she would not marry him."

37

"Her 'wild ways'?"

"Hal said ye could see clean to her hips when she mounted her horse!" Ambrose sounded indignant.

"She must be very clever then," murmured the copper-haired fellow beside him, "for I've spent half my life looking and never yet seen—"

"And her wild ways with the kerchief and other things." Ambrose was on the defensive now.

His tall friend looked as if that were most instructive. Actually he was reminding himself that the orange-plumed hat on his head and the full-sleeved shirt of fine linen on his back were both borrowed from Hal, and therefore refrained from the ribald comment he would ordinarily have made. But one thing he could not let pass. "Her wild ways *with the kerchief?*" he demanded, fascinated.

Ambrose looked hunted. "That sheer lawn thing the young ladies wear across their bosoms above the bodice—I think Bess calls them whisks or pinners." He was floundering beyond his depth now and when Stephen looked baffled, he raced on, trying to explain his aversion to the beauteous Imogene. "Her guardian, old Lord Elston—he's not here tonight, for his health is poor, seldom goes out—admits to all who will listen that he doesn't know what to do with Mistress Imogene. 'Tis said he's given her an ultimatum: the next time he betrothes her to someone, she'll ne'er break it off, she'll to the church to be wed if he has to drag her there trussed up like a capon. My sister Bess likes her—I don't know why—but you wouldn't, Stephen. Anyway, she's too young by half, too—arrogant," Ambrose finished grandly with the firm conviction of extreme youth.

Stephen could guess that the dazzling Imogene must have ignored young Ambrose as "a mere child." How that must have rankled! Still he was moved to protest.

"'Too young'?" he demanded in astonishment. "Why, she looks to be all of sixteen."

"About that," agreed Ambrose sullenly.

"Then I'd say she was ripe for the plucking." Stephen's broad russet-clad shoulders gave a slight start as the lady in question swung around and he got a full front view, though her face was still hidden flirtatiously by her fan. "I like her gown," he muttered appreciatively.

"That's another thing Hal chided her for," said Ambrose, his tone severe. "Goes too far, she does. Not that—" he added scrupulously—"she goes *all the way*, I didn't mean to say that." His face grew brick red at Stephen's sardonic grin.

"Ye mean she's the type to say 'Lud, sir, I hadn't meant to let you take such liberties—what will the world think of me with my skirts up like this?' and dash away, leaving ye to gnaw at your knuckles?" he wondered wickedly.

Ambrose's crimson face grew a shade deeper. "I *meant*," he said in a smothered voice, "well, look at her, bare to the nipples!"

"Past that," murmured Stephen, leaning forward the better to view this gorgeous piece. "They're showing."

"There, you see?" Triumphantly. "Any other girl would have worn a sheer gauze kerchief, or whisk or whatever they call them, to cover herself for modesty—as I don't doubt *she* did until she got here and her chaperon had her usual fainting fit and had to go and lie down! 'Twas after she got rid of poor Mistress Peale, I'll wager, that she took off the kerchief and tossed it over the battlements—as I've seen her do twice before!"

"Ye can criticize that?" demanded Stephen incredulously, dazzled by the distant display of pink-tipped white bosom rising above the dainty ruffled silk. "Why, man, all the fashionable ladies at court do peep out above the bodice the same way."

" 'Tis not right," insisted Ambrose. " 'Tis not such a display as a young lady of rank and fashion should make. Nor yet should she lie to poor Mistress Peale about it—saying the wind took it, indeed! Though she's a friend of my sister's and I've known her all my life, for she lives on the Isle of Tresco, just to the northwest of us—" he made a vague gesture toward the stars and the sea, his anguished gaze still riveted on the disturbing vision before them—"I do fear for Bess in Imogene's wild company, for she'll come to no good end with her blatherskite ways."

"If she's wild enough company, I should rather think she might make it all the way to the Lord Protector's bedchamber," murmured Stephen, but Ambrose, carried away by his own tirade, did not hear him.

"Some say 'tis old Lord Elston's fault. He's allowed Imogene to run wild ever since she came here to live with him. She's been his ward since her parents were killed when they got in the way of a volley of shot during the civil wars. Happened in their own garden too, in Penzance! Shows a man never knows where he can be safe. And because they were royalists, all the property that would have been hers was confiscated by the Lord Protector. Lord Elston would be poor as a churchmouse, too, if he did not somehow manage to keep on the good side of the Puritans, although who could stomach—damme, ye're not a Puritan by chance, are ye, Stephen?" he finished weakly, a note of horror creeping into his voice.

"Never," said Stephen in a deep consoling voice, but he gazed at his young companion in some wonder. A lad who'd condemn a lass for being high-spirited and flashing a bit too much bosom or ankle? Faith, he seemed more like an old gentleman of eighty-three than a young buck of nineteen summers!

Still, from the wisdom he'd acquired in his twenty-seven adventurous years—the last ten of them spent as a rover—Stephen reminded himself that it was Ambrose and Ambrose's older brothers, fine sailors all, who had pulled him out of a churning ocean that wild night a week ago when his light craft had piled up on the black sawtooth rocks of the Scillies. It was Ambrose's family who had generously taken in the stranger who had washed up on their beach with a cut head and been nearly reclaimed by the sea again as the great waves thundered in. Stephen had collapsed on the beach, half-conscious, and been vaguely aware that there were boots about him and that strong hands were dragging him across the sand away from the reach of the clutching waves. Sick and dizzy and weak from loss of blood, for he had been near swept from the deck when the mast broke and fell on him, he had come to for a moment when they'd laid him down. He had looked up just as a white flash of jagged lightning had rent the sky from end to end, weirdly illuminating the beach and the wild sea and the black rocks—and had seen above him a lovely face. Wide concerned blue eyes had looked down into his, and a wealth of fair hair streaming down mermaidlike in the wild spray from the waves frothing against the rocks had lightly brushed his wet face.

"An angel!" he had gasped in astonishment. "So I've gone to heaven and not the other place!" And had sunk back into unconsciousness.

Two days later, when he was sitting propped up with pillows in a big square bed and a beaming Ambrose had ushered in a serving girl carrying hot broth, he had asked where he was and who Ambrose was and who the "angel" was he'd seen when he was half-drowned.

"Ye're on Saint Mary's, the largest isle in the Scillies, and this is the Castle of Ennor, or what's left of it," Ambrose had grinned. "For there was fighting here during the civil wars and some of the walls were blown up. I'm Ambrose Duveen and 'twas my brothers and I saved ye—though not your boat, I'm afraid. We saw her go down in deep water. And—" his eyes did not quite meet Stephen's—"there's no angel here save my sister, and none have yet called Bess that."

"Your sister? Blond and blue-eyed, is she?"

"Dark-haired and gray-eyed."

A mirage then, a vision born of being hit over the head with a falling mast . . . perhaps an angel for all that, hovering over him, promising him glory in death.

"I'm—"

"Your name I already know," Ambrose had beamed. "For ye gasped out that ye were Stephen Linnington of Devon before ye lost consciousness."

So he had told them that much. . . . The knock on the head must have been worse than he thought. He felt of his scalp gingerly, winced. "I'm late of Hampshire," he supplemented, fabricating as he went. "Although 'tis true I was born in Devon."

Ambrose's broad pleasant face took on a disappointed look. "Too bad," he blurted, "for we've kin in Devon. Though in truth," he added earnestly, "we see them but seldom."

Very seldom, Stephen Linnington hoped fervently. For he'd left Devon in his teens with two musket-carrying fathers in hot pursuit, each claiming he'd debauched their daughters—as indeed he had. Under pressure from his own father he'd have been only too happy to make amends by marrying one, but he found it hard to choose between pretty Peg and lightsome Molly. To run had seemed the best course—and Stephen Linnington had taken it.

BOLD BREATHLESS LOVE

His flight had carried him north to Yorkshire, where he'd fallen in with bad company, and one night while drunk he had married a highwayman's sister. But he'd married her under an alias, and did that count? Anyway, she'd fled with the highwayman one stormy night when the king's men surrounded the tavern where they'd taken shelter, leaving Stephen to the law, and once he'd escaped jail he'd not known where to find her. Fate and a strong horse had carried him to Lincoln, and there he'd taken up with a pretty barmaid and because she'd plagued him so, he'd married her, too. Since then he'd ranged the north and west of England, his hot temper and stubborn pride getting him into more trouble than his strong sword arm could get him out of.

As matters stood, the tall gentleman from Devon was wanted in York for murder and in Lincoln for bigamy and in half the rest of England for this or that infraction. He'd been locked into stocks for drunkeness, and pilloried for roundly cursing a constable—and from that event he still bore a slight scar over his right eye. In London they'd have locked him up in Newgate forever for debt had he not eluded his pursuers by leaping off London Bridge into the Thames and swimming away from the shots that rang out in the night. Homesick for the land of his birth, though long estranged from his family, who in shame told everyone he was dead, he had journeyed south again into Devon—and fared no better there. There the young adventurer with the wicked gleam in his turquoise eyes and the ready hand on a sword hilt had swaggered his way into a dice game and from it acquired a boat. He had departed on that boat in a hurry when his remarkable luck at last came under closer inspection and he was accused of cheating. Dodging bullets again, he'd intended to sail for Falmouth and try his luck there, but a storm had come up and carried him clear to the Scillies. When his boat shattered against the ugly black rocks the young man with the tarnished past had been lucky to escape with his life.

The Duveens little knew the character of the man they had so generously offered their hospitality and—Ambrose at least—their friendship. From his clothes, his bearing, the tone of command in his voice, they knew him to be a gentleman and as such they accepted him. It would have astonished them to have learned the truth about him.

Stephen Linnington thought the less they knew of him the better and in the big square bed he had cursed himself silently for having gasped out his real name along with a gurgle of salt water. Even a half-drowned fool like himself should have known better than that, he thought. All the names he'd used as he roistered across England, and here, but a short sail from Devon, he'd given his real name! Faith, his family would not thank him for that if they heard about it!

Always generous hosts, the Duveens had told Stephen he was welcome to stay with them as long as he liked. He'd been grateful for that, since his head wound was giving him dizzy spells. But now he was feeling fit again, and Hal—the only Duveen with a shoulder span that matched his own—had lent him a clean ruffled shirt and a sweeping hat with orange plumes—his own shirt having been torn and his hat lost when his boat went down. And Ambrose Duveen had taken him along to the ball at Star Castle and was bent on scorning the best-looking girl there.

"Whatever her morals, will ye introduce me to Mistress Imogene Wells, Ambrose?" His expression intense, Stephen bent toward his short young friend so abruptly that his thick shock of copper hair cascaded over his wide white collar.

"Well," said Ambrose in an undecided voice, "I'll introduce ye, of course, because Imogene *is* received everywhere still, although there do be wild tales about her.''

"Let us hope they are all true," muttered Stephen fervently, for it had been all of two weeks since he had lain in a pair of yielding white arms, and he'd been too aware of the kindness of his hosts, the Duveens, to try to seduce their daughter, Bess. Tonight might change all that! He squared his russet velvet shoulders jauntily and strode forward beside Ambrose to meet the daring beauty, Imogene.

But the introduction, brief as it was, went unheard in his ears. For the face that was turned toward him, suddenly revealed as the pink plumed fan was wafted away, caught him up as stunningly as a blow.

"Faith, 'tis my angel!'' he murmured in disbelief. For the lovely piquant face that was looking up at him half expectantly, half arrogantly, was not one he was likely to forget. It was the face he thought he'd dreamed. Those wide delft blue eyes with their dark-rimmed irises, shadowed by long dark lashes, were the same that had looked down upon him with concern that might when he'd lain half drowned on a strange beach. Those softly curving lips that smiled provocatively at him now had then been a straight, worried line, and those flaunting wings of brows now so slightly lifted, perhaps by disdain, had been lost in a curtain of long, tumbled hair that had streamed down, fair and wet as a mermaid's.

Stephen Linnington, the rake who had held so many women lightly in his arms and had left them all, looked into those lovely blue eyes and was lost. All of his being seemed to converge in a sudden rush of feeling centered on this slip of a girl whose dainty chin was upraised defiantly beneath the burning pressure of his hard, masculine gaze. For a moment as the music of the *viola da gamba* struck up, she looked uncertain, panicky almost, as if she might suddenly turn and run away from him, but he seized her hand in his strong fingers and swept her away without asking into the dance.

The light that seemed to leap from Imogene's blue eyes to Stephen's turquoise ones was more than a trick of the wavering torches, her slight yet frantic gesture away from him was no coquettish pose. For Imogene felt the same bolt pass through her that had impaled Stephen. All her innermost feelings seemed to surge up in a rush toward this russet-clad stranger with the copper hair, and she felt again the same winds of fear that had brushed her like dark wings the night she had heard the Duveen boys calling out and had come running alongside Bess to find Stephen lying on the beach. Bess had shouted, ''I'll go prepare a bed!'' but Imogene had leaned over the fallen figure, and when the lightning flashed she had been looking down into his eyes.

Never had she been so attracted to a man's face. Bold, and yet—tender. With humor about the mouth. And when he had opened his eyes and gasped, ''An angel!'' she had trembled.

That night, when the stranger had been made comfortable, and lay, still unconscious from his wound, in a big bed in a room down the hall from her own—for she was visiting Bess Duveen at Ennor Castle—that night she had dreamed the dream again. It was an old nightmare from her childhood, when the loss of her parents, shot down in their pleasant garden, was still fresh.

In the dream it was summer—the kind of lovely summer day it had been when the volley of shot had found her parents in their Penzance garden. Seven-year-old Imogene had seen them fall and had been visited by the same nightmare intermittently from that day.

But in the dream she was not in Penzance but in some place strange to her. She was creeping down a tall white sand dune and below her was the silver glimmer of a gray and glassy ocean. And upon that ocean—or beyond it—something was waiting for her, *something she had to reach*. Suddenly the sounds of summer were stilled and out of nowhere came a screaming wind. Over the white brow of the dune a dark cloud rushed down upon her and she ran terrified before it, toward the silver ocean. And now as she plunged into the gray surf, she saw what she must reach. It was a sailboat beating toward her and in the boat stood a tall man with copper hair, calling to her. She could not hear what he was saying, but as the surf broke about her she called his name—a name she could never remember later when she woke. Now she was flailing through the water toward him pursued by that onrushing black cloud and the sea had changed its silvery surface—it was suddenly alive with sharks. This way and that she plunged desperately to avoid them and now the largest was streaking toward her—and she saw death in its open jaws.

At that point she always waked—and on this night also, just as those teeth were closing down, she had waked with a choked scream and found her faithful maid, Elise, who'd been sleeping on a cot at the foot of her bed, shaking her. Elise had been Imogene's nurse almost since birth; now her kind face was worried.

"Ye were dreaming again," she said roughly. "Was it the same dream?" And at Imogene's nod, her voice grew energetic. "'Twas all that lobster at supper and those rich pasties, and then the storm and that ship foundering."

"No." Imogene's eyes were dark pools and she hugged her knees in her arms, shivering. "I think I saw my future, Elise—and it was dreadful."

Elise felt fear trickle through her. She was remembering that Imogene had had a Scottish grandmother, and didn't the

Scots have The Sight? Perhaps Imogene *had* seen something . . . something waiting for her out there. Elise's protective arms gripped Imogene the tighter.

"There, there." Elise's comforting arms were around her, her gaunt form holding Imogene close as she stroked the girl's bright hair. " 'Twas only a dream."

"No." Shuddering. " 'Twas real. It just—hasn't happened yet." And then, lower still. "That man on the beach tonight, Elise—he looked like the sailor in my dream."

Again fear bit at Elise. "We must leave," she told Imogene decisively. "Tomorrow morning. Perhaps the food here does not agree with you. We must go back to Tresco." She had not added—although she felt it—*we will be safe there*.

And so they had gone back to Tresco the next morning and forgotten the stranger on the beach—until tonight at the ball at Star Castle. Beautiful Imogene could not be expected to miss *that*.

And now, looking up into the stranger's hot eyes, when all the attraction he had for her had been borne in on her again, she had remembered the dream. . . .

She had flinched away from him, but he had seized her hand. And now she was whirling headily in his arms to the plaintive music of the *viola da gamba* beside the rooftop parapet of Star Castle, with the hot torchlight nearby and the cold starlight reaching down from a sky of midnight blue velvet. All her senses had come alive and every nerve seemed twanging like the strings of the *viola*.

For a breathless moment she hardly dared look at him, for too much in that wickedly smiling face attracted her—she who had been served notice by her guardian that another broken betrothal would not be tolerated. She'd known for a month now that Lord Elston was planning a great marriage for her, a marriage to Giles Avery, only son of the greatest fortune in Cornwall and—chafing at the restrictions of her life in the Scillies—she wanted that marriage.

Intuition had told her that the stranger, lying sodden and bleeding on the beach, could spoil all that.

He still could.

But the whirling motion of the dance had freed her from her sudden tremor and her old boldness returned. Her head was lifted haughtily in a little gesture of defiance as she spoke to him.

"D'you take all your castles by storm?" she asked tartly as they reached the center of the stone floor. "For indeed I had promised this dance to Giles Avery—see him, over there in the violet taffetas? He's glaring at you."

Stephen's whiplike fencer's body turned slightly that he might view the violet-clad dandy who was indeed glaring murderously in his direction. He was sharply aware that his own russet velvet doublet and trousers were in poor case, having been somewhat damaged by his shipwreck.

"The paunchy lad taking snuff?" he drawled. "Faith, he looks to be not much of a menace."

Imogene sighed—she had often had the same thought. "Giles's sword arm may be weak," she retorted, "but his purse is one of the heaviest in Cornwall—and at least he is young. My guardian is determined that I shall make a 'good' marriage and I think he has paraded every old bachelor and widower in the district before me! But he tells me I must make up my mind soon else I will be too old to attract a man, for I'll be seventeen in June." Over Stephen's broad shoulder she beamed a fetching smile at the snuff-taker. "Ah, there, Giles has asked Bess to dance. That's better!"

"Seventeen in June—a great age indeed," Stephen said

with becoming gravity. "I can see that you must make haste. But does a deep purse weigh with ye so mightily then, Mistress Wells?"

Imogene gave him a sharp look and then laughed; her perspective had been restored. "It might, for I've a mind to see the world—London, Paris, Rome. All the places Giles promises to take me once we're wed."

"London is drab these days," pointed out Stephen. "The Puritans have closed the theaters. One dare not dance there or celebrate Christmas or even kiss one's wife on a Sunday!"

The very toss of her head was a challenge. "What?" she mocked. "You do not dare kiss your wife on a Sunday?"

Goaded by her beauty, her neatness, he accepted the challenge.

"Stephen Linnington has no wife." There, the words were out! And, he asked himself, was it not so in truth? A highwayman's sister who had married him—and God knew how many others—that she might pick his pockets while he was drunk; a tavern maid who'd wed him because she thought a "gentleman" must have lots of money—and had burst into tears and turned him out of her room when she found he had not! And both of them he had wed under other names. No, he told himself, it was the very truth: Stephen Linnington had no wife—at least, no wife of the heart.

"You speak of yourself in the third person," she said critically, trying to still the wild burst of joy she felt at this avowal that he was single. "As if you view yourself from some distance."

"Perhaps I view myself from a distance because I cannot stand a closer view." His deep voice was bitter, disillusioned.

Imogene sighed. "Perhaps we can none of us stand close inspection. . . ." And then, because that well might bring Giles

Avery back into the conversation, she added hastily, "I have heard that things are bad in London and I do pray for the king's speedy return."

Stephen looked surprised. "A king in exile's not likely to return soon with Cromwell set so firmly in the saddle."

Imogene gave an irritable shrug that made her firm young breasts tremble deliciously. Stephen was hard pressed to draw his eyes away from their pale entrancing gleam. "Cromwell's an old man," she said. "He'll die soon and who then will take his place as Lord Protector? That bookish son of his? No, the king will be back on his throne, you'll see, and London will bloom again."

And you plan to be at his Court. Somehow. That yearning note in her voice made Stephen Linnington wish he had spent his wasted years chasing gold instead of petticoats. If he had, he might have had something to offer this blazing beauty.

"We've met before," he observed. "Ye do not remember me?"

"Oh, but I do. I was visiting Bess Duveen at Ennor Castle the night your boat sank and you nearly drowned. But I left the next day. You were not yet conscious."

"Yet when I mentioned seeing an angel, Ambrose did not tell me 'twas you," he grinned.

Imogene laughed on a wicked note. "Ah, but that's because Ambrose considers me a devil, not an angel. And he fears I will contaminate his sister, the gentle Bess." She glanced across the room at Bess, her sleek heavy black hair bound up and her mauve satin ball gown blending perfectly with the violet taffetas of the bored young man who was whirling her about.

"Could that appraisal of Ambrose's be due to the fact that he presumed on your favors and was set roundly back on his heels?" Stephen wondered.

"How could you know that?" In the torchlight Imogene turned an astonished expression toward him.

" 'Twas a fair guess." Grimly.

"Ambrose had heard stories about me. All grossly untrue. And—and I had reason to slap his face and so I did." She looked indignant.

Stephen's eyes dropped to those winking shell pink nipples, just peeping out from the top of her pink silk bodice. How the sight maddened him! Still, a lady of fashion—even one so young as this—was not to be judged by the daring cut of her gowns or her "wild way with a kerchief." In spite of this resplendent display, Imogene might well be more innocent than a lass whose collar reached to her chin.

"I thought as much," he murmured.

Imogene was looking at him with a new respect, that he should understand how it was. And suddenly, under the pressure of her friendly, almost comradely gaze—her quarrels became his quarrels.

"If any have offended you, my lady," he offered, his turquoise eyes narrowing and emitting a wicked gleam, "I'd be glad to take care of the matter." Lightly his strong fingers caressed his sword hilt.

She shook her head. " 'Tis whispers only, and who knows where they start? Or why?"

Because you are too beautiful, he answered her silently. *Because others less fortunate envy you all that you are*.

At that moment dark-haired Bess Duveen drifted by with Giles Avery, who turned to glare pointedly at Stephen.

They heard Bess laugh. "Come now, Giles," she chided gently. "There's too much heat in your glance! Stephen Linnington is a stranger here and Imogene doubtless gave him this dance to

52

welcome him to our shores—on which he landed so strangely, as ye may have heard.''

''I've heard your brothers fished him from the sea and I wish they had left him there!'' growled Giles, clenching her hand so hard his numerous jeweled rings bit into the flesh and left her wincing.

Stephen heard that last before Giles turned on a polished boot and whirled Bess away from them amid the dancers. His sardonic face turned dangerous.

''Indeed I might sharpen my sword on that young puppy!'' he observed in a steely voice and two nearby heads swung curiously in their direction.

''No—forget Giles,'' said Imogene quickly, aware there were listening ears in the throng about them. ''Is this your first time in the Scillies?''

Stephen nodded, his intent gaze still following the violet-clad dandy.

''They're called the Islands of the Sun,'' she told him, giving him a look through shadowed lashes as he swept her to a less crowded part of the floor. ''And by some the Isles of the Dead because of all the old 'standing stones'—the menhirs. There are two tall menhirs that stand above Saint Warna's Bay—that's at Saint Agnes, our southernmost island—they're called Adam and Eve, and sometimes on summer nights I've prayed to them and asked the old gods to send me a lover, someone to remember before I'm wed to such as—'' she jerked her head a trifle toward the sulky young gentleman in violent taffetas across the floor.

'' 'To remember before'—!'' Startled, he turned his gaze back to her.

''And now,'' she mocked, ''you'll say I'm not a lady and

53

that I deserve no better than I'll no doubt get!"

His turquoise eyes kindled. "No, I'll say if ye admit ye pray to the old gods, ye're like to be dragged to some Puritan marketplace and burned on a Tuesday."

"But we're not Puritans here," she protested, "we're royalists."

"Do not be saying it so loud," he cautioned, with the wisdom of the hunted. "For the Puritans rule England this night and I'm told the Lord Protector has built himself a castle somewhere in these isles."

" 'Tis on Tresco, the island where I live," she told him carelessly. "Take the road on the western side, pass Hangman's Island and ye'll come to it. It fronts toward the sea. They tore down most of King Charles's castle on the hill above it, for the building of it."

So this lighthearted wench could mock the Puritans standing beneath their very walls. His wild rover's heart went out to her.

"Why should ye give yourself to such a man as the young snuffbox lord yonder, if ye do not wish to?" he asked bluntly, for now it concerned him.

"I told you—for gold," she said pensively. "I don't want to dance any more. Have you seen the view from the battlements? I could point out the different islands."

Stephen would have gone anywhere with her at that moment—to Cromwell's castle, or to hell. He swung her out of the dancers, and as she turned, her pink silk skirts wrapped luxuriously about his legs for a moment. A warning bell tolled through him. This was no tavern wench to be taken lightly. He closed his ears to the warning. Together they reached the crenellated wall. He swung her up and they stood looking over the parapet.

"To the right is Penninis head," she said, pointing with a milk-white arm across the midnight blue of the sea. "And see, there is Saint Martin's and Tresco and the Round Island." But the tall gentleman beside her did not choose to follow where her finger was pointing. His heated gaze was on the rise and fall of her gleaming bosom. "And there—" she turned a little and so spoiled his view of her breasts—"there's Bryher and Samson and Broad Sound—and over there are the Western Rocks, and there is Annet and there is Agnes. My maid, Elise, is from Agnes, and she has told me horrible stories ever since my cradle days of the wreckers there who set out false lights and caused many a ship to break up upon the rocks."

"So many islands," he murmured, ignoring the dark shapes that rose against the sea's dark glimmer and leaning over to breathe deep of the perfume of her soft fair hair. "I had not thought there were so many."

"Perhaps a hundred and a half," she said, seemingly unconscious of the tumult she had roused in his breast. "And all of them older than time. Tresco is the prettiest, I think. It is full of flowers and tropical fruits. And past Cromwell's castle there's Piper's Hole where the mermaids dwell."

"The mermaids . . . I thought you were a mermaid when I looked up out of the blinding salt water and saw your face and your dripping fair hair."

"You did not," she corrected him lightly. "You thought I was an angel—you said so, and I'll hold you to it, for you're the first to have thought it!" She glanced around. "Ah, I see Giles has found us. You'd best ask Bess to dance so she won't be left standing as he whisks me away from you."

"When," he wondered, "will I see you again?"

She gave him a wicked smile. "Tomorrow my chaperon will be indisposed. Mistress Peale is always indisposed after a ball, for she drinks too much and spends the next day in her bed. I shall visit the Isle of Saint Agnes with my maid, Elise, who wishes to see her ailing sister—if the weather be fine. If you should happen to borrow a boat and sail to Agnes, we could climb Kittern Hill and see the great stone they call the Old Man of Gugh.''

''And perhaps Adam and Eve—your wishing stones.''

She laughed. ''And perhaps Adam and Eve. Ah, there you are, Giles,'' she said, taking Stephen's hand and springing lightly down from the battlements with a swirl of silken skirts. ''You did forget our dance but fortunately the Duveen's guest, Mr. Linnington, rescued me. Have you met Mr. Linnington, Giles? Stephen Linnington, Giles Avery.''

The dandy in violet taffetas, about to make some sharp remark about those who stole dances intended for another, found the wind taken out of his sails by Imogene's chiding remark. He choked an acknowledgment to the introduction and whirled Imogene away as the music struck up. Over that stiff violet shoulder, Stephen could hear Imogene laughing.

''Will ye do me the honor, Mistress Bess?'' he asked absently and they were off across the floor.

Bess's wide gray eyes were looking at him gravely. ''You must forgive Giles, Stephen. He's wild in love with her, you know. 'Tis said their betrothal will be announced at any moment.''

Stephen's only response was a slight tightening of his arm muscles—those long ropy muscles that could split a man with a sword. If Bess noticed that, she made no comment, only continued to consider him with those large, grave eyes and a slightly pensive air. Preoccupied with thoughts of Imogene, Stephen was not to know the effect he had had on dreamy Bess, who thought him in all ways wonderful and dreaded the moment he must leave the Scillies to take up with the life he had left behind him when he was shipwrecked on their shores. For the moment she was content to dance with him and pretend that Stephen was in love with her and that tomorrow—some lovely rose-scented tomorrow—he would ask her to be his wife. She felt shy with him and she cast down her eyes and thrilled to his lightest touch.

Ambrose came up and introduced him to some other people. Bess was swept away and Stephen found himself dancing with a succession of young girls whose names he could not even remember. And then he was dancing with Bess again, but he found himself looking over her shoulder at Imogene, who was smiling winsomely at a new partner. When the dance ended, they all found themselves together in a group containing stout Lady Moxley, who considered herself the leader of island society. Lady Moxley's outdated farthingale bumped against Stephen as she turned a ceruse-whitened, disapproving face to the beauty in pink silk. "Have ye lost your whisk, then?" she asked tartly, eyeing Imogene's dainty exposed bosom with disfavor. "For I thought ye were wearing one when ye arrived."

"I was," declared Imogene in a blithe voice. "The wind took it. 'Tis probably floating away to sea by now."

Lady Moxley sniffed and Ambrose, catching Stephen's eye just then, gave him a significant look. But Stephen took that opportunity to return Bess to her brother and claim Imogene for another dance.

"Did ye mean what ye said about sailing to Saint Agnes tomorrow?" he asked.

"If the weather be fine. . . ." Her gamin smile mocked him.

"And if it be not fine?"

"Then," she shrugged deliciously, "ye must try and find me, must ye not?"

"Or perhaps," he suggested equably, "we could see each other rather sooner. After the guests go home, you could slip away and I could help ye look for your blown-away kerchief below the castle walls. 'Tis a clear night. It should be easy to find it."

" 'Slip away'?"

"Aye. Don't tell me ye've never done it."

She gave him an irritable look. "Of course I have." *No need to tell him that nothing had come of it, that she had enjoyed slipping away with an ardent swain on occasion and amused herself with his hot kisses. Sometimes she'd even let an eager questing hand wander too far—but always she'd stopped prudently short of endangering her virginity.*

His turquoise eyes gleamed. This was better than he'd hoped.

"I'll wait for you beneath the castle wall."

She tossed her head so that her golden curls bounced. "I won't be there."

"And how will ye comfort yourself when ye're married to yon exciting lad in violet?" he prodded. "Ye'll have only your memories then, my lass! And wouldn't you like to remember a search for a kerchief and perhaps a moonlight swim?"

She gave an irritable shrug that set her delectable breasts in motion again. "Giles will be—manageable," she snapped. "We're not betrothed—yet. But if we were, he'd swim with me in the moonlight anytime I chose."

Stephen snorted. "Now, perhaps—though I doubt me you'd be willing to shock him by bringing up the subject. But after ye're married—never! For then ye'll be his possession, tightly guarded. There'll be no slipping out then! Indeed, he'll probably sleep with one leg over ye to make sure ye don't stray!"

"You're—impossible!" she gasped.

"Nay, 'tis Giles that's impossible. Look at him, every hair in his yellow wig combed and pomaded to perfection. Think how elegant he'll look when he takes it off and sets it carefully upon a wig stand and ties up his shaved head in a ribboned cap and comes to bed?"

He was laughing at her! How Imogene would have liked to strike the smile from that bold countenance, for wigs were a sore point with her. She thought her guardian, so dignified in his great curled periwig, looked ridiculous without it, his head seemed shrunken inside his beribboned nightcap. How often the image of some shaven-headed dandy had risen up before her with distaste, for she knew that men of fashion who wore wigs kept their heads shaved. And Stephen Linnington, with his elegant head of thick gleaming copper hair—all his own, obviously—was bent on enjoying her discomfiture.

"I shall be too busy unloosing my ropes of diamonds and pearls to notice Giles's wig!" she retorted.

Before he could taunt her further, the dance ended. Seething, Imogene fairly pulled Stephen toward Giles, who was standing between two of his friends: a slender, dark, rakish lad in fawn brocade whom Stephen identified vaguely as Mowbrey, and a smirking thick-lipped youth in wine satin whose eyes never left Imogene's rapidly rising and falling breasts.

Giles stepped forward to claim the next dance and Imogene, with a vengeful look at Stephen, allowed Giles to take her hand. " 'Tis so hot!" she complained, fanning herself energetically with the pink-plumed fan that dangled on an ivory chain from her wrist. "A dip in the sea would be cooling. Think you that I in my chemise and you in your smallclothes could swim out to the point?"

"Mistress Imogene!" Giles gaped at her and cast a horrified look at his grinning friends. "Surely, ye jest!" He almost stumbled over his own boots as he made haste to lead his spirited lady out upon the floor.

Imogene's face was flushed, and to Stephen's regret, her reply was lost in the music as a scandalized Giles Avery bore her away from them, but Mowbrey's lip curled as he turned away. "Giles does not know our lustrous Imogene if he thinks she jests!"

"What?" murmured his companion avidly, turning to join him. "And has she gone swimming with you in her chemise?"

"Better than that, in her altogether. She—" A sudden burst of laughter from a coquettish girl floating by drowned the rest of his comment but from his companion's sudden sputter of laughter Stephen had no doubt what it was.

He strode after the pair, clamped his heavy hand down on the speaker's shoulder and spun him around.

"I think you besmirch a young lady's reputation," he grated and dusted his knuckles bruisingly across the lad's surprised cheek.

"What business is it of yours, sir," gasped Mowbrey, turning pale as he looked up into that dangerous face, "to eavesdrop on a private conversation?"

"I make it my business. Take back your lying words about Mistress Wells."

" 'Tis no lie!" Bluster, now that a group was collecting around them. "For all know that she—"

A sudden hard blow to his mouth rattled his teeth and he ended his comment by spitting blood.

"Admit ye lied about Mistress Wells!" thundered Stephen.

"I will not!" The cornered youth gave a wild look around him, saw that there was no escape from the eager onlookers who pressed forward. "I—I demand satisfaction, sir."

"Good, I'll give it to ye at sunup. Ambrose—" for Ambrose

Duveen had pushed through the spectators—"will ye be my second and make the arrangements?"

"A duel, Stephen?" Ambrose looked shaken.

"Hardly that. I'll be teaching a young puppy to guard his tongue in the future—if I decide to give him a future." Stephen fixed his quarry with a gleaming eye. "Pray well this night, Mowbrey—it may be your last opportunity!"

Turning first white and then red, his brocaded opponent looked about to leap forward, but the thick-lipped youth restrained him. Looking excited, he pulled Mowbrey away, while the lad pulled back crying, "Do not drag me off, Cowles! Faith, I'll humble the fellow here!"

"Listen to Cowles," advised Stephen in a cold, carrying voice, "or ye're like to take not one drubbing but two!"

Ambrose tugged at Stephen's arm. " 'Tis madness to quarrel with Tom Mowbrey," he said in an undertone. "His father's Lord Constable and if ye should chance to kill him, he could make trouble for ye!"

"I've no mind to kill him," growled Stephen, moving away through the throng with Ambrose tagging after. "Just to let a little of his hot blood for him."

"In heaven's name, why?" cried Ambrose. "Ye met him only this evening, what could ye find time to quarrel about?"

"I liked not his insinuations about Mistress Wells," said Stephen shortly.

"About Imogene?" Ambrose's eyes widened. "But *everyone* knows—"

He found his words cut off by a strong hand that cruelly twisted the lace at his throat. "Say not one word about Mistress Imogene Wells," came Stephen's level voice, "or I'll forget ye're a friend and cross blades with you!"

Ambrose paled—and swallowed as the strong fingers were

withdrawn from his windpipe and he could breathe again. "So it's that way now, is it? 'Twixt you and Imogene?"

"There's naught between us."

"Yet you're her champion?"

"Aye," growled Stephen, "and in this Godforsaken place she needs one."

Ambrose bristled, and then chewed that over mentally. Stephen, he told himself sorrowfully, like so many others, had been instantly stricken with desire for Imogene; it was a malady from which many had suffered yet all had recovered. Doubtless Stephen would, too. He went away to find Cowles and make arrangements for tomorrow's duel.

"You mustn't do it," Bess told Stephen wildly. She had hurried across the room when she heard the news of the impending duel, which had flashed like wildfire through the crowd. "His father is—"

"Lord Constable. Ambrose told me."

"But he can make *desperate* trouble for you!" cried Bess.

"Mistress Bess." Stephen's voice softened at her obvious disarray. "I've had trouble made for me by experts. I doubt me this Lord Constable can make my problems any worse."

"But they say the quarrel was over Imogene and she isn't yours to defend! She's—"

"Mine to defend. Exactly right," came a Cornish voice and Stephen swung around to see that Giles and Imogene—a rather pale Imogene—had joined them.

"That's as may be," drawled Stephen. "Meantime I'll fight my own battles on behalf of any lady I please."

"Imogene," appealed Bess. *"Do something!* Stephen may be killed!"

"I did not ask him to fight for me. Indeed, I've no wish to be brawled over like any tavern wench!"

Before Bess could more than sputter her indignation, Ambrose stuck his head between them. "We should go home now," he told Stephen decisively. "For ye'll need your sleep to have a strong sword arm tomorrow. I see Mowbrey has already left."

"I won't be accompanying you." Stephen looked straight at Imogene. "For whether death strikes me down tomorrow or no, I've a mind to stroll for a while beneath the castle wall before coming back to Ennor to sleep."

"Ye're mad!" cried Ambrose. " 'Tis already late and Cowles and I have arranged for a dawn engagement beneath this same wall! Mowbrey will spend the night with Cowles, who lives but a short distance away, and you—oh, I must insist!"

"Insist all ye like," grinned Stephen, his narrow gaze still playing over Imogene's rapt face in which the color was rising. "But I've a mind to cool myself off with a moonlight swim and I may not be back till late. Indeed, I may not be back at all, but wait for my opponent here beneath the wall he's so fond of."

Bess protested unhappily and Ambrose left them, shaking his head. But as Giles reached out to pull her away, Imogene, whose gaze had been locked with Stephen's, shook her head as if to clear it.

"Whoever is mad enough to wander the night," she declared ringingly, "*I* shall be sleeping. For whoever is heavy-eyed, *I* at least plan to be fresh for tomorrow's battle!"

Stephen grinned but Bess gave Imogene a look of pure horror for her heartlessness.

And the ball went merrily on.

CHAPTER 2

Now that the ball was over, Imogene Wells, who, along with her maid, Elise, and her chaperon, Mistress Peale, were houseguests at Star Castle, could not sleep. She tossed in her unfamiliar bed and told herself that Stephen Linnington had been but baiting her, toying with her—he was not even now strolling beneath the stone walls and perhaps gazing up at the battlements, wondering if she was leaning over them searching for his lean figure in the darkness. She told her strumming heart decisively that she did not care a fig about that silly duel to be fought tomorrow. Tom Mowbrey was no swordsman, and Stephen, with his lean fencer's body and that determined gleam in his turquoise eyes, could doubtless handle him. Softhearted Bess had been merely hysterical that a houseguest of the Duveens might come to harm.

Still, Imogene could not sleep.

Suddenly, goaded by the thought that he might really be

out there waiting for her, she rose from her bed, rose stealthily, not to disturb Elise, who lay snoring soundly on a nearby cot. Quickly she slipped into a sky blue linen kirtle and doublet. She was about to tie on the huge detachable sleeves that were so fashionable, sleeves through which her ruffled white lawn chemise sleeves could be thrust, when a sudden thought occurred to her. A smile pricked the corners of her mouth and she dropped the big sleeves and snatched up a white lawn whisk and stole from the room.

Soundlessly she made her way up to the battlements where the sleeping musicians, much the worse for drink and sleeping it off stertorously beside their instruments, lay sprawled. She tiptoed by them and leaned over the parapet, her eyes searching the dry moat for a dark figure . . . there was none. All the world seemed gone to bed.

The only safe course was to go back to bed herself because she knew in her heart, although it annoyed her to admit it, this man could be dangerous—to her. He could change the course of her well-ordered humdrum life.

Still the thought of him down there somewhere in the moon-streaked darkness tempted her and she lingered, leaning pensively on her arms on the parapet in the moonlight staring out at the dark islands and the dark, glittering sea stretching ever away.

There was more to life than these islands and a guardian who was determined to marry her off, she told herself rebelliously. And—she sighed—she had so little time, for in June she would be seventeen.

Until June . . . she had only till June and then her guardian would force her into marriage with Giles Avery. Not a betrothal she could lightly break—*marriage*. Marriage to the heir to the greatest fortune in Cornwall. *And wasn't that what she wanted?*

she scolded herself. She toyed with the thought of marrying Giles, imagining how it would be.

There would be a garlanded wedding, a boisterous wedding with guests from afar and bride's ales, and ribbon favors to be cut from her gown. And while the guests went on roistering there would be . . . a wedding night. Her eyes darkened at the thought, for she knew in her heart that she could never love Giles. They would be close together in a big bed with the curtains drawn around them, sinking in a smothering feather mattress, flesh pressed against flesh. . . . She hugged her arms around her body, feeling suddenly cold in her light linen doublet.

But this was the way things were done—in Cornwall and all the rest of England. And who did she know who had married for love? It was customary for parents or guardians to arrange marriages for the young before . . . *before they could break free and make their own choices*, her rebellious heart told her.

She pushed aside the thought. *Think of all that lies ahead*, she told herself desperately. *Think of the fine clothes, the jewels, the balls* . . . no, with Giles there would be very few balls; he did not really care much for dancing—fine clothes, yes, and strutting about like a peacock, taking snuff—but dancing, no. He had often told her it was too fatiguing.

Looking out over the far dark islands, she saw how it would be: Handsomely gowned—and considered lucky for a girl with no dowry—she would go to live at Giles's family's Tudor manse near Lands End and after the wedding trip he had promised her, she would probably never see any more of the world at all. She would spend her life—when she was not being ordered around by Giles's mother—attending Giles's needs, bearing his children, and watching a paunchy young man grow into a portly middle age. Of evenings, when her feet were tapping to dance, she would have to sit demurely plying her needle and watch Giles work over his account books or smoke his pipe—and make conversation with his parents, whom she had met once and found unutterably dull. Or for a real treat Giles might ask her to play cards with him, for he had told her—with sparkling eyes, as if it were an important state secret—that at his home they played cards twice a week. It was their sole revolt against the Lord Protector's puritanical hand.

And on lovely nights like this, long after Giles had lurched off her unresisting body and lay snoring beside her, she would rise from her bed and stand silently at her window, as she was standing at this parapet now. She would look out through the trees at the great standing stone they called the Blind Fiddler. And hear ancient music strumming through the night, calling to her as her own wild blood sang. And ancient laughter mocking her for having gone so docilely to her prosaic destiny.

A small sob rose in Imogene's rebellious white throat at this stark assessment of her future and was immediately choked back.

Till June, she told herself fiercely. *She had until June. She was her own woman until then and she must make the most of it.*

Almost as a reflex gesture of defiance she tossed the sheer white lawn whisk she was holding over the parapet, watched it float away, gossamer white in the moonlight, on its slow descent to the dry moat below.

She should certainly have gone back to bed then, but she did not.

Instead she turned and ran back on light feet the way she had come, avoiding her own doorway and following the great Jacobean stairway down. Quietly she made her way out of the sleeping castle and on soft slippers reached the dry moat and looked around her.

Everything was perfectly quiet. The petrels and cormorants and auks and great black-backed gulls that screamed and wheeled over the islands in the daytime were still. Nearby, the moonlight picked out yellow lichen on the gray stones, and at her feet was a mass of bluebells and other wild flowers scenting the warm night air.

Imogene took a deep breath. From the silence, it seemed indeed that all the world had gone to bed.

She felt a sharp prickle of disappointment.

He was not here.

Well then, she would try to find her whisk and go back to bed.

She walked about, staring down at the grasses and wild flowers that luxuriated in the dry moat, stirring them with her foot. The whisk should have fallen about here. It was white and would be hard to miss.

Suddenly, from out of the shadow of the castle walls a man's arm shot out, a man's hand seized her wrist.

Imogene choked back a scream.

A low laugh followed the hand, then a smiling face, and then a body was thrust out of the darkness. The moonlight beamed down into a pair of reckless turquoise eyes.

"So you vowed you wouldn't, but you came anyway." Stephen's voice was triumphant.

Still tingling from her sudden fright, Imogene tossed her head and her bright curls rippled in the moonlight. "I came but to look for my whisk," she said airily.

"The first? Or the second that came sailing over the castle wall just minutes ago? I found them both."

So he'd been watching after all. . . . "You should be home in bed," she mocked. "For that terrible swordsman, Tom Mowbrey, is like to run you through tomorrow."

"Is he a good blade, then?" A genial grin spread across Stephen's face. "Faith, I'm glad to hear it. 'Twill make the event more sporting."

She laughed up at him. "No, Tom's no blade at all. I'm sure he'd never have challenged you had he not felt pushed into it because everyone was looking. You—"she frowned—"you must not kill him, Stephen."

"Why? Because his father's the Lord Constable?"

"No. Because he's a fool and not worthy of your steel."

"A better reason." Caressingly. "And doubly a fool for insulting you."

She sighed. "I do not know that I've been insulted."

"A taste of the blade will make him watch his tongue in future."

She leaned forward. "Tom Mowbrey is spiteful because I scratched his face once!"

"And how did you come to do that?" wondered Stephen. "Come, let us walk down to the sea while you tell me."

"First you must tell me what he said."

" 'Tis not for your ears."

"Of course it is! It was *about me,* wasn't it?"

"He said, Mistress Imogene—"

"Oh, call me Imogene. You might as well, you're fighting a duel over me in the morning!"

"He said, Imogene—"Stephen had taken her elbow and was guiding her footsteps over the rocks—"that ye'd gone swimming with him in your altogether. I bade him take back the lie and he refused. I bloodied his teeth a bit for that."

"I was not in my altogether!" she flashed.

He gave her a sharp look. "Then it was partly true?"

"Yes, part of it's true," she admitted gloomily.

Stephen frowned. He'd not have called Tom a liar if he'd known he was telling the truth. "What part?"

"I did go swimming with him in my chemise and petti-coat—on a dare. But my wet skirts wrapped around my legs and near drowned me and Tom was hard put to pull me in to shore. When I lay on the beach, coughing water, he thought to revive me by taking off my clothes."

"I could see he might." Ironically.

"But I was in no mood to let him do it, half-drowned or no, and when he tore my bodice, I clawed his face. 'Tis the clawing he resents, for I left a mark on his cheek he was hard put to explain."

"And I'll leave my mark on him, also," said Stephen blithely. "To remind Master Tom not to trifle with you again."

They had reached the ocean now, a black mirror reflecting the dark sky and the big white floating moon and the scattered diamonds that were the stars.

"You shouldn't be fighting for me, Stephen," Imogene said, troubled. "Giles is right, if anyone fights for me, *he* should be the one."

"And you think he would fight for you?"

"Probably not," sighed Imogene. "It would be too—enervating. He'd make it up with Tom some other way."

"Then it grieves me to deny you, my lady," Stephen said softly. "But young Mowbrey is intent on having a lesson in self-defense."

Her white teeth bit into her soft lower lip, for she felt suddenly to blame for everything. She had taunted Tom, hadn't she? She had brought it all on herself. And this duel tomorrow . . . "Will nothing dissuade you?" she asked wistfully. "Is your mind so made up?"

"It is, my lady." He was standing so close his breath brushed her cheek. "And with your permission I will wear one of these two whisks I found as a favor upon my sleeve."

Giles, she told herself, even had he succeeded in supplanting Stephen in tomorrow's duel, would never have thought of anything so gallant. "Of course you may wear it," she said with a little catch in her voice, for she was all too aware of his heady masculine presence only a breath away. "And I'll tie it about your wrist myself!" she added vigorously, taking the proffered whisk.

She moved to do it and felt a shakiness start in her fingers and move through her whole body as she touched him, a heady giddiness as if her knees might buckle. It was hard to meet his eyes, whose intent gaze seemed suddenly more brilliant than the stars.

"There," she said breathlessly, giving the whisk a little pat. " 'Tis done."

He looked down upon her work, smiling, and then at her face, now turned slightly away from him as if she could not bear to look at him. With a gentle finger, he turned her face back to him.

"And would ye take that dip in the sea with me, my lady, that Giles turned down?" His voice was rich, caressing; it went through her like the strum of a *viola* string.

"No, I—no, I must not." She moved uneasily as if to ward him off.

"I had hoped . . ." His voice was melancholy. "Hoped that since I might well die on your behalf in the morning that ye'd grant me this small favor."

" 'Die'?" Her gaze flew to him, saw that his eyes, perhaps laughing, were shadowed now. She choked back a rich laugh. "Poor Tom is like to turn and run!"

"And yet . . ." He reached forward to touch experimentally a tendril of her fair hair. "I'm told a peer of England was once killed in a duel with the king's fool—and the fool no higher than a man's knee. 'Twas a lucky arrow shot.''

"I take your meaning." *A man could slip, a lucky thrust could breach his defenses, even the finest of swordsmen were cut down in the end. . . .* This duel, which had seemed at first but a joke, had suddenly assumed alarming proportions in her mind. Her cheeks had grown hot and now she looked away from him, out past the white beach and the piled-up black rocks through which the surf poured, out across the open ocean.

Then abruptly she seated herself upon a large flat rock, lifted her skirts and reached for her slipper. "Turn your back," she ordered crisply. "For I've no mind to risk drowning with my legs caught in a twisted-up chemise!" And then, to that stalwart back, "I'll call when I'm ready."

That call came moments later from the surf. Stephen turned to see Imogene's white arm waving to him from the dark water. And on the rocks nearby lay, neatly arranged, all her clothing.

His lady was swimming naked!

Eyes alight, Stephen shucked off his clothes, taking especial care with the whisk her gentle fingers had knotted so carefully around his wrist. Sweeping plumed hat, russet velvet doublet and trousers, flowing shirt, boots and stockings and smallclothes, all were left in a pile beside the blue linen kirtle and doublet and the dainty white chemise and slippers. Tossing back his copper hair, he ran barefoot lightly down into the surf to join her, his lean, muscled body gleaming pale in the moonlight.

She had the grace to turn her head until he was in the water up to his waist. Then she turned a smiling face and unexpectedly drove a great splash of water into his face with her open hand.

Laughing as Stephen ducked and choked, Imogene knifed into the waves like a dolphin, to come up farther away from him with a tantalizing wave of her hand, for she had swum some distance underwater.

Delighted with his playful mermaid, Stephen leaped forward and with strong strokes swam out to her. "Ye did not tell me ye were such a swimmer!" he approved.

She laughed, tossing back her wet hair as she faced him, treading water. "Tom Mowbrey thought I could not swim—'twas he near drowned me. Left alone I'd have wriggled out of my tangled skirts and made it back to shore."

"How did ye learn to swim so well?" he wondered, for swimming was an unusual accomplishment for a young lady of fashion.

"I used to slip out of the house at night and swim alone along the beach—and then return before morning and be heavy-eyed and sleepy at breakfast." Her laughter rippled. "My guardian, Lord Elston, decided I was coming down with something and had his doctor try to give me a tonic—woodlice steeped in wine. I spat it at the doctor!"

" 'Woodlice'!" Stephen grimaced. "Faith, I'd have spat it at him, too!" But he wondered . . . *how often had Imogene slipped out and been gone all night? And had she always been alone?* "I take it ye're not afraid of the dark?"

The wet fair head tossed again. "I'm afraid of nothing!" Contemptuously. *But that wasn't quite true. She was afraid of the dream.*

In the water his hands clasped about her naked waist. "And did you always swim alone?" He had to know.

Her eyes seemed to darken. She shoved a hand against his shoulder, brought a bare foot up against his thigh, and with a sudden jerk that submerged them both, broke free. When they came up, she gasped, "I gave you no leave to touch me!"

But he had felt the tremor that went through her at his touch and that encouraged him.

"I'm going ashore now," she said in a shaken voice and Stephen matched his stroke to hers as they swam leisurely back together, following the moon's path over the dark gleaming water.

She had not answered him as to whether she'd always swum alone. Perhaps there'd been others for whom she'd shed her chemise and plunged into the dark water? Perhaps dashing Imogene was no longer a virgin? The thought both tormented and tantalized him.

"Turn your back and stay in the water till I call you," she ordered peremptorily over her shoulder and grasped one of the big rocks, used it to steady herself, for underfoot the sand was shifting, trying to pull her back into the water. She was half out of the water when his fingers closed, gently but urgently, upon her shoulder. The wet face she turned to him in the moonlight was young, vulnerable, the eyes alight and lustrous; it was a face of surrender and he knew it.

"I'd dance with ye, my lady, in a way I could not at the castle ball," he murmured, and put an arm around her, lifted her up, wet and dripping, and carried her to the smooth, flat rock where their clothes lay. With a careless gesture, he brushed them off to the sand, then stood her very carefully upon her feet. She stood before him, glowing, trembling like a young colt not yet broken to the saddle, and his warm smile gave her confidence.

Together, naked and barefoot, they danced atop that broad, flat-topped rock. Danced to a music that throbbed only in their own ears, their wet bodies touching, vibrating to a shared and tantalizing rhythm.

Laughing, exultant, Stephen clasped two strong hands about her waist and swung her up above his head. Laughing, she threw her arms about his neck in wild abandon as he swung her down again and felt her breasts crush softly, lovingly, against his hard-muscled chest. As her body slid down his, rasping like watered silk, she was no longer laughing. Her lips were parted, her eyes were wide and luminous, and she collapsed against him with a little moan.

He picked her up then and carried her back into the surf, and there, lying in the sand with the lacy foam breaking over them, he made love to her. Imogene had no will to resist him. It was the softness of the night, she told herself wildly. The dark glitter of the water had worked some alchemy in her head. She felt herself borne along by large forces, irresistible, strong . . . strong as the moontide, washing in toward them.

And suddenly she faced reality—and what it was she wanted. She wanted this man—Stephen Linnington. Not Giles Avery with all his wealth or silent Hal Duveen—though she had fancied Hal's mighty muscles for a season until he had turned out to be both stupid and prudish—she wanted *Stephen*.

And if she did not let him take her now, the chance might never come again. Stephen might be hurt in tomorrow's duel—there was always the chance of that—he might leave the island; her guardian was old, he might take sick and send for her suddenly and she would have to hover about his bedside until the copper-haired man from Devon left the Scillies forever.

No, it was now—or perhaps never.

Reckless Imogene, acting on impulse—and perhaps the pressure of destiny—sighed luxuriously in Stephen's arms. And stopped struggling.

The change in him was immediate. A tremor went through his strong frame and for a moment his lean body tensed as his senses twanged like a bowstring.

Her new attitude toward him, the yielding way she fitted her body to his, spoke to him clearly. *Take me*, her body told him, *for I am yours*.

Never one to hesitate, Stephen caressed this new pliant creature in his arms, whispered in her ears words that could scarce be heard above the roar of the surf, for the moonswept tide was coming in. And Imogene clung to him, whispering unheard words in return.

To Imogene, giving herself to a man for the first time, this was a wedding night, for on this night she gave her heart as truly as any bride to Stephen Linnington. Through a crack in the black rocks, the surf foamed white, incoming with the tide. Like a bridal veil, it spilled over her pale wet hair spread out around her like a fan, poured over her shoulders, her gleaming breasts. It foamed over her narrow feet like white satin bridal slippers and spilled over her long white legs like lustrous stockings. Pouring through that crack in the rocks, the water caressed her feverish body like cool silken undergarments and found secret places to gurgle and ripple and flow. It caressed her white form in the moonlight—as Stephen's questing hands and eager lips caressed her. Together they lay on the sand in the roiling incoming surf, rocked and lifted with each incoming surge as if they lay upon the ocean's great throbbing breast—merman and mermaid, creatures of some long lost time when there was only the sea and the rocks and the sand.

To Imogene the pain that rent her suddenly and left her gasping was a small price to pay for the wild emotions that surged through her, triumphant, joyful, and she responded to Stephen's lovemaking with an ardor that thrilled and surprised him.

He had shattered all her defenses and Imogene was content to lie in his arms and let him do as he would with her. And in those arms she learned, learned fervently and gloriously, what it was to be loved by a strong, vigorous man in his prime.

To Stephen she was a miracle, a dream come true.

Her skin was smooth and wet to his touch. His fingers slid along it as if it were watered silk. His own body had the sheen and feel of heavy satin, and above her lissome, yielding body that clung to him so confidently, so luxuriously, his own form rose and fell in an ancient rhythm. His passion mounted as their foam-washed bodies tangled, surged, blended. A bird flew dark across the moon and what he saw below him must have seemed like two long graceful silvery fish beached in the surf and writhing—or a mermaid and a merman mating against the backdrop of the black primordial rocks.

As the bird swooped low over them—curious perhaps— Stephen lifted his head, alerted by the sudden shadow that swept across the sand—and caught his breath at the sight of her, eyes closed and lips parted, the moon shining magically across her wet gleaming breasts, silvering her gleaming knees that rose convulsively to slide along his pale gleaming thighs.

With a low yearning sound in his throat he fell back upon her and their bodies surged and pressed and retreated to a rhythm as old and as splendid and as engulfing as the ocean's rhythmic boom against the rocks.

And when they lay still at last, motionless, exhausted by the splendor that had claimed them, their ardor spent, their passion fled like retreating surf—lay like enchanted beings, resting before stealing back to the world from which they had come—they were silent with the wonder of it all, for they both knew in their secret hearts that this night had changed them for all time.

For better or for worse, after tonight neither of them would ever be the same.

CHAPTER 3

Stumbling through the semidarkness on the way to his duel with Stephen Linnington, Tom Mowbrey was having second thoughts. He chafed at thick-lipped Cowles's steady flow of conversation beside him, and frowned when his wine-clad friend pointed out how hot it was already and how wise he'd been to insist that the meeting be at dawn, when there was still some coolness in the salt air. But he spoke up when Cowles insisted that Tom would surely win because he was the younger and therefore the better man.

"We know nothing of this Linnington fellow," he told Cowles sulkily.

"That's true, but then we've never heard of him as a swordsman." Cowles paused complacently to brush a blowing leaf from his wine satin trousers.

Tom Mowbrey swung on him in a fury. "We've never

heard of half the blades in England but that's not to say they aren't good men!"

"Ah, I didn't mean to downgrade Linnington." Cowles saw his mistake and hastily tried to make amends. "I but said ye'll triumph over him this day with no trouble."

Mowbrey stumbled over a rock and cursed as a gull rose nearby with a scream and took off, circling overhead. How could Cowles, who had not a nerve in his stupid body, know what he was thinking? "Best not to crow until the match is over," he said sourly and begged his friend to leave off talking to him.

Cowles nodded sagely. A man needed time to plan his strategy; that was perfectly right and proper.

But in truth Tom Mowbrey, as he stormed along the uneven path, was flaying himself for his ill-advised words last night and wishing himself anywhere in England but the Scillies at this moment.

His nervousness, as they neared their destination, increased.

"Ah, I see they're here already, waiting for us," said Cowles, looking down into the dry moat with satisfaction, and Mowbrey could have cried with rage.

Below them in the dawn's pale light they could see Stephen Linnington in the clothes he had worn the night before, and Ambrose Duveen, who hailed them with a wave of his hand, sprucely dressed in shades of olive and lime.

"There's the detestable creature," muttered Cowles, and Mowbrey's dark head and scowling visage swung around to see what he had not noticed before—Imogene Wells, looking disheveled and unusually gorgeous in her sleeveless blue linen doublet and wide skirt, with her full, elbow-length white chemise sleeves spilling, lace-pointed, around her slim forearms. She was seated on a big rock, watching them approach. She looked cool, Cowles thought, and almost dreamy.

"I hate her," choked Mowbrey almost with a sob, and felt a pulse pound in his temple.

"All in good time," soothed Cowles, seeing that the sight of the woman in the case had upset his friend. "After ye've bested her champion, ye can go over and have a word or two with Mistress Imogene if ye like."

After . . . . a chill went through Mowbrey. Down below them Stephen had tossed aside his plumed hat and had removed his doublet in the heat. At the moment he was standing there in the flowing full-sleeved shirt he had borrowed from Hal Duveen. He saw Cowles and Mowbrey coming down the path and with a casual gesture unsheathed his blade and tested the tip meaningfully. Mowbrey noted with alarm how his big shoulder muscles rippled as the light breeze blew his thin shirt against them. He tugged unsteadily at his lacy cravat. "This damned heat," he complained, his voice uneven. "A man could suffocate."

Cowles was instantly solicitous. He must keep his man cool-headed—and if possible, cool-bodied—until this contest was over. "Here, Tom, give me your doublet and cravat," he urged. "And your hat as well."

"Perhaps ye'd like my boots too!" Testily.

"It would be better if ye took them off."

"What?" Mowbrey was indignant. "There may be thorns hidden in this stuff." He kicked violently at the bluebells.

"As ye wish," agreed Cowles, willing to agree to anything. "But the wide tops of your boots could trip you or throw you off balance."

"Linnington is wearing his boots—I will wear mine!" cried Mowbrey. "Think you I want to land on a thorn just as I'm parrying a thrust?"

Bickering thus, they joined the waiting company to find Stephen—who had already tested the dueling ground—seating himself and peeling off his wide boots.

"*Now* will ye take yours off?" hissed Cowles, who had just come to the unpleasant realization that this contest might not be the vision of chivalry he'd pictured it to be.

"I will not!" rejoined Mowbrey. "I told ye there are thorns—"

"Then die with them on!" snapped Cowles, impatience at last overcoming friendship.

It was the wrong thing to have said. The dark-haired youth paled perceptibly and sat down suddenly on a rock. "Perhaps ye are right," he muttered. "Here, help me get them off, Cowles."

The seconds were getting ready, testing the blades, bustling about, when Imogene's clear voice rang out.

"Your quarrel is with me, Tom Mowbrey. I'm the one who scratched your face. Why fight a stranger?"

Tom Mowbrey, standing now in his stockings and testing his toes gingerly upon the grass and wild flowers, turned a vengeful gaze toward the calm blue and gold vision who sat perched on a rock, with bluebells caught in her hair, carelessly swinging one leg, and chewing on a grass blade.

"I'll have a word with you later, Mistress Imogene!" he retorted.

"Not," said Stephen silkily, interposing himself between them, "if I have anything to say about it. And I advise you to keep your mouth closed during this engagement or I may shorten your tongue for you!"

A bloody film seemed to go over Mowbrey's eyes and he would have leaped at the speaker had not Cowles restrained him.

"If ye cannot keep quiet, Mistress Imogene, we must ask

ye to leave," Cowles told the girl impatiently. "Ye can see the effect your remarks are having on Tom!"

Imogene gave a careless nod and tossed away the grass stem she had been testing with her white teeth. "I but thought to save that fine brocade suit Tom is wearing from a slash that will have to be mended by his mother's tirewoman," she said lazily.

Stephen chuckled at this irrepressible remark by his lady and flexed his arms and shoulders. His body felt wonderful—relaxed, happy. As well it should, after last night, he told himself. Out of the pink dawn another hot day was peeping. Soon the sun would be beating down, pouring its molten gold down upon the beach—and here before him was a brash lad, ripe for a lesson at arms. Stephen had never felt better. He stepped forward to confront the dandy in fawn brocade who stood glowering before him.

Imogene tensed as the two men saluted. At the signal, Mowbrey, too eager to make his mark—sprang forward. His first wild thrust—from which Stephen stepped back in some amusement—managed to nick a blowing edge of Stephen's shirt and Tom leaped back, panting and jubilant.

"I've pinked him!" he crowed, flinging down his blade.

Stephen cast a sardonic glance down at the slight tear in the white linen. Hal's shirt . . . a pity. He leaned upon his blade and studied his foe. "Shall I strip to prove ye have not?" he demanded.

"Of course not," cried Cowles. "There's a lady present. We'll take your word!" He reached joyfully for the sword Tom had flung down, proffered it with a flourish, for he felt that at last Tom was catching on, taking command of the match. "Here's your blade, Tom. Have at it, man!"

Choked with rage, Tom Mowbrey took the blade—in a hand that trembled—and with a snarl that Cowles mistook for a killer instinct, charged again. His charge was easily checked as Stephen, experienced swordsman that he was, pushed him back almost contemptuously.

Imogene was leaning forward, holding her breath. She watched Stephen seem to lead his opponent around in a semicircle upon the grass, testing his defenses, learning his weaknesses. Like Ambrose and Cowles, who were also watching intently, she was puzzled by Stephen's seeming consideration for Tom Mowbrey, who leaped and panted and strove most manfully to inflict some wound upon his foe that would end the match—for this was not a duel to the death, and the first to draw blood would emerge the victor.

Suddenly Stephen leaped in, his blade twinkling so rapidly that a sweating Mowbrey was hard put to follow its passage. As Mowbrey parried desperately, their clashing blades slid up their full length until the two men were hilt and hilt, staring into each other's eyes. Mowbrey thought he saw leaping death in Stephen's and jumped back, appalled.

Ah, what a fool he'd been to tear that shirt! This man meant to kill him!

Imogene for a mad moment had had the same thought and caught her breath as she leaned forward.

Terrified and cornered now, Mowbrey sprang to the attack once more and this time Stephen gave ground, gracefully, allowing Mowbrey to wear himself out with his wild lunges.

"Ye have him, Tom, ye have him now!" exulted Cowles from the sidelines, and Tom Mowbrey, had circumstances permitted, which in this wild melee they did not, would gladly have flung his sword at his friend's empty head. He was panting and badly winded as he came out of the last exchange of thrusts—and, even worse, badly scared.

Now Stephen was smiling—a steely smile that made his

white teeth flash like a wolf's, Tom thought—and stalking his young foe about the trampled grass and wild flowers. He had, with seeming leisure, assumed command of the match.

Unwillingly, Tom gave ground. His opponent seemed to be probing him, seeking to pink him at some particular spot—and at that moment, catching sight of Imogene's frightened face, Tom Mowbrey was certain that spot was the breastbone. The thought terrified him further and made him reckless. Winded, he staggered back, and then, born of desperation, he made a sudden wild thrust, skidded on the grass and went down on one knee. As Imogene screamed, he jumped up—hardly noticing in his excitement that Stephen had graciously stepped back to let his opponent rise to his feet. With the last of his strength, Tom lunged forward, his whole body extended.

In an instant, his strong experienced opponent had crashed his blade against his, the sword flew from Mowbrey's half-numbed hand and the point of Stephen's blade was menacing his throat.

White to the lips, Mowbrey staggered back. "No, don't kill me," he whimpered. "I take back what I said about Imogene!"

Instantly the deadly point of that blade flicked upward and as he flinched, believing it aimed at his eyes, he felt a sharp pain in his cheek.

Stephen stepped back, eyeing the small cut with satisfaction. It was exactly where he had meant to place it.

" 'Twill make but a small scar," he told a shaking Tom Mowbrey critically. "But 'twill replace the scratch Mistress Imogene once gave you—and serve as a reminder whenever you look in the mirror, which I take it is often, to guard your tongue when you speak of her."

Imogene, delighted that the duel had ended with so slight a wound, proffered the other white whisk Stephen had found.

"To bind up your wound," she said negligently.

Looking as if he might any minute be sick, Tom Mowbrey struck the whisk away and charged off, forgetting his boots.

"Wait!" cried Cowles in an anguished voice. He seized Tom's boots and doublet and cravat and hurried after him.

But Tom had gone no more than a dozen paces before he gave a howl and began hopping around on one foot, cursing Cowles, the terrain and all present with incoherent rage—the sole of his stockinged foot had managed to connect with a thorn and it had pierced both his flesh and the remnants of his self-control. In the distance he could hear Imogene's taunting laughter.

His pride rubbed raw, sobbing with rage, Tom Mowbrey stumbled home beside a mortified Cowles. When his friend tried to comfort him by saying he could meet Stephen again on some other occasion when he "felt better" and thus rescue his honor, Tom struck him in the face and hobbled away on his thorn-pierced foot.

He would lay the whole matter before his father, he vowed angrily—how he had been laughed at, made a fool of—and all over a careless word about wild Imogene Wells. He would enlist his father's aid in checking up on this brash Linnington fellow who had sprung forward to champion her. And if there was anything, *anything* in this fellow Linnington's past that could be held against him, he would pounce on it and bring him down!

But back at the dry moat, over which the sun was now spilling its gold, the lovers gave him not a thought. For them the day was already wonderful and their spirits soared like the seabirds.

Ambrose, flushed and smiling that his man had won the day so handily, said he was away to breakfast and wouldn't Stephen like to come with him?

Stephen's smiling eyes never left Imogene, who was looking glorious. "Go on without me," he told Ambrose. "I'd have a word with Mistress Imogene."

"Aye, I guess ye've earned it," agreed Ambrose gloomily, and strode back to Ennor Castle and his breakfast, where he found Bess white and pinch-faced, waiting for him.

"Well?" she cried, running toward him. "What happened? Tell me!"

"Nothing happened." Ambrose yawned and pushed past her toward the dining room. "I told ye what a fool ye were to think ye should go and watch. Stephen pinked his man—on the cheek; the Lord Constable won't like having his son marked, I'll wager—and the duel was over. Like that!" He snapped his fingers.

Bess sank against the nearest wall as if her legs would not support her. "And Imogene?"

"She was there with him when I arrived," he called back over his shoulder.

Then she could . . . have been there with him all night. Bess brushed the thought aside as too awful. She followed her brother into the dining room, watched him sit down and seize a roll. "Did she try to stop it?" she asked weakly.

"No—yes, I suppose she did." Like his sister, Ambrose was always scrupulously honest. "She asked Tom Mowbrey why he would fight with a stranger when his quarrel was with her?"

"I am glad to hear it. What was his answer?"

"That he would have words with her later—at which point Stephen leaped into the breach. D'ye know, Bess?" Ambrose had grown thoughtful as he munched. "I do think he's in love with her."

Bess felt each word strike her separately. "Oh, he couldn't

be,'' she protested in a faint voice. "He only met her last night—and saw her but once before when he was barely conscious.''

"Still, I think he may be. Their heads were very close together when I left them.''

Had Ambrose but known it, hardly had he left the lovers before their heads were quickly jerked apart at a loud "So there you are! I've been searching the castle for ye!''

Imogene whirled to face her maid, Elise, who, hands on her brown homespun hips, was staring at her with disapproval.

"I came down early, Elise. To watch the duel being fought over me.''

Duel? Elise gasped. "Is anybody dead?''

"No, but Tom Mowbrey has been well humbled for the night when he tried to—'' Imogene broke off, her eyes sparkling. "Go back and say you could not find me, Elise.''

"But I can't do that! They will report ye as missing to Mistress Peale when ye don't show up for breakfast, and she'll wail for search parties!''

"Then tell everyone I'm having the vapors over the duel that was fought—and won—by Stephen Linnington when he vanquished Tom Mowbrey in my behalf. Tell them I was so exercised that I've taken to my bed and you'll bring my tray to my room, for I've no mind to be scolded today—by Mistress Peale or anybody else!''

Elise knew Imogene's impulsiveness and stubbornness all too well. "Ye'll be back for supper, then?''

Imogene cast a shadowed look at Stephen. "I doubt it,'' she said softly.

"But I was to visit my sister Clara today on Saint Agnes. What if Mistress Peale should ask for you after I'm gone?''

"Go tomorrow, Elise, and I'll go with you. Stephen will

borrow Hal's boat and take us there. And tell Mistress Peale that I've promised Bess Duveen we'll go to visit them tomorrow and she must rest in bed and conserve her strength, for she knows how the stairs at the Duveens' always exhaust her—*that* will keep her from getting up and trailing to my room to pester me with questions!"

"Giles Avery will be asking for you."

Imogene shrugged. "Put him off."

Elise hesitated. She had always helped Imogene before in hoodwinking Mistress Peale and her elderly guardian but today Imogene looked different. She was glowing. As if she had some great important secret that she could use to triumph over everyone.

Elise was afraid for her.

"I'll do my best," she said in an altered voice.

"Thank you, Elise." Imogene blew her a kiss and took Stephen's hand.

With a sober face, Elise watched them saunter away among the rocks until they were hidden from her view. Then, shaking her head, she went back to the castle, mentally girding herself to ward off Mistress Peale's querulous wonder as to where was Imogene?

But the strolling lovers had already forgotten her. Hand in hand they walked among the bluebells—laughing, because Imogene had just said mockingly that it was too bad Tom had not pinked Stephen as he had claimed, for then she could have taken him to the fabled spring in Hell Bay at nearby Bryher Island, a spring where the sun never shone and the waters healed all wounds. Her eyes met his as she said that, and there was a mystical glory in them and a contentment, as if for him she would heal all the wounds of life.

And seeing that look, Stephen winced—and saw himself

for a fleeting moment as others must see him. In a flash of honesty, he faced, momentarily, the truth: He had *wanted* to believe the worst of Imogene, to believe her wild and wanton, for he had burned to hold her in his arms. He had *wanted* her to be wild, and when he had overheard that careless talk about her—all lies, as he now well knew—he had half convinced himself of the truth of it.

He had seduced a virgin.

What was worse, a virgin of breeding and sensitivity, who'd undoubtedly expect him to marry her.

Which of course he could not do, having already two wives, although at the moment he could not pinpoint the location of either.

"Are ye sorry?" he asked abruptly. "About last night?"

"Never!" Her voice rang with sincerity. And whatever happened to her in the future, she knew that was true—she could never be sorry about last night. "Are—are you?" she asked hesitantly.

"Never!" He swung her up in his arms and kissed her lips and carried her away with him down toward the beach.

Lying content in his arms, Imogene's heart sang.

The duel was won, her virginity lost—and not regretted.

It was a magical day, that day she spent with Stephen. They lounged in secret places hidden among the rocks of the beach, they sought the lonely places that only lovers know—lovers and seabirds, shrieking their lonely way on the gossamer currents of the salt wind in the azure dome of the sky.

As the day wore on, in shadowed clefts of the old gray lichened rocks they laughed and made love and teased and forgot there would ever be a tomorrow. In late afternoon they found a shabby fisherman roasting his catch in the ashes of a little fire—and for a few coins, gladly taken, they joined him in his dinner. Then they strolled farther and swam and made love in the shadow of a beached forgotten wreck, half buried in the sand. Lying beneath the bleached bones of the old hull, they slept for a little, lulled by the heat of the late afternoon sun.

Imogene woke first, with a start. The sun was going down. It burned low in the west and like a dying ember it gave all the sky a last red glow. As she watched, the red glowing ball was suddenly eclipsed—and she realized that her view of the sunset was blocked by an enormous flight of seabirds, returning home to the Isle of Annet, where they bred at this time of year. Now her eyes followed their path across the darkening sky.

She sat up, running her fingers through her long hair, and smiled down at the man stretched out long and lean beside her. She hated to wake him and yet she must go back before a search was actually mounted. Elise could cover for her only so long. Still she hesitated, unwilling for this lovely day to end. And so she idled, tracing patterns in the sand with a lazy finger as she looked down on Stephen's face. He looked so young and vulnerable as he slept, she thought.

Strange . . . she had always expected to be taken in bed—that first time. But now she hugged her bare silver knees in ecstatic remembrance . . . last night had been perfect; she wouldn't have had it any other way. Indeed, she felt a ridiculous sense of triumph over other mortals, as if she had risen above them in some way with this new joy, this new ecstasy.

Lying back on the sand again, she studied the darkening sky overhead and told herself playfully that after they were married—for she never for a moment doubted that they would marry—they would live in the sea, swimming endlessly, tirelessly by day and beaching themselves by night, making love till first light.

Her fantasies were lovely. They gave her a glow that made

Stephen's eyes light up in wonder when he came awake at her touch.

She was headed for tragedy but she did not know it. Not yet.

CHAPTER 4

From her vantage point atop the low hill, Elise watched the lovers lingering by the sailboat they'd beached at rugged Saint Agnes Isle.

Three weeks had passed since the ball at Star Castle, three weeks in which reckless Imogene Wells and the tall, sardonic gentleman from Devon had managed to slip away and meet almost daily. Three harrowing weeks for Elise, who had had to cover for Imogene, first at Star Castle and then at Ennor Castle, where they had gone to visit the Duveens. At Ennor they had lingered a scandalously long time, to Elise's way of thinking, for poor Mistress Bess Duveen, who'd always worn her heart on her sleeve, was plain as day in love with the Linnington fellow, who couldn't see her for the dust.

Elise hoped that impetuous Imogene would soon forget Stephen Linnington and find some new toy, but she wasn't so sure that was going to happen. At least Giles Avery, continually rebuffed by Imogene when he came to the Duveens to call on her, had gone away, back to his Tudor manse at Lands End it was presumed, so she could breathe easier on that account. For Mistress Peale might wander about asking plaintively where Imogene was, and sweet Bess Duveen might guess their whereabouts—but Bess was Imogene's friend and would never cause her trouble, not even on Stephen's account. Giles had been a different matter altogether. Elise had been cold with dread that he would come upon Imogene and Stephen in some compromising position and shout it to the world.

If that were to happen, Imogene would be ruined. Her only chance then would be if Stephen Linnington would choose to marry her—and so far as Elise could tell, he had not offered.

Her jaws closed with a snap.

Men!

She turned away from the sight of the golden beach and blue sea and bluer sky. Tall and gaunt in her serviceable brown homespun, she strode the short familiar distance from the shore to the stone hut where her widowed sister Clara had lived alone these five years since her husband had died. On Elise's strong arm was swung a basket filled with fruit kind Bess Duveen had sent Clara. But on her forehead rode a worried frown, and her unseeing gaze passed without interest over the rugged familiar mass of Saint Agnes, southernmost of the Scilly Isles. Beyond lay only Annet, tiny islet of the seabirds; and past Annet a spattering of dark rocks dotting the ocean's blue unruffled face.

It was storied ground over which she walked, wild and beautiful, with sea-scarred and sea-blasted black rocks rising in weird shapes, and lonely cliffs, sea-sculpted and desolate. To others it was a place of legends and mystery—but not to Elise. To her it was home, had been since that long-ago night when Spanish raiders had surprised the little village of Mousehole on the mainland where the young Elise lived, and put the town to fire and sword. After that terrible day, all that had been left of the Meggs family had been eleven-year-old Elise and her younger sister, Clara, who had fortunately been visiting her aunt, who lived in a hunt on Saint Agnes, when the Spanish came. To this hut the two refugee children from destroyed Mousehole had been welcomed and here on Saint Agnes they had grown up and, after the death of her aunt, young Clara had married. On that day Elise had realized how small was the one-room hut, how little privacy would be afforded the shy married pair.

Determined to do something about it, Elise had found herself a job in Penzance on the mainland. And into her empty arms had been thrust tiny Imogene, to care for and to love.

Elise was fiercely protective of Imogene, for in her secret heart she considered Imogene to be *hers*, just as if she, Elise, had borne her. And now that Imogene's own parents were dead and Imogene had been thrust into the household of an unfeeling guardian who spent his days puttering among his roses and his nights, by candlelight, with his nose in musty leather-bound books, Elise felt that mother instinct even more strongly.

It was her love for Imogene that had brought Elise here today.

Her thoughts were abruptly cut off, for she had reached the hut. Through the open door she saw Clara bent over a ball of yarn. As Clara heard her step, she dropped the yarn, darted around the spinning wheel and ran toward her sister.

"Elise, 'tis good to see you." Always more demonstrative than Elise, Clara hugged her.

"How have ye been, Clara?"

"Well enough. I burned my hand baking fish in the hot coals—" she indicated her bandaged left hand—"but 'tis near mended now."

"Ye should not live here alone," observed Elise, casting her eye around the spotless one-room cottage, so barren except for the few objects of serpentine work, gift of a brother-in-law who worked as a stone-carver on the mainland.

"*Ye* should have married," countered Clara. She shot a fond, sad look at her husband's musket, which she polished once a week and which still reposed on the rude mantel, and his well-worn clothes, which she could not bear to part with and which still hung on a nail in the corner.

" 'Married'?" For a moment the smell of sweat and blood and musketry came back to suffocate Elise and she was eleven years old again and back in Mousehole, lying in the dirty street. She felt again a Spanish knee pressing against her childish stomach, holding her down, and then the burning thrust inside her that sent yet another racking spasm of pain through her childish body. In memory she could hear her own thin scream and see, like a vision of hell, the roof of the burning Church of Saint Paul on the hill fall in with a crash and a shower of sparks like fireworks. A burning timber landed in the dusty street nearby and the soldier straining above her cursed thickly as another soldier, waiting his turn at Elise, kicked it away with his boot. Her encounter with the first soldier left her bleeding and nauseous. By the tenth the pain had become a steady agony that wavered and peaked, and her sobbing scream had become a continuous keening wail like that of a dying animal.

Mercifully, an officer had come running by just then barking a command in Spanish and the little knot of soldiers had all scrambled up from their ring around the tortured child and hurried away to carry their hell to the nearby town of Newlyn. They had gone on to ravage Penzance, those two hundred men from the squadron of Spanish galleys, before they were turned back by organized resistance—and in retaliation the English had later attacked and burned Cadiz.

But none of that, no promise of vengeance to come, had mattered to the little girl, with her family murdered, lying more dead than alive in Mousehole's bloody street. She had crawled back to the low wall that surrounded the smoking ruin of her family cottage—and fainted.

It was there the searchers had found her and sent her to her aunt on Saint Agnes who had nursed her back to life.

But though Elise's body recovered, her soul did not. Men had done this to her! Ever after, when a man looked on her with kindness, she would remember the day the Spaniards came and a look of menace would come over her face and a caustic note creep into her voice that would take him aback.

That day in Mousehole had marked her life.

Now, in answer to her sister's query, she said in a level, contemptuous voice, "No, I should not have married."

Clara sighed. It was always like this with Elise. "Come sit here." She lifted a basket of mending from a bench and beckoned Elise to it. "What of Mistress Imogene? Even here on Saint Agnes, I hear of her escapades."

"They are none so bad," sniffed Elise. " 'Tis her beauty makes her the object of envy, and her guardian cares nothing for her. His head is always bent over his books—he sees not that she is a young girl, with a young girl's dreams."

Clara looked surprised to hear Elise mention dreams. What could grim Elise, who had urged her not to marry, know of a young girl's dreams? She gave her older sister a speculative look. " 'Tis a hot day, Elise. Here, I'll pour ye a tankard of cider." She was passing the cottage's one tiny window when she paused, glanced down toward the beach. "I see ye've brought Mistress Imogene and her lover with ye," she said in patent disapproval.

"Ye'll not be calling him her lover," Elise said crisply. "I've told the Duveens ye're sick and Stephen Linnington volunteered to sail Hal's boat over and bring me to see you. Mistress Peale was feeling poorly again and let Imogene come along with me." Her voice sharpened. "Remember that, Clara."

Clara looked uncomfortable. "Ye should not involve yourself so in Mistress Imogene's affairs, Elise," she grumbled. "If Lord Elston were to hear that ye encourage her in her escapades, ye'd be dismissed."

"He'll not be hearing it, unless you speak of it!"

"You know I won't. And I suppose they're safe enough here on Saint Agnes, whatever they do, since I'm the only person living here at the moment now that old Mister Drureton has died. But what of the Duveens? Don't they notice that an affair is going on under their noses?"

"The Duveens think of nothing but sailing—save for Bess. And Bess Duveen is Imogene's friend—though I do think she's in love with Stephen, too."

Clara threw up her hands and rolled her eyes. "He charms them all!"

"I am worried, Clara." Elise sighed and sat down. "I do not know how it will all end."

"It will end with her pregnant!" said Clara energetically.

"Ah, do not say that, Clara." Elise's hand shook on the tankard Clara had given her and she took a quick gulp of cider.

Clara's hands were on her hips; for once she had her bossy older sister on the defensive. "I thought you told me her guardian had his heart set on marrying Imogene off to Giles Avery."

Elise, heartened by the cider, gave a vigorous nod. "He

does. And thanks be to the Almighty that Giles Avery has gone back to sulk at Lands End. He was angry that Imogene paid so little attention to him and left in a huff.''

"But he may return," pointed out her sister.

"Time enough to think about that when it happens. How are matters with you, Clara?''

Clara waxed voluble about how matters were with her. She sat down—glad to have someone to talk to, to complain to—and kept Elise's attention focused on her.

So neither woman noticed the sailboat with one man aboard that was heading for Saint Agnes Isle.

On the beach Stephen and Imogene might have noticed it, had they not been so preoccupied with each other. Imogene was talking, dreaming aloud of the future—*their* future. "And will you take me home to Devon to meet your family, Stephen?" she wondered.

"Aye," lied Stephen. "Soon." His voice was easy but he could not meet her eyes, for in this short time he had come to love her and it went hard with him to have to always be lying to her.

"Will they—like me, do you think?''

"How could they not? There'll be no maid in Devon half so fair!''

She gave him a look of pure enchantment. "And will we be married there? Or here in the Isles?" It was a bold thrust, for Stephen had never mentioned marriage.

Hypnotized by her beauty, by his overwhelming desire for this slim girl in the blue dress, by the absolute *rightness* he felt about their being together, Stephen leaned toward her and planted a light kiss on her forehead. "We'll be married wherever you like, Imogene," he told her recklessly.

There, he had said it at last! Triumph welled through

Imogene. *We'll be married wherever you like* . . . now the only other question was when.

"After I've met your family?" she guessed.

"Yes." He felt relief spreading through him, for there were many ways to delay such a meeting—not that it could ever come about, for he had learned from the only sister who still spoke to him when they met that his father had changed his will and cut him off with a shilling. "After you've met them would be best."

So in love was she, she had half hoped he would say, "We'll be married as soon as may be and meet my family later." Oh, well, perhaps this way was best. "I'm sure I'll like Devon, you've told me so much about it," she said in a slightly quenched tone. Then, her spirits rising, "Come, Stephen, we must plan our lives. Let us walk down to Saint Warna's Bay and make our plans where the two tall stones, Adam and Eve, can see us—for 'twas they who sent you to me!" She laughed at her own fancifulness, grew serious again. "Are they very formal in Devon? Will they really like me there, do you think?"

"They will *love* you in Devon, Imogene," he said huskily. *And so they would,* he thought bitterly, *could he but bring her there as a bride . . . which he could not.*

"I shall wear white to be married unless you think it—not appropriate?" She gave him a shadowed, questing glance.

"I think it *most* appropriate." His voice deepened. "In my heart you will always wear white, Imogene."

And Imogene, strolling beside him, asked herself if anyone had ever been so happy.

In the sailboat, Giles Avery—never a good sailor and cursing now as he tried to handle a borrowed boat he could not manage very well—was having trouble with the wind. His spirits had leaped when in the distance he thought he spied

Imogene's blue dress upon the shore near where the boat that must have brought her to the island rested—and now, looking up, he saw that he had lost the wind. He gave an oath as he stared at his drooping sails in disgust.

For Giles brought exciting news to the Isle of Saint Agnes and to the girl in the blue dress.

He had interpreted Imogene's apparent lack of interest after having at first smiled at him so brightly—and her frequent disappearances—as coyness. She was baiting him, he told himself, urging him on with these coquettish feminine wiles to seal the pact that would lead them to the altar. For Giles, young peacock that he was, and with wealth to boot, had never doubted his own desirability.

Having decided this, the impatient youth had promptly journeyed to Lands End to get his parents' approval. It had been hard won, for his mother had had her heart firmly set upon a marriage to someone other than a penniless beauty—some heiress perhaps to unite their fortunes, or someone who would have Court connections if by chance the rightful king returned to claim his throne, or at the very least a decorous, obedient maiden who would cast her eyes down and do her mother-in-law's bidding without question—which she doubted beautiful, restless Imogene Wells would ever do, for on the one occasion on which she had met Imogene she had thought her far too spirited.

But eventually, by dint of much persuasion and pleading—and at one memorable moment even bursting into tears—Giles, spoiled darling that he was, had won his parents' consent. Yesterday his father had journeyed with him to Tresco to make suitable arrangements with old Lord Elston, who was as eager for the match as was Giles. The betrothal agreed upon, the two had spent the night as Lord Elston's guests and today Giles's father had returned to Lands End. But Giles, chafing that Imogene still lingered on as a houseguest of the Duveens—a family he did not like overmuch—had taken himself to Saint Mary's to bring Imogene the glad tidings in person. There at Ennor Castle a subdued Bess Duveen told him Imogene had gone to Saint Agnes to spend the day, and Giles had promptly borrowed a boat and followed.

Now he sat, becalmed and fuming, in a stationary boat upon a glassy blue surface, still as glass. Already he was suffering from the heat in the splendid gold-laced saffron satin doublet and matching trousers he had worn to impress Imogene.

And having time upon his hands, he suddenly wondered how Imogene had reached Saint Agnes. Hal Duveen had not sailed her there, for he had seen Hal in the distance as he clambered aboard this hastily borrowed boat, and waved at him. And Imogene herself was no sailor. Surely her maid had not . . . his teeth clenched. That Linnington fellow! *He* would have brought her. Well, they would be well rid of *him*, for now that they were betrothed, he meant to forbid Imogene to have anything further to do with Stephen Linnington. And he had a perfect excuse, for had not that Linnington fellow insisted on dueling with Tom Mowbrey over her? A young lady about to marry into the pretentious Avery family could not be too careful about scandal. Imogene must be made aware of that! Giles gave a vengeful look up at the wilted sails and at the sun beaming down furiously overhead. He could feel a trickle of sweat running down his backbone and he'd no mind to look wilted when he arrived. Finally he tore off his doublet and stood in his white ruffled shirt peering toward the island where that bit of blue cloth he had glimpsed had long since disappeared.

And so Giles fumed and sweated in the heat while the lovers strolled out of his sight.

Holding hands they wandered down to one of Imogene's favorite haunts—Saint Warna's Bay on the island's south coast. At first it was hot, but as they reached the bay the wind came up, blowing Imogene's hair back from her hot neck and cooling her pink cheeks.

And although the lovers did not know it, that same wind lifted and billowed the sails of Giles Avery's borrowed boat so that it sped like an arrow toward the island with a panting and wilted Giles aboard.

"Now we will cool us, my lady." Stephen tossed back his copper hair with an indolent gesture and smiled down upon Imogene. "In the water, for there's no one to see."

Imogene shot a look around the deserted bay and gave him back an impish glance. "You just want me to take off my clothes!"

"That too," he admitted with a grin, and sat down and began removing his boots.

"I think I'll just sit on the beach and wait for you," she decided, wanting him to beg her.

"As you like." He gave her a steady look. "But I'm for a swim."

A little nettled that he should choose not to urge her, Imogene sat down and fanned herself with her hand. She watched Stephen undress, admiring the sleek ripple of his strong back muscles as he pulled off his shirt, the breadth of his shoulders, the leanness of his hips and thighs as he pulled off his trousers. He caught her watching him and grinned, then strolled down the sand and into the surf.

For a moment she pouted. He might have insisted a bit that she swim with him! Then, plagued by the heat and with her whole being yearning to join Stephen in the water, she stood up and swiftly shed her clothes. For a moment she stood, stretching luxuriously in the sunlight, and looked up at the two tall stand-ing stones . . . Adam and Eve. So must the original Adam and Eve have felt in the Garden. And who was to say this was not Eden?

Smiling at her own thoughts, she ran down to the surf and swam out toward that wet copper head, shining in the sunlight.

"I see ye have changed your mind," he approved as she joined him.

"A woman's privilege!" She splashed water at him and turned and swam away from him. Stephen knifed through the water after her and together they swam lazily in the clear water, brilliant blue beneath an endless blue dome. In the sparkling sunlight they were playful as young dolphins. Suddenly Stephen dived under and as she looked about for where he would come up, his hand darted impudently between her thighs, causing her to jump and swallow a gulp of sea water. In retaliation, as he came up dripping and laughing, she reached out and playfully ran combing fingers through his thick copper hair, now dark and wet and gleaming—and suddenly, twining her fingers in that strong mass, jerked his head under.

Almost as a reflex gesture, he reached out and pulled her under with him and they turned end over end in the water, for they were both nearly unsinkable. Suddenly Imogene felt Stephen's teeth playfully graze her bottom and she surfaced with a shriek and struggled free and swam away in mock terror to shore. She ran from the water and shook a shower of silvery drops from her wet body—and stood on the hot sand, looking over her shoulder and laughing.

That lighthearted shriek was to cost her much, for Giles Avery, who had at last reached the island, had left his boat beside theirs and had been walking about, fanning himself with his plumed hat, searching for sight of her. He had been about to turn back and climb the hill and ask for her at Clara's cottage. Had he done so, Clara would have managed to hold him there drinking a cooling tankard of cider while Elise slipped away and found the lovers and warned them—and all might have been well. But his head came up at that playful feminine shriek and he turned about with a frown.

Walking softly now, he began to comb the coastline, studying those weird rock groupings that might shelter a man and a girl.

All unknowing, thinking herself and Stephen as alone as the tall frowning menhirs of Adam and Eve on the hill above the bay, Imogene, splendid in her naked loveliness, stood on the beach shaking sea droplets out of her wet hair while Stephen came ashore behind her. The sun glanced warm down upon her slender shoulders and she glanced up at the hill with a half smile toward the two great standing stones the ancients had erected . . . the old gods were true, they had indeed sent her a lover—and what a lover!

Behind her Stephen paused in the surf to study her loveliness. It was a sight that shook him: the straightness of her back, the soft feminine jutting of her hips and buttocks, the long graceful line of her legs. As he watched her, hardly daring to breathe, for she seemed to him like a delicate bird poised for flight, droplets from her long wet hair slid glittering down her white hips and legs to dampen the sand below.

Imogene turned to regard him with a look of splendor in her eyes. Seeing the answering gleam in his, she spread out the blue linen kirtle she had removed before their swim and he joined her on it, stroking her breasts.

God, how soft her skin was, he thought, how magnificent

her body! How gloriously she returned his passion—kiss for kiss, sigh for sigh, tremor for tremor. He reveled in that.

For Stephen—so experienced with women—it was, achingly, as if it were the first time, with all the ecstasy and hesitancy and delight. That was the way it had been for him that night with her at Star Castle, that was the way it had been for him every time since. And now some inner wisdom told him why: Many women he had had—and some had loved him—but now for the first time he loved, truly loved, in return.

He was in love with Imogene. He'd known he should let her alone but—he hadn't been strong enough to resist her feminine charms. Now he knew with fear in his heart that he could deny her nothing. Fear, because his own reckless neck might well be marked for the gibbet and he must be careful not to take lovely Imogene Wells with him.

But if Stephen was having dark thoughts, Imogene was not. She nipped at his ear and giggled as he—firmly nuzzling her right breast with his tongue—retaliated by twisting his fingers in the pale wet triangle of silky hair between her thighs and wringing as if to dry each strand while she wriggled and laughed and slapped playfully at his hands and tried half-heartedly to resist him.

Then the playfulness ended as their lovemaking became more serious. Imogene's eyes were dark pools as Stephen's arms gripped her to him and he drove within her in a turbulence of passion that even he had never known.

They were like two splendid animals, straining, sharing, evenly matched—thoroughbreds both.

Rising on peak after peak of ecstasy, they were oblivious to all but each other.

Until the toe of a boot landed cruelly on Stephen's pale gleaming buttock and a voice choked with rage—and perhaps with pain as well—cried, "So this is what you've been doing—behind my back!"

CHAPTER 5

In a single violent leap, Stephen catapulted off Imogene's yielding naked body and landed on one hand and one knee in the flying sand as he whirled to face his unknown attacker.

Startled—and still throbbing with emotion—Imogene looked up with a gasp, to feel hot sand sting her face as a pair of wide boots shot across her field of vision. She had a sudden bewildering impression of a flash of saffron trousers and a saffron doublet vaulting over her probe body. From her appalled position on the sand, she could see from below Giles Avery's crimson contorted face and hear the choking sob in his voice as he shouted hoarsely at Stephen, "I'll kill ye for this, damn ye!"

Hardly had Giles cleared her body before Imogene jack-knifed up and spun to her hands and knees. Her head swung around in time to see Stephen uncoil like a spring from the position in which he had landed and hurl himself full length through the air toward his sword, which lay a little distance away in the sand. His long body slid in the sand as his hand sought and found his sword hilt.

Giles had already dragged out his sword and was rushing forward, even before Stephen was airborne. In his blind rage, he apparently intended to run through a naked unarmed man with the point of his blade.

Frozen in terror for Stephen, Imogene screamed.

Neither man paid the slightest attention to her. It is doubtful if they even heard her. Bent on attack, Giles hurtled forward. Bent on defense, Stephen, landing in the sand, got his sword free of its scabbard in a smooth lightninglike gesture and brought up his blade's protective point just as Giles lunged.

To Imogene, wildly intent upon the scene before her, it all seemed to happen in slow motion. It seemed to her an eternity—although actually it all happened in split seconds—before Stephen's blade cleared its scabbard and flashed in the sun. Giles was almost on him; she was sure he would run Stephen through the body, and her heart almost collapsed in her chest.

Lying fully extended in the sand, with only a split moment between him and death, Stephen twisted his body to the side as he brought up his blade. Almost upon him, Giles was charging true as a bull to a red cape and never deviated from his path in the slightest. But that last-moment twist of Stephen's muscular body was to prove his undoing. Giles lunged forward, missed Stephen by a hair's breadth—and drove his point deep into the sand.

Too late he saw Stephen's defensive blade snake up. He could not stop. With a howl he impaled himself upon it, the very momentum of his charge driving the point through his body and out the other side.

Imogene rose with a shriek and ran to the combatants.

As she reached them, Giles was slithering down the bloody

blade to the sand and Stephen, very pale now, had caught him gently by the shoulders and was trying to ease him up and off the blade before it sliced a wider path through Giles's trembling body.

"There," he said, expertly withdrawing the blade. "Now to see how bad ye're hurt."

Pettishly, Giles struck Stephen's hand away from the red stain now spreading across his saffron doublet. "I want no favors of you, Linnington! Nor of you, Imogene!" His bloodshot eyes glittered at her shrinking naked figure. "Brazen doxie! And to think I came to bring ye news we were betrothed!" he lamented, wincing as he moved. "The shame of it!"

"Ye'd best not be talking of shame," observed Stephen, ignoring Giles's protests and tearing open Giles's doublet and shirt. "For that's a bad wound ye've got, and we must get ye to a doctor and speedily!"

"I'll go nowhere in your company!" flashed Giles, spitting up blood and coughing.

Stephen noted that bad sign with a frown. "Then I'll bring a doctor here," he said quietly and began to pull his clothes on.

"I'll stay with him," said Imogene, kneeling on her bare knees beside Giles in the sand.

"Lying doxie!" He jerked his head away from her and the motion sent him into a paroxysm of coughing.

"Let him alone," said Stephen sharply. "Every time he moves the wound bleeds worse. Rip off the bottom part of your chemise. Perhaps we can stanch the blood with that."

Giles, lying in an expiring heap upon the sand, managed to control his cough and gave Stephen an evil look. "I'll see ye hanged for this!" he bellowed.

"Come, come," muttered Stephen, adjusting his trousers and pulling on his boots. "Love is no hanging matter!" He turned to Imogene. "Hurry with that cloth. He's sinking!"

"It—won't—rip!" Imogene, bent over her chemise, gave the fabric a jerk. "There." She managed to tear off a long strip and was handing it to Stephen, when Giles, with a murderous glare, suddenly lunged toward Stephen's sword, which lay withdrawn and bloody upon the sand.

The effort cost him his life. He doubled up, choking, before he ever reached it. And coughed out his life in Imogene's white arms there on the sands of Saint Agnes.

Stephen, well aware that it was too late to seek medical help, had remained. "The lad meant to run me through at the last," he muttered. "He'd more spirit than I thought." He sounded regretful.

"Oh, how can you say that?" cried Imogene, so upset she hardly knew what she was saying. "He sneaked up on us and tried to kill you!"

Stephen was frowning down at the youth whose blood ran red upon the sand. "The fault was mine."

" 'Twas *not* your fault! Giles leaped on you when you were naked and unarmed."

"With *you* locked in my arms." Stephen's lean face twisted into a sardonic smile. "Oh, there's no doubt whose fault it is. I seduced the girl this boy loved and he caught me at it. There's no doubt at all where the fault lies."

She was staring at him. At that moment she looked very frail and helpless and his heart went out to her, caught up in something she had not bargained for. "I mean, you couldn't *help*—you weren't trying to kill him, Stephen."

"True, it was an accident. I meant to do no more than defend myself—as I would have with an irate husband."

He was speaking as if Giles had property rights in her! Imogene's head went up indignantly. "I had no way of knowing my guardian had betrothed me to Giles! Indeed, I would not have consented!'' Her voice trailed off at the sad little smile that was playing around his mouth.

"The unlucky thing—for us, Imogene—is that it happened here on this near-deserted island. For there was no challenge flung, no witnesses, and so under the law it will be accounted murder."

She sprang up. "*I* am a witness!"

His sardonic smile deepened. "Think you your word will be of much account in this matter? The lad who lies here dead at our feet is heir to the greatest fortune in Cornwall—an only son. Think you his parents will rest until the man who killed him is brought down? They will drag you before the Lord Constable and ask you what you were doing that so enraged their son. And when you tell them, they will say that you were not a witness but a co-conspirator, an accessory to murder—and perhaps worse. I must save you from that. I'll put the lad's body in his boat and tow it out to sea and sink it. Pray God I'm not seen doing that. And then I'll sail away on Hal's boat, and when the Duveens come looking for you, you'll say we quarreled and that you left me on the beach and went into the cottage with Elise and her sister, and that I must have sailed away in anger, but you did not see me go. You'll say you saw naught of Giles Avery. That way, if the law decides there's been foul play, 'twill all be on my own head—where it belongs—and not yours."

"I'll not do it," she said staunchly, snatching up her torn chemise and stepping into it. "I'll take the same path you tread and tell the same story. And if you run away, I'll go with you."

He gave her a fond look. He hated to see her dressing, for he knew it was the last he would see of her lithe, lovely body. "Well spoke, Imogene," he said gently, "but we both know it cannot be."

"Why not?" She was pulling on her kirtle now, unmindful that it was damp and covered with sand. "Why could you not take me to your family in Devon? We could be married there and since I gather they have influence in Devon, they could protect us."

Stephen winced at the open simplicity of that thought, and tried to tear his tormented gaze from the white legs that flashed tantalizingly as she tried to brush the sand from her skirt. In another day, another time, it could have happened that way. But he had found love at the wrong time, in the wrong place, in the arms of another man's betrothed. Even so, they might have worked something out—he'd had wild dreams of late that he might somehow find the highwayman's sister and the tavern maid and buy them both off and divorce them and so return to Imogene once again an eligible bachelor—but by sending Giles to the island to catch them making love, life had dealt them both a cruel blow.

They could swear on all the Bibles in the land that there had been no concerted effort to kill Giles, that it was an accident brought on by the very heat of Giles's nature, but who would believe them? And disbelief could well bring Imogene beside him to the gibbet.

His jaw hardened. Whatever transpired, he was not going to let that happen.

"You cannot come with me, Imogene," he told her with finality.

She flinched as if he had struck her, and her fingers, fumbling with the hooks of her blue linen doublet, were stilled. "You mean," her voice trembled as realization flooded over her suddenly, "you will not return to the Scillies?"

Stephen was bending over Giles's fallen body, but now he straightened up and spent a long time studying her, as if to fill his eyes with her for all time. Every nerve in his body ached to tell her she could go with him, she could walk his path, they would fare well or badly, but they would be together—always.

Had it been last year, had it been some other woman, he might have done just that.

But knowing Imogene had changed him. For Stephen Linnington, late of Devon, late of York, late of half of England, had looked into a pair of clear delft blue eyes and seen himself mirrored there—not as he was, but as he once had been: a man of birth and breeding, a man a young lady of rank and fashion might give her arm to, might dance across a castle floor with— might even choose to marry. And now on the hot beach of Saint Agnes Isle, with reality crowding in upon him, he felt a sharp pang of sorrow for his misspent youth. Bitterly, he wished himself a stripling again, with all the world before him.

But he could not bear the heartbroken look on her lovely face as she slowly hooked up her linen bodice.

"I will come back to you, Imogene," he said slowly, knowing even as he said it that he would not.

"You promise?" A wisp of a sound.

"I promise." He would burn no more in hell for this lie than for his other sins, a list too long to count.

She flung herself into his arms, her soft breasts crushing themselves against his chest, her body a sweet heavy burden, her hair smelling of lemons and the salt sea.

"I will not let you go!" she cried brokenly.

He held her to him as a dying man might hold onto life and caressed her hair, her slim body. He cupped her wistful face in both his hands and looked deep into her eyes. " 'Twill be only for a little while," he soothed her, for her safety depended on her carrying this off coolly and with determination. Tears would only bring suspicion on her. " 'Twill only be until the hue and cry dies down and I've time to make my arrangements. Then I'll don a black wig and a new name and sail back to the Scillies some fine night and snatch you from your guardian's house on Tresco and we'll away like the wind. Show me a cheerful face, Imogene. Remember, ye must not be found when they come looking for you, as indeed they will, with dark circles under your eyes or a tearstained face. You must say I mean nothing to you, that we quarreled over some trivial thing and that you had no idea I would sail away and leave you here, but when you came out of the hut, I was gone.''

"But that's as good as pointing a finger at you, that you killed him, for there'll be those who know Giles came here to find me, and they'll put two and two together.''

He nodded soberly, feeling her skin like silk beneath his yearning fingers. "Even so, you'll do it. For if I'm to come back for you, Imogene—and see me again, you will, never doubt it—there must be no thought that you were implicated in a murder. For you've a memorable face and figure and men would remember having seen you—we'd have no chance at all to escape them if they should come looking for you. My own looks are easy changed.''

She tried to believe him, tried to see the merit of his argument as he gently put her away from him—but could not.

But she could see one thing clearly. He had hoisted Giles's body to his shoulder and was swinging along toward the place where they had left their boat. She ran along beside him, silenced by the urgency of his long stride.

"There—that must be the boat Giles came in, there beside ours.''

Stephen nodded and shifted the dead boy's weight. He felt ashamed that he should have killed the lad, but for the life of him could not see how he could have avoided it. Pray God no fishermen came by this way to see Imogene here with him. Working fast and silently he put Giles's body in the boat that had brought him and made fast a line so that the one boat could tow the other.

Imogene tried to help but she was half blinded by her tears. The wind was drying them on her cheeks even as they fell.

But in the cottage above the beach where the two boats lay, Clara, passing before the window, had suddenly exclaimed, "There are two boats down there!"

Elise had leaped up. Crowding past Clara, she saw Stephen carrying an inert body, clad in saffron, saw that he was putting it into the other boat, lashing the two together with a towline. In a moment he would cast off.

She pushed her sister away from the window. "You saw nothing—nothing. Remember that!" she cried harshly, and ran out of the cottage and down toward the beach.

The sails of Stephen's boat had already caught the wind by the time she reached there. Imogene stood on the beach hugging her arms about her as if she were chilled, with the taste of salt tears and Stephen's lips still lingering on her trembling mouth.

"What's happened?" cried Elise sharply. "Why is Mister Linnington sailing Hal's boat away and towing that other boat along?"

Imogene turned a face to her that was suddenly older. "You don't want to know, Elise," she said sadly. "Don't ask. What we must tell them is that I left Stephen outside and came into the cottage and we talked for some time and when we looked out again the boat was gone—that's all we know. We must stand by our stories, Elise—Stephen says my life depends on it."

"Your—life?" whispered Elise.

"My life."

Elise's arm went around Imogene protectively and together they watched Stephen sail away. Imogene would never know what it cost him to leave her there, how it took all his willpower not to turn the sailboat around and pick her up and take her with him and never let her go.

But he kept his head turned resolutely toward the blue water ahead. Whatever he had told her, there was no turning back. If he left her now, she would soon forget him—like any other bad dream, he told himself—and marry some likely young lord and have the kind of life that he could never give her.

Forlorn, with the wind whipping her blue skirts, Imogene stood on the beach, pushed back her blowing blond hair, and watched the billowing sails until they disappeared over the horizon. She was blinking back tears and she had to hold on to Stephen's promise with all her being: *I will come back for you.*

And he would do it. He would, she knew it.

But once his boat was gone and she and Elise were staring out over an empty sea, she returned abruptly to reality.

"How will we get back to Saint Mary's?" practical Elise was asking.

"We won't, until they come for us. Will your sister mind keeping us overnight? For I doubt the Duveens will realize we aren't coming back and delay coming for us until morning."

"Clara will be glad of the company, but 'twill be crowded, for she's only the one room."

Imogene gave a laugh that was half a sob. "This day I've caused one man's death and perhaps another to be hanged—I'd not sleep this night had I the softest bed in England!"

So the man she'd seen slung over Stephen's shoulder was dead. Elise had no need to ask if it was Giles. She moved closer to Imogene as if to protect her.

It was harder to protect Imogene from her guardian's wrath.

As Imogene had predicted, a boat came from Saint Mary's the next day, seeking them, wondering why they had not returned. The boat was piloted by Hal Duveen, who swore manfully when he learned that Stephen Linnington had left the women here and sailed away—in Hal's boat—they knew not why.

"Ye must have *some* idea!" he insisted.

"No, we have not," said Elise stoutly. "We were all three of us in Clara's house and Clara was showing Mistress Imogene how to make lace, when I chanced to look out the window and saw that the boat was gone. We waited, but Mister Linnington did not come back for us." Her voice sharpened. "Is that not the way it happened, Clara?"

Clara had always felt dominated by her older sister. She felt dominated no less this day. "Yes—that is how it happened," she said faintly.

"I quarreled with Stephen," Imogene admitted in a troubled voice. "But it was over a small thing—I did not expect him to be so affronted that he would leave us here."

" 'A small thing'?" Hal's voice sharpened and he gave her a suspicious look.

Imogene had the grace to color up and a look of understanding came over Hal's face. So Linnington had tried to go too far with the wench! And then gone off in a huff when she'd rebuffed him! Devil take the fellow!

Shaking his head and muttering, big Hal conveyed them back to Ennor, where Bess Duveen's gray eyes turned dark with fear when he told her what had happened. "But Giles Avery sailed to Saint Agnes to see you, Imogene," she protested. "Did you not see him? He stopped by here for you and I told him you had gone there. He said—he said that he and his father had just left your guardian on Tresco, and that your guardian had agreed to your betrothal.'' Her voice faltered.

"He must have changed his mind and sailed somewhere else,'' said Imogene flatly. "For we did not see him. And my guardian would surely have spoken to me before he betrothed me to Giles.''

But though the women might stoutly maintain they had not seen Giles Avery or his boat, there were several others who had. During the next two days, a story of sorts was pieced together: Giles had sailed for Saint Agnes Isle in fair weather. The Duveens had seen him start out. Some fishermen had chanced to notice two sailboats lying together at Saint Agnes later that day, and another fisherman had seen Hal Duveen's boat towing another away from the island.

They could not prove foul play, but they inferred it. A nasty scandal broke over Imogene Well's pretty head. Her guardian sent for her and she went back to Tresco in disgrace with Bess's last words to her, "Oh, Imogene, what have you led Stephen into?'' ringing in her ears.

She found her guardian, Lord Elston, not at his musty, leather-bound volumes, but pacing the floor with his hands clasped behind his back, lost in thought. He looked up as she entered the familiar book-lined study with its big trestle table and worn leather-covered chairs.

"So ye're back.'' He gave her a gloomy look from under bushy eyebrows. "I knew ye would be nothing but trouble, Imogene.''

"Why?'' she was startled into asking.

" 'Tis your beauty,'' he said heavily. "It goads men and infuriates women. One or the other, they'll always be making trouble for you. 'Tis why I tried so hard to marry you off.'' He took a turn around the room, ended up before her, a formidable old man with bushy hair and eyebrows. "I've known since you were eleven that suitors would be banging at the door. What I never guessed was that you'd turn all of the steady ones down and take up with a rakehell." He sighed deeply. "Well, you've ruined yourself in the Scillies, my girl. My only hope is to send you away until the talk dies down and hope that I can arrange a good marriage for you with someone who knows nothing of this affair—say in the north of England."

"Send me—away?" faltered Imogene, for she had not considered this possibility. How would Stephen find her, if she were sent away?

"As far away as possible," he said dryly. "Mistress Peale has relatives in Amsterdam on her mother's side. We're not at war with the Dutch right now, thank God. I'll send you both there."

"But—but I don't want to go to Amsterdam."

The bushy brows came together fiercely. "The divil be damned if ye don't want to go! Ye'll to Holland, my girl, if I have to send you there in irons!"

Amsterdam! It seemed a world away. Imogene felt stunned. "Can I—can I take Elise?" she wondered.

Her guardian's wrath had abated as swiftly as it had appeared. "Aye, take Elise," he said wearily. "I suppose ye'll need a maid if ye're to appear as gentlefolk over there. Between them—" his expression hardened and he reached for his pipe—"Mistress Peale and Elise should be able to keep ye in check." He took a long time lighting his pipe. "Though they've not," he added in a more thoughtful tone, "done such a good job of it before!"

Imogene's cheeks crimsoned. She supposed she deserved that but it was hard hearing it. It was as if—as if Stephen had somehow smirched her with his love—and nothing could be further from the truth. Their love had ennobled them, made them better than they were before. She couldn't find the words to tell him that, this dry old man with his pipe and his books, and she didn't try, for she knew it would be no use. Why, if she told him Stephen Linnington had promised to come back and marry her, he'd probably lock her up! She stumbled out into the sunlight, where Elise, looking worried, was waiting for her.

"Elise," she said dully. "We're going to Amsterdam." Her tears broke through then. "Where Stephen will *never* find us!"

"There, there, of course he will." Elise held Imogene in her arms and patted the girl's slender back awkwardly. "For he's a resourceful man. He'll be back for ye, ye'll see."

But in her heart she could not help wondering if it would be best if he never came back, if the copper-haired gentleman from Devon went back where he came from and forgot lovely Imogene so that—in time—she could forget him.

PART TWO
The Golden Temptress

A toast to the sweet worldly women
Who lure men from home and from grace,
Who lure them forever to follow
A smile and a beautiful face.

Amsterdam, Holland, 1657

CHAPTER 6

It was the beginning of another glorious day in Amsterdam: A day when billowing clouds, gray and soft as goosedown, would chase each other lazily across a blue and turquoise sky, and the sun would shine down, scattering gold upon the shoppers who strolled along the Kalverstraat. But for now the dawn was just breaking. Its pink light frosted the tall pink chimneys where storks built their gigantic nests, and picked out sleepy vendors stumbling along in wooden shoes, bringing their carts of flowers and vegetables to market. It shone on flower-laden boats in which sat wide-trousered men and women in white peaked caps, gliding along the canals. In another few minutes the sun would gild the carved lions and crowns and sea monsters that decorated the hoisting beams that protruded from the elaborate facades of warehouses and private houses alike, for the tall, narrow, elaborate homes of the merchants had enormous attics, and goods were hoisted into them from the canals and stored there—a feature that made the face of Amsterdam different from that of any city in the world.

In the room she shared with snoring Mistress Peale and her maid, Elise—a room taken upon their arrival in Amsterdam last evening—Imogene Wells could not sleep. She tossed and turned and at last, as the dawn's first light pinked the sky, she rose from her unfamiliar bed and threw wide the casements, leaning out over the sill to look down curiously into the magical darkness of the narrow street below.

She had been despondent on the voyage, sure she would never see Stephen again. Mistress Peale had been seasick the whole time and blamed Imogene bitterly for her plight. It had been a relief to sail into the great port city and disembark, a relief to walk on dry land again and spread out their trunks and boxes in the relatively large quarters of the inn the captain had recommended—the Roode Leeuw, or Red Lion.

And with the change from monotonous ship's fare, the release from travel over an uncertain ocean, and the exploration of Amsterdam ahead of her, Imogene's spirits had soared. She would see Stephen again, of course she would! *Somehow* she would get back to the Scillies, Stephen would come for her as he had promised, and they would be away on the wings of the wind!

And because of that certainty, there was a glory in Imogene's delft blue eyes, and on a note of hope and happiness she began to sing softly, a lilting Cornish lullaby, to the dark narrow street below.

Suddenly the casements of the room next door flew open and a dark head stuck itself out. Imogene turned in surprise and found herself looking into a pair of amazed dark eyes set in a narrow face. Her disheveled hair haloed gold around her face in the dawn's pale light and her winsome smile flashed mischievously into the dazzled face of the stranger.

"We are alone with the dawn, mynheer," she said blithely—and disappeared from his view as Mistress Peale mumbled sleepily, "Don't be standing at the window in your night rail, Imogene—ye'll catch cold."

She had had a devastating effect on the stranger, but Imogene, with all of Amsterdam waiting for her outside, promptly forgot him.

At Mistress Peale's insistence she dressed that morning in a rustling lemon silk dress, trimmed in blue ribands that matched her eyes—and with a white lawn whisk drawn carefully across her bosom to conceal anything the gown's low cut might reveal—for this morning they were to call upon Mistress Peale's relatives in Amsterdam, who, hopefully, might invite them to visit and thus relieve them of the difficulties—and the expense—of living at an inn.

Imogene, intent on all the strange sights that greeted her along the street of orange-brick buildings, was not aware that her exit from the inn's oaken door was avidly watched by a handsome young man in rich black brocade. No sooner had she passed than he turned in excitement and clutched the arm of a passing chambermaid. "There—that's the girl I saw this morning," he muttered in an anxious undertone. "Can you tell me who she is?"

But the chambermaid did not know and young van Rappard, afraid he would be rebuffed by Imogene's formidable chaperon if he tried to introduce himself, hurried to follow them out and match his pace to theirs at a suitable distance as he followed along behind the strolling ladies.

What a charmer she was, in her yellow silks! Like a lovely

little yellow bird he had once possessed, singing its heart out every dawn through the bars of its wicker cage. The young patroon from America bumped into passersby and had to mutter a dozen pardons as his neck craned to see every move of the lissome young woman ahead. Now she was crossing a hump-backed stone bridge over one of the canals, pausing a moment to watch a flower-laden boat disappear beneath, now she was fingering some cloth at a waterside stall, now pointing out a pasty to her impatient chaperon.

Lord, how he would like to buy her that pasty! His fingers itched on his purse and he was hard-pressed not to shoulder his way through the throng and boldly introduce himself with a flourish of his sweeping plumed hat.

But prudence forbade that. So, although he was chafing with impatience, he followed them unseen to a handsome address on the Herengracht, where the ladies were turned away from the door. Van Rappard's ears stuck up at that. No welcome for the English beauty and her entourage? And now the chaperon looked quite put out.

Even though she realized that her letter sent from the Scillies had not had time to reach Amsterdam ahead of them, Mistress Peale was indeed discomfited when the servants at the Schillerzoons' majestic residence, to which they had been so carefully directed by the innkeeper, told them the family was away at their farm outside Haarlem and it was uncertain when they would be back. But Imogene was secretly glad. Now she could explore this unusual city without additional Dutch chaperons —perhaps more efficient than the English!—to hamper her.

"We can come back tomorrow and inquire," she told Mistress Peale, and pulled her away as she hesitated on the steps. "Today we can shop and wander about."

Verhulst van Rappard sauntered after them as they wandered

about, pursuing this vision in lemon silk as he might some distant goddess.

Imogene was unaware she was being followed. She was delighted with everything she saw. If only Stephen were here! For instinctively she knew he would share her approval.

And well he might, for in the 1600s Amsterdam was unique. It was a wayward town, a tolerant international town where worldly women wore the latest fashions—silks from Italy and the Orient, pearls from the Caribbean and the Far East, musky perfumes from the Orient, and beaver hats from the New World. They decorated their houses with Flemish lacework and their tables with thick soft rugs from the Near East they called "Turkey carpets" and set on their wide, tall mantels, above the spotless dust ruffles, silver candlesticks that had been seized by Dutch privateers from Spanish treasure galleons—for Holland was endlessly at war with Spain. Beside canals crowded with water traffic moving everything from cabbages to lumber, men stopped by market stalls and conversed in a dozen languages—and every day fortunes were being made in the Exchange. An exciting town to visit, an exciting town to live in.

Even Imogene, desolate at being sent here, away from Stephen, felt that excitement.

At one of the waterside stalls that lined the canals opposite tall narrow houses with gardens in the rear, Imogene had paused to admire a beautiful blue fan with peacocks painted on it. She was trying to buy it but the stolid woman who ran this stall spoke only gutteral Dutch and Imogene could not find out the price. She rummaged in her purse, pulling out a variety of English coins, but the stall-woman only shook her head—she wanted to be paid in Dutch money.

It was just the opportunity Verhulst van Rappard had been waiting for. He strode forward and bowed impressively before

Imogene. "Permit me, mistress," he said in his excellent English. While they watched he paid out the coins to the woman in the stall and presented the fan to Imogene with a flourish. "With my compliments."

"Oh, but I couldn't accept it!" she said, startled. "I'm most grateful to you, sir, but I don't know you." Although his face *did* look vaguely familiar. "So I couldn't possibly—"

"Permit me to introduce myself," he said impressively. "Verhulst van Rappard, patroon of Wey Gat in New Netherland—in America. And the fan is but a small tribute. I will be desolated if you will not accept it, for—it matches your eyes."

Mistress Peale, frowning at this forward gentleman, was somewhat mollified by the title "patroon." But to accept a gift from a gentleman—and a stranger at that! It was not to be thought of! Before Imogene could frame an answer, she cut in. "Come along, Imogene, you don't need a fan!" She was plucking at Imogene's skirts as she spoke and awkwardly backed into a wide-trousered man carrying two baskets of live ducks suspended from a wooden yoke slung across his shoulders. He staggered backward as Mistress Peale backed into him and the yoke fell off his shoulders. The baskets fell to the street, the ducks let out enraged squawks, passersby stumbled over the fallen man and his quacking load—and Mistress Peale gasped at the havoc she had unwittingly wrought.

"Allow me," Verhulst said smoothly, once again pressing his advantage. He bent over the fallen man, proffering money. The man looked up from dusting off his trousers and trying to rescue his ducks. At sight of the coins he began to grin and scrambled up, seizing the money.

"I have paid this man for his ducks," Verhulst said, turning to Mistress Peale. "And now I am suffering a surfeit of food, for he insists on taking the ducks to my inn and I cannot eat all these ducks. Unless you ladies will join me for dinner tonight at my inn, the Red Lion?''

"But we're staying at the Red Lion, too," cried Mistress Peale.

Imogene gazed at Verhulst in amusement. Now she knew where she had seen him—this morning, from her window. She made him a delightful curtsy. "We would be delighted, mynheer. I accept for us both." And then, in a wicked aside, "You have been following us, mynheer!"

"I admit it," said Verhulst solemnly. "For this morning your face dazzled me and I have been attracted to it like a moth to a flame."

Imogene laughed. It might be fun to have a light flirtation to pass away the time here in Amsterdam until she could return to the Scillies—and Stephen. "You should have spoken to us sooner," she mocked, "for we could hardly understand the servants this morning at the Schillerzoons' when they told us the family was away."

"Indeed I should," he said gravely. "For I am a man who desires to spend his time in the company of beautiful things." *And I have seen nothing so beautiful as you in Amsterdam*, his gaze told her.

Mistress Peale, at first shocked that Imogene should accept an invitation from a stranger, no matter how fortuitous his appearance, was mollified at dinner when, over orange duck and green sallet and tansies, Verhulst told them casually that he was in Amsterdam to acquire treasures to decorate the great house he was building on the North River in New Netherland. His father had begun it—he would complete it. No, he was not married. Or betrothed. His parents had been killed by Indians, scalped—the ladies shuddered—and he, an only child, had come into his patroonship early. Mistress Peale listened to his almost faultless English and studied as if hypnotized the handsome gold chain that swung on his black satin brocade doublet, the rich Flemish lace at his throat and the ruby that sparkled from it, the bloodstone signet ring set in heavy gold on his finger. She wondered if he had come to Amsterdam to acquire a wife as well.

To acquire a wife had been the last thing Verhulst had been thinking of. But now, sitting across the table from the English beauty clad in a lustrous gown of pale amber silk and with a whisk so sheer he could see the pearly sheen of her breasts through it, he wasn't so sure. Not only Verhulst but all the diners in the common room were captivated by this dainty display.

"We should have had a private dining room," Verhulst told them, vexed by all this neck-craning interest Imogene had aroused, "but I asked too late; they were all taken."

"It is no matter," said Imogene eagerly. "It is very pleasant to sit among travelers from all over the world and hear a dozen languages spoken."

She exaggerated, for, except for one table where two plumed-hatted gentlemen argued in vociferous French, only Dutch was being spoken at the nearby tables. But Verhulst cared nothing for that—he was warmed by her approval.

"Tell me about Wey Gat," encouraged Imogene.

And Verhulst did.

When the young patroon had ceased speaking, she sighed. "I don't wonder you are in Amsterdam to acquire treasures for it. As you spoke I could almost see the wide river running between sheer cliffs and big, rounded mountains all covered with a virgin forest—the waterfalls spilling over the dark rocks, the deep mossy places—oh, we have nothing in the Scillies like it. Surely such a place is a treasure in itself."

But Verhulst van Rappard had for the moment forgotten

the thick-piled rugs from the Orient, the delicate teakwood screens and rustling Italian silks and heavy plate and delicate China he had come to Amsterdam to acquire. For of all the treasures he had seen, Verhulst wanted Imogene herself the most. How she would grace his fine rooms at Wey Gat! A golden woman, her supple beauty enhanced by her negligent feminine gestures as she talked. And there, to his fevered imagination, she would be a golden bird, singing for him . . . only for him. His young face hardened. He meant to acquire this English beauty, as he had acquired priceless paintings and sculptures and rare spices. He meant to ship her home carefully with himself to guard her and spend his life admiring her as she wandered through the spacious halls of Wey Gat. His imagination raced ahead: Occasionally, he told himself, he would exhibit her to guests, as he did his other treasures. Imogene, smiling at him across her orange duck, would have been astonished and indignant to know that Verhulst had just decided that she was to be his golden songbird and Wey Gat her gilded cage.

The next day Verhulst escorted them round to the Schillerzoons' again, and this time they were back, having arrived home late yesterday evening. Vrouw Schillerzoon was a tall, determined woman who viewed Mistress Peale—a distant relative of her husband's—with some dismay, but nevertheless ushered them all into her spotless parlor, a dark, rather forbidding room that Imogene guessed rightly was used only for special occasions. The young patroon Vrouw Schillerzoon welcomed with suspicion, for her husband had had recent dealings with the New Netherland Dutch—dealings in which he had lost money. And she gave Imogene Wells one startled look and promptly sent her only marriageable son back to Haarlem to oversee some things at the farm—Vrouw Schillerzoon had no intention of letting her son Hans, so easily smitten, marry anyone but the daughter of their next-door neighbor, whose father had ships that would be convenient to transport Mynheer Schillerzoon's considerable merchandise.

All in all, it was an uncomfortable afternoon they spent sitting on straight chairs in Vrouw Schillerzoon's immaculate parlor, but their hostess made them promise to return next day for supper, and Mistress Peale left in consternation.

"She did not even invite us to spend the night," she mourned to Imogene after they had returned to the Red Lion.

"She's afraid I'll seduce her son," grinned Imogene. "Did you notice how quickly she sent him from the room, and then told us he was away to Haarlem?"

"Do not speak so!" cried Mistress Peale. But she was afraid that Imogene was right. Hans Schillerzoon *had* disappeared from their sight rather precipitately. "As if you would have such an ill-favored lad!" she added venomously.

Imogene laughed.

Snubbed by the Schillerzoons, who could have opened up Amsterdam society to them, Imogene and Mistress Peale spent their days in leisurely sightseeing with the young patroon to guide them.

From the wedding-cake spire of the Zuiderkerk to the medieval Waag, with its five-foot-thick walls, that housed the guild-chambers, they saw it all. At the Schreierstoren, the Weeping Tower, they watched sobbing women clinging to their sailor husbands for a last farewell before they departed on long voyages.

"I am told the stones here are always moist from their tears," Verhulst told her soberly. "For the women know that many of these men will not come back. And yet my father sailed away on such a voyage, and I am a patroon because of it."

And because of it your parents lie far away beneath alien

soil, thought Imogene, *chopped to death by Indian hatchets*. But it was too lovely a day to quarrel. "You told me you were going shopping," she said, for the great variety of Amsterdam's shops fascinated her.

Verhulst's eyes lit up. She was taking an interest in his purchases, in his home across the sea. That was a good sign! He promptly escorted the ladies into the busy Warmoesstraat, which was the main street of the city, found a draper and let Imogene pick out the window hangings for the great double living room at Wey Gat.

"The green damask is handsome but I like this amber velvet best," she told him, fingering the rich stuff lingeringly. It seemed to run through her fingers like water—like a caress; she hated to remove them from its gleaming surface. "Here, touch it, mynheer."

Verhulst's hand brushed hers as he took the gleaming fabric from her. Imogene hardly noticed that brief contact, but Verhulst was shaken by it.

"Yes, you are right, it is beautiful." *And how your hair will shine against it in the candle's glow!* he thought, and promptly bought an amount that made the shopkeeper's eyes shine.

"Perhaps we should decide on draperies for—a lady's bedroom next." Verhulst stumbled over the words, for he had almost said "your bedroom."

" 'A lady's'?" Imogene turned a mischievous glance toward him. "But I thought you were not married, mynheer."

Above the rich Florentine lace at his throat, Verhulst flushed happily. How different was this English girl's steady blue gaze from Rychie's scathing look! "I am not, Mistress Imogene, but one day I hope . . ."

"Will not your bride prefer to choose her own things?"

"I am sure her taste will coincide with yours."

Imogene ignored that as a pretty compliment but insincere—as pretty compliments were prone to be.

"But the room should accent her coloring," she mocked him. "Have you already decided what color her eyes will be, this bride you have yet to meet?"

"Yes," he told her with decision. "I have decided that her eyes will be blue."

Imogene gave a peal of laughter and Mistress Peale, fingering some fabulous gold-shot silk from India and wishing she had the price, turned and gave her a reproving look.

"Then why not this sky blue satin?" suggested Imogene. Sky blue . . . she had been wearing a doublet and kirtle of sky blue linen that first night Stephen had made love to her . . . and again, the day he had killed Giles Avery by accident and sailed away from her. Her face clouded as she bent over the fabric.

"Is that what you would choose for your own bedroom?" he asked, studying her.

"Oh, yes, if I could afford it, which I cannot!" Imogene wrenched herself back to the present. "It is much prettier than these murky-looking damasks, and handsomer than these flowered calicos. And you could have curtains made of this fine white lawn. Are they casements?"

He nodded. "And they look down the bluff to the river and across it to the bluffs on the opposite shore. It is a wide, airy room with a high ceiling and polished floors."

"It sounds lovely." She was still trying to tear her thoughts away from Stephen. "If you have not completed the fireplace, you should give it a French mantel. I saw lovely ones of white marble in a shop down the street."

"I will attend to it," said Verhulst gravely.

Imogene shot him a surprised look, wondering if he was laughing at her.

"I thought perhaps a Turkey carpet?" he suggested later, when they were considering a shipment of rugs just brought by a tall-masted East Indiaman from the Orient.

"These two are the most beautiful." Imogene stroked the thick, soft pile of two rugs from China with extravagant designs of dragons and birds set in muted jewel colors against a background of cool Chinese gold.

"I will buy them for the drawing room," said Verhulst instantly, eager to please her, although he himself had thought a dark red would be richer. He turned to the shopkeeper. "Do you have a blue one for my lady's bedroom?"

The shopkeeper, thinking by "my lady" Verhulst meant Imogene—as indeed he did—hurried to show them an assortment of blue rugs and Imogene chose one of medium blue with a wide dark blue border and a trailing design of white flowers lavished across it, as if it were a painting instead of a floor covering.

Verhulst bought it.

He did not stop there. He bought wallpaper from France depicting hunting scenes in the forest of Versailles, where elegant bewigged gentlemen and wide-skirted ladies riding side-saddle followed the hounds through sun and shade beneath magnificent old trees. He bought numerous pairs of heavy knobbed brass andirons and delicately worked brass fenders, sumptuous table linens of Holland flax trimmed in heavy lace—on all of which he ordered his monogram to be embroidered. And because Imogene liked them he bought a pair of branched candlesticks of baroque silver so heavy that the boy who carried them away to be packed staggered beneath their weight.

"You are making that young man spend too much money," chided Mistress Peale after they had returned to the inn.

"Nonsense. Mynheer van Rappard told us he was in Amsterdam to acquire treasures for his house. And he asked for my advice."

"I am sure he would not have bought that elegant silver tray and pitchers and those pearl-handled fruit knives and all those blue and white China plates if you had not raved over them."

"He is but seeking a woman's opinion, and I am glad to give him mine."

He will be seeking more than your opinion, thought the older woman shrewdly, but she let the matter rest.

"And besides . . ." Imogene was letting Elise dress her for dinner in ivory silk and wondering if she dared push her whisk down any lower, for Mistress Peale had insisted she wear one because they were "causing a sensation in the dining room" as it was. "We are not going shopping tomorrow. Mynheer van Rappard has promised to show us the countryside. We will see the *polders,* as the farms here are called, and their windmills. Verhulst has promised to show me a thousand windmills, and I shall hold him to it!" she added blithely.

When she repeated this threat to Verhulst next day, he threw back his dark head and laughed. "Mistress Peale doubtless thinks we would be better off counting the thousand ships moored in the Damrak, ships that could carry you both back to England!"

"Yes," smiled Imogene. "Perhaps she does." She had sometimes found herself looking longingly toward the Damrak, from whence one day a stout ship would carry her back to England—and Stephen. But she would not tell this fiery-eyed young Dutchman that.

But even though Mistress Peale pronounced herself entirely enervated by their day in the country, Imogene was delighted with everything. Verhulst pointed out wagon wheels perched atop chimneys to attract storks, and great creaking windmills with giant sails that turned lazily above a landscape flat as a floor. He showed her fields of tulips and canals adrift with swans, and dikes that rose above that landscape so tall that great white ships seemed to sail by them on dry land. She brushed aside Verhulst's apologies for not having been able to find them a *kermis*, or fair.

"It doesn't matter," Imogene sighed, stretching her slim arms luxuriously—an imminent peril to the tight blue flowered calico of her bodice. "We didn't need a *kermis*, it's been a perfect day." She smiled at the sight of a sturdy peasant and his wife, harnessed to a *pakschuyt*, or water dray, dragging it home from market along the canal in the waning light. The woman, in her wooden shoes and peaked white cap, was singing softly in Dutch and her song floated out to them. It had a dreamy quality in the summer dusk. Imogene did not know what future the world would mete out to her and Stephen, but if only she could be as happy as that woman, gladly dragging her heavy burden back home alongside her man. . . .

Perfect, thought Verhulst ecstatically. His lady had called the day *perfect*. Surely that must mean—!

He was still basking in the memory of her casual remark when they returned to the city, and just before they reached their inn, a man nearly bumped into them, hurrying by. He was so oddly dressed that Imogene remarked on him.

Verhulst turned to look at the black-clad figure with its wig and air of importance and long black crape streamer billowing from his black-plumed hat.

"He is an *aanspreeker*," he told Imogene. "It is his duty

to go and invite people to attend funerals.''

"But don't they come anyway? Must they be invited?"

"No, they do not come unless the *aanspreeker* brings them an invitation.'' He held open the inn door for her. "And those who attend are given rich gifts.''

Imogene thought this very odd—but on a par with the church service which they had attended with Vrouw Schillerzoon, where the women had clustered in the center of the church and the men had drifted to the sides and the nobility had sat in elaborately carved circular pews, each built around one of the lofty columns. "I suppose that is why they call some people 'pillars of the church,' " she had murmured irrepressibly later and Vrouw Schillerzoon had given her a black scowl, for though the Schillerzoons were wealthy, they were not yet possessed of such a pew.

So the pleasant days passed for Imogene in Holland. She went everywhere, saw everything, and shopped for household items that were far beyond her reach. And Verhulst pranced and postured before her, assuming noble poses that made him—in his own mind—appear emphatic, or imposing, or charming.

He would have been astonished and indignant to know that Imogene, her mind and heart still filled with Stephen Linnington, scarcely saw him at all.

But her chaperon did.

He is very taken with her, this rich young patroon from the Americas, she wrote ecstatically to Imogene's guardian, Lord Elston. *I feel sure he will offer for her!*

The letter had scarce been posted before Verhulst made his offer. Earnestly he described again the noble setting of the great house at Wey Gat, the beauty of the Dutch colony of New Netherland, the gaiety of its people. But the headstrong English beauty gazed back at him from her wide blue eyes and saw but one thing: *Here was a way to return to the Scilly Isles and be reunited with her Stephen! Hang the betrothal, once back in the Scillies she and Stephen—who must have come back by now—would run away together.* The wrong she was doing the intense young Dutchman never once occurred to her. Her reckless heart told her this was the way, straight as an arrow, to Stephen's arms—and Imogene had always followed her reckless heart.

"I'll marry you, Verhulst," she promised after she had kept him staring at her in agony, and hardly breathing, for a suitable time. "But not here. Back home in the Scilly Isles."

She never meant to go through with her bargain, of course. Verhulst was only to be her passage back to the Scillies—and Stephen.

CHAPTER 7

"Oh, ye'd not do it, Imogene! Ye'd not marry this Dutchman!" Elise protested in horror when she heard it. "Ye can't!"

"Can I not?" The two women were alone in their room at the Red Lion, for Mistress Peale had bustled away downstairs. Now Imogene turned from looking into her small silver mirror, for she was pushing back an errant curl that kept falling over her forehead. With raised eyebrows she surveyed Elise. "And why not, pray?"

"Ye *can't* marry with him—and him believing ye're a virgin!" gulped Elise.

The hand mirror slapped down upon the bed with a force that would have broken it had it not landed on a soft surface. "Hold your tongue, Elise! You'd no right to be spying on me!"

"I've not spied on ye." Elise shook her dark head vigorously. "But—I know ye, Imogene, and your blood runs hot. You and

Stephen Linnington were often alone. I knew what was going on.''

Imogene bit her lip. "You'll not say anything to Mistress Peale?''

"I didn't then and I won't now,'' Elise told her sturdily.

"Then naught stands in the way." Imogene's voice was casual. She went back to arranging her hair.

Elise stepped back to study her. "Ye don't intend to go through with it, do ye?'' she said slowly. " 'Tis only a way to get back to Stephen Linnington?''

The mocking look Imogene flung at her was answer enough. "If my guardian does not send for me, I must find my own way back,'' she told Elise.

"But this Dutchman is in love with you. You will hurt him.''

Imogene shrugged. "There are plenty of women in the world, Elise. He will find someone else.''

Elise went away, shaking her head. She had never been able to win an argument with reckless Imogene.

Back to the Scillies they would certainly have gone, for Verhulst had already arranged passage for them all, had not a letter arrived in Amsterdam that same day. It was brought by a sea captain who had touched at Saint Mary's Isle in the Scillies; he had had the letter from Bess Duveen's hand and had promised faithfully to deliver it to the Red Lion in Amsterdam—for Imogene had written to Bess her first day in Amsterdam, hoping for news of Stephen.

I knew you would want to know this, Bess wrote, and her falling tears had blurred the ink of some of the words. *For we have just heard by way of friends in Penzance that Stephen Linnington has been killed in a duel somewhere in Cornwall. We do not yet have the details, but they had it from friends farther north. The Lord Constable is furious, for now that Giles Avery's body has been washed ashore and he was found to be run through by a sword rather than drowned as had been thought, he was planning to pursue Stephen for Giles's murder— and demand that you be brought back and questioned, for he felt you knew more than you had told. I write you this as a friend, Imogene—and I pray it reaches you. Stay in Amsterdam, for he will try to make someone suffer for the deed and it could well be you. I know Stephen would never kill Giles except in self-defense and that he must have left the Scillies to shield you from your part in the affair, but I have not spoken of this to anyone, not even to my brothers—nor will I, you may depend upon that.* Here the quill pen had paused over the paper, for Bess could not bring herself to repeat to Imogene the vile rumors that were spreading about Stephen—that he was a bigamist, a murderer, a cheat. *If I find out more about Stephen's death,* she had written in an unsteady hand, *I will let you know, for I know he was as dear to you as he was to me.*

Imogene read the note and fainted.

All that day she stayed in her room at the Red Lion and wept. That day and the next and the next. Not all of Verhulst's entreaties—faithfully relayed through an anxious Mistress Peale—would budge her.

"I have told him you had bad news from England," Mistress Peale told her nervously on the fourth day. "That a distant cousin in York to whom you were devoted has died in childbirth and that it has given you a migraine. May heaven forgive my lies! He says to tell you that he respects your grief."

Imogene, still in her night rail, her legs drawn up in her locked arms and her chin resting on her knees, stared out at the endless blue of the sky over Holland. Her face was drawn and reserved and she gave only the barest indication that she had heard. The letter that had turned her life upside down, now read and reread and stained with her tears, lay at her bare feet. Stephen was gone . . . gone. She would have to live all of her life without him. Everything that was said to her seemed to be spoken in a kind of nightmarish dream.

If only I had stayed, she found herself thinking. *If I had only insisted on going with him, done anything—flung myself into the sea, forced him to take me with him, perhaps I could have prevented the duel that killed him.* She bent her head and drenched her night rail with her tears, for these were bitter thoughts. Her guardian, in a pensive mood, had once muttered, *If I had my life to live over.* . . . Now at last she knew what he meant.

Every hour that passed made her more remote. Her body—which refused to eat or sleep—was trapped in Amsterdam, but her spirit had fled to England and memories of Stephen. Once again she felt his every caress, knew the burning passion of his kisses, lost herself in the glow of his turquoise eyes, felt his arms enfold her.

"Her grief is so strong I am afraid she will die of it," worried Elise to Mistress Peale.

"Oh dear, oh dear," sighed Mistress Peale, who had not been allowed to read the letter that lay at Imogene's bare toes, and had not been able to wring from Imogene the source of her woe. "I do not know how much longer I will be able to hold the young Dutchman off. He is growing very restive—I do believe he thinks I am keeping Imogene from him! Certainly I cannot think of any more lies to tell him. Grief, you say? For what does she grieve? What is wrong with her?"

Elise, who had been told simply, *He is dead,* and loyally kept silent, looked with pity at that straight defiant back across the room. The brilliant light from the casements spilled over

Imogene's cascading golden hair, haloing it. In the delicate night rail her slender figure looked slight and lost. "She will not talk to me about it," Elise told Mistress Peale sturdily. "But at least she has stopped weeping."

"Yes, but now she sits and stares straight ahead of her and ignores what we say! She will not talk to me."

"I know, I know," frowned Elise. "But it will pass."

Behind her, Imogene could hear them talking. And now, through her grief, had come shafts of reality. There were decisions to be made, bitter decisions. And she alone could make them.

She could not go back to England.

She could of course linger on in Amsterdam—provided the wealthy Avery family did not send someone to seize her from Amsterdam's streets and kidnap her and drag her back to the Scillies to answer for her "crime"; such things had happened before and would happen again. She could linger here living on what her guardian sent her. But Lord Elston was old and when he died all his property would be inherited by a nephew who—when she had slapped away his impudent questing fingers that had found their way into her bodice—had developed a deep dislike for her. When he inherited, Imogene's allowance would be promptly cut off and Mistress Peale summarily returned to the Scillies. After that she would find herself dependent upon the charity of such as Vrouw Schillerzoon.

Or she could try to find honest work. And that would be difficult, for Amsterdam was a town of fierce guilds that protected their own and kept out outsiders seeking work. She had no special skills, she was not a clever seamstress, or adept at baking. She knew no foreign languages, she did not even know how to milk a cow. She had not the temperament for a servant.

Grimly then, she assessed her assets: Beauty—she had

that. A good seat on a horse—and what did that matter in a town where all the traffic went via canal? An aristocratic if provincial upbringing—she wore clothes admirably, she was expert in light banter, she danced well.

It all added up to one thing, and the answer rang through her tired head like a tolling bell: A woman like her really had only one choice: She must marry.

On the fifth day she waited until Mistress Peale had gone downstairs, clucking, to breakfast, and then rose with decision and dressed. Her mirror showed her a pale, determined face with dark circles under her eyes, which she whitened with ceruse, and added a touch of "Spanish paper" to rouge her pale cheeks. But she was dry-eyed and in control of herself when Mistress Peale came back up from breakfast much perturbed.

"Your young Dutchman was much exercised that you did not come down to eat—again," she told Imogene severely. "I told him you still suffered from your migraine, but I could scarce restrain him from sending up a doctor."

Imogene brushed that aside. "Mistress Peale, you cannot winter in Amsterdam, your health will not stand the cold."

"But—but we are all going home, are we not?"

"No, *you* must return to the Scillies, where the weather is mild. Verhulst has already paid for your passage. But—I will not be going with you."

"What?" cried Mistress Peale, scandalized. " 'Tis one thing to excuse yourself from dinner, but quite another thing to excuse yourself from an ocean voyage! Your young Dutchman will hardly relish taking *me* back to the Scillies and leaving *you* here!"

"You will be going back alone."

Startled by the expression of sudden pain on Imogene's lovely face, Mistress Peale's great girth sank down upon the bed. "What—what has happened?" she faltered. "You did not tell me what was in the letter that upset you so."

"Bess has written me that the Lord Constable will take me into custody as soon as I arrive—and doubtless he will torture me also, to make me say I had some part in killing Giles Avery."

"In—in killing Giles Avery?" Mistress Peale's voice rose on a note of hysteria. "But he was drowned at sea!"

"It would seem he was not. His body has been found and 'tis said he died of a sword thrust. The Lord Constable believes Stephen Linnington killed him—and that I had some part in it."

"Then—" Mistress Peale recoiled in horror—"you can never go home!"

All night, once her first grief was spent, Imogene had been wrestling with that problem. It was true. While the Lord Constable lived she could never go home.

"I am not going home," she said quietly. "I am going to marry Verhulst van Rappard, a man who loves me, and go with him to America."

Verhulst was delighted that Imogene had changed her mind about going to the Scillies, for he did not relish spending any time in England—Amsterdam was the place! He was more than delighted to be rid of Mistress Peale, although he was resigned to taking Imogene's dour maid to America.

Now that Imogene was to remove herself from Amsterdam a married woman, Vrouw Schillerzoon suddenly warmed to them all and offered her big front living room with its shadowy drapes and polished floor, for the nuptials.

Dryly, Imogene refused. She did not like Vrouw Schillerzoon and she did not intend to start her new life—for that was what she meant it to be, a new life in which she would try to change, mend her reckless ways, and be a good wife to

Verhulst—in Vrouw Schillerzoon's front parlor. To Verhulst's amusement, she told a startled Vrouw Schillerzoon that she had decided to be married adrift in a flower-decked boat and float down the glassy waters of the canal toward the sea, a bride.

"You are a romantic, Imogene," Verhulst teased, but his face was flushed with pride in the proud lovely girl who sat so still beside him, coolly facing down Vrouw Schillerzoon, who was muttering darkly that any girl who chose to be married on a *kanaalboot* needed a *dokter* for her head.

"Perhaps," Imogene agreed casually with both of them, but she was glad when they took their leave of the affronted Dutch housewife and she could prod Verhulst to tell her more about America. For she must not look back—*she must not*. Verhulst was her future.

"I will *show* you America, Imogene. But you know it will not do, this marriage in a *kanaalboot*. We will be married on shipboard by the captain of the *Kierstede* on our first night out. The ceremony can be held on deck, if you like, where the sea wind will blow your hair and ruffle your bridal veil."

" 'Bridal veil'? But I have not bought one."

"I have bought one for you. It is of fine point lace, sheer as a spider web, white as the ocean's foam—I but quote the shopkeeper, who is something of a poet."

A bridal veil . . . Imogene felt she was not entitled to a bridal veil, but she could hardly refuse to wear one, since Verhulst had already bought it for her.

"A marriage on the ship's deck—yes, I would like that," she said in a faint voice—and beat back the thought of the white sails beating from island to island in the Scillies, and Stephen beside her on the swaying deck. This marriage would open the door to a new life—what did it matter where the ceremony was held?

But having decided that, Verhulst seemed in no hurry to board. And had Imogene been less stunned by the news of Stephen's death, which seemed every day less real to her so that she moved in a kind of unhappy dream, she would have wondered about that. They let the *Kierstede* sail without them, although its hold would transport many of the treasures Verhulst was shipping to America, and took passage on the later sailing *Hilletje*—on the pretext that they must see Mistress Peale off.

Standing on the dock, Imogene watched her crying chaperon waving from the deck—and felt the last bit of England she had known was slipping away from her. "I will miss her, truly miss her," she murmured, and beside her Elise sobbed into her apron.

"Come, come," said Verhulst in some surprise. "It isn't the end of the world. Mistress Peale will come and visit you at Wey Gat."

"No." Imogene shook her head and dabbed at her misty eyes. "She will never do it. Mistress Peale was seasick the whole way here. She will not attempt a long ocean voyage again."

There was a measure of relief in Verhulst's eyes. "Then I must cheer you up," he said firmly—and took Imogene on a round of shopping that left her dizzy.

"I am not going to be presented at Court, Verhulst," Imogene protested in some amazement when he presented her with three dozen ostrich plumes in assorted colors.

For a moment his dark eyes went murky and she sensed anger boiling up in him—she had touched his pride. "You will be the wife of a patroon, Imogene," he said silkily. "Remember that. And we have excellent hatters in America. Your plumes must always be fresh and match your costume."

Seeing how important the trappings of splendor were to

him, Imogene went meekly into a round of fittings that left her pinpricked and exhausted.

"Of course," Verhulst told her cheerfully, "there are plenty of good tirewomen in New Amsterdam, downriver from Wey Gat, so we should stock up on materials as well." And promptly insisted that she choose several dozen lengths of dress materials—the more expensive the better.

They had just come out of a cellar shop where Imogene had chosen several lengths of jewel-toned velvet—deep ruby red and vivid sapphire blue and the haunting green of emeralds, all of which Verhulst had insisted on, as well as his usual selection of rich lustrous blacks for himself—and several lighter tones of gold and saffron and lemon that Imogene felt would be a relief against the brilliance of Dutch dress. As the shop door closed behind them with a jangle of its bell, Imogene looked up and saw a man regarding her from the street with a narrow smile.

He was not at all an ordinary sort of man. He looked, she told herself dispassionately, like a brigand—but he had the air of a commanding general. There was authority and lean, lithe strength in every line of that tall frame. Strength—and a wildness she recognized, with a sudden stirring of her own wild heart, in those narrowed eyes, gray as the northern seas, that were even now mentally stripping her. The tall gentleman had a thick shock of dark hair, hair of so dark a brown that it appeared black expect where the sun struck it and highlighted it to a rich, glowing bronze. He was dressed in the Dutch style, with wide pantaloons and fine leather boots with wide tops, and he stood easily balanced with his legs wide apart as he considered her. There was a heavy pistol thrust casually into the yellow silk sash that swept down from his broad shoulder, and his finely shaped hand rested negligently on the hilt of a very serviceable-looking sword. His clothes looked a bit the worse for wear—except for his linen, which was spotlessly clean. Lace spilled snowily at his throat in sharp contrast to the strong jaw of his sun-browned face, and she saw that his brow and cheekbones were darkened by the sun almost to the color of his russet doublet—which made those narrowed gray eyes startlingly light.

She was startled when the gentleman spoke to Verhulst.

"Ah, mynheer, I did not expect to see the Patroon van Rappard in Amsterdam," he said affably. His voice was resonant and deep-timbred.

Beside her, Verhulst froze. His tone, she thought, was notably uncivil. "Good day to you, Captain van Ryker." He would have pushed on but van Ryker stepped neatly in front of him and that broad chest barred their passage.

"I believe I have not had the pleasure," he said suavely, smiling at Imogene.

Verhulst was obviously nettled. "Mistress Wells, this is Captain Ruprecht van Ryker."

"Captain van Ryker." Imogene acknowledged the introduction as the tall gentleman swept her a deep bow that spilled his dark shining hair down across his shoulders. He straightened up and his smile deepened.

"You are English, Mistress Wells—I can tell from your accent. Cornish, perhaps?"

She gave him a quick, wicked smile, for it occurred to her that he knew very well she was English, that she and Verhulst had been speaking together in English when they had emerged from the shop. And because his bold direct gaze irritated her, she said, "You are right," and added innocently, "I thought you must be English also, Captain van Ryker, since you addressed Verhulst in that tongue rather than in Dutch."

His smile deepened still further. *"Touché,"* he murmured in French. "A very good sword-thrust, Mistress Wells. I see you would make an admirable opponent. Perhaps we will cross blades again sometime?''

''I doubt it.'' Imogene gave a shrug that dismissed him and all his kind from the face of the earth—there, let *that* be the answer to his knowing grin that seemed to be peering into her chemise!

''My betrothed and I are heavily occupied, for we set sail with the tide,'' said Verhulst impatiently. ''This is our last day in Amsterdam and we have many last-minute errands—you will have to excuse us.''

'' 'Betrothed'?'' murmured van Ryker, his dark brows lifting. ''Yes, I can see you would be heavily engaged to keep such a headlong lass in check.''

''What do you mean by that?'' demanded Verhulst, his thin face reddening.

''Why, nothing, nothing at all,'' was the urbane reply. ''Save that Mistress Wells has a tongue as sharp as a rapier and a smile that would melt stone. Come now, there cannot be so great a hurry. Where are you staying? I would drink a draft with you, mynheer—and with your lovely betrothed.''

''We are staying this night on board ship,'' burst out Verhulst. ''And as I told you, we are very busy, for we have boxes and baggage to see to.''

''Ah, yes—boxes. Do not let me interfere with the loading of luxuries for the bride, mynheer.''

Verhulst gave Imogene's arm a peremptory tug and they were off into the crowd even before she could acknowledge the captain's ironic bow. She glanced back to see his ice gray eyes following them.

''Who was that?'' she wondered. ''Faith, he was a formidable-looking gentleman. Is he one of your neighbors, Verhulst?''

" 'Formidable'?" Verhulst sounded annoyed. "Indeed, he is formidable—reputed to be the best blade in the Caribbean. But one of my neighbors he is not. Why, he's—he's nothing but a damned pirate! I didn't want to present you, Imogene, but there was no other way. The fellow was like as not to run me through if I angered him."

" 'A pirate'?" Imogene looked surprised. She had seen occasional pirates roaming the streets in Cornwall, but they had been a raffish lot, they had lacked this man's style, his presence. "He is Dutch, then? But he spoke such excellent English."

"Oh, yes, I understand he is Dutch but he speaks a dozen languages excellently. The fellow's something of a scholar, I'm told—reads books all the time in his great cabin."

"I would have thought a pirate would find something else to amuse himself with," she murmured. "Women, for example."

Verhulst snorted. "He does not lack for those either! Come along, Imogene, we do not want the fellow to catch up to us."

"What, is he following us, then?"

"I do not know—no, don't look round, he's like to join us!"

"And why would that be so terrible?"

"I told you, because he's a damned pirate!"

"His gaze *was* overbold," agreed Imogene instantly.

"I am glad you noted that." Verhulst spoke with vigor. "Such men walk the streets of New Amsterdam freely—but *I* do not receive them at Wey Gat."

All that day Imogene, who had gone through the days since word of Stephen's death like someone in a dream, found herself haunted by the stranger's bold glance—as if he saw through her to her very soul and marveled at what he found there. Something about him had disconcerted her and she found it hard to concentrate on what Verhulst was saying, something about this being their wedding day.

Their wedding day! Somehow the thought was remote, it was happening to somebody else, not to her. But as the day wore on and the sun dipped gold in the west, she found herself grateful to the bold stranger for one thing—he had taken her mind temporarily away from Stephen, who was lost to her, and away from Verhulst, who tonight would be shocked to learn that his English bride was not a virgin after all.

Nervously clenching and unclenching her hands, Elise, dressed in her best—a rustling gray silk that Imogene had insisted Verhulst buy for her in Amsterdam—stood by that night on the deck of the *Hilletje* when the captain read the marriage ceremony that united Imogene Wells with Verhulst van Rappard, patroon of Wey Gat. Nothing short of death or dismissal would have separated her from Imogene, but her back was rigid with fright for the young girl whose drifting white veil blew with the sea breeze.

And Imogene, standing almost in a trance with the salt wind fanning her hot cheeks and the white shrouds flapping from the masts above as the *Hilletje* beat her way into the North Sea, listened more to the creaking of the great ship than to the words the captain was speaking. She looked not toward the thin, intense young man beside her, but out toward the white stars winking down from a black velvet sky and heard an inner voice repeating over and over: *A new life, a new life. . . .*

But practical Elise was almost hysterical when, after toasts had been drunk and a late wedding feast consumed, she readied Imogene for bed in the cabin she would share with her new husband. Elise's bony hands shook as she slipped the beautiful white lace-trimmed night rail Imogene had bought in Amsterdam for this occasion, over the girl's bare white form.

"What will you tell him?" she mourned, giving the soft floating material a tug that carried the white night rail down below Imogene's delicately molded breasts and past her supple hips to brush against her slender white feet. "Oh, what will you tell him?"

Imogene loosed her fair hair and it fell in ropes of gold down around her shoulders. She shook it out. "I will tell him I had a riding accident," she flared. "I will tell him whatever I choose. Verhulst will believe me—you'll see."

"Why?" persisted Elise. "Why will he believe you? Why will he not think something else?"

"Because," sighed Imogene, combing her hair vigorously with a sculptured silver comb so that it glimmered in the light of the cabin's swinging lamp, "I am a very convincing liar." She wished for a treacherous moment that it were not so, that she could start this night, this new life without lies, without deception. The comb paused in her hand. "Do you think perhaps I should tell him the truth?" she wondered wistfully.

"Oh, no, don't do that!" Elise dropped the slippers she was holding—dainty white satin bridal slippers that had been worn on deck earlier—from nerveless fingers. "Promise me you won't do that," she pleaded, near hysteria.

"Very well, I promise," snapped Imogene, Elise's fright restoring her own courage. "Anyone would think you were the bride, not I! For heaven's sake, get you to your cabin, Elise." She nodded toward the tiny cabin next door that was to be Elise's on the voyage. "Verhulst will be arriving at any moment and he will hardly expect to find you still here."

"I will not sleep a wink," cried Elise brokenly, for the tension of what was soon to come had set her nerves on edge and rubbed them raw. "I will listen at the door—call me if there is trouble."

"You will not listen at the door. If there is trouble—" Imogene's voice was ironic—"it will be a bit late to call on you. I will have to deal with it myself."

Elise scurried away, her control completely gone. She was bent over and wringing her hands. Her sister Clara, who had always considered Elise a tower of strength, would have been appalled to see her at that moment. "Not a virgin," she was muttering to herself. "Oh, who knows how this Dutchman will feel about that?"

The same as other men, came Imogene's silent answer. But she felt a quiver of fear go through her—and of shame. Because she had not been fully honest with her Dutchman.

She plumped the fat bed pillows and lay back against them, trying to arrange herself fetchingly. Wild thoughts coursed through her mind. She could pretend to virginity, of course, she could twist about, cry out, feign tears. She could insist on keeping the lamp on—then she could watch Verhulst's face and see if he believed her.

No—her face was stained with color at the thought. She would do nothing so humiliating. She would murmur something about "A riding accident . . . you must understand . . ." at an appropriate moment, and hope that Verhulst's blood would run hot enough with desire that he would forget—or at least forgive.

Perhaps she should tell him that she had fallen as a child while climbing on the rocky cliffs and torn herself. He must know that Cornwall and the Scillies abounded with cliffs and jutting sawtooth rocks.

But then he probably knew nothing about Cornwall. The problem was—how much did he know about women?

Time passed.

Imogene, biting her lips—more from nervousness than to

make them red—told herself petulantly that Verhulst would consider her lack of virginity of no importance. Had he not stressed time and again how he had always meant to marry a lovely woman to grace his handsome home, to receive his friends? *That* was what was important to Verhulst, not virginity!

She felt perspiration breaking out on her forehead and almost panicked. She *must* seem fresh and dewy! Everything depended on it. For Imogene was steeped in the knowledge handed down from Eve that a lovely woman, fresh as springtime and delicately scented, could hold out her bare white arms and bend a man from even his firmest intentions.

She dived from her bed and seized a fine linen handkerchief and feverishly rubbed her damp palms across it, blotted it against her face. Now the barest brush of attar of roses, so that the scent of the damask rose would rise faintly from her silken body.

Her face was flushed and her thoughts hammered at her: *Could I tell him that it is not the custom in England? That only the poor go virgin to their marriage beds?* Oh, no, he would never believe that. He would ask *who*—and I cannot speak about Stephen, not yet. Perhaps . . . not ever.

Tears stung her eyes and were hastily brushed away. A crying bride? Never!

Back in the bed she lay down atop the coverlet, stretched out one white arm over which a wash of sheer lace spilled, and turned a bright expectant smile toward the cabin door.

No, she could do this better. She slid one leg up, bending a white knee invitingly so that the skirt of her night rail slid up along her hip, and blew out the lamp. There, that knee would shine silver in the moonlight.

And so Imogene waited, looking infinitely desirable and

frozen in fear, with her heart pounding in her chest—and waited, and waited.

At last the cabin door swung open.

Verhulst van Rappard stood there, a dark shape in the doorway.

BOOK II
The Sea Rover

A toast to the lean sea rover
Who hides with his wolfish grin
The terrible cost of all he has lost
And all that it meant to him.

CHAPTER 8

The sun shone bright on the clean-scoured boards of the *Hilletje*'s deck and a fair wind billowed her shrouds. Barefoot sailors whistled as they went about their chores and the few passengers—most of them New Netherlanders on holiday, for Holland had trouble getting the contented Dutch to migrate to their raw American colony—strolled about, taking the morning air.

But one passenger was not strolling. Elise, her face so white and pinched that passersby assumed her to be seasick, leaned against the ship's rail, watching not the blue sea with its frothy white-capped waves but scanning anxiously each passenger who emerged on deck. She was watching for Imogene and her imagination was so harrowed by wild thoughts of what the girl's wedding night must have been that she started forward with a convulsive protective gesture when Imogene at last came out on deck and walked toward her.

As the full sight of Imogene sank in on her, Elise sank back against the rail and her fearful eyes surveyed the young girl in amazement. Imogene was wearing a wide-skirted dress of ruffled yellow calico that billowed in the salt breeze over a sky blue silk petticoat. Black velvet ribands decorated her low square-cut neckline and crisscrossed her V-shaped bodice. Saucy black velvet bows accented her wide yellow calico oversleeves and peeped from the frothing lace of her white lawn chemise cuffs. She sauntered toward Elise on soft yellow slippers, looking as if she had not a care in the world, and wished her a smiling good morning.

Still, Elise—whose kindly heart had almost stopped at sight of Imogene out of very real fear for her—could not bring herself to trust this casual stance. Imogene was bold; she well might be trying to carry off a disaster by ignoring it.

"Was it—was it all right?" Elise whispered hoarsely, clutching Imogene's arm. "I kept trying to listen at the door—"

"You shouldn't have done that," chided Imogene, lowering her voice as two passengers walked by. She acknowledged their greeting, then turned and studied Elise's haunted face. "You do look as if you haven't slept all night, Elise. Best take a nap today."

Elise gasped at this offhand answer. "I couldn't hear anything," she protested. "Your voices were too low. And I hoped, I hoped—oh, was it all right?" she entreated. "How did he take it? Has he turned against you? What did you tell him?"

Imogene acknowledged the simpering bows of a passing Dutch vrouw and her daughter, then turned a puzzled face toward the far blue waters, stretching away in the glittering distance. She waited until the two women were out of earshot. "There was no need to tell him anything."

" 'No need'? But he must have wondered when he—"

"He told me he was seasick, but I think he was drunk," said Imogene dispassionately. "He did not touch me. Not once. I think—" she frowned—"I really think he must be afraid of me."

So it was all postponed for some other possibly more terrible time. Elise looked as if she might faint. "He did not touch you? *Not at all?*"

"Verhulst was taken suddenly ill," Imogene told her tersely.

" 'Ill'?" Wild new thoughts coursed through Elise's terrified mind. "Oh, I do hope it is not the plague!"

Imogene gave her a very steady look. "I do not think it is the plague," she said evenly. "But even in the moonlight I could see how pale his face was as he unlaced his doublet. I thought at first that he must be a poor sailor and was seasick but . . . now I am not so sure." Her voice dwindled as she remembered the maddening slowness with which Verhulst had undressed, how careful he had been always to keep his back turned to her, how at one point he had sought to steady himself by grasping a chairback . . . indeed, he had seemed afraid to turn and face her. And when at last he had, his expression had been unreadable. She could not bring herself to tell Elise that her bridegroom had all but tottered to the bed or that his heavy breathing—which she had mistaken for unbridled passion and braced herself—had been merely a symptom of his distemper. For at the bedside he had paused as if to study and memorize each feature of his young bride, so temptingly displayed upon the bed.

Imogene had tensed. This was the moment.

Then: "Move over, Imogene," he had said huskily. "There's not enough room." And almost collapsed beside her, face down into his pillow.

She had waited, confused and anxious and annoyingly pinned down—for Verhulst's body, when he fell forward upon the bed, had caught the spreading length of her night rail with his hip and now the fabric lay beneath him, effectively holding her. She was so stunned by his behavior that she hesitated to pull the material out from under him. Could it be that he was *disappointed* at the sight of his bride in her night rail? Her worried gaze had scanned the silver sheen of her knee, rising from a foam of lace. No, she was sure she must present a desirable picture to any man there in that moon-drenched room. What, then, was the matter? Beside her the steady stertorous breathing remained muffled by the pillow that hid her bridegroom's face, and his thin figure in the handsome damask nightshirt continued to lie beside her, unmoving.

When the tension in her had mounted to a point where she felt she might scream, she had given the material of her night rail a little tug to wrest it from beneath him and he had lifted his head a little and said in a hoarse voice, "Ye'd best to sleep, Imogene."

Imogene came back from reliving last night. Elise was speaking to her.

"Then you were up with him all night?" Elise prodded.

Up with him? For all she knew, her bridegroom had slept the night away! Toward morning she had drifted into a fitful sleep, studded by nightmares that had kept her restless and moaning.

"No, no," she said. "I was not up with him at all. I tried to lie very quietly beside him so that I would not disturb him, but once I turned over in bed and my bare leg brushed his thigh, for my night rail had ridden up and he groaned—*groaned*, Elise, as if I had hurt him!"

"*Groaned* at such a light pressure?" Elise was scandalized.

Imogene nodded and frowned. In her concentration she

failed to notice the sweeping bow of an immigrant from Leyden who would later report to the captain with a chuckle that the patroon's young bride must have passed an enjoyable night—indeed, she had looked quite tired when he passed her on deck this morning!

"This morning I asked him what was wrong," Imogene told Elise.

"And what did he say?"

Imogene remembered waking up in a tangle of covers and looking through eyes still glazed with sleep at the astonishing sight of her bridegroom, fully dressed and trying to tiptoe out of the cabin. She had sat up with a start, pushing back her tumbled golden hair. The ribbon holding her night rail had become tangled in the bedclothes and with her sudden rise it had broken so that the loosened white fabric had slid down off her shoulder exposing one pearly breast to his gaze.

In the doorway Verhulst had stiffened. "You must cover yourself," he had told her in a strangled voice. "I am about to open the door."

"I can see that you are," she had answered tartly. And then she had asked him what was wrong. Was she not beautiful enough? Did he, who had been so hot to wed, regret his bargain? Did he no longer desire her? She had watched the red rise into his sallow cheeks, heard the slight tremor in his voice as he answered before hurrying from the room. How eager he had seemed to escape her!

She could not tell Elise all that!

"When I asked him what was wrong," she said carefully, "he told he he was not sure, but that all night he had felt very unwell. And as there is no doctor on the ship, he wishes you to move in with me and he will take your smaller cabin during this voyage. That way he will be able to sleep without being disturbed.'' Her voice grew ironic. "It seems I passed a restless night when finally I dropped off to sleep.''

Elise gasped. A groom on his honeymoon demanding separate quarters from his bride? She could hardly credit it! "But if he is so ill,'' she protested, "will he not want you by his bedside to take care of him?'' She caught her breath as out of the corner of her eye she saw Verhulst himself swinging across the deck toward them in the clear morning light. His costume was unusually striking—for him. For above his usual black velvet trousers he was wearing a black-figured velvet doublet with a yellow silk lining against which the heavy gold chain he habitually wore around his neck glittered. Yellow tassels adorned his wide-topped black Spanish leather boots and yellow ostrich plumes waved gracefully from his wide-brimmed black hat. He looked very fit.

"I am not sure what is wrong,'' muttered Imogene, turning to survey her resplendent bridegroom. "But you can be very sure he does not want me at his bedside.'' She faced him now with a bright smile, for she had promised herself in Amsterdam that she would be well and truly his mate, that she would forget old loves and be to him all that a wife should be. "Good morning, Verhulst,'' she said. "You are looking much better.''

Did a shadow pass over his face? Or did she only imagine it?

"I am a little better,'' he admitted, "although I fear me the pains may return tonight.''

"Perhaps it was something you ate yesterday? We could speak to the ship's cook.''

"No, do not do that,'' he said crossly, returning the bow of a passenger across the deck. "I do not wish to appear infirm. Come, Imogene, we must meet our fellow passengers.''

So he did not wish to discuss his malady, whatever it

was. . . . Imogene fell silent, allowing Verhulst to propel her toward a portly lady and gentleman in dark fustian, who were striding energetically about the deck. With a frightened look at the patroon, Elise drifted away, murmuring that she would remove her things to Imogene's cabin and replace them with the patroon's.

"What is the matter with that woman?" muttered Verhulst as they crossed the deck. "She looks at me as if I were the devil!"

"She is seasick," supplied Imogene imperturbably. "It has damaged her expression. She will be better shortly."

"Let us hope so. You understand, Imogene—" his tone was low and hurried, for they had almost reached the little group of passengers beaming at the new bride and groom—"these people are of no importance and you will invite none of them to Wey Gat, but during the voyage one must be pleasant."

Imogene sighed. "I understand, Verhulst—during the voyage." She met the dazzled gaze of a teenage girl who doubtless was already dreaming of being invited to some great ball given by the patroon—and felt like a hypocrite as she returned the girl's smile.

Soon she was engulfed in small talk, but Verhulst would not permit her to talk long to anyone. "You must not become involved in their affairs," he told her privately. "It is beneath the dignity of a patroon's wife."

Verhulst's ideas of a social life were difficult for her to adjust to. Nor did his "health" improve. Imogene slept alone . . . .

The sea lanes plying between New Netherland and Holland were busy this time of year, and on their twelfth day out Imogene and Verhulst were standing by the captain on the poop deck while he held forth on the difficult art of navigation. Imogene was not listening. The salt wind was blowing her hair and she was studying a fleet and beautiful ship with a golden hull that had come up suddenly out of nowhere and seemed to be pacing them.

Suddenly a shot came across their bow in the sea just ahead.

The captain looked startled and muttered something in Dutch that sounded like a curse. Imogene turned to Verhulst in alarm. "What does it mean, firing across our bow? Is not that ship flying the Dutch flag?"

"It means he wants us to stop," frowned Verhulst. "And that ship may be flying a Dutch flag but she is a pirate ship all the same. That ship—" he gave her the Dutch name in English—" is the notorious *Sea Rover*."

In bewilderment, Imogene turned to the captain, who had recovered his composure and given orders to bring the *Hilletje* about.

There was a hail from the other ship, and a shouted conversation in Dutch between the two captains followed. Imogene, with the sun shining in her eyes, could not see the *Sea Rover*'s speaker but the sun glanced blindingly off his metal breastplate. Was he dressed for battle, then? She felt the general unease that spread through the clustering passengers, who by now had all swarmed out on deck.

She was further bewildered as Verhulst leaned forward, his thin face white with fury. "I won't do it!" he cried.

To this outburst, the *Hilletje*'s captain gave a chiding answer. "Be reasonable, mynheer. That is a ship of forty guns out there, set to sweep us broadside. If the gunports were to open and the guns to speak, we are all dead men. All her captain asks is that you and I and your lovely bride share a glass of wine with him aboard his ship."

Share a glass—? Imogene's mouth dropped open. Speechless, she turned to Verhulst.

"It is that damned pirate, van Ryker," he explained between clenched teeth. "He intended to make us drink with him in Amsterdam and now he has caught up with us on the high seas—insolent dog!"

Imogene's laughter pealed with pure relief—and with a hint of malice too, for Verhulst's neglect had nettled her. In these last moments she had been imagining dreadful things, like being seized by armed men and made to walk the plank. When Verhulst had cried, "I won't do it!" chills had gone up her spine. "If that is all he wants," she said blithely, " 'tis an easy thing to accommodate him and we'll be none the worse for it save that we may lose a few minutes of sea time."

"The lady is right," agreed a tall-hatted passenger who had crowded up beside them. "We must do whatever this pirate wants, else he may blast us out of the water."

"Yes—we must!" cried one of the Dutch ladies. "I have met Captain van Ryker. If he insists, my daughter and I will accompany you to his ship." She gave her homely, marriageable-age daughter's arm a tug. "Stand up straight!" she hissed.

"Captain van Ryker requests only the company of the patroon and his bride—and myself," sighed the *Hilletje*'s captain—for the lean buccaneer's popularity with the ladies was well known; not a house in New Amsterdam but would gladly receive him.

"I will have to dress," stated Imogene, smothering a laugh. "This gown I have on will hardly do for such an occasion." She looked down at the becoming slate blue velvet skirt that swept away from a tight velvet bodice heavily embroidered in a deeper blue. The bodice had a deep-cut square neck that was chastely filled in with a whisk whose sheerness had distressed Verhulst.

"You will not change—you are already dressed far too well to board a pirate ship," objected Verhulst testily. "If you were wearing jewels, I would have you take them off!"

"As you like." Imogene shrugged with a ripple of big detachable velvet sleeves that exposed their ice blue satin lining. She shook out the frosty lace of her full white lawn chemise sleeves that spilled fashionably down from her elbows. "Then I am ready to confront this—pirate," she declared merrily.

"You are *sure* you would not feel safer with two other women along?" The Dutch lady's gaze was on her petulant—but marriageable—daughter.

Imogene managed to keep a straight face. "I feel sufficiently protected by my husband and Captain Verbloom," she said and watched the lady's lips tighten. "Well, Verhulst? Captain Verbloom?" She turned to the *Hilletje*'s captain. "Do we go over straightaway? Or do we wait until this impatient gentleman shoots off our masts?"

Captain Verbloom met her mirthful look with some annoyance, for he had a fuming patroon on his hands and several dazzled ladies aboard who would be only too overjoyed to accompany them on this visit to the dangerous Captain van Ryker's ship. "Now will do well enough," he growled. "And I will remind you, ladies—" he encompassed them all in his warning—"that Captain Van Ryker and his men may be very popular in New Amsterdam, but now we are *at sea*." His emphasis was significant.

"Are you implying they are so desperate for female companionship that they must stop us in mid-ocean to ravish us all?" demanded Imogene lightheartedly. "For they are but recently out of Holland, which teems with willing wenches! Indeed, I would think them to be still resting from their exertions!"

There was a titter of laughter among the women.

"Imogene!" choked Verhulst. His face was scarlet.

Imogene turned to him. "What, would you have me confine my opinions to the weather and the wine?"

"At least do not express them so publicly," he muttered.

Imogene cast her eyes down demurely. It was the first time on this tiresome voyage that she had truly enjoyed herself. With sparkling eyes she climbed into the ship's longboat beside her smoldering husband. This was adventure! A sudden gust of wind caught at her hair and as she reached up to keep it from streaming into her eyes, she managed to catch her fingers in her whisk and with a blithe gesture tore it from her throat and let it fly away into the waves. Verhulst made a wild snatch for the whisk and was saved from going overboard only by the *Hilletje*'s captain, who seized him around the waist and hauled him back into the boat. In horror, Verhulst's gaze rested on the newly bared expanse of his wife's lustrous breasts. Why, her nipples were almost showing! He drew in his breath with an angry sob. Imogene, amused by the situation she had created, gave him a sweet, innocent smile. She was beginning to suspect Verhulst of faking his nightly "pains" that kept him from her bed and at the moment she did not care that her young husband looked almost apoplectic. She watched with interest as a sailor from the *Sea Rover* dived over the side and swam toward the floating whisk.

It would be, of course, too wet to wear. . . .

Captain van Ryker had doffed his metal cuirass by the time they boarded, and handed her on board the *Sea Rover* with aplomb.

He was, she noted, extremely well dressed, and wondered if that had anything to do with her. He would of course, since sending a shot across their bow, have had time to change into the gray trousers and silver-shot doublet he was wearing. His linens, as in Amsterdam, had a fresh-donned look and the smile he shot her was a brilliant flash of white teeth in his sun-bronzed face. His narrow gaze hardly rested on the snowy gleam of her bosom at all—although heads all around the deck craned with interest, and Verhulst's sallow face was suffused with angry color.

"Captain Verbloom," said van Ryker affably. "Mynheer van Rappard and your lovely bride—" he swept Imogene a low bow—"how nice of you to accept my hospitality."

"Hospitality offered with a shot across one's bow from a ship of forty guns is hardly to be ignored," responded the *Hilletje*'s captain dryly.

Van Ryker's dark brows shot up. "But I sought only to attract your attention," he said suavely. "You had somehow overlooked my signal."

A bit of telltale color rose in Captain Verbloom's cheekbones and Imogene realized that he had deliberately chosen not to return that signal. The captain coughed.

"Can we not get this over with, van Ryker?" asked Verhulst testily. "You have stopped our ship and dragged us over here for some purpose other than to drink our health, I would imagine. And if we linger long enough on the high seas, the Spanish men-of-war will find us and shoot us all out of the water."

A steely glint appeared in the gray eyes that studied Verhulst and the answer was stern. "While you are under my protection, mynheer, you may rest assured that you will be safe from Spanish guns. And you are right, I did invite you here for another purpose besides drinking your health—although it will be my pleasure to do that too, since I was thwarted of it in Amsterdam." He turned to the *Hilletje*'s captain. "I had word from a passing ship that there is a Spanish squadron prowling far north of their usual run, perhaps to strike at Dutch shipping from New Netherland. Since you have rashly chosen to sail alone, rather than with a sister ship, it is my intention to give you safe conduct by convoying you myself to New Amsterdam harbor.''

Captain Verbloom was taken aback at being chided for his rashness by a buccaneer but pleased at this surprising offer of protection. "My sister ship broke her rudder at the last moment," he explained.

"You should not have sailed without her."

"Aye, you are right." Ruefully. "I had not expected Spaniards so far north. 'Twill be a comfort to my passengers to know that we are protected by a ship of forty guns."

"And now perhaps ye'll all share a glass with me in my cabin?"

Even Verhulst was somewhat mollified by this mention of a prowling Spanish squadron, for he had no illusions as to their fate if they were gunned down by a passing Spanish ship, and this offer of escort was a handsome one. "The damned Spaniards have no business to claim this western ocean as their own domain," he muttered.

"Ah, but they do," was the urbane reply. "And I do not think ye'd like a season of rowing in their galleys."

" 'A season'?" Captain Verbloom seized on that eagerly. "I'm told you had a season of rowing in their galleys, Captain van Ryker. What was it like?"

"Hell," said van Ryker shortly, and for a moment Imogene glimpsed a wolfish glimmer in the gray eyes and knew why this lean buccaneer hated the ships of Spain. She'd heard stories of agonizing death by torture of English prisoners in Spanish jails—and other slower deaths as galley slaves, chained to the oars of some majestic galleon. So van Ryker had been one of those. . . .

The thought temporarily silenced her banter as van Ryker presented the ship's officers. Together with Barnaby Swift, the ship's yellow-haired master, and Raoul de Rochemont, the ship's mustachioed French surgeon, they followed the dark buccaneer captain across a well-scoured deck to his great cabin in the *Sea Rover*'s stern. Imogene was glad they had been speaking in English for her benefit and surprised and impressed by the ship's magnificence, for not only did the brasswork glitter from polishing, but the shining table about which the debonair buccaneer captain seated his guests was of solid carved black oak, the seat into which she sank was cushioned in rich garnet red velvet tasseled in gold, and the wine that the cabin boy was even now bringing had the golden gleam of fine Canary.

Even Captain Verbloom was startled by the sumptuousness of the high-ceilinged great cabin with its wide bank of windows in the stern. He had not dreamed that buccaneers lived so well. . . .

Amid the gilt and the handsome furnishings, there were heavy gold candlesticks, and Imogene, studying her host narrowly, remarked on them.

"Seized from some Spanish ship, no doubt?"

His smile mocked her. "As was the ship herself. She was not always called the *Sea Rover*. She was *El Cruzado*—the *Crusader*—out of Barcelona."

He looked like a crusader himself, she thought, with his reckless smile and serviceable sword that never left his side. "You—took her, then?" Somehow she was surprised. She had expected this ship to have been built in Amsterdam for the East India trade.

He nodded, and she saw lights flicker in his gray eyes as he remembered the battle. "And refitted her to my taste. She is faster now."

"I'll wager there's a story there," Captain Verbloom, making up for his earlier churlishness, said heartily.

"Yes . . ." Their host looked restive, and as their glasses were filled by a cabin boy in the leather breeches and coarse cotton shirt that marked him as a *boucan* hunter, Imogene sought to change the subject.

"And what do you keep behind all those doors, Captain van Ryker?" she wondered, studying the built-in cupboards with sturdy wooden doors that adorned the great cabin. "Braces of pistols to subdue a mutinous crew? Or treasure to astound us?"

Her tone was impudent and van Ryker quickly set down his glass and in two long strides crossed the room and threw open the doors of two of the cupboards to reveal rows of well-thumbed leather volumes. "This is the treasure I keep in my cupboards," he remarked expressionlessly.

"Then it is true that you are a great reader," observed Verhulst, sounding surprised to see it proved.

"I study navigation—and other things. I take it you are no great reader, mynheer?"

Verhulst shook his head, "I prefer a game of chess."

"Aye," agreed Captain Verbloom instantly. "I regard myself as a good player but the patroon has beaten me twice already—and we have only played three times."

"Indeed? And yet you are renowned for your mastery of the game, Captain Verbloom. All the world knows it."

The captain's chest expanded at this praise and—being obviously regarded as a superchampion beating a world-renowned champion—so did Verhulst's. Imogene watched them narrowly over her wine, wondering what game the buccaneer was playing with his carefully directed flattery. She doubted if it had anything to do with chess.

"Well, you must give us a game, mynheer," declared the

buccaneer smoothly. "Raoul here accounts himself a good player."

"I will be glad to." Verhulst seized on the opportunity to safely beat these pirates.

"And perhaps Captain Verbloom will oblige Barnaby here." Van Ryker indicated the ship's master.

Amusement sparkled in Imogene's blue eyes. She saw where this was leading. But van Ryker's gaze was innocent as he took from another cupboard two handsome ivory chess sets and placed them before the participants. He observed with concentration the first move and then said casually, "While you concentrate on your game, gentlemen, I will escort Mynheer van Rappard's bride on a tour of the ship, for I am sure she is curious—as all women are—as to how buccaneers live."

Verhulst looked up from the board in angry surprise, but Imogene rose with a careless, "Why not? It will be cooler on deck and the wine has made me very warm." Her level gaze reminded Verhulst that it was he who had insisted she wear this heavy velvet gown when she would readily have changed to something cooler and more elegant in silk.

Verhulst subsided but his hand trembled slightly as he moved his queen on the chessboard, and watched his young wife sweep from the room in the company of a "damned pirate."

CHAPTER 9

As the lean buccaneer captain courteously showed her around his handsome ship, Imogene could not but remark on the shining brass, the well-scoured floors, the fresh gilding and signs of care that were everywhere apparent.

"She's a beautiful ship—I can see you're very proud of her."

"Aye, that I am." His voice took on a rich caressing note. "She's a formidable man-of-war but for all that she's a lady. . . ." The sudden intimacy of his smile told her he was speaking of more than just his ship, he was speaking of *her*. Out of the corner of her eye she noticed that the *Sea Rover*'s crew were making themselves scarce and wondered grimly if they were following their captain's instructions. Did he expect to overwhelm her with his charm on a stroll down the deck in broad daylight?

"You said she was a Spanish ship originally?"

He nodded. "I've never found out her origin—she's Portuguese-built, I think, although she sailed out of Barcelona. She's fast, she's seaworthy, she rides a gale the way a mare I once knew took stone fences—in stride." His dark face was closer now, she could smell the faint scent of Virginia tobacco and another headier odor—the light fruity smell of the fine Canary they'd been drinking. "God took a hand in her design, I think,"

he said softly, "for she's the best I've ever seen of her class."
His hand brushed hers and she felt a rippling tingle race up
her arm.

Imogene snatched her hand away. Best of her class indeed!
This impudent pirate was doubtless comparing her with a dozen
captured wenches, wondering how *she'd* ride the gales! Conscious that her breast was heaving a trifle fast and that his gaze
was resting pleasantly upon its white expanse, she tried to
compose herself and considered this buccaneer captain curiously.

She had not really looked at him in Amsterdam, she now
realized, but here in the setting most familiar to him he seemed
larger than life, as vivid as the sunshine that gilded his strong
profile. The dark face that now leaned so tauntingly close was
enough to give one pause: saturnine, with lean planes, and lit by
unreadable gray eyes, features as eagle-strong and clean-cut as
his sinewy body clad in a well-cut suit of French gray velvet, the
doublet slashed and shot with silver with the gray silk of the
lining peeking fashionably through. His lean legs were encased
in boots of fine Spanish leather and over their wide tops cascaded a wealth of frosty Flemish lace. A great jewel—she guessed it
to be a South American emerald—shone from the froth of lace at
his throat. Save for the thick gleaming dark brown hair that fell
to his broad shoulers and swung in response to his restless
gait—hair that was patently his own in a day of fussy curled and
pomaded wigs—he was elegant as any courtier. An amused
smile curled her lips at the thought and the tall man beside her
was quick to note it.

"What makes ye smile, my lady?"

Imogene hesitated. She felt curiously locked in time—
locked in by this man's absolute concentration. Around them lay
an almost deserted deck. The sun hung steady in the sky; not a

sail flapped. From the ship came the gentle moaning of great timbers lazily skimming the blue water.

In that moment, as he hung intent on her answer, Verhulst might never have been—nor Captain Verbloom, nor the *Hilletje*. For the space of a sigh the golden woman and the buccaneer stood alone in eternity.

Now in a softer voice, she gave him a frank answer. "That you're a pirate, sir, and yet you look, you sound—" her voice was rueful, for neither her husband nor any of the wealthy passengers aboard the *Hilletje* were half so urbane—"as if ye'd just escaped from the side of the Queen of England! What were you—before you became a pirate?"

It was his turn to look amused. "The side of the queen, ye say? Nay, I've never been there . . . nor yet to Court. And my past's of no interest. It's not where we've been, but where we're going that counts. But you called me a pirate and that I'm not—I'm a buccaneer, my lady."

"There's a difference?" she mocked him.

"Aye, a world of difference." He considered her gravely. "Were I a pirate, as you suggest, I'd seize yon ship—" he indicated the *Hilletje* with a careless nod of his dark head. "I'd toss your husband overboard—or ransom him, as pleased my fancy—but in either event I'd take you to my cabin for my pleasure."

Imogene's color rose. Her breath came a little faster and she wielded her fan with unnecessary speed. "And as a buccaneer?" Her voice was a trifle frosty.

"As a buccaneer, my lady, I protect all women—and prey only on the ships of Spain, which would deny us the right to sail these waters either in peace or war."

Imogene's eyebrows elevated. "Then if I were a Spanish

lady captured from some galleon or galleass?''

The gray eyes looked calmly into hers. ''Ye'd be safe from me and from my crew. I'd give ye safe conduct as far as Cuba or some other Spanish shore, set ye into a longboat manned by captured Spanish crewmen to row ye into Havana harbor—whose guns even such a ship as the *Sea Rover* has no wish to challenge.''

''Indeed? And an English lady?'' Imogene's fan waved a trifle faster in the sudden calm. ''Would you take *her* to Tortuga or Port Royal and ransom her there?''

''No, I'd set her on the first England-bound ship we passed—or America-bound, as pleased her fancy.''

Imogene digested that. Plainly, chivalry was not dead—it lived on in this tall fellow at her side who could, with a single deep-voiced command, turn his guests into captives and do with them as he would. . . . Now that she knew he would not do it, she was perversely sorry—danger appealed to her.

''We are all glad to discover you take such a view,'' she mocked. ''Else we might be even more traveled before we finally reached American shores—we might have reached them by way of Tortuga or Port Royal.''

''Are you saying you'd have liked that?'' His voice was soft but his eyes took on a sudden keenness as his head bent down, the better to consider her.

She was treading on dangerous ground now. Something throbbed painfully in Imogene's chest, a hint of summer madness that had no place in the heart of a new bride.

''No—of course not,'' she said breathlessly.

Still those bold eyes considered her. ''I'm half of a mind not to believe you,'' he said in a quiet voice. ''For 'tis my belief that you yearn to go adventuring and that you've already discovered that the young pup you've married is too dull a man for you.''

"You're wrong!" She turned her head away from him lest he see the sudden hunger in her gaze—hunger for a life such as Verhulst could never give her, for a man such as Verhulst was not, would never be.

Van Ryker gave a low disbelieving laugh that angered her. And along with that laugh the wind came back, filling the *Sea Rover*'s sails with a crack like thunder.

"I am surprised you have lived so long," Imogene flashed, almost losing her footing on the suddenly rolling deck. "Pursuing married women as you do, surely some husband must have shot you by now."

"Grazed me only," said van Ryker carelessly. He took her arm to steady her against the swaying deck, held it firmly when she would have wrested it away from him. He resumed his pacing with Imogene reluctantly in tow, shot her a sudden look. "Did you really yearn to see the crew's quarters and the galley? You've missed those."

"No."

"I thought not." Ironically.

"And what do you mean by that?" Imogene's fan fluttered furiously.

"Just this." He stopped and she, too, stopped perforce. "That a woman's soul sometimes speaks through her eyes."

"And you think mine has?"

"Can you deny it?" he challenged.

"Captain van Ryker," said Imogene, exasperated. "If you harry the Spanish half so diligently as you harry the ladies, I am not surprised at your success—you *exhaust* your victims!"

He threw back his head and laughed; at that moment his saturnine face looked very young. "Forgive me, my lady, but you look very fresh and the chase has hardly yet begun."

"Consider it ended." Imogene froze him with a glance "I

came on deck only because the fresh air was welcome."

"Aye," he agreed half humorously. "In your company, more welcome than wine."

In spite of herself, a smile curved Imogene's lips at this outrageous buccaneer, pursuing her as if he were a courtier and she a lady-in-waiting at Court. "You make a pretty compliment—for a pirate," she admitted.

He ignored the word "pirate," continuing to smile down at her, and her eyes took on a wicked sparkle. "That was a beautiful lie, Captain van Ryker—about the Spaniards being sighted."

Her thrust went home. He gave a slight start and his smile deepened. "Ah, well," he said equably. "Buccaneers are as other men, once they meet a beautiful woman."

Her voice was mocking. "You would lead me to believe that you pursued the *Hilletje* out of Amsterdam on my account?"

He had led Imogene to the poop deck and now they were standing by the rail with the wind ruffling their hair and rattling the shrouds above them.

"And would you believe it if I said I had?"

"No."

"Good," he said with a wry smile. "I see you are nobody's fool. I had business that kept me in Amsterdam, but the *Sea Rover* is a fast ship and overtook the *Hilletje*. When I saw her there, I remembered you were aboard."

"And how did you know that? I do not remember that Verhulst told you in Amsterdam the name of our ship."

His smile was wary now. "I made inquiries," he admitted.

Imogene did not know why she should feel so perversely pleased. "And so you pursued a bride and groom into the Atlantic," she murmured.

He grimaced. "I would put it some other way, of course."

"Of course. You know that you have made my husband furious by neatly trapping him into a game so you could spirit me away?"

Van Ryker shrugged. "Such fury will throw him off his game. Barnaby will win—and then of course your husband will seek vengeance and will have to accept Barnaby's challenge to another."

"You are wrong, he will postpone the next game to see where I have got to."

"Shall I wager you on that?"

"Why not?" He was standing very close now, and the wind whipped her slate blue skirts against his gray velvet trousers. Suddenly Imogene found it hard to breathe. Her voice was not quite steady.

"A kiss, then," he murmured, "if I am right?"

"A kiss with Verhulst watching? He would fling you a challenge no matter what the cost!"

"A kiss at our next meeting," he said inexorably. "I assure you that I will find the opportunity."

She caught her breath. So there was to be a next meeting. . . . "And if you lose?"

"Then I will pay a forfeit. What would you have me do?"

"Admit you followed me from Amsterdam, admit that you have stalked us, stayed behind us until we were well out to sea, admit that yours was the ship whose topgallants the watch saw endlessly on the horizon."

"I admit it now," he said softly, and his face brushed her bright hair. "What else would you have of me?"

Her voice sharpened. "I would have you tell me how many women you have loved—and left."

He straightened up and grinned down at her. "Too many to

count," he said lazily. "But if I lose this wager, I promise I will try to tally them up. And now, before we drive your husband to desperate deeds, shall we return to my cabin?"

He had timed their reentry well. Verhulst was losing badly. He gave Imogene an angry look when they entered, and was sulky as he finished his game, soundly beaten.

"An off-day, mynheer," consoled van Ryker, offering the seething patroon another glass of wine. "But Barnaby will be glad to give you another game, won't you, Barnaby?"

Barnaby nodded his yellow head and Verhulst, almost choking on his wine, said grimly, "And this time I will beat you, for now I have taken your measure!" He cast a menacing look at his young wife and the debonair buccaneer captain.

Barnaby was setting up the board when van Ryker stopped him. "But not tonight. The wind is coming up and Captain Verbloom would not care to be absent from his ship if we should run into a gale."

"No indeed!" Captain Verbloom jumped to his feet in some alarm.

"So we will postpone your game with Barnaby until tomorrow night when you will be my guests for dinner."

Verhulst looked trapped. Imogene felt vaguely sorry for him.

"It seems calm enough," observed Captain Verbloom in surprise when they came out on deck.

"Ah, but the wind freshened strongly when the lady and I were on deck earlier. I felt you would not wish to take chances with your ship."

"Of course, you are right," agreed the *Hilletje*'s captain, but he gave the patroon's English bride a sharp look.

"What did that man say to you when you were alone?"

stormed Verhulst when they had reached the relative privacy of the *Hilletje*'s deck. All the passengers were crowded at the other end of the ship, watching a school of porpoises break the water in long, graceful leaps.

Imogene, strolling dreamily beside him, thought of her wager—already won by the pirate captain. She owed him a kiss when next they met and the thought of it stormed through her mind like the prow of a ship, breaking white water. She looked out over the sunlit waters to where the golden *Sea Rover* ran lightly alongside them, giving them sea room, but keeping them ever in sight. "Nothing much," she said. "He is an interesting man, Verhulst. I wonder why he became a buccaneer. I asked him, but he would not tell me."

"Doubtless he will tell you tomorrow evening!" Verhulst tripped over a coil of rope and cursed.

"I doubt it," she said ironically. "I do not think he tells people very much about himself. He reads his books and he seizes Spanish ships and their cargoes—a strange life for such a man."

"I do not know what you mean by 'such a man.' " Verhulst felt injured and was inclined to quarrel. "But it does you no honor to be speculating on the life story of a damned pirate!"

Imogene gave Verhulst a slanted look. "He is not received, then, in New Amsterdam?"

"Oh, yes, he is received in New Amsterdam. Half the women there are in love with him and there'll no doubt be a ball in his honor when we come ashore. But *we* will not attend."

Perhaps we will, thought Imogene rebelliously. *Perhaps I will dance a measure or two with this "pirate captain."* She turned and gave her husband a straight look. "How is your health tonight, Verhulst?"

Verhulst was taken aback. "I feel well enough," he stuttered. "But—" he saw with alarm where this was leading—" 'tis only afternoon and the pains may yet return. I had best keep to my cabin tonight in case they do."

"You might try Doctor de Rochemont," she suggested in a level voice. "Perhaps he could help you."

"A ship's doctor on a pirate ship?" Verhulst was aghast at the idea. "I'd as soon consign myself to the devil!"

Imogene gave am impatient shrug. Her husband's neglect of her was becoming legendary! At least she now had something to occupy her mind—the dangerous buccaneer captain whose ship was pacing them across the western sea.

It was with exceeding care that she dressed for dinner the next night.

Elise disapproved. "Consorting with pirates!" she muttered, offering her a simple gray petticoat.

"You sound like Verhulst," reproved Imogene. "No, not that one—I'll wear the yellow satin petticoat."

"But it is one of your best petticoats!"

"So it is." *And perhaps this is the occasion for it. . . .* Imogene held up her slender arms and let Elise slip the delicate petticoat down over her head. The material fell sensuously, sliding over her chemise, stroking her like the pressure of a man's casually questing hand. Van Ryker's dark intent face swam suddenly before her vision. She stood rapt, remembering what it had been like to walk beside him down the *Sea Rover*'s sun-washed deck.

Elise expressed her disapproval by fastening the waistband with a jerk that made Imogene gasp, then bent to spread out the gleaming material so that it billowed in wide folds over the light chemise. Imogene fluffed out her big sheer chemise sleeves and gave the bodice a sharp tug downward.

"Any further down and you might as well not be wearing a chemise!" warned Elise tartly.

"Elise," said Imogene, "you manage your own necklines and I will manage mine."

"Your husband is taking you to a strange wild land full of savage Indians," scowled Elise. "And you will have much to explain to him, when he is over his distemper and comes at last to your bed. It is not wise to anger him now—he may remember it!"

"My husband is neglectful." Imogene's voice became muffled as Elise slipped a heavy white lace overskirt down over her head, fastened it at the waist and began tucking it up artfully so that the yellow satin petticoat showed to best advantage. "Perhaps a little spirit of competition will wake him up!"

Elise considered Imogene with fear in her eyes. Competition! And her a bride! Still . . . the circumstances *were* unusual. She was silent as she helped Imogene into a separate bodice of heavy white lace backed by yellow satin. It was cut dangerously low. "Your breasts may pop out," she sighed.

Imogene's reckless chuckle frightened her. "I will take that chance."

As she was combing Imogene's long golden hair, Verhulst came into the cabin. He was dressed in somber unrelieved black and surveyed his wife with an unsmiling face. "You are very richly gowned for dinner with a pirate," he growled.

"We must keep up appearances, Verhulst. Do you not consider yourself above Captain van Ryker in the social scale?"

Verhulst looked startled. "Of course, but—"

"Then we must look the part, must we not, so all the world

will be aware of it? I see you have removed your ruby ring.''

" 'Tis a ship of thieves, Imogene!'' he burst out.

"But they will not steal from us,'' she pointed out. ''They steal only from the Spaniards, who would kill us all if they caught us daring to sail 'their' seas. I think you should put the ring back on and look as magnificent as you can and face down these—pirates.''

Verhulst studied her uncertainly for a moment, then abruptly he did as he was bid. But when he came back he pushed Elise aside. ''*I* will fasten Imogene's whisk,'' he growled. ''I will pin it securely. This time it will not blow away. Have you not one less sheer?''

"No.''

"I can see through this one,'' he grumbled.

Over his head as he bent to pin the whisk to her bodice, Elise met Imogene's mocking eyes. Imogene was wondering irrepressibly what Elise would say if she told her she had lost a kiss on a wager to the buccaneer captain who waited for them on board the *Sea Rover*. The thought kept her eyes sparkling all the way up on deck.

Captain Verbloom was thoughtful as they climbed into the longboat the buccaneer captain had sent over for them. It was easy to see which way the wind was blowing—Captain van Ryker's conquests were legendary. He only hoped he could avert bloodshed between the lean buccaneer and the hotheaded young patroon while they were on the high seas. Once they were all in port in New Amsterdam, he'd wash his hands of the lot of them. This high-spirited beauty in her white lace and yellow satin could strip in public if she chose, or take a pirate lover to her bed—it was all the same to him. But . . . these potentially explosive trysts were costing him sea time.

Pursued by his grim thoughts, he watched the rippling bronzed muscles of his buccaneer escorts row him across the ocean to the waiting *Sea Rover*.

CHAPTER 10

Captain van Ryker was at the ship's rail to greet his guests and hand them aboard. He was dressed in the same gray velvet trousers and silver-shot doublet he had worn yesterday, but Imogene noticed that his shirt was different. There was heavy point lace spilling over his cuffs today and matching point lace on the boot hose that spread out stylishly over the wide tops of his leather boots. Plainly, the captain was meticulous about his linens.

Imogene, as van Ryker sprang forward, edging out Verhulst to help her over the side, gave him a mischievous look. From the recklessness of his answering smile, she half expected her impetuous buccaneer to demand satisfaction on his wager then and there and for a heart-stopping moment she braced herself to be swept up into his arms, expecting him to grasp her to him under the pretext that she had missed her footing and he needs must save her.

But he did no such thing. Instead he assisted her over the side with courtly grace and no duchess could have been handed onto a ship with more respect.

Even Verhulst, scowling that he had been shouldered away, could not fault his performance and looked mollified.

The evening was well advanced when they all sat down to a sumptuous dinner served on such a dazzling array of plate that Captain van Ryker felt constrained to admit to the admiring captain of the *Hilletje* that it was "a part" of his share from the raid on Maracaibo.

That brought about an enthusiastic discussion of that famous raid, during which Imogene, toying with her food, studied that dark face with its strangely light eyes. In this light they looked silvery . . . like the sea on a moonlit night. She frowned at herself. These were dangerous thoughts she was thinking, but she was lulled by a kind of magic. Above her head a ship's lamp swung to and fro and the sun had sunk rosily in the west. Soon stars would be shining through the bank of windows at the far end of the great cabin. Around her were maps and cutlasses and pistols, and behind the cupboard doors—books. Traitorously she wondered what it would be like to be a buccaneer's woman and hear the roar of the guns and the shouts of the men on deck, and wonder if her lover was still alive . . . or did one wait in safe harbor in Tortuga or Port Royal for him to sail back to one's arms?

She roused herself. Van Ryker had leaned across the table and was speaking to her. "I was wondering if you would accept a tortoise-shell comb for your hair?"

Imogene turned to Verhulst with a questioning look. "I do not see why not," she said impulsively before he could say no.

Van Ryker rose and went to a heavy brass-trimmed sea chest, opened its high curved lid and lifted out an intricately

wrought high-backed Spanish comb. "With my compliments."
He handed it to Imogene with a smile.

Imogene let his gaze hold hers. "Perhaps you will instruct
me in how to wear it?"

He leaned forward. "If you will permit me?" He set the
comb expertly into her elaborate coiffure. "It is to be worn like
this."

Verhulst made a strangled sound, which Imogene covered
with a light laugh. She wondered idly if this gift of van Ryker's
would wreck Verhulst's chess game.

"And is this too from the raid on Maracaibo?" she wondered.

"No," he said soberly. "It was a gift to me from a lady
who said she wished it were rubies."

Captain Verbloom, deep in wine, gave a coarse laugh.
"Faith, ye must have made a deep impression on her, van
Ryker!"

" 'From a lady'?" said Imogene uncertainly. He had taken
her by surprise.

"From a lady I rescued from a sinking boat and set ashore
dangerously near Havana. She was grateful. She took this comb
from her long black hair and insisted that I take it—and give it to
someone who would wear it well."

Someone who would wear it well. . . . Imogene felt the
blood pound in her ears. "And was it your guns that sank her
boat?" she wondered.

Van Ryker shook his head. "No, it was her husband who
set her adrift alone in a leaky longboat. He was punishing her for
taking a lover."

Across the table Verhulst's teeth closed with a snap. "He
was right to do it!"

Imogene gave Verhulst a cold look. "And did you return
the lady to her lover?"

Van Ryker shrugged. "There was no lover save in her husband's overwrought imagination. I returned her to somewhere near the estate of her uncle, who would, with persuasion, return her to her family in Spain."

Captain Verbloom gave the young patroon a droll look. That look said Verhulst would come off second best whether fencing with the buccaneer with tongue or sword. He settled back to serious drinking—at least this buccaneer captain was making a dull voyage interesting!

Imogene, who was sure van Ryker had invented the whole story and had actually bought the comb in the marketplace at Tortuga or Port Royal, tried to hide her amusement. She was playing with fire, but the game had her full attention.

To her surprise, after dinner as they sipped their wine and the chessmen were set out, Captain van Ryker did not try to hurry her on deck, but sat there drinking his wine and considering her from beneath shuttered lids. *He is waiting for me to indicate that I will make good my wager,* she realized, feeling the blood pound in her temples even as she admired his restraint. Wickedly, she was tempted to let him wait. But—that would not be fair. He had made her the wager in good faith and won. She had accepted the wager in a reckless moment because—now she admitted it—because she had wondered what the touch of his lips would be like, what it would be like to be held in the arms of such a dangerous man.

Across his glass he was regarding her a trifle sternly.

Imogene rose gracefully. "I feel a little faint," she announced. "I think perhaps it is the smoke in this cabin. No—" as the gentlemen present made to put out their pipes—"do not do that. Nor do I need your services either, Doctor de Rochemont," for the ship's doctor had risen. "A turn around the deck, and I will be quite restored. Do not let me interrupt your game,

Verhulst. Captain van Ryker can escort me on deck."

"Well done," van Ryker applauded her when they had reached the ship's rail. "I had thought to arrange something myself if you did not."

"A fire in the hold perhaps?" she taunted. "Something that would occupy Verhulst's attention?"

"Nothing so dramatic. We are towing a log, which would have fouled the rudder a few moments from now and brought everyone's attention to that part of the ship. As it is, I will give the order to cut the log loose." He waved his handkerchief as a signal and Imogene heard feet slap along the deck.

She laughed. She felt lighthearted, young, a girl who had never met Stephen Linnington or married Verhulst van Rappard.

"And you are a terrible liar, Captain van Ryker," she chided him. "Spanish lady indeed! Where did you get the comb—at the market in Tortuga?"

" 'Twas a gift from a well-wishing friend," he smiled. "I seem to remember trading a pair of gold bracelets for it. Of course, she offered something to boot. . . ."

"I'll wager she did!" Her saucy look challenged him. "What was it, van Ryker?"

He touched her bright hair yearningly. "Something better than gold."

"Nonsense," she scoffed. "What, to a pirate, is better than gold?"

"To a buccaneer—many things."

"Name one!"

"The gold of your hair for one." He kept his finger twined around the lock of hair he had appropriated and his voice was lazy. "Am I correct that you have come to pay your wager, Imogene?"

She did not even notice his use of her first name. "What

wager was that?'' she asked innocently. ''Did I make you a wager? Faith, I cannot remember.''

His fingers tightened on the lock of hair and his voice deepened caressingly. ''Dishonorable wench,'' he grinned. ''I'll help you remember! A wager's a wager!''

She turned her laughing face up to his and the moonlight struck down full upon her, deepening the lights in her blue eyes, silvering the gold of her hair, highlighting the wicked witchery of her smile. Her beauty struck him like a blow.

Very gently he bent his dark head and his lips brushed hers. Imogene felt her senses stir and her body stiffened.

''You could have been mine,'' he murmured. ''*Would* have been, had I not been such a fool as to let you go in Amsterdam. . . . I knew when I saw you that I had found my woman.''

His words—and the deep rich resonance of his voice as he said them—were more intoxicating than wine. Rocked by a bright surge of desire, Imogene set both hands against his chest and pushed him violently away from her. She was bewildered by the sudden strength of her own feelings for this buccaneer who meant nothing to her—nothing.

'' 'Twas but half a kiss,'' he protested, amused.

''Perhaps I am but half a woman,'' she said shakily. ''Unworthy of the man I have married, that I would make such a wager with you. Come, van Ryker, ask of me something else— these ear bobs, perhaps. They should please a pirate.''

''But I would have the original wager—the sweet taste of your lips. And since ye persist in calling me a pirate, faith, I'll just take it!''

Before Imogene could move to thwart him she was crushed against his silver-shot doublet, and her senses twanged like a bowstring when the arrow is loosed as she felt the deep, strong throb of his heart. She struggled and tried in vain to turn her head away from his dark face but his strength was inexorable. His strong right hand cradled her fair head, holding it firm that he might devour her lips at his leisure, and his sinewy left arm held her waist like a vise as he bent her pliant struggling form toward him. The pressure of his mouth was more insistent now and against her will she gave a violent start as van Ryker's impudent tongue parted her panting lips and probed luxuriantly behind them.

There was a ringing in her ears that blotted out the creaking of the great ship's timbers, and behind her closed eyes warning lights were flashing brighter than any ship's lantern on the clearest night. Her knees felt as if they might give way at any minute. All her defenses were crumbling! Panic rose in her.

Suddenly the buccaneer let her go and as she staggered away from him he caught her by the shoulders and held her at arm's length, studying her with a fierce intentness.

"You do not belong with the young patroon," he said quietly—and his complete command of himself in this moment when she felt all in disarray, panicked by the tumult of her own emotions, infuriated her.

"Who are you to say that?" she cried, half blinded by the magnificence of the figure he cut as he stood there, his leonine head bent, dark shining hair spilling over the broad wingspread of his shoulders, keen gray eyes ardent in concentration.

His words hammered at her softly, like blows delivered through a pillow and their meaning cut through to her heart. "I am the man you should have had, Imogene. I say that you and the patroon are ill-mated—you, the sleek, long-haired cat, he, the thin, yapping terrier."

Still trembling, Imogene blinked at this rude assessment.

Her combative spirit rose. "What right have you to judge me or my marriage? Do you know me so well, and this our third meeting?"

His arms fell away. "You are right," he sighed. "I am in no position to judge you, Imogene."

It was surely the moment to put him in his place, to question his use of her given name. But she could not do it. Not with the feel of his lips still burning her own. Not with her heart still fluttering strangely beneath the pressure of his hard hypnotic gaze.

"You speak of my marriage," she said, feeling defensive. "But what do you know of it? Perhaps in my place—" she gave him a shadowed look through long lashes—"you would have done the same thing."

"I might," he agreed, "for we are very alike."

His words startled her. Alike? Her gently bred self and this pirate captain raging across the seas? Why, they were nothing alike! He had—he had but seduced her for the moment into wild thoughts unbecoming to a married woman.

She stepped back. "I regret that I did not win my wager," she said coldly. "For I would have enjoyed a tally of the women you have loved and left."

Van Ryker reached out and caressed her hair, running his fingers through the gleaming locks at her throat, brushing the white column of her neck as he did so. She knew she should have pulled away, but she did not. Something held her there, immovable as stone while inside her blood coursed wildly through her veins, seeming to crash against a cliff at his every touch.

When he answered, it was in a rich, low voice. "The answer would have been easy, Imogene. I have never left a woman I loved."

The question seemed dragged from her; it left her lips reluctantly. "Then you have not loved at all?" Those wide velvet shoulders moved in an indifferent shrug. "I have held women in my arms and thought for a season that I loved them."

"But—" Why was it so important to know? "You were wrong?"

"Yes." He chose his words carefully. "I was waiting for something, someone. And now that I have found her—" his cool gaze raked her and she could almost feel it, like a touch, sliding along her arms, her bodice, savoring her lips—, "I shall not let her go."

"Captain van Ryker!" gasped Imogene. "I would have you remember that I am a married woman!"

"That bothers you?" he mocked, and she caught a gleam from his white teeth in the moonlight. "Faith, 'tis a condition I can rectify." Casually he touched his sword hilt. "You are easily widowed."

"Do not joke about such things," said Imogene crossly. "In spite of what you may think, I take my vows seriously."

"Then what are you doing on the deck of a buccaneer ship with me?"

"You are right," she flared, turning away. "I do not belong here. I will take my leave at once!"

"Ah, but wait." He caught her wrist in a strong grip, detained her while he stared down into her lovely, vulnerable face. "I would not take you with a broadside and you know it. Come now, admit it," he wheedled. "You feel the same as I do."

Imogene, with her veins still aflame with the wild longing that had been awakened by his touch, gave him a sulky look. "Suppose I do?" she challenged. "What would that matter?"

"It would matter a deal—to me." His voice was soft, caressing, but he still held her firm.

"Very well," she said tartly. "I admit it. You have had your victory. And now we can both forget it as I return to my husband and you return to your various loves."

"A spitfire!" He laughed. "You remind me of a kitten that once found its way aboard and into my cabin. She spat at me and flexed her little claws every time I tried to pick her up, but after I had stroked her fur for a while she came to trust me and she began to purr."

"And you think *I* will purr for you? You are mistaken, Captain van Ryker!"

"Stranger things have happened." She could not fathom the look in his eyes.

"What—what happened to the kitten?" she asked, because she could not meet the frank desire in his gaze.

"I took her ashore and gave her to a little blond girl in New Amsterdam. On my next call there, the little girl ran to the dock to inform me that kitty is the mother of half a dozen kittens herself now—in assorted colors, for she fancied several toms."

What is happening to me? Imogene asked herself wildly. *Why am I having this ridiculous conversation with this man?*

"Captain van Ryker," she said in a steely voice. "I command you to let me go at once."

"And if I do not?"

"Then I will scream for my husband and if you hurt him, I promise I will never speak to you again!"

His fingers relaxed their grip and she stroked her half-numbed wrist. "You are devilish strong," she complained. "I don't doubt you've left marks on my wrist!"

" 'Tis not marks on your wrist I'd be leaving, but marks on your heart!"

She would have flung away then but—she must make clear to him her true situation, and why she had married Verhulst. Why it should be so important for this buccaneer to know her reasons she did not ask herself, but it was.

"Captain van Ryker," she began earnestly, "whatever you may think of my husband, he saved me from a very unfortunate situation. I could not have gone back to England, for—for there was another man and I was implicated in a murder there. I would have been questioned, perhaps tortured, perhaps—hanged."

He flashed her a keen look. "And did you kill him?"

"No. My lover did. It was an accident. My lover fled—and now he is dead." It was a relief, telling him these things that she had kept locked up inside her. She had thought never to tell anyone; it was a surprise to hear her own voice saying them.

"And then you met van Rappard?"

She nodded.

"And told him all this?"

He had trapped her! "No," she admitted in a strangled voice. "Verhulst would never understand. Of course I did not tell him."

"Then why," he wondered silkily, "are you telling me?"

"Because—because you are a man beyond the law and are not likely to turn me over to the authorities. And being what you are, you can understand."

His dark brows lifted. "Beyond the law . . . and being what I am . . . I see." His voice roughened. "And this story is not for van Rappard's tender ears?"

She gave a helpless gesture. "It would only hurt him, and Verhulst is in love with me—I think."

"You do not know?"

She turned her head away. She was certainly not going to discuss her sleeping arrangements with this sardonic pirate!

"I see you don't wish to discuss it?" he prodded.

"No," she said, muffled. "But no one can be sure of love."

"A profound statement from one so young," he mocked, and Imogene, grateful for his change of mood and reluctant to return to the great cabin and the patroon, her husband, lingered yet another moment by the rail.

"How," she asked curiously, "did you become a pirate?"

"Correction—a buccaneer. And it is too long a story to tell you now."

"Your ship's doctor is French, your ship's master English— and you, Captain, speak English far too well!"

He met her challenging gaze with a smile. "I see that I have met my match in you," he sighed. "And you make me wish for other days, better days. Tomorrow night I will arrange a ball in your honor."

A ball! On a pirate ship in mid-ocean? Imogene was laughing at this fantasy as she swept back into the *Sea Rover*'s great cabin, where a flushed and concentrating Verhulst had just triumphed over Barnaby Swift at chess.

CHAPTER 11

Imogene's color was high. "Captain van Ryker has promised to arrange a ball in my honor—here on the *Sea Rover* tomorrow night," she told them merrily as she swept in, turning slightly to let her wide yellow satin skirts ease through the cabin door.

Amazement looked back at her from four pairs of eyes, but van Ryker was unperturbed. "There are other ladies aboard your ship," he told Captain Verbloom in an unruffled voice. "Perhaps you would be good enough to invite three of them—one each for Barnaby and Raoul and myself to dance with—and one for yourself, of course."

"They are all married, save for the Widow Poltzer and her daughter, and I do not know if they dance."

Imogene remembered the Dutch lady with the marriageable daughter who had been so anxious to accompany her on board the *Sea Rover*. "Oh, I am sure they both dance," she put in hastily, her blue eyes asparkle with merriment.

"But even so," protested Captain Verbloom, who greatly mistrusted this "buccaneers' ball," "we would still be lacking two ladies!"

"Two of the ladies on board the *Hilletje* have husbands too seasick to leave their cabins," pointed out Imogene with an innocent look at Captain Verbloom.

"Good. Invite their husbands as well," said van Ryker with a careless gesture.

"But the ladies cannot go dancing without their husbands," protested Captain Verbloom.

"They would of course be heavily chaperoned," put in Imogene, managing to keep a straight face. "By the rest of us."

Verbloom felt the situation was getting out of hand. He only growled as Captain van Ryker gave Imogene a benign look. "We will see who shows up," the buccaneer told her. "For if the weather remains fair, we will have dancing on deck tomorrow night."

Verhulst was speechless. He fairly tottered from the *Sea Rover*. But he found his voice once they had returned to the *Hilletje* and discovered they were expected to dine on board the *Sea Rover* as well.

"Did you incite van Ryker to this?" he demanded of Imogene. " 'Tis bad enough that he spirits you away every time I sit down to the chessboard, but now we must needs eat all our meals with him and he is even giving balls in your honor!"

"Not *really* in my honor," protested Imogene airily. " 'Tis more a diversion in his rough life at sea. Anyway, why do you care? The food on his ship is far better than ours and he and his officers are good company."

"Why do I care? Why would I *not* care? I do not wish to be *forced* to dine with anybody."

Imogene forbore telling him that van Ryker would undoubtedly be delighted if he stayed home and let her go alone. . . .

Verhulst must have guessed what she was thinking. His exasperated voice followed her as she moved away. "And do not imagine that I do not know why this 'ball' is being given, Imogene! It is so that Captain van Ryker can find an excuse for holding you in his arms."

His untouched bride gave him back an uncompromising look. It was on the tip of her tongue to tell him that Captain van Ryker had already done *that*, but she forbore. "Do you think I should wear my flame satin or my green silk, Verhulst? I would like to outshine the other ladies—as becomes our position."

She was mocking him! "Wear what you like!" Verhulst stormed out of the cabin.

He was still sulking next day as Imogene dressed for dinner on board the *Sea Rover*.

"I told you," warned Elise, who had noticed the angry glances the patroon was directing at his bride, "that you are driving him too far."

Imogene, who had already decided to wear the flame satin—it was cut lower—gave a reckless laugh. "We are sailing across an empty ocean toward a strange new land where I will never see my buccaneer again, Elise. Do not begrudge me an evening of frivolity! Besides," she added, "balls call for music and musicians are not that easy come by in mid-ocean. I am curious to see how van Ryker will contrive it!" She turned to Elise with narrowed eyes. "*You* are a single woman. Would *you* like to attend the ball tonight?"

Elise looked so taken aback that Imogene laughed. "Why not?" she prodded. "Come, 'tis your chance to dance with a buccaneer and wave a fan with the best of them!"

"I could not," protested Elise. "The patroon would dismiss me from his service!"

"He will not," said Imogene sturdily. "And you can wear one of my dresses."

"They are all too short for me."

"So you will be very daring and show a bit of ankle! We will make up for that by giving you a very heavy whisk!"

"I do not know how to dance."

"These buccaneers will teach you! Hurry, we will let out the hem of my green velvet. The material is soft, no one will be able to tell it was let down. We will touch a bit of Spanish paper to your lips and cheeks to make them red and a touch of ceruse to your nose to make it whiter. I will sweep up your hair and garnish it with green satin ribands—you will be an elegant lady, Elise, as elegant as any there."

Elise looked quite dazzled. She had never attended a ball, never danced a measure. Imogene made it all seem quite within her reach.

"First we must get *you* gowned," she said huskily, opening one of the trunks that held Imogene's ball gowns. Her gaze on Imogene was soft. She begrudged Imogene nothing—certainly not an innocent flirtation with a handsome buccaneer—but only feared for her. Now she smiled and shook her head and dressed this young girl she so loved in her most stunning costume yet.

Imogene's gown was of gold-encrusted flame-colored satin, cut so low that even the Dutch dressmaker who had stitched it had been scandalized, and it had wide gold-encrusted oversleeves that reached almost to her elbows, from whence spilled out the delicate ruffles of her chemise sleeves. Steadying her feet on the lightly swaying floor, Imogene turned before a mirror Elise held up, saw how the flame of the dress brought out rich coral highlights in her fair hair. She stuck out an embroidered satin slipper, pirouetted, and laughed. A duchess could not have looked more elegant, she told herself contentedly, and turned her attention to Elise's outfitting.

Once that was accomplished to her satisfaction, she told Elise to follow her in a minute or two and went up on deck to find Verhulst.

She found him in loud-voiced conversation with the *Hilletje*'s captain, asking him why the devil should this round of unwanted entertainment be allowed to go on and on?

"Mynheer," that gentleman was telling the young patroon earnestly as Imogene approached, "we are fortunate indeed to have the protection of the *Sea Rover*. Captain van Ryker is a buccaneer—not a pirate; he will not attack any ship save the ships of Spain—"

"Ha, that is not the impression you gave when you cajoled us aboard her in the first place!"

"Captain van Ryker is a man first and a buccaneer second, and a man may strike back if he is offended."

"So it is his forty guns that move us after all!"

"I am saying that there are plenty of pirates who ply the sea who are not so nice as van Ryker," explained Captain Verbloom patiently. "They would fire on a Dutch ship as quickly as on a Spaniard. Surely it is a little thing that Captain van Ryker has asked of you—your company for dinner and at some sort of impromptu 'ball' that he has arranged. All of the passengers are very grateful for the added protection of his escort, and this will be a diversion, an outing for the ladies. I see that several of them are on deck already dressed for the occasion."

Verhulst's gaze swung to the little knot of passengers containing several bright-colored gowns, who were buzzing some distance away. The Widow Poltzer and her marriageable daughter were there, stiff with finery in shrieking shades of pink, and one other pensive lady in red and gray taffeta who looked as if she might take flight at any moment.

"And here is your wife," added Captain Verbloom, blinking at the opulence of her flame satin gown.

Verhulst cast a bitter look at Imogene's gorgeous garb. "I would have a word with my wife, Captain," he said testily. "If you will excuse us?"

Captain Verbloom bowed to Imogene and went to join the other passengers.

Verhulst, left alone with Imogene, gave her whisk—through which her bare bosom and peeking pink-tipped nipples were plainly visible—a bitter look.

"Do you not have a whisk less sheer?" he asked her impatiently. "This one is less than nothing."

Imogene, who had searched through all her whisks to find the sheerest, shrugged. "What, would you have me wear a linen table napkin? I have nothing else, Verhulst. If you do not like it, I can leave it off."

"Oh, no, ye'll not do that!"

"Indeed, and why not? 'Tis all the fashion at Court."

"This is not the Court," he grated, "but a pirate's ship we go to, Imogene. These are desperate men. Do not inflame their passions!"

Desperate men . . . Imogene thought fleetingly of that lean sardonic face, those searching gray eyes, the courtliness of this captain whom the world called a pirate.

"I feel I will be safe aboard the *Sea Rover*," she stated. "And to make doubly sure, I have made certain arrangements."

He stared. "What arrangements?"

"You will see." Imogene looked around for Elise, but did not see her yet.

"In any case," he warned her testily, "see that this time ye do not lose your whisk, for I was not there to anchor it on ye!"

"Have no fear, Verhulst," said Imogene coolly, with a snubbing look. "I assure you I will not lose it, for this is my best whisk!"

She turned and strolled back toward the captain with Verhulst in his somber black clothes fuming in her wake. "I see we have one lady whose husband is too seasick to accompany her, Captain Verbloom, but where is the other?"

"The other refused to come," said Captain Verbloom shortly.

"Ah, I feared as much." Imogene pictured the portly lady of whom they spoke—she would as soon swim to the *Sea Rover* as dance aboard her! "But I have found us a substitute." She turned with a dramatic gesture. "Here she comes now: my maidservant and good friend—Mistress Elise Meggs."

Both the captain and the patroon were silenced by the sight of Elise, striding toward them down the deck. She was of a formidable height and she moved like a battleship, bearing down on them stiff as a ramrod in her finery and wearing a self-conscious frown that might give any man pause. She was sumptuously dressed in Imogene's green velvet gown, the deep hem of which had been let down and hurriedly stitched—it would hold for this one night. That gown now swished above a petticoat of heavy weighted gold taffeta that rustled alarmingly as she walked. The shoes that peeked out from beneath the petticoat's hem were her own best yellow leather ones, for Imogene's dancing slippers were all too small, and the wide ruffles of her sleeves—her arms being longer than Imogene's—were a trifle too short for the current mode, but her fasionably low-cut bodice was filled in with a whisk so heavy it could have served as table linen. Its modest folds managed completely to obscure any inch of Elise's bosom that might have been exposed to public view. Feeling that even this might not be enough to ward off the lascivious eyes of pirates, Elise had added one other touch after Imogene had left the cabin—and it was this addition that held Imogene in spellbound fascination and caused her to choke back her laughter.

Elise was wearing a wide stiff ruff around her long thin neck. It was terribly out of fashion, for no one wore ruffs any more except old ladies; it was yellow-starched and looked as if it had seen better days, but Elise had dragged it out of her own trunk and was wearing it triumphantly. Her blue eyes flashed as she approached and curtseyed to the patroon and the captain.

"What charade is this?" Verhulst was aghast. "This woman is wearing your gown, Imogene!"

"So she is," said Imogene carelessly. "This is the 'arrangement' I spoke to you about, Verhulst. I felt that it might be well to have a woman to attend me tonight, in case there is heavy drinking at the ball, and it seemed more prudent for Elise to attend as one of the guests. That way she cannot be fobbed off to some distant cabin to 'wait for me.' "

Verhulst gave Imogene an uncertain look. Her suggestion made excellent sense—if indeed she meant it. He took another look at Elise's rouged lips and cheeks, her whitened nose, her stiffly piled hair atremble with green satin ribands, her shining eyes—for Elise had dreams, too, even if they were repressed, and this was her first ball. Verhulst forbore a shudder.

It was with trepidation that the patroon of Wey Gat climbed into the longboat beside his wife and her newly resplendent maidservant.

On board the *Sea Rover*, they were all amazed to view the change that had been wrought overnight. It seemed a carnival ship. Colorful Chinese paper lanterns hung precariously from the yardarms, a portion of the deck had been hung gaily with colored ribbons, and after dinner the lanterns were lit and cast a magical glow of red and blue and green and gold across the delighted company. Dinner was served in great style by two grinning ship's boys clad in maroon and gold livery.

"Stolen undoubtedly," Verhulst muttered, gazing gloomily at the livery.

To Imogene's embarrassment, van Ryker heard him. He leaned forward across the table, cocked a satirical eye at his guest. "From Spain," he said lightly, "and not from Holland."

The marriageable daughter tittered and was promptly silenced by a black look from her mother. The lady who'd been half a mind not to come nervously knocked over her glass and was drenched by its contents. She leaped up with a cry and as the Widow Poltzer and her pink-clad daughter dabbed cluckingly at the spilled wine with their table napkins, Captain Verbloom desperately launched into a rather incoherent story about a mermaid he had glimpsed one night off the Hebrides and this diverted the guests from the patroon's lapse of manners. The company drank a whole array of fine wines and, thus warmed, wandered out on deck where two scarred buccaneers in leathern breeches and clanking cutlasses played on the *viola da gamba*, and a half-dozen others with good voices sang in a jumble of languages and stamped bare feet upon the deck.

"Allow me to exert a host's privilege and claim the first dance." The buccaneer captain, flamboyantly dressed tonight in black and silver with a wide scarlet baldric from shoulder to hip, stepped forward past a pouting young lady in pink to claim Imogene.

She gave him a dazzling smile and stepped forward to take his hand. It was a very steady hand but she felt a slight tremor go through it at her touch and was perversely glad. With Verhulst seemingly impervious to her charms, it was balm to her spirit to see flickering lights in van Ryker's usually cold gray eyes and know they burned for her. Although she would go back to the *Hilletje* when the ball was over, her reckless heart rejoiced that she should be here tonight with the dangerous Captain van Ryker, whirling with him across a deck surrounded by watching buccaneers in the light of the Chinese lanterns that lit the bizarre scene.

The Widow Poltzer was mollified when Barnaby Swift, whom she personally considered the most dashing of the buccaneers, for she had always had a penchant for yellow hair, led out her blushing daughter. She stood beside Captain Verbloom, who had elected not to dance, and watched enraptured, sure that with every simper her daughter was making way with the stylish young buccaneer. What matter that Barnaby's dancing did not come up to the cut of his suit? He was a bachelor, was he not? That fact she had already established at the dinner table. And her Geertje followed him well. See how well the girl looked! Her pink skirts were bouncing with the exertion and her sallow cheeks were taking on a deeper color. And the young buccaneer had spoken to her again—his lips were moving! And now Geertje was laughing—ah, this could ripen into something! The Widow Poltzer bobbed her head raptly in time to their steps so that her fat cheeks wobbled. Each time Barnaby whirled Geertje about so that her skirts flew and exposed her pink-striped petticoat, her mother gave an ecstatic little cry and tapped the captain's arm with her fan until that gentleman, tiring of this unceasing tattoo, eased away from her side and asked Elise to dance.

It was too great an honor for Elise to refuse—the captain of the *Hilletje*, an eminent man, dancing with her! She let the dour captain lead her out and they stomped miserably upon each other's feet until the captain admitted defeat—neither of them, he told Elise calmly, could dance a step. They belonged at the rail, not out on the floor.

As he led a crestfallen Elise back, the Widow Poltzer claimed his attention again. "Are they not a lovely couple?" she cried, pointing with her fan at her daughter and Barnaby Swift.

The captain growled an unintelligible response that sounded like "humbug." Drat, he was back with that idiotic woman again, crowing over her daughter dancing with a buccaneer as if he were a prince of the blood!

He looked about for help and saw with relief that de Rochemont was heading for them. There, now he would be rid of her! But de Rochemont turned instead to the lady on his other side. He had noted the droop of Elise's green velvet shoulders as she was led in defeat from the floor. Now he made her a sweeping bow.

"If madame will do me the honor?"

Elise was overcome—first the captain, now this handsome French doctor with his tweaky little mustache!

"I—I fear I am no dancer, sir," she gasped.

"If madame will forgive a paraphrase," said de Rochemont smoothly, "there are no women unable to dance—there are only awkward men unable to dance with them." He gave the furious Captain Verbloom a withering look that said the French did it better and the next time the Widow Poltzer tapped him on the arm Verbloom bellowed, "What is it, mevrouw? What do you want?"

Elise, her eyes glazed in fright and fixed on de Rochemont with the rapt fascination of a snake for its trainer, gave the Frenchman her hand—doubtfully. Stiff in every bone, she allowed him to lead her out on the floor and so expert a dancer was he, so nimble on his feet, that she trod on him only once. Flushed with her triumph and beaming, de Rochemont exchanged partners with Barnaby Swift—that little pink mouse of a Geertje Poltzer was showing surprising animation—and Elise was off on the floor again for another try at high life.

Over van Ryker's broad shoulder Imogene smiled affectionately at Elise. She was confident she was giving her old friend an evening she would never forget.

Captain Verbloom, driven too far by de Rochemont's jibe and this infernal tapping, stomped over to the lady with wine spilt upon her dress and asked her ringingly if she would tread a measure with him. The lady gave a harried look round at the circle of buccaneers and asked in a hoarse stage whisper, "Do you think we should? With all these cutthroats about?"

"I think they'll not harm us until the music stops," said Verbloom grimly. "Our antics are providing them too much amusement." He danced his frightened lady past the Widow Poltzer, who—now that Barnaby Swift had claimed her daughter for a second measure—was almost jumping up and down in delight. Her jowls shook, her eyes gleamed, all the fringe on her ruffles danced, and her big breasts were aquiver with excitement. The captain tore his eyes from the sight and glared at two convulsed buccaneers, holding each other up as they watched her and wiping their eyes with quiet mirth. *They'd be laughing over this night in the grog shops of Tortuga for years to come,* the captain predicted with an inward groan.

His wine-drenched partner trembled whenever they whirled too near the throng of watching buccaneers lounging about the edge of the "dance floor" and once, when one of them turned and accidentally rattled his cutlass, she gave a short sharp scream. Verbloom was grateful to be able to return her to the Widow Poltzer, who gave a delighted little skip as Barnaby led out her daughter again.

"Don't they make a lovely couple?" she gushed.

"Who?" cried the wine-drenched lady nervously. "Oh, do look at that man with one loop earring over there? Have you ever seen such a vicious scar? It reaches clear down his chest into his belt. Oh, dear, why ever did I come?"

The Widow Poltzer's jowls wavered to a stop as she gave her an affronted look. *She* at least knew why *she* had come. Mothers of marriageable daughters—especially if those daughters were not well endowed in either face or fortune—must seize every opportunity and these buccaneers seemed well enough mannered men. She sniffed contemptuously as the wine-drenched lady cringed against her.

"It is a romantic setting," she said heavily.

" 'Romantic'?" Her friend's voice rose in a little protesting shriek. "Romantic?" She gazed across the deck at what seemed to her a sea of devilish faces. "I shall be glad to get back to the *Hilletje,*" she said faintly.

The Widow Poltzer had already forgotten her. "There! See them there!" she cried triumphantly, tapping the lady's arm sharply with her fan. "He's going to ask her again—oh, no, he's not! The doctor has claimed her. But he's heading this way— he's going to ask one of *us* to dance!"

Her friend shrank back and Barnaby, driven by van Ryker's stern instructions earlier that his ship's officers must dance with all the ladies, bowed low before the Widow Poltzer and requested the honor. She was so excited she did not wait but grasped his hand and led him out. Every second of the dance she spent asking him pointed questions about his background, his present situation, his expectations.

Barnaby blinked at this barrage. It had been a long time since the young buccaneer had been badgered by the mother of a marriageable daughter—the fleshpots of Tortuga and Port Royal were hardly teeming with respectable young ladies and those few who were there were more apt to be closely chaperoned and guarded against buccaneers, who were considered to have a short life expectancy, than thrust into their arms.

Under questioning, he allowed weakly as how he had a little nest egg "put away" and was rewarded by a roguish beam of approval as the Widow Poltzer missed a step to give him a smart tap with her fan. "And how do you like my little Geertje?" she demanded. "Is she not a pretty thing in her pink dress? And all made of the very best materials—nothing but the best for my Geertje! See how the doctor looks at her? Why, I swear he's quite taken!"

"She's very pretty, ma'am." Barnaby felt the lace at his throat growing uncomfortably tight. His face reddened as she crowed, "Ah, I knew you two would get along well! Geertje isn't right for that Frenchman—she's always fancied blond men!"

With a sigh of relief Barnaby returned the Widow Poltzer to her wine-drenched friend and firmly claimed Elise for the next dance. Across the floor de Rochemont gave Barnaby a nod of approval; he had been about to ask Elise again himself but he was not sure he was nimble enough to dodge for any length of time her heavy feet—best to let young Barnaby suffer for a while. He turned affably back to the Poltzer girl. A foolish twit, but pretty enough now that she looked animated; she would doubtless give some man a bland and uneventful life. Now, the confection that swayed in van Ryker's arms was something else, but the Frenchman knew better than to interrupt *that* duo.

Across the floor the Widow Poltzer's gaze sharpened. That handsome Frenchman, de Rochemont, had danced twice with her daughter! She puffed out her fat cheeks in perplexity. The Frenchman was not so young as Barnaby of course, and he was not blond, but doctoring was a moderately good trade—in this boisterous age, they were always in demand to bind up a wound! Was it possible that a ship's doctor made a better living than a ship's master? She must ask Captain Verbloom tonight as they were rowed back to the *Hilletje*. Ah, it promised to be a lovely voyage with perhaps a wedding at the end of it!

From the rail where he stood beside Captain Verbloom, Verhulst van Rappard turned his sulky gaze from the sight of his wife dancing and laughing with the lean buccaneer captain and glanced upward at the colorful paper lanterns, swaying more perilously now that the breeze had freshened.

Beside him, Captain Verbloom's gloomy gaze was upon the handsome pair who overshadowed all others on the dance floor. Resplendent as peacocks, he thought grimly, sure of themselves, evenly matched. And—reluctantly he admitted it—made for each other. Anyone with half an eye could see it.

He listened to the wailing music, and looked keenly around him. There was a feeling of excitement in the air, and Verbloom was not immune to it. Perhaps, he reasoned, it was engendered by the tall buccaneer captain, raptly swaying with the dashing lady in flame and gold. In any event, it could become a problem. Nights like this might be all right in the Caribbean but something was being ignited here on the cold northern seas. It was a powder keg that could blow up in all their faces.

He chewed thoughtfully on his lip for a moment, then turned with a sigh to the young patroon. "Mynheer van Rappard." The words came reluctantly. "I would look to my wife, if I were you. Perhaps she should feign an illness and find herself unable to attend further functions aboard this vessel."

Verhulst, who had been hoping wistfully that one of the candle-filled paper lanterns might fall and ignite the ship, thus giving this damned pirate something to think about beside Imogene, turned to Verbloom with a startled glance.

"It is not that I wish the *Sea Rover* to abandon us," explained the *Hilletje*'s captain sheepishly. "But after all this is your wedding voyage. I can see that you would prefer not to spend it in the company of a man who looks at your wife as if she were a goddess."

Or a glass of wine to be swallowed up and forgotten, thought Verhulst, gazing truculently at the magnificent black and silver figure who swung Imogene so lightly across the swaying deck. "I'll claim her now," he muttered. "There's no reason why she should dance with him all night!"

He would have shouldered forward but the *Hilletje*'s captain detained him with a hand on his arm. "Not yet," he advised. "Best to let matters go on as they are. No harm's been done."

"You aren't suggesting he might make off with her?"

Captain Verbloom had indeed been considering that possibility; he did not want the matter on *his* head. He cleared his throat. "This is a formal evening and you have nothing to fear, mynheer. But—after tonight I would be careful." He looked around him uneasily. "I marvel at this buccaneer captain's control of his men," he muttered. "We might be aboard a ship of His Majesty's Navy, for the discipline I've seen! But this flaunting of skirts before the faces of men long at sea is dangerous. Tomorrow our buccaneer may decide to give a general ball and insist that all the passengers aboard the *Hilletje* attend! With so many women milling about, there could be an incident. . . . Heed my warning, mynheer—urge your wife to take to her bed and feign illness."

"Will van Ryker not send over that damned French doctor?"

Captain Verbloom turned to consider Raoul de Rochemont, who had led Elise out upon the floor again and at the moment was achieving a kind of martyrdom by keeping a set smile on his face as she trod heavily on his feet. It was true the *Hilletje* had no doctor on board; the buccaneer captain might well insist on sending de Rochemont over in a boat. "Even so," he frowned, "the lady can fake some illness and pretend her head pains her too badly to leave her bed."

"From the look of van Ryker," said Verhulst moodily, watching the flame satin skirts sweep in and out past the buccaneer's wide-topped boots as the pair of them whirled across the floor, "he might decide to come and get her!"

Captain Verbloom gave him a wounded look. "On one thing you can rely, mynheer: No unwilling woman will be taken by force from aboard my ship!" His chest expanded as he spoke and sparks flashed from his eyes. "Nor do I think it will come to that. Captain van Ryker may show a marked preference for the lady but if she does not wish to see him, he will remember that he is after all a Dutchman and a civilized man. He will stay aboard his own vessel. Besides, if he attacked a Dutch ship, the port of New Amsterdam would be closed to him and he would not want that—the captain has a profitable trade with the burghers there."

"I hope you are right," gloomed Verhulst, for he saw crowded about the rails, watching the dance proceed, the sturdy forms of the *Sea Rover*'s battle-scarred buccaneers, victors of many a bloody rough-and-tumble on sea and shore. The crew and passengers of the *Hilletje* would stand scant chance against them even if the *Sea Rover* chose not to use her forty guns.

The dance went on. The ship's master, who stumbled over his own feet—and the ship's French doctor, who danced delightfully, for all that his toes were numb from the punishment Elise had given them—dutifully danced with all the ladies.

And again and again the dark captain claimed beautiful

Imogene van Rappard for his partner.

Imogene was enjoying herself. She smiled winsomely up into the buccaneer's rapt face.

"Do you have anything on board the *Hilletje* that you value?" he asked her suddenly.

"My clothing and jewels—don't tell me you intend to ransom me!" she laughed.

"Your clothing I can easily replace in the markets of Tortuga."

"Easily," she mocked. "But then there's Elise—I value her; she is my maidservant."

Van Ryker's thoughtful gaze sought out Elise, flushed and intent and nervous in her velvet dress, alternately stomping on Barnaby Swift's feet and wincing as he awkwardly trod on hers. He ignored Imogene's blithe, "They appear to be having a good time—and they're well matched, since it's obvious neither of them have ever danced before."

"The woman can be brought along on some pretext," he told her. "Possibly to look for some trinket you will tell your husband you have lost on my ship. But place in your purse or wear any jewels you particularly value and bring them with you tomorrow."

"And why," she wondered in a lazy voice, although her heart was of a sudden stilled, "would I do that, Captain van Ryker? Particularly since I have no reason to suppose I will be on board the *Sea Rover* tomorrow! These trysts in mid-ocean are slowing down our voyage—Captain Verbloom complained of it only this morning."

His strong hand tightened on hers. "Ah, you will be aboard, Imogene. And bring with you your valuables—for I plan to carry you away with me when next we meet."

Imogene's heart lurched to a wild racing rhythm and she missed a step. Deep inside she had always known what he intended, but now he had spoken of it in words and she was faced with a decision. No longer could she play at misunderstanding him or indulge in wild fantasies. He was asking her to make a choice between him and Verhulst and her heart and her head were not of one mind on that.

Time—she must play for time.

"Do you always take all your castles by storm?" she asked coolly, as she had asked once before in England of another man.

There was a controlled violence in van Ryker tonight and it came through in his voice, like a surging tide. "Never have I seen a fortress so worth storming—nor one I so desired to storm."

"And have you no thought of my reputation, sir?"

He cast a wry meaningful look down at her almost transparent whisk. "Do you value your reputation so much, then, Imogene?"

She could not meet his direct challenging gaze. Her heart was thumping in her chest. Verhulst had never spent a night in her bed since their wedding night—and then he had not touched her. It was becoming clear to her that he did not intend to. Hers was an empty marriage, hers were empty arms, and this dark, intense buccaneer was offering her a life of romantic adventure that appealed to her reckless heart. She could feel the pull of his masculine virility, the pressure of his hot gaze, which even the sea breeze, which had freshened in the last hour, did not dispel.

"Of course I value it," she whispered.

His arm tightened about her. "Remember what I have said," he warned. "For the next time we meet I will press my suit more forcibly."

Half frightened, half fascinated, Imogene stared up at him. "You—you have naught to offer a woman!" she protested.

"If you mean I have no home but the sea or a buccaneer's lair, you are right. But that can be rectified. For you, Imogene, I would change many things . . . my whole life."

His words tore at her, tumbling her emotions into tumult. The spell of the moonlight and of muted buccaneer voices lifted in song and the haunting strains of the *viola da gamba* were upon her. She felt hypnotized by it all, swept along by a tide that was too strong for her.

"May I interrupt?" It was Verhulst's harsh voice. "Captain Verbloom feels we must be going. He says a gale may be coming up."

Van Ryker lifted his head and sniffed the air. "He may be right," he said, and reluctantly let the woman in flame-colored satin slip from his arms.

"Until tomorrow," he told her, and Verhulst gave him a smoldering look.

"I would like to challenge him," he muttered as they climbed into the longboat.

"I wouldn't if I were you," murmured Imogene. "He's said to be a notable blade—I think *you* told me that."

"Nevertheless," growled Verhulst.

"He has asked us to dine with him again tomorrow. Would you slaughter your host?"

Captain Verbloom heard that and turned on Verhulst a look of blank astonishment. Did the young patroon fancy his swordplay to be in a class with van Ryker's? Faith, a thrust or two would disabuse him—before he died on the point of van Ryker's blade, of course. Verbloom shuddered. "Perhaps we will not be dining aboard that *Sea Rover* tomorrow night," he said with a pointed look at Verhulst.

"I can't imagine why we would not," said Imogene. "Unless a gale blows up in the night."

But a gale did blow up in the night. Imogene woke in darkness, jarred almost from her bed by the lurching progress of the ship, and listened to the wind whistling through the shrouds. By morning the squall was well upon them and Captain Verbloom looked out at the gray sky, and dashed stinging rain from his eyes.

"Your lady need not feign illness after all," he told Verhulst with some satisfaction, "for there's no question of dining aboard the *Sea Rover* tonight. Faith, 'tis the first time I've ever been glad to see rough weather!"

Imogene, too, felt a sense of relief. The storm had pushed off the time when she must make a decision. Tension had been building in her ever since van Ryker had kissed her. It had made her realize with sharp physical force how very much she wanted him. Although she had kept a stern grip on herself—that reckless self that wanted to throw itself into his arms whatever the cost—she had been unable to stay away from him, flying ever nearer to disaster as a moth to the flame. And after van Ryker had told her calmly that he meant to carry her away with him, her battered nerves had almost reached the breaking point. *Carry her away* . . . she was not ready for that. She felt a strong physical attraction for him certainly, an almost overpowering attraction; she found him a fascinating man whose depths she had not plumbed but—she had made a bargain in good faith with Verhulst and she meant to keep it.

She was almost glad that tall seas kept the ships apart all the way to New Amsterdam's harbor. Verhulst was jubilant.

But Imogene landed with fear-shadowed eyes—and not because of a lean buccaneer with taking ways. For the morning after the ball she had waked and been sick. Every morning that week she suffered from a black nausea—she who had ridden out the stormiest seas in the Scillies and never felt even a touch of seasickness.

"I don't know what can be the matter with me, Elise," she gasped, when the morning before they were to dock in New Amsterdam's harbor the blackness struck her again.

"I do," Elise said grimly. "Ye are pregnant."

Imogene, never very regular, had neglected to consider this possibility. Now the two women stared at each other in mounting horror.

"Pregnant since before ye left England, I don't doubt," declared Elise in a gloomy voice. "Pregnant by a lover who's dead, and with a husband who comes not to your bed. What will ye do now?"

"I don't know," said Imogene. She was very pale but her voice was steady. Only the whitened knuckles that gripped the side of the bunk betrayed how trapped she felt. She gave Elise a compassionate look—poor Elise, caught up in her troubles. "I will make my decision on shore."

BOOK III
The River Bride

A toast to the bride of the river!
Her feelings, her love she must hide
Forever and ever and ever. . . .
A toast to the river bride!

PART ONE
The Patroon's Lady

A toast to our reckless lady,
She who must finish the game,
Who stares at the stars through pride's rusted bars
From a life of glamour—and shame . . .

New Amsterdam, New Netherland, 1657

CHAPTER 12

When the tempest blew itself out and land was at last sighted across the still rough seas, Imogene, so depressed during the voyage, found her spirits rising. For disembarking she dressed herself with care in a tailored French gray broadcloth, wide-skirted, narrow-waisted, heavily trimmed in black braid—save for its opulent virago sleeves, which spilled forth an enticing billow of white lawn and lace, it made her look more like an expensive matron and less like an expensive wanton, she told herself grimly—and topped off her costume with a rakish wide-brimmed gray hat aflutter with white plumes. She arranged the froth of white lace at her throat that spilled out over her fitted bodice, gave her wide-tiered gray broadcloth oversleeves a last shake and pulled on delicate gray leather gloves.

"How do I look, Elise?" she demanded. "Would I do credit to a patroon?"

"Ye would do a duke credit," sighed Elise, straightening

out a heavy broadcloth fold in Imogene's skirt. "Ye look like a woman with a future," she mourned, "when indeed ye have none!"

"Take heart," said Imogene cheerfully. "All is not lost—at least not yet. Come out on deck. Let us view this new capital of the western world!"

But Elise was not to be cajoled by Imogene's blithe flippancy. "I can see no reason to be light of heart," she muttered. "Ye should be crying. Had ye already told him, he'd abandon us on the dock but—what happens to us when we reach Wey Gat?"

Imogene, turning down the cuffs of her leather gloves to show their intricate beading, flashed her a confident smile. The morning sickness had left her, the air was fresh and clean, a whole new life awaited her. And if it did not—well, time enough to worry about that when it happened. At least she would know today. For although she would not tell Elise, who was half mad with anxiety already, Imogene did not intend to wait until they reached far Wey Gat to tell Verhulst he was to become the "father" of a child not his own. She meant to tell him right here in New Amsterdam. Now, today!

Buoyed up by the excitement that decision always brought her, Imogene tripped lightly forth upon the deck to find the passengers milling about expectantly, waving and pointing at the town, although it would be some time before they landed.

She made her way through a heated argument between two guests who had attended the buccaneer's ball on board the *Sea Rover*.

"How can ye say poor Barnaby Swift drinks too much?" the Widow Poltzer was demanding passionately of the lady who had that night been drenched in wine and who now stood stiff and disapproving. "When ye've seen the lad but once? Why, your own husband wasn't seasick on this voyage—he was drunk! He's nothing but a tosspot!''

''Ye'll not say that of my Amos!'' came the furious reply. ''Throwing your daughter at those—those cutthroats! 'Tis a marvel we weren't all raped!''

Imogene pushed her way between the antagonists, who moved back, like spitting cats, to let the patroon's elegant lady pass. The buccaneer's ball would not soon be forgotten, she thought with a pang, although the Widow Poltzer might be overvaluing her homely daughter's charms if she thought she'd already captured Barnaby Swift—New Amsterdam must abound with pretty Dutch girls who'd catch a buccaneer's eye.

Along with the others, she stood by the rail. But unlike them, her gaze was not upon the town that lay ahead, but upon the rakish *Sea Rover* that had kept them in sight no matter how wild the tempest. Van Ryker . . . guarding her. She pushed the thought away.

Verhulst shouldered up to join her. He looked very assured now that New Amsterdam was in sight. Rubies flashed from his thin fingers, a pigeon's blood ruby winked from the lace at his throat—there was even a ruby pinning the gray ostrich plumes that floated above his wide black hat. Aside from his jewels and the heavy gold chain he habitually wore, those gray plumes and the Florentine lace at his throat and his white lace-point boothose, the young patroon was clad in unrelieved black: cut-velvet doublet, wide ribbanded breeches, shining black boots.

''Ye should be wearing the sapphire pin and earbobs that I bought you in Amsterdam,'' he said, giving Imogene a critical look.

''I'll get them,'' she promised meekly and hurried back to her cabin to open her little chest of jewels. She must be prompt in fulfilling all Verhulst's small requests, she thought with a sudden attack of nervousness, for she had such a large favor to ask of Verhulst—that he accept her child as his own. Was it too much to ask of a man? she wondered as she slipped on the sapphire earbobs.

It had been done many times of course, she told herself firmly. Had not King Arthur's father accepted his wife's bastard child? But that of course was rape, not a lover. . . . In the Scillies, a woman on Saint Mary's had wed a Cornishman from the mainland when she was already large with child by another. *He* had accepted the child cheerfully as his own—but *he'd* been about to be carted off to debtors' prison and his errant bride was an heiress. Imogene sighed . . . she knew of no case exactly like her own.

She went back on deck to join Verhulst, who gave her a look of proud approval now that she was wearing the earbobs.

Tonight, she told herself. *Tonight, she would tell him.*

Like a mother hen herding along a single chick, the mighty *Sea Rover* shepherded the fat wallowing *Hilletje* into port, but once assured of her safe arrival shot around her and docked first. When the slower *Hilletje* finally docked, the buccaneer captain and crew of the *Sea Rover* was nowhere to be seen; they had gone into the town.

Verhulst was delighted with that. He seized Imogene's hand in his own black-gloved one and—leaving Elise to cope with the baggage—hurried her ashore, muttering that *this* time they'd seen the last of that damned pirate!

Imogene, almost running to keep up with her husband's long stride, looked about her and got her first close view of this new land that was to be her home.

What she saw was a Dutch town that almost—but not quite—might have been set in Holland, not America. It was dominated by a fort and a huge windmill. And there was a crowded jumble of little buildings side by each, made of yellow- and orange-colored brick, which raised their tall step gables in rows. Atop these houses were saucy weathervanes—roosters and stiff metal soldiers and little iron ships in full sail. Imogene was impressed with the enormous anchoring irons of the houses they passed—sometimes formed in the shape of the owner's initials. And because these water-bred Dutchmen preferred to transport their goods via water rather than over land, there was a canal down the center of Broad Street, which Verhulst called the "Heere Graft." They followed this street past a bridge that spanned the canal where a group of full-breeched Dutch bur- ghers stood gossiping. Their talk ceased as they bowed to the patroon and his lady, but as they passed Imogene heard someone murmur, "Ach, he's brought home a beauty!" and then some- one else said something she could not hear and they all laughed. Imogene had learned just enough Dutch to understand that remark about her beauty and she turned to ask Verhulst what else had been said, but his face wore such a forbidding expression that she forbore.

Between the first bridge and the second, which she could see up farther, Verhulst told her, was the home of Vrouw Berghem, a widow who had been in her youth a close friend of his mother's.

"I will leave you with Vrouw Berghem while I make arrangements to load the sloop for Wey Gat," he told her.

"But what will Elise do?" cried Imogene, stumbling over a cobblestone. "She will not know where to find us!"

"Neither will Captain van Ryker," said Verhulst grimly. "Imogene, watch where you are going! Elise will be waiting at dockside with our baggage. I have only to find the *Danskammer*—"

"The what?"

"My sloop, the *Danskammer*. Her *schipper*, Schroon, is probably asleep in some grog shop. He must have been waiting for me these ten days past while we were held up in mid-ocean by—"

"Captain van Ryker," supplied Imogene resignedly.

"Ah, I see you recall what caused our delay." His voice was sarcastic and Imogene's eyes flashed. Quickly she reminded herself that whatever Verhulst said to her, whatever he did, she had done far worse by *him*. If only he could find it in his heart to forgive her!

"We will be gone from this place by tonight," he promised her as they reached the front stoop of Vrouw Berghem's yellow brick residence. "The setting sun will find us sailing upriver toward Wey Gat."

But big, buxom Vrouw Berghem, who seized Verhulst unceremoniously in a bearhug that left him wincing, had other plans for them.

"You'll not be leaving before the Governor's Ball?" she protested after she had embraced them both and Verhulst had tried to break away, explaining his haste to be gone. Seizing them both by the hand she ushered them into her *voorhuis*, that seldom-occupied front room filled Dutch fashion with her finest possessions. She spoke in English for Imogene's benefit. "Why, 'tis being held tonight and Peter Stuyvesant will be very upset if you do not show him the courtesy of attending! All New Amsterdam knows that your sloop has been waiting for your return this past week or more, and only this morning I met Governor Stuyvesant on Pearl Street—" she called it "Perel Straat"—and he said 'twas a pity you had not yet returned, as the ball would make a fitting reception for your bride! And within minutes your ship was sighted! Besides, you cannot take this poor girl upriver without letting her see something of our city first! Stay overnight with me and tomorrow we will all take the ferry to Breukelen, if we can get the ferryman to answer the blast on the horn! 'Tis a horn that hangs from a tree at the waterside,'' she explained to Imogene, ''and the ferryman will come and row us across the river unless the wind blows strong enough that the sails of the windmill—you saw it near the fort—be taken in; then he will not come until the wind dies down. But I think tomorrow will be a fair day, don't you?''

''I would love to see Breukelen,'' said Imogene eagerly, who at all costs did not wish to leave for Wey Gat until she had come to some understanding with Verhulst. ''And everything else New Amsterdam affords. I really think we should go to Governor Stuyvesant's ball tonight, Verhulst. It would be foolish to offend him. And we are not in such a great hurry, surely, as all that. Wey Gat will wait for us.''

''Of course it will wait,'' coaxed Vrouw Berghem. ''And what better opportunity to show off a new bride than a Governor's Ball!''

Verhulst's dark eyes flickered for an instant and Vrouw Berghem beamed. The bride's entreaties might fail but she knew her man. His eyes had lit up at the thought of parading his English beauty before the town; she had him now. ''And I am sure your bride has brought lovely clothes that will be the envy of all,'' she added slyly.

''And jewels,'' murmured Verhulst, considering. ''There are pirates in the town,'' he objected.

''When are there not pirates in the town?'' Vrouw Berghem was astonished. ''But they will not harm us. They sell their wares and are gone—we remain.''

''You are right,'' agreed Verhulst in a stronger voice. *''We remain.''* He gave Imogene a hard look. ''We will attend the ball tonight, mevrouwen, and we will accept your hospitality for the night as well." Vrouw Berghem clapped her hands and Verhulst turned away looking as if he might regret his decision. "I will go and bring my wife's maidservant from the dock," he said shortly.

"And my jewel chest and a trunk of ball gowns," Imogene called after him. She turned with a smile to Vrouw Berghem. "Men sometimes do not think of these things."

The big woman gave her a wry smile. "Verhulst will. Sometimes I think that boy concentrates too much on clothes and not enough on the people who wear them."

Imogene thought that was a fair assessment of her husband; she wondered if he would be able to change. . . .

With Verhulst gone, Imogene turned curiously to Vrouw Berghem. "How did you know Verhulst was bringing home a bride? We were not married till we boarded the *Hilletje*."

Vrouw Berghem winked and put a finger to her lips. "Of course I did not know—I had it from Captain van Ryker when we met on Perel Straat!"

Imogene's lovely mouth formed a grin. "Then it was not the Governor you met there but Captain van Ryker?"

Vrouw Berghem nodded sagely. "What men do not know does not hurt them," she said with a shrug. *If only that were true!* thought Imogene. "Verhulst was obviously distracted by his homecoming and so he did not question what I said. Oh, he may puzzle about it later but you are not to tell him! If pressed, I will say that I had a premonition that Verhulst would come home married and told the Governor so and—"

"And *he* said it would make a fitting reception for a bride!" finished Imogene, laughing. She was delighted with her hostess. "Mevrouwen, you may be sure I will not give you away!"

"Good, then I see we shall be great friends."

"And you must come and visit us at Wey Gat. Could you not sail upriver with us when we go?"

Vrouw Berghem hesitated and shook her head. "Some other time perhaps. Wey Gat is indeed a beautiful place but—I rarely visit there."

"Why not?" wondered Imogene.

Vrouw Berghem met her gaze frankly. "I think it is the dogs."

" 'The dogs'?"

"That savage pack of dogs Verhulst keeps, ever since his parents were scalped. I hear them howling at night and I think of some poor devil being torn apart by their fangs. It interferes with my sleep. I have told Verhulst so, but he only shrugs and says he wishes to keep them near the house—in case of need."

"You mean—" Imogene's blue eyes widened—"the dogs are trained to hunt *men?*"

"Yes—and to destroy them. I am told they are very good at their work." Vrouw Berghem repressed a shudder. "Oh, you must not be alarmed—they are kept in check. Verhulst has an excellent kennelmaster. His name is Groot. But I like to walk about, and their presence—even if I cannot see or hear them—makes me uneasy. Come now, enough about dogs. Let me show you my house."

Imogene told herself she might not be seeing either Wey Gat or its savage pack. When Verhulst heard what she had to say to him, he might go storming upriver without her! Meanwhile she enjoyed being shown through Vrouw Berghem's spotless home and being instructed in the ways of a Dutch housewife.

That wide stoop at the front door flanked by two high-backed wooden benches, Vrouw Berghem told her, would be filled, on any average evening, with neighbors come to gossip. Tonight of course the neighbors, like themselves, would be too busy—they'd be dressing in their best for Governor Stuyvesant's ball. And that divided front door, like all the front doors along the street, was very useful—it kept the dogs out and the children in. Of course, *her* children were all married and gone, so now it served to keep other little feet from dashing inside, dragging their wooden shoes or Indian moccasins across her well-scoured floors.

Imogene remarked on the exceeding whiteness of those floors and Vrouw Berghem told her importantly that the white sand with which those floors were scoured was replaced daily. She herself swept it into the interesting patterns that she saw there. When Imogene admired the frosty white ruffle that stretched across the top of the high mantel with its decorative blue and white tiles, her hostess told her she would find those in all the Dutch houses. And those "crow steps" atop the gable ends of the house—those were for the convenience of the chimneysweeps, who could run nimbly up them carrying their brooms.

Life was different here, she told Imogene, proudly exhibiting her *kas,* or linen chest, as she chattered. Many things were dear but at least beaver and butter were cheap. It was a pity that Imogene would not be here on Saturday, for only last year Saturday had been established as market day and boats loaded with produce would come from the Bronx and Long Island to Vrouw Kierstede's shed, where they would sell their wares. There would be homespun duffel-cloth for sale and linsey-woolsey, and the Algonkins would bring venison and lobster and oysters. She warned Imogene against buying lobsters over a foot long; those five and six feet long were not so tasty for table— here Imogene blinked, trying to imagine dealing with a six-foot-long lobster—and the smaller oysters were better, too, although some were so large as to be a meal in themselves, up to a foot in size.

As she talked, Vrouw Berghem energetically removed a small blue Oriental rug she called the "table carpet" from an oaken table and spread a linen cloth upon it and soon Imogene was sharing with her hostess a tasty snack of crullers and headcheese washed down by tall tankards of fresh milk. There would be only a hasty supper tonight, Vrouw Berghem confided, for they must on to the Governor's Ball!

"Do many pirates really roam the town?" asked Imogene, when her sprightly hostess stopped for breath.

"Do many—?' Vrouw Berghem was surprised. "But of course! Without them we would pay much higher prices for our goods! But they are not truly pirates, you know, they are buccaneers and plunder only the Spanish. You can sleep sound in your feather bed—they will not hurt you."

Imogene was not worried about sleeping sound in her feather bed. "My acquaintance with buccaneers is meager," she admitted.

"But very selective!" sparkled Vrouw Berghem. "Captain van Ryker told me he met you on the high seas when he stopped the *Hilletje* to warn Captain Verbloom about the Spanish squadron."

Imogene studied the folds in her skirt. "Will Captain van Ryker be at the Governor's Ball tonight, do you think?"

"Oh, I am sure he will. He is very popular with all the ladies and will certainly be invited, for Governor Stuyvesant thinks highly of him."

Imogene frowned. She had almost hoped not to meet Van Ryker again. Certain now that she was pregnant, she had been thinking long thoughts, and this buccaneer captain, attractive though he was, did not figure in them. She had a husband to placate, a baby to think of. Reckless she might be with herself but with her child—never.

Her delicate jaw hardened and she hoped nervously that tonight van Ryker would do nothing to alienate Verhulst, for she had promised herself that tonight she would tell him—and take the consequences, whatever they were.

It was late before Verhulst arrived. He strode in with Elise and big Schroon, the *Danskammer*'s skipper, following him. Schroon was a blond, blue-eyed giant with a rolling gait, who balanced Imogene's trunk of ball gowns on his broad leathern-clad shoulder as lightly as if the trunk when empty did not weigh some seventy-five pounds. Trailing him came Elise, her arms wrapped firmly around Imogene's jewel case, as if she feared someone might steal it. She looked exhausted. Imogene sprang forward to take the jewel case from her and asked wonderingly why she was so late. Elise whispered that she had lost the proper trunk in the maze of piled-up luggage and been roundly scolded by the patroon for doing so. As a punishment, he had made her wait, standing on tired feet, until every piece of luggage was stowed aboard the *Danskammer;* she had not eaten a bite since their meager breakfast.

Imogene gave Verhulst an angry look and promptly spoke to Vrouw Berghem who told Elise in a hearty voice to make free with her kitchen, she would find plenty to eat out there!

After the hasty supper her hostess had promised, Imogene, with a somewhat recovered Elise helping her, chose her ball gown from the big trunk with exceeding care.

Verhulst was taken aback by her choice. "But that is your wedding gown!" he protested.

Imogene nodded soberly. "Even to the beaded white silk gloves I wore. But I am wearing my hair differently. Do you like it swept back this way, Verhulst?"

Verhulst ignored Imogene's question and only glanced at the white plumes caught with diamonds that waved atop her elaborate coiffure. "But why a wedding gown?"

"It's obvious, isn't it?" she sighed. "It will tell all of New

Amsterdam—all who may think they see a wild light in my eyes—that I am married.''

He digested that slowly. *All of New Amsterdam.* . . . ''You have guessed that van Ryker will be at the ball tonight,'' he divined.

She nodded. ''This gown will remind even a buccaneer that I am a married woman.''

For a moment that narrow, sensitive face lost some of its autocratic coldness. ''A good thought, Imogene,'' Verhulst said slowly. ''And here is a gift that I was saving for some great occasion. It may as well be tonight, since it will well become your gown.'' From somewhere he produced a small blue velvet casket and from it took a shimmering necklace of diamonds, let it slip like water through his fingers into her hand.

Imogene gasped with delight as she held it up. ''But—but this is fabulous, Verhulst! Something a queen would wear!''

''Or the bride of a patroon,'' he said haughtily. ''Here, I will clasp it around your neck.''

Imogene stood back and considered her reflection in the mirror. The diamond drops he had given her in Holland on her betrothal winked from her ears like the diamond clips that he had given her on her wedding day and which now held in place the waving white ostrich plumes in her hair. But the necklace he had given her now for some reason obscure to her eclipsed them both. Against her white throat it was a stunning fiery blaze. Not a woman at the Governor's Ball but would envy her! She gave her young husband a grateful look, thinking guiltily how he had taken her on faith and of the blow she yet must deal him.

''It's lovely, Verhulst,'' she said huskily. ''Much better than I deserve.''

''Untrue,'' he protested vigorously, and then in a lower tone with a glance at Elise's turned back across the room,

"Although I *did* consider throwing it in the sea a time or two—once when you left me playing chess in the great cabin of the *Sea Rover* and went up on deck with van Ryker, and again when you kept dancing with him."

In a sudden burst of emotion at this—for him—unusual declaration, Imogene threw her arms around him and kissed him. "You have no need to be jealous of Captain van Ryker, Verhulst. I will be true to you as long as you live—I promise."

Verhulst stiffened. Gently he disengaged her clinging arms. She felt somehow she had embarrassed him. "We must hurry if we are to be on time, and you should not disarrange your hair," he told her in a smothered voice.

Imogene thought he looked flushed and uneasy. She was puzzled by this reaction to her impulsive hug. Surely a display of affection from a bride should be welcome?

They went downstairs where Vrouw Berghem, dressed in a shrieking shade of magenta embroidered in aqua and green was drawing on her gloves. She did not look up. "Rychie ten Haer will be at the ball," she said, apropos of nothing.

Verhulst's arm, on which Imogene's hand rested, gave a slight jerk and Imogene turned to look sharply at him.

"And who is Rychie ten Haer?" she wondered.

"No one of interest." Verhulst spoke too quickly. "Rychie ten Haer is the daughter of a patroon who lives downriver from Wey Gat. Last year she married her cousin, Huygens ten Haer. Rychie was—a frequent visitor to Wey Gat."

Vrouw Berghem's eyebrows lifted in perplexity. All the river knew of Verhulst's pursuit of Rychie ten Haer and how she had spurned him. Saffron-haired Rychie had a sharp tongue and she had always comfortably considered Verhulst her possession, no matter how badly she treated him. Perhaps she herself should have warned the bride!

But Imogene, sensing trouble, was not to be put off. As they walked toward the Governor's mansion inside the fort, with stout Vrouw Berghem in her eagerness to reach the festivities preceding them by some distance, she brought up the subject again.

"What is this Rychie ten Haer to you, Verhulst? I must know who these people are, and why mention of some of them upsets you."

Verhulst, his nerves already rubbed raw at the prospect of this unexpected meeting between the girl he had loved and the girl he had married, turned on Imogene with a snarl. "If you must know, Rychie is a girl to whom I once offered marriage. And," he grated—for anyone on the river would tell Imogene, since Rychie had laughingly spread the story everywhere herself—"'Tis well known she laughed in my face."

He strode on angrily but Imogene stood frozen for a moment in astonishment, looking at his elegant black velvet back. So the patroon's daughter had laughed in his face? Well, it was plain to see the wound still hurt. Ah, poor Verhulst! Her heart went out to him.

"I look forward to meeting this Rychie," she said grimly, catching up with her stiff-backed husband at the Governor's open front door.

Verhulst gave her an incoherent answer and together they went inside where candles glittered and lavishly garbed guests moved about. They were greeted by their host, Peter Stuyvesant, the bluff Dutchman who had governed the colony for ten years now, standing with aplomb on his silver-studded wooden leg. Proudly he told Imogene that the city's population now numbered above a thousand. But he did not wait for her comments. Instead, he turned and immediately entered into a near shouting match with a guest who insisted the Dutch upriver were selling guns to the Iroquois, "guns which will be turned on us, myn-heer, mark my words!"

Imogene, more interested in the people who would be her new neighbors than in local politics, was relieved when Verhulst bore her away, into the thick of the crowd. She had indeed chosen the right costume to make an impression on New Amsterdam society. With her billowing ostrich plumes and glittering diamonds highlighting her pure white gown, she made a dramat-ic entrance into a room full of brightly garbed Dutch ladies, who all turned to look at her. Red, saffron yellow, brilliant shades of pink and blue and green—in the whole gamut of colors that swirled about her, Imogene was the only lady present who had chosen to wear unrelieved white.

Cool and fragile she stood beside the black velvet figure of her husband, and tried to look as chaste as her snowy gown.

She had taken her wedding vows almost in a somnolent state with her mind and her heart still fixed on Stephen Linnington. And during the voyage to America she had let a handsome buccaneer sway her. But tonight, before God and assembled New Amsterdam at the Governor's Ball, she told herself firmly, she would pledge her troth to Verhulst anew and take her wedding vows again—in her heart. For tonight—tonight she would tell him, and if he forgave her, she would never leave his side. But however the dice were cast, she was Vrouw van Rappard now, wife to the patroon of Wey Gat, and she was going to be all that was expected of her!

Beside her, Verhulst viewed the assemblage haughtily. Imogene watched him, puzzled. He was not like a man greeting old friends after a long absence. He wanted only to parade, to preen before these people against whom he seemed to nurse some deep private grievance.

No matter, she told herself sturdily. By her own graciousness she would make up for any lack on Verhulst's part.

Beautiful, graceful, elegantly gowned—and new to them all and thus of consummate interest—Imogene swept all before her that night. The Dutch gallants vied for dances, the older ladies remarked to Verhulst how pretty his young wife was and how pleasant, and the older gentlemen made her elaborate compliments—often in Dutch, which had to be translated, as Imogene extended her hand daintily to be kissed. Her voice was gentle, her smile was just right—not too warm, not too cool. The Governor's guests crowded about her, seeking introductions, and Verhulst, proud owner of this paragon, beamed as first this *jongvrouw* and then these *vrouwen* and this *mynheer* begged an introduction to his lovely bride.

One hung back, waiting with smoldering eyes for them to come to her. And Imogene knew without being told that this was Rychie ten Haer. Across the room she considered her rival dispassionately. Rychie was a big girl, as tall as Verhulst. Her thick coarse hair of brilliant saffron yellow looked as if it belonged in long braids, goosegirl style. It lacked the silky fineness, the luster of Imogene's fair hair. Rychie's complexion, unlike Imogene's sheer pink and white coloring, was pale honey, and her eyes, lacking the soft depth of Imogene's, were sharp and blue as china plates—and as hard, Imogene decided. Rychie's smile was brittle and the staccato way she waved her ivory fan betrayed agitation. Her low-cut gown, fitted skillfully to her fine, if overlush, figure, was impossible to miss. It was of scarlet satin heavily trimmed with black and yellow bows and it made her appear, in contrast to Imogene's glittering white, both tawdry and overdressed.

From her spot across the room, flanked by a little clot of

faithful admirers, Rychie watched Verhulst and Imogene and whispered behind her fan. From time to time Imogene looked out from those who crowded around her and guessed that saffron-haired Rychie was hating it, all this fuss being made over Verhulst van Rappard's new wife.

With calm eyes she studied Rychie, flouncing about.

Inevitably, they would clash. . . .

CHAPTER 13

Imogene looked up and forgot about Rychie. Captain van Ryker had entered the room.

He was flanked by his ship's doctor and his ship's master, and their arrival created some stir. Imogene saw that he was wearing the same gray and shot silver in which he had entertained them aboard the *Sea Rover*. But tonight he wore a broad gray satin sash, slung from one shoulder, in which were stuck a brace of large pistols. And that was not a delicately made dress sword that swung against his lean gray velvet thighs but the same serviceable blade that she had seen him wear aboard ship. Obviously, whether on land or sea, the captain went prepared. She watched as van Ryker and his officers were warmly greeted by Peter Stuyvesant, who introduced them to several blushing young ladies and their beaming mamas.

A sudden abortive movement in the crowd caught Imogene's attention. The Widow Poltzer had seized her daughter by the arm and was pushing her way energetically forward. Imogene hid a grin. Barnaby Swift had not seen the last of them!

And then van Ryker turned from greeting his host. His hawklike head lifted and his cold gray eyes swept the room.

And found Imogene easily: the most beautiful girl in the room and clad dramatically in white.

His gray eyes lit up. In half a dozen strides he had reached her side and was asking her to dance.

Imogene would have been glad to turn him down, for a little distance away she could see Verhulst watching her, but to have done so would have been to make a scene. She gave the tall captain a bright defiant smile and let him whirl her out onto the floor, where people paused to watch this magnificent couple who seemed made for each other—the man a lean gray wolf, the woman a flaunting golden lioness.

"I had expected you to be staying at the inn," he told her.

"We are staying with friends."

A smile quivered at the corners of his mouth. "So van Rappard thought it best to keep you away from any public house where I might abduct you!" His gaze roved carelessly over the pearly expanse of her bosom, the soft molding of her white bodice about her ripe young breasts. "As well I might," he added softly.

Imogene took a deep breath. She lifted her head and gazed directly into his eyes. She almost flinched from their hot light; she felt scorched by it. She moistened her lips. This was going to be difficult, but what she had to say had to be said.

"Captain van Ryker, we are on shore now—"

"Does that make a difference?" he demanded. "Are you telling me that you danced with me aboard the *Sea Rover* through *fear?* For even if you tell me so, I will not believe it!"

"No, of course I did not dance with you through fear," Imogene protested, feeling that he was already getting the best of her. "But you must understand that I am married, these are my husband's friends. I must not appear to—"

"Falter in your marriage vows? But you have already faltered in your marriage vows! I could tell that when I took you in my arms aboard the *Sea Rover*."

Imogene's cheeks grew hot. "Nevertheless, we must not see each other again."

Van Ryker's lean face lost its lighthearted look, his square jaw hardened perceptibly. "And what has brought about this sudden change of heart?"

Imogene certainly did not intend to tell him about the baby, nor about her strong feelings of guilt toward Verhulst. "We must each lie in the bed we have made," she told him sharply. "Certainly I intend to lie in mine."

It seemed a long time before he answered that. Barnaby danced by with the Widow Poltzer's simpering daughter, and Verhulst, prodded by duty, led Vrouw Berghem out upon the floor. Over van Ryker's shoulder, the French doctor, de Rochemont, gave his captain an enigmatic smile—Imogene would have given a deal to know what he was thinking. She saw a sea of new faces as van Ryker swung her around so that her satin skirts billowed out and heads turned to admire them.

"Forgive me for saying it," he drawled, "but even though you flaunt yourself in bridal white, you do not have the look of a woman who has found happiness in her marriage bed."

Imogene gave him an affronted look. "If you say anything further about my marriage bed, I shall assuredly slap your grinning face."

"Ah, but then your husband would of necessity challenge me to a duel and you would very promptly become a widow. Is that what you seek?"

How she yearned to strike that impudent visage! But she dared not. Van Ryker was right. If she were to strike him, Verhulst to defend his honor would be obliged to fight it out with him.

"Verhulst was right," she burst out. "You're nothing but a damned pirate!"

A steely light replaced the amusement in his gray eyes. "Damned perhaps, but a pirate—no. I seem to remember telling you that I am no pirate, but a buccaneer."

"I fail to see the difference," sniffed Imogene, intent on baiting him.

"Ah, there is a very great difference. Pirates are mad dogs who attack everyone. Buccaneers attack only the ships of Spain, who would deny us our right to sail these waters. In fact they deny your right to sail them—and the right of the patroon your husband. Spain has decreed that the waters of the New World belong to *her*. It is for freedom from this tyranny that I fight."

"And to make yourself rich," scoffed Imogene.

"What an interesting comment to hear from one who has so recently sold herself for gold." His calm gaze rested insultingly on the diamond necklace about her throat.

"How dare you suggest—"

"I do not suggest; I but state the obvious."

"You insult me, sir!"

"Then I will take it back," he ground out, "if you will look into my eyes and tell me how much you love your husband."

"I'll tell you no such thing," panted Imogene. "let me go or—"

His grip on her was steely. "Come now, we mustn't make a scene. Remember van Rappard's tender hide. At least—" his glance had grown frosty—"you didn't sell yourself for English gold, it was for Dutch gold."

How dare he show contempt for her! "Even if it were for Spanish gold," choked Imogene, " 'tis no concern of yours!"

"Ah, if it were for Spanish gold, I would feel obliged to share it—in ransom."

"*Damn* you, van Ryker!" She was almost sobbing, her

BOLD BREATHLESS LOVE

face flushed—and not just from his maddening words, but from the tumult within herself that just being near him brought her. In fury she had raised her free arm to strike him when she was suddenly aware that from across the room Verhulst was staring at her in consternation.

"Before you damn me too much—" the buccaneer's hand shot out and grasped her wrist in a paralyzing grip before it could so much as brush him—"let me tell you, my fiery lady, that my men surround this place. I could take you out of here and none could stop me."

Involuntarily, Imogene shrank back. "These people won't let you take me—not from the Governor's mansion!"

Van Ryker's gray eyes glinted. "I would snatch you from hell if I had a mind to," he said caressingly. In her impotent fury at being held here at his pleasure, Imogene did not realize that the buccaneer was stalling for time, waiting for some word, some gesture, some indication that she *wanted* to go with him. A stolen bride would be one thing, an unwilling captive something else. . . .

The dance had ended, the musicians were taking a break. In their rapt concentration on each other, they had whirled to a stop beside a little knot of people and as Imogene stepped backward, oblivious to everything but her attempt to elude van Ryker, she trod on someone's foot and there was a little cry of pain. She quickly turned about to say she was sorry—and found herself looking into Rychie ten Haer's wide china blue eyes. On Rychie's broad face was a malicious smile, but she ignored Imogene's swift apology and turned her attention to the man who kept his grip on Imogene's wrist.

"Captain van Ryker," Rychie smirked. "Assertive as usual?"

The lean buccaneer turned to Rychie with a frown. Like

most of the gentlemen here, he had been a time or two the object of Rychie's amorous attention. A vivid lass, he thought, but crude. "In what way, Mevrouw ten Haer?" he asked her courteously.

Rychie tittered. "Why, in holding onto a lady's arm so tightly after the music has stopped!" Her fan fluttered.

Van Ryker's dark brows lifted. "I always hold onto that which is—"

Imogene knew he was about to say "which is mine" and cut in sharply, her high sweet voice overlaying his deep resonant one. "You are Rychie ten Haer, are you not? I am Imogene van Rappard. None have thought to introduce us—and Verhulst has told me so much about you."

"Has he indeed?" Rychie looked startled, for she could think of nothing in their relationship that had done Verhulst much credit.

"Yes," said Imogene with composure. She was trying—without appearing to do so—to wrest her arm from the buccaneer's grip. But he still grasped her wrist firmly, even though the folds of her lovely white dress now concealed the silent struggle. "Verhulst has told me that since I am a newcomer to your country, that I must guard against making mistakes." Rychie bridled, expecting a compliment. Imogene's voice went lazily on. "And that you are the one to consult on mistakes—having already made them all."

Impaled upon that barbed remark, Rychie's saffron head came erect like an animal scenting danger. Out of the corner of her eye, Imogene could see Verhulst moving toward them. It was a calculated risk, this attack upon Rychie. Verhulst already looked thunderous and there was no doubt as to the reason, for the whole room must have noticed his wife's violent interchange with the buccaneer captain. If only she could deflect his wrath from van Ryker to this woman who had once rejected him! From the suddenly startled expression on Verhulst's face, Imogene guessed that he had heard her remark to Rychie.

Now Rychie's gaze flicked coldly over the diamond necklace circling Imogene's neck and moved with precision to her detractor's lovely face. Her voice rose. "It is a pity you do not speak Dutch, Mevrouw van Rappard—"

"An omission easily remedied," shrugged Imogene. "Languages come easily to me." It was not the truth, but it would serve.

"—for we Dutch have a word to describe your comment," continued Rychie contemptuously. *"Wartaal!"*

She flung the word at Imogene, who looked blank.

Van Ryker, amused at this sharp exchange between the two women, leaned down and murmured in her ear, *"Wartaal* means 'gibberish.' "

"Yes, I am sure you are an expert at *wartaal,* Mevrouw ten Haer," Imogene agreed gravely and Rychie simmered. "I am told your husband is an old friend of Verhulst's." It was a stab in the dark; Imogene had no idea whether Verhulst even knew Huygens. "Are we soon to expect the pleasure of your company at Wey Gat?"

Rychie had recovered her aplomb. "I doubt it," she responded airily. Her carrying voice rose over the listening throng. "For we are expecting an heir in the spring." Her taunting smile played over Verhulst and Imogene saw him quiver. Her whole being sprang hotly to his defense. Why should this woman who had spurned him be allowed to hurt him so?

Her anger rose and with it her reckless nature. She flung caution aside. If Verhulst was too proud to do it, *she* would vanquish his enemies. She would do more than that—she would resolve her future. With Verhulst's face pale before her, she made up her mind. She would not wait until tonight to tell him—she would risk everything on a single throw of the dice.

Imogene's voice, too, could have a carrying quality when she was aroused. Now in the room suddenly hushed by Rychie's barb, that voice rang out.

"We, too, are expecting an heir at Wey Gat," she told Rychie, and her head lifted proudly as she spoke. "*Our* child will arrive *before* spring."

No sooner were the words out than she regretted them. This was hardly the way to inform Verhulst that he was soon to give his name to a child he had not fathered! She should have whispered the words in her bedroom—with her eyes downcast. But—it was done, and as always in time of trouble, Imogene's natural courage stiffened her spine. Not daring to look at Verhulst, she turned with steadied casualness to smile calmly up at the tall buccaneer captain beside her.

If Rychie ten Haer was taken aback by Imogene's calm announcement, there was one in the room who was stunned by it.

Verhulst van Rappard lifted his periwigged head and stared in wonderment at his beauteous bride. The coolness of her thus to counter Rychie's malice! And oh, the magnificence of her lie! What matter that she had lied thus publicly? In later months if the subject came up, Imogene could claim she had lost the baby. He forgot his jealousy of van Ryker that had brought him raging across the room. His sensitive lips trembled and his dark eyes filled with tears. Imogene, his beautiful Imogene, had defended him! She loved him after all. . . .

And there was another in the room whose body froze to

rigidity and whose countenance became oddly still at Imogene's bold pronouncement. Captain van Ryker was looking directly down upon Imogene as she spoke, flaunting her soon-to-be motherhood at this spiteful young Dutch vrouw. He kept his hold on Imogene's wrist there concealed by the folds of her skirt but his gaze switched suddenly to the glowing face of the young patroon.

Could it be that he had misjudged Imogene? That the tremulous physical response he had felt in her was but a sham? That she was actually *in love* with this taut dark lad whose heart glowed in his eyes when he looked at her?

The music struck up and Captain van Ryker abruptly tightened his grip and swept Imogene past Verhulst into the dancers without so much as a by-your-leave.

"Let me go," murmured Imogene furiously, her cheeks flaming. "Everyone is looking at us!"

"Tell me that you love that frail lad with the great fortune that you're married to and I'll let you go," he challenged her.

Imogene lifted her head. Van Ryker had spun her into the middle of the floor and now from across the room she found herself looking into Verhulst's narrow face—a face made radiant by gratitude and pride. Ah, she could not bring herself to hurt him as spiteful Rychie once had! On the moonswept deck of the *Sea Rover* beneath a sky glittering with stars she had harbored wicked thoughts about this buccaneer captain and trembled in his embrace, but now—now there was her child to think of. A child who must have a name and who could not be brought up aboard a pirate ship, whether its captain claimed to be a buccaneer or no!

She tried to still the mad beating of her heart and forced

herself to look defiantly into van Ryker's eyes—those cold gray eyes that sparkled now with silver lights.

"*I love Verhulst.*" She spaced the words. "*I love my husband.*"

Blood surged into the captain's dark face and retreated, leaving it pale. "*I do not believe you!*" he grated.

"Then believe this!" She wrenched her right hand free and struck him hard across the face.

CHAPTER 14

For an instant the room stood breathless. Attracted by the crack of Imogene's palm against the buccaneer's cheek, the guests at the Governor's Ball turned to stare curiously at the tableau unfolding before them.

Captain van Ryker had stopped in mid-whirl and now Imogene's white skirts billowed in satiny folds about his wide-topped boots. They were oblivious to all the world, these two, held by fury and by something else—something Imogene was too proud to recognize and the captain too proud to assert. The blood pounded in van Ryker's head as he looked down at the tormentingly beautiful woman who had struck him, and evil thoughts coursed through his mind, telling him that his buccaneers were ready outside to storm the hall and he could carry her away to his own domain—a ship that rode the restless waters of so many seas. He could take her by force—none here could resist him, and sail away with her never to return. He had *not* been wrong, he had felt the fire in her those nights aboard the *Sea Rover*—he *knew* that she desired him.

A wolfish smile spread over van Ryker's dark countenance. *He would do it.* Though he be damned in hell forever, he would do it!

But at that moment from outside came a sudden rattle and a ringing of bells and hoarse cried of *"Brant! Brant!"* and the whole assemblage, mesmerized by the sight of the patroon's English bride standing rigid in the grasp of the tall buccaneer, stirred as if a great wind had shaken them.

"What has happened?" demanded Imogene.

"The rattle watch has discovered a fire somewhere," van Ryker drawled and the wolfishness of his smile and his gleaming eyes told her he had no care for the fire, nor if all of New Amsterdam burned to the ground this night—his mind was on something else: *Her!*

Someone jostled her arm; it was Verhulst.

"Imogene . . ." he said unsteadily—and she knew in that instant she had been right to fling her announcement of an heir to Wey Gat in Rychie's face. Verhulst had forgiven her; she could tell from the gentleness of his touch. There were unshed tears in his eyes—and suddenly dark anger as he turned to van Ryker. His voice grated. "I know not what you said to my wife to make her strike you, but I add my blow to hers!" He drew back a black velvet arm and his knuckles dusted the captain's strong jaw.

Standing steady with both boots planted, van Ryker was unshaken by the blow. The only change in the buccaneer's sardonic face was a deepening coldness in his ice gray eyes.

"I demand satisfaction!" cried Verhulst recklessly.

"Verhulst—" Imogene would have intervened but van Ryker interrupted.

"You will have your satisfaction, Mynheer van Rappard—in

the morning.'' Those white teeth gleamed. "At the moment, I take it you're to the fire to keep New Amsterdam from burning down?''

"As *you* should be!'' cried Verhulst, needled by that taunting tone. He staggered as someone, fire-bound, bumped into him. "Imogene, get you to Vrouw Berghem. I will join you later.''

He hurried past, swept onward by the sea of outrushing male guests, and Imogene turned to the buccaneer beside her with leaping fear in her eyes. Van Ryker really meant to duel with Verhulst—he would kill him!

"This duel,'' she said tensely. "It cannot go on.''

"Indeed?'' Sardonic brows elevated. "And how do you propose to stop it? You could see for yourself your husband is hot for my blood.''

"He is not! He was goaded into it. All know you are the best blade in the Caribbean—Verhulst said so himself. It would be murder!''

Van Ryker shrugged. "A blow was given. 'Tis my right to demand satisfaction.''

"Your 'right'!'' Her laugh rang out discordantly. "'Twas *I* who struck you. 'Tis from *me* you should demand satisfaction!''

"That too,'' he said, studying her from shadowed eyes.

Imogene felt a little thrill of fear go through her. Van Ryker was determined, resolute, a man to reckon with. And tomorrow, if swords were crossed, he would leave Verhulst van Rappard lying in his blood on New Amsterdam's cobbles. Unless . ... unless she stopped him.

The buccaneer had caught her thought. "You could easily save this madman you have married,'' he suggested.

"How?''

'You could go with me now.''

"That I'll not do!'' she grated.

He shrugged. "Then your husband must take his chances."

Suddenly her pretty teeth flashed in a tight little smile.

"You fear the fire, Captain van Ryker?" Her taunting voice had little teeth in it.

She saw his dark head jerk slightly, for he was startled by her words. "I fear nothing," he said calmly. *But it was not true,* he thought. *He feared her loss, this lustrous woman who had come into his life like a shaft of white moonlight and brought to mind old forgotten dreams.*

"Verhulst does not fear the fire," she said recklessly. *"He* has gone with the other men to fight it. And yet you linger here?"

"No, I'm to the fire." He clapped his hat more firmly upon his head. " 'Twill give ye time to pack your most precious belongings."

"That I'll not!"

His eyes flashed. "You will, if you prefer not to be made a widow!"

Imogene drew a deep shaky breath that disturbed the lace on her bodice and made van Ryker catch his breath at the sight of that rippling white skin. She stared up into his eyes—and he was lost in their depths.

"I'll come by for you once the fire's quenched," he promised huskily.

"You'll find the door barred!"

"A barred door has seldom stopped me."

"And anyway, you don't know where we're staying!"

"At Vrouw Berghem's." Her grinned at her.

Imogene was quivering with rage; she felt her world wavering. This wild, dangerous—and maddeningly attractive—man was offering her a choice of sorts: She could go with him willingly—now; or she could wait and be widowed in the morning. And the worst of it was that the very thought of the *Sea Rover* sailed through her mind languorously; perfumed winds stirred her sails, and commanding her was a man of steel, a man to stir the heart. . . .

She brought herself up sharply. Verhulst had forgiven her, the road ahead was safe for her baby. Only this tall fellow stood in her way.

"I hope a burning brand falls on you!" she told him through clenched teeth.

"And well it may," he agreed equably. "But ye'll still have time to pack while my men and I deal with the fire."

All about the room the women stood in little groups, whispering and staring at them. Imogene was suddenly sharply aware of what all this talk would do to Verhulst—Verhulst, who had shown only sympathy and pity and unselfish kindness when she had announced before the whole room that she was pregnant!

"If you carry me away, van Ryker, it will be fighting and screaming. For I'll not go with you willingly—whether wife or widow!"

"As you will," he said carelessly.

With a quick bow he strode away and Imogene was left alone with the other women in a hall from which the men had gone, some of them carrying hastily caught-up leathern buckets that had been passed out among them. Automatically she rubbed her benumbed wrist—still tingling from van Ryker's touch. Her heart was pounding, for deep within her she was fighting a feverish desire to do as he had bade her, to pack and sail away with this insolent buccaneer.

A thought she must not brook—ever!

Her face was flaming as Vrouw Berghem bustled up. She was talking even before she reached Imogene. "What a night!" she cried. "Vrouw Poltzer is wailing that her poor daughter could have snared young Barnaby Swift if it were not for this cursed fire, and that awkward de Puyster fellow caught his spurs in my overskirt as he dashed out with his bucket. He ripped the hem right out—see?'' She turned mournfully to exhibit her torn magenta skirt and paused at sight of Imogene's upset expression. "Whatever did Captain van Ryker *say* that so upset you?" she wondered, round-eyed. "And Verhulst struck him! Ach, there'll be trouble over that, I don't doubt."

"A duel," said Imogene dully. "In the morning."

" 'A duel'! But that must not be! No wonder ye stood here wrangling with the captain! He's a fabled duelist, all New Amsterdam knows it and Verhulst would be a fool to fight him. Why, van Ryker would kill him!"

"I told van Ryker it would be murder," sighed Imogene. "But he would not back off."

"Yes, well, men are like that," said her hostess resignedly. "They are always throwing themselves onto knives or swords or cutlasses for their precious honor! Would they were not so touchy!" She pondered a moment. "Well, there are no two ways about it," she said energetically. "You must get Verhulst away from here, upriver to Wey Gat. It is a stronghold—even Captain van Ryker would hesitate to pursue him there!"

Imogene thought van Ryker might well pursue her to the gates of hell, but she was ready to seize on any means of escape.

"You are right," she agreed quickly. "We must get Verhulst upriver—tonight. I will go home and pack. We must leave at once for—for van Ryker has promised he will come and break your door down and take me away with him."

"What?" Her hostess was the very picture of indignation; her magenta ruffles shook with it. "Why, I can't believe it of Captain van Ryker! I shall certainly deny him admission to my *voorhuis* in future if he does any such thing—yes, and I will pass him in the street without speaking too! Break my door down, indeed!''

The comic contrast of denying future admission to a man who had already broken down one's door was lost on Imogene in her eagerness to leave. Making a swift excuse to their hostess, the two women hurried out, leaving behind those whispering little clusters of women to speculate and gossip. One claimed she had heard the buccaneer captain tell the patroon's bride that he would carry her off. There was a general flutter of protest at that, and several ladies announced that they would call on Vrouw Berghem in the morning—*she* would know the truth of the matter!

Meantime, Imogene and her hostess were on their way back to Vrouw Berghem's. They could see the fire in the distance, a red glow that lit up the night sky.

'' 'Twill be one of those illegal wood-and-clay chimneys that's caught fire,'' predicted Vrouw Berghem as they hurried along, holding up their skirts. ''People *will* build them in defiance of the law, and they're always bursting into flames like torches and igniting the thatched roofs nearby. You'll not be troubled with *that* at least at Wey Gat—the chimneys there are of heavy stone like the house and the roofs are of slate.'' She gave her skirts another hike that showed her striped stockings. ''There's none about to see our legs, so hold your skirts higher, for this ground is terrible uneven.''

Imogene, whose skirts already brushed her knees, wished her plump hostess could move faster. ''The bells are still tolling,'' she noted.

''Yes, from the church and from the Stadt Huys. You heard that shout of 'Throw out your buckets'? By now the men and boys will have formed a bucket brigade—I suppose it is the same in England?''

Imogene was spared an answer as Vrouw Berghem stumbled on the uneven ground and she reached out to catch her.

"Thank you," gasped that lady. "I think I'd best slow down." She held on to Imogene's arm. "I did not yet congratulate you on the child," she panted. "When it is born, you must invite me to the christening. I have a beautiful silver porridge spoon I brought from Holland that will be perfect for the baby!"

"You will be my child's godmother," Imogene promised her warmly. "And I hope you will not wait until my child is born before you visit us at Wey Gat."

Vrouw Berghem, who knew they'd been married on shipboard, was mentally tallying up the months. It didn't work out.

"Verhulst looked so—so happy," she said vaguely.

"Yes, didn't he?" Imogene was at a loss to explain that to herself. Startled, yes, perhaps even forgiving—but happy? Did Verhulst so desire a child that he would make himself believe—? No, it was not possible. But did he perhaps really believe the child was his? It was a thought that made Imogene almost lose her footing. More than one night on shipboard he had reeled into his cabin drunk. Could he perhaps believe that he had fathered her child on one of those nights?

If that were the case, he would be disabused of it once the child was born and he counted the months since they had boarded the *Hilletje* and gone through a wedding ceremony!

No, she would *make* him believe it! The child could be passed off as premature. There was no need to shatter his happiness—Verhulst need never know! Imogene's fingers, guiding Vrouw Berghem's faltering footsteps, clenched down on that lady's elbow so sharply that Vrouw Berghem gave a little cry.

"I am sorry." Imogene was instantly contrite. "I was—I was thinking of something else and as my thoughts seized me, so I seized your elbow. I hope I have not hurt you?''

'' 'Tis all right,'' Vrouw Berghem assured her. ''Our one thought must be to get you and Verhulst away before morning.''

''But cannot the *Sea Rover* overtake us on the river?'' wondered Imogene, seeing a new problem loom up.

Vrouw Berghem bridled. ''None can overtake our river sloops! They are famous everywhere for their speed. They are truly flyboats, for they fly across the water. And the *Danskammer* is renowned for her speed—she has won races!''

So the buccaneer captain might glower, but morning would find her far beyond his reach. Imogene told herself she was content, but tiny teeth of regret gnawed at her. Van Ryker *was* dashing, he was handsome, he was bold, he was the kind of man every woman wanted—all but herself, of course.

They had reached the house now and Imogene hurried in to rouse Elise, change to traveling clothes, and to pack.

''He's coming for you, isn't he?'' asked Elise, rubbing the sleep from her eyes.

''Who?'' Imogene tried to sound airy and failed.

''That pirate captain! I could see it in his eyes!''

''Yes, he's coming for me. Here. He said so.''

''I knew it!'' Elise was frenziedly grabbing at this and that, stuffing everything into the big trunk. ''And these foreigners will hand you over to him, mark my words! They won't want to dispute with a ship of forty guns! A few broadsides from the *Sea Rover* and that claptrap little fort would be a pile of rubble! Quick, off with your dress, I must pack it. And ye must put on something sensible, if we're to fight pirates!''

''Elise, he won't be here until after the fire is quenched. He will find us gone.''

Elise, in the act of pulling off Imogene's overdress, stopped and gave her a hopeful look. '' 'Gone'?''

"Gone upriver aboard the *Danskammer*, which Vrouw Berghem swears is too fast a sloop to catch."

" 'Upriver'? But—" A new terror lit Elise's pale eyes. "But you have not told your husband—"

"Yes, I have told him," said Imogene shortly. She struggled out of her tight bodice. "I announced it at the ball." Her voice was grim.

Elise stood frozen. "And how did he take it?"

"He seems overjoyed about it." Imogene could not but sound puzzled.

Elise's mouth gaped open. "Over—overjoyed?" she whispered. "I can't believe it!"

Neither could Imogene, but she felt she had no choice. Fate had dealt better with her than she deserved—it had given her a paragon for a husband.

"Verhulst is to duel with Captain van Ryker at dawn," she said, and at the sudden jerk of Elise's bony shoulders, she added grimly. " 'Twas my fault. I'll thank you not to twit me with it!"

"To 'twit' you!" Indignantly, Elise took the bodice Imogene thrust at her. "Your husband dies at dawn and you'll thank me not to twit you with it?"

"We will elude this pirate," said Imogene through her teeth. "Here, let me do that, Elise—you're stuffing everything into the trunk the wrong way. I'll finish the packing. You go and find Verhulst—he'll be among the men at the fire."

" 'The fire'?" Elise had heard nothing of a fire. She had slept soundly through the clamor and just now realized that, outside, church bells were tolling. "And where is that?"

"You'll find it by the glow. Manage to speak to Verhulst privately and without Captain van Ryker seeing you. Tell him we are packed and ready to leave at once. Hurry!"

But Elise returned limping and dirty, having tripped over

270

one of the leathern fire buckets and catapulted into a puddle.
."The patroon would not speak to me," she reported sadly.
"He shouted at me that fires were men's work and to get me
gone."

"Perhaps Captain van Ryker will not come tonight," Vrouw
Berghem tried to comfort her. "After all, there is this duel.
Having been challenged, the captain will not wish to appear to
evade a meeting with Verhulst. He will have his honor to think
of."

" 'His honor'?" asked Imogene contemptuously. "The
honor of a buccaneer?"

Vrouw Berghem sighed. In her opinion Captain van Ryker
was a very honorable man. And now he was about to steal
another man's wife. By force. She could not understand this
change that had come over him.

"I hope you are right and that he will wait," said Imogene,
biting her lips. "It will give us more time to get away."

Elise watched her fearfully. She could not understand any
of this but it all had the wrong ring to her. It was inconceivable to
her that a man so proud and autocratic as the young patroon
should be happy about the baby. Perhaps it was best that they
have the duel after all. Then they would have only one man's
rage to worry about!

It was some time before Verhulst returned, exhausted, to
tell them that a barn and a stable had caught fire and it had been
difficult to rescue the animals. He was covered with soot and
grime, one sleeve of his velvet doublet shredded, his trousers
torn.

"But your beautiful suit is ruined, Verhulst!" cried Vrouw
Berghem, overwhelmed by this new disaster.

"No matter." Verhulst was pale and tired. He turned a
smoke-grimed face toward the women and suddenly took in that

both his wife and Elise were dressed in traveling clothes and Elise was clutching Imogene's little chest of jewels. "What's this?" he demanded in amazement.

"We're leaving," explained Imogene. "Tonight." She nodded toward the closed trunk of ball gowns. "We can send for that later."

"Yes," echoed Vrouw Berghem energetically. " 'Tis madness for you to even consider dueling with Captain van Ryker. You must find Schroon and tell him you are leaving at once. The *Danskammer* will carry you out of van Ryker's reach to Wey Gat. There you can hold him off—or you can take your wife and flee inland, hide with some friendly Indians!"

Verhulst stared at them as if they had all gone mad. Whatever else he was, the young patroon was not a coward. "I'll not run away!" he cried angrily. "What do you take me for? And why should I hide my wife among friendly Indians? Have ye both taken leave of your senses?"

"Verhulst." Imogene gave Vrouw Berghem a chiding look. "No harm has been done me. I became angry at something Captain van Ryker said—a small thing."

"*What* small thing?"

"Oh, 'twas nothing, some remark I took badly. I was—was angry at Rychie and I took out my anger on the captain. I should have asked his pardon."

At the memory of how she had taken his part with Rychie before all of them at the Governor's Ball, Verhulst's angry face softened. "I will not send my seconds to Captain van Ryker," he said. "That much I will grant you, Imogene. But if his seconds come looking for me, they will find me. Right here. I will not run. Not even to please you."

Vrouw Berghem and Imogene looked at each other in despair. Bravado was all very well, but they both knew that for

Verhulst to meet the lean buccaneer in mortal combat was madness.

"I'm to bed," said Verhulst tiredly, clomping past them on muddy boots to mount the stairs. "And unless I am roused by Captain van Ryker's seconds, I desire that you let me sleep late. And tomorrow afternoon I will take you both to see Breukelen."

In silence, they watched him go.

"I think what we all need is some hot buttered rum," declared Vrouw Berghem in a voice of doom. "Perhaps *that* will get us through these next hours."

Verhulst was sound asleep when Imogene came up to bed. She was careful not to disturb him, for if he was to fight a blade as dangerous as van Ryker in the morning, he would need all his strength—and more. Instead, she sat down in an uncomfortable wooden chair and spent the last hours of darkness studying by candlelight her young husband. He lay boyishly with his arms outflung, sprawled across the coverlet in utter fatigue, still dressed in his ruined velvet suit.

She knew now, if she had not known before, that she should not have married him. For her heart did not go out to boyish figures such as Verhulst, but to strong, determined, sardonic men. Men like Stephen Linnington. Men like—she was forced to admit it—Captain van Ryker.

Verhulst was good, she told herself gloomily. It would have been natural enough for him to have turned on her, but he had not. Instead he had accepted the fact of the baby almost with joy. So kind . . . she did not deserve a man so kind.

Through the dark hours as she sat stiffly, watching him, she made up her mind.

She would not let this foolish, kindly boy die for her—as another foolish boy had died for her in England. Not even her unborn child could ask that of her. Verhulst had done a noble thing—he had forgiven her the great wrong she had done him. He should not be repaid by death on the point of a buccaneer's gleaming sword!

Silently Imogene rose and stole stealthily down the narrow stairs. Dawn was near breaking now; a false dawn's pale light was graying out the stars. With care she unlatched Vrouw Berghem's front door and let herself out into the night.

She would elude the watch, find van Ryker at whatever tavern or inn he was staying. She would go with him wherever he would take her—if only he would spare Verhulst. She would leave no note. She would go out of the patroon's life as she had come into it, leaving behind her jewels and her furs. Let Verhulst think badly of her, it was what she deserved. But at least he would not die, this heedless boy, in defense of her honor. She could give him the gift of life, she who had so nearly brought him death.

Tomorrow, she thought, as she slipped silently along New Amsterdam's dark streets, tomorrow she would sail aboard the *Sea Rover*—for she had no doubt that van Ryker would promptly quit the town before the guns of the fort could be brought to bear on him and he be forced into battle with his erstwhile friends, the Dutch burghers.

Tomorrow—she took a deep breath of the cool sea air— tomorrow she would become that creature she had scorned to become—a buccaneer's woman.

PART TWO
The Prisoner of Wey Gat

A toast of the woman brought low
By loving unwisely too well,
Who ends up with nowhere to go
But her own deep private hell.

The North River, New Netherland, 1657

CHAPTER 15

Leaning on the rail of the *Danskammer*'s high quarterdeck, Imogene van Rappard stared up at the mighty Palisades moving languorously by on her right. They had left the sea gate—that point where the North River met the East River—behind them. And now, with a cool breeze whipping her fair hair, Imogene stood awed into silence by the grandeur of the high-flung basalt escarpment that lined the river's eastern bank. They had been sailing by it for miles. Across the glittering water on the western bank was a forest brilliant with all the colors of fall, but Imogene had eyes only for the towering stone battlements that guarded the eastern bank, rising like a curtain wall before her fascinated gaze. *Henry Hudson discovered this*, she thought. *He sailed for the Dutch, but he was English.* She felt a sudden glow of pride for the valiant man who sailed out of England for far places, men like . . . Stephen Linnington. Men like—Captain van Ryker, whose English, she thought wryly, was far too perfect for a Dutchman.

Captain van Ryker. . . . Imogene's features tightened perceptibly. Three days had gone by since the night of the fire and the Governor's Ball. Two moons had risen and set since Imogene had wended her stealthy way to the dark wharf to strike a bargain with the buccaneer captain—a bargain that, she knew, would save her husband but sweep her out of his life forever.

For a husband would never take back a wife who had gone willingly into the arms of a buccaneer, sailed publicly away with him on his ship. She would not expect him to. Nor, in this case, a little wisp of a thought plagued at her, *would she want him to.* . . . And again as she hurried toward the wharf she heard the musical call of the islands and felt warm breezes washed with sun sweep over her.

But she had come to an amazed halt at the wharf. Dawn was breaking by then and in its pale light the billowing white sails of the *Sea Rover*—pinkened now by the rising sun—stood far out to sea and a southward sweeping wind was carrying her buccaneer fast away from her.

Imogene's senses had wheeled full circle and settled back with a thud.

He had sailed without her. He had not even said good-bye.

Her throat felt dry and some wild thing that had sung in her heart was stilled—perhaps forever.

The lean buccaneer was gone.

Almost at her feet a bundle of ragged clothes that turned out to be an old man who must have slept the night on the dock, rose up and stretched. He smiled at Imogene blearily through a matted gray beard.

"Were you here when she left?" Imogene indicated the pink sails far away.

"The *Sea Rover, jufvrouw?*" He called her "young lady" in his rough Dutch even though he had answered her in English. Along the wharf many languages were spoken.

She nodded.

"Aye. Sailed with the tide, she did. Her captain—I know him well; many's the coin he's tossed me—came back from the fire looking grim and told his men to upanchor and away. Buccaneers is like that—sudden fellows." He gave her a sympathetic look. "Was there someone on board her you wanted to see before he left, *jufvrouw?*"

"No—no one," she said quickly and turned away.

Torn between relief and regret, Imogene went home through a town already stirring with the dawn, to find Vrouw Berghem up, wearing a starched apron, vigorously sweeping the front stoop. She looked up in surprise at the sight of Imogene.

"I found the front door unlatched," her hostess explained, "and I thought Verhulst must have gone out seeking the captain."

" 'Twas I who sought the captain," sighed Imogene. "I hoped to persuade him against this duel but I found him already gone. The *Sea Rover* was far out to sea when I reached the wharf."

Vrouw Berghem gave a great sigh that shook the starched folds of her white apron. "Thank heaven for that!"

"Verhulst would not have approved of my going. You'll say nothing of it?"

"Of course not. 'Twas exactly what I would have done in your place. Come in, we'll have a bowl of Indian porridge together."

Imogene was eating the Indian porridge and meditating on the sudden fellow who had told her last night he'd make her a widow and today was a fast-disappearing dot on the horizon when Verhulst came down the stairs, stretching and yawning.

He was wearning another dark velvet suit, very like the one he had ruined last night, and he looked at Imogene, still attired in the traveling dress she had donned last night, in some surprise. "You're up early!"

"I didn't go to bed last night," she admitted. "I was worried about you."

Her husband's chest expanded. "No need. Van Ryker's seconds haven't been about, have they?"

Imogene shook her head.

"The *Sea Rover* has sailed," put in Vrouw Berghem importantly, setting a place for Verhulst. "And good riddance to it!" She was about to add, *A man who'd duel with a boy!* but thought better of it.

" 'Sailed'?" Verhulst looked astonished. "Did you say she'd *sailed?*"

"Late last night," said Imogene. "With the tide."

"Well!" Verhulst's velvet doublet expanded still further. "So he was afraid of me, the damned pirate!" He chuckled, his opinion of his skill as a swordsman going up several notches.

Imogene looked quickly down at her plate. She was silent as Verhulst consumed his Indian porridge. Whatever van Ryker's reason for leaving so abruptly, she knew it was not fear. . . .

She could not know that after the tall captain and his buccaneers had helped the men of New Amsterdam subdue the rapidly spreading fire, he had looked at himself and his motives in the afterglow of the blaze—and been chagrined at what he saw.

He now faced squarely the unpleasant truth: He was trying to drag with him to the Caribbean an unwilling woman—a woman who had flirted with him lightly on the high seas, it was true, but there he was a man to be reckoned with, which gave him, he supposed, a certain romantic allure that might attract a lovely woman. Here on dry land this same woman clearly preferred another man, a man both wealthy and titled who could give her a safe, secure life—her husband. *Had she not blithely announced to all the world that she would soon be bearing Verhulst's child? Had she not told him to his face that she loved her husband?* The words had cut van Ryker to the heart.

Van Ryker stamped out the sparks from a still-smoldering ember and cursed himself for a fool. He had forgotten what he was—a buccaneer, a man with a price on his head, a man with a short life expectancy. Who could blame a woman for not choosing such a man? And he had gone chasing after her like some enamored schoolboy. . . . How she must be laughing at him!

The leathern buckets were being collected now, the livestock—happily unscorched—herded away from the vicinity of the ruined stable. Tired men were stumbling back to home and vrouwen. Van Rappard was nowhere in sight—*he* of course had good reason to hurry back: Imogene was waiting for him.

The captain glared about him. In his exasperation, he had an urge to throttle someone.

"Do we go back for the lady?" Barnaby's voice at his elbow.

"No, we do not," was the curt answer.

"But I thought ye said—"

The captain swung around, presenting a smoke-blackened visage. So wicked was his countenance, so burning his eyes, that his ship's master fell back in alarm.

"We're leaving!" roared van Ryker. "Pass the word that anyone not aboard within the hour will be left behind!"

Barnaby sprang to carry out that command but he gave his captain's broad departing back a puzzled glance. For himself he was glad enough to leave New Amsterdam, for the Widow

Poltzer was too hot on his heels for comfort and he'd no wish to marry her daughter—or anyone else for that matter. But the captain . . . he'd never seen him so taken by a woman. Barnaby sighed. It was as well they were leaving. If the captain had carried out his stated plan to seize the patroon's wife and make off with her, the port of New Amsterdam would be closed to him—and to a buccaneer that was important, for the Dutch burghers paid a high price for goods.

Van Ryker strode away from the partly burned stable, now drenched and smoking. Scowling, he headed for his big seaworthy ship in the harbor. Let the Dutch patroon make what capital he could over the fact that van Ryker had evaded a duel with him. Doubtless, he told himself sardonically, Verhulst would tell Imogene her buccaneer was a coward. Somehow he doubted that she would believe him. She might even believe the truth— that he had made her a parting gift of her husband's life. And if any other man dared to suggest he had run away from an encounter—here van Ryker's bold countenance became an implacable mask of menace—he would carve the truth on his impudent body with his sword!

Now brisk and businesslike, van Ryker gave curt orders to round up any stragglers among his men, to drag from the taverns any who were drunk. Thank God they'd finished their provisioning this day, for with the mood that was on him he'd no mind to miss the tide.

And with that tide the *Sea Rover* left New Amsterdam behind her and took to the sea lanes, prowling far southward to harry the Spanish Main. Word drifted back north of his exploits, but the Dutch Coast of New Netherland saw him not.

But when he sailed van Ryker carried with him a token to remind him of Imogene—the sheer white whisk she had "accidentally'' lost on the way to his ship that first night. It had been fished from the water and carried to him and carefully washed and dried, and now it lay among his shirts, a sweet reminder of what might have been.

He would find other ports to sell his illicit goods, he told himself—Tortuga had a vast waterfront market where everything from salt to slaves were sold. And if he prowled north again to New Amsterdam, he would finish his business with the Dutch burghers quickly and sail away again—he would hold himself back, he would resist the urge to sail upriver to Wey Gat and gaze again upon the winsome wench who had stolen his heart.

None of this Imogene knew, but her pensive thoughts were on van Ryker as the Palisades towered by.

She started and tried to erase any sadness from her face as behind her Verhulst spoke. He had come up behind her so silently that she had not heard him. Now at his voice her body swung around toward him with a pliant gesture of submission, telling him mutely how grateful, how very grateful she was for his understanding and support.

But Verhulst was not looking at her. His gaze was concentrated on the river's eastern bank with its vivid splashes of red and gold and crimson. ''Fall is late this year, Imogene. We should have lost the leaves long before this.''

''I am glad summer has hung on,'' she told him gravely. ''The colors are lovely—much more brilliant than they are in England.''

Verhulst gave her a look of proud approval. He wanted his English bride to love this land—as he did. ''Are you warm enough?'' he asked solicitously, reaching out a black velvet arm to touch the azure satin ribands at her elbow. ''That broadcloth dress is thin for a breeze as stiff as this."

"I wore it because you admired it," she smiled, touched by his obvious concern for her.

"And so I do—it matches your eyes."

"Then I shall keep on wearing it all the way to Wey Gat," Imogene laughed, "and so keep your favor!"

"My favor you have already," he said, suddenly grave. His voice grew husky, humble. "I was proud of you at the Governor's Ball, Imogene."

She thought he might have said more, but big Schroon, the *Danskammer*'s *schipper*, called out suddenly and pointed to something on the western bank. From Schroon's first hearty *"Welkom aan boord"* she had liked the big, smiling Dutchman. Now as Verhulst hurried over to big Schroon's side, Imogene's gaze followed those spatulate pointing fingers. On the west bank, just moving into the cover of the trees, was a party of buckskinned Indians, moving silently, single file. Perhaps they were on one of their hunts, in which whole tribes participated— Verhulst had told her about these autumn hunts—before the winter cold closed in.

But Imogene's attention soon left the spot where the Indians had melted into the forest. She went back to studying her husband's back thoughtfully. He presented a slim, richly clad figure as he talked earnestly to the huge *schipper*, whose great bulk looked sloppy in his wide homespun trousers and coarse loose shirt. Behind those dark eyes, who could know what Verhulst was thinking? And yet, he had been so considerate of her, so anxious after her welfare and comfort ever since that reckless moment when she had boldly announced her pregnancy to strike the malicious smile from Rychie ten Haer's sneering face.

He is pleased about it, she told herself firmly. *Else why mention how proud of her he had been at the Governor's Ball? And yet,* a little voice tugged at her, *he has not spoken of the baby directly, nor asked me how I came by it. Does he not wonder who my lover was? Is it conceivable that he just accepts it and does not care. . . . I had expected him to speak of it when we came home after the fire—but he said nothing, just went to bed. Of course, then he was expecting to duel with van Ryker in the morning. Still, in all the time that we visited Breukelen and toured the fort and all the other sights New Amsterdam had to offer, he has not spoken of it. I kept thinking he would bring the subject up, that he was waiting for a propitious time, but he has not. . . .*

Imogene told herself she must count herself lucky, but she could not help being puzzled by Verhulst's bland protective behavior. She toyed with the idea of bringing the subject up herself but some deep female instinct for self-preservation bade her to accept his indulgence and let the subject alone until he himself saw fit to bring it up. She had come to see in Verhulst's personality a certain instability. Sometimes he laughed too loudly, or became too excited, or too depressed. She thought he was too intense.

It was enough, she told herself, that he accepted the baby's coming—more than she had hoped, that he should welcome it. Elise was still frightened, but Elise would come to realize that in marrying Verhulst she had chosen a remarkable man, a man of rare understanding and patience. Strange . . . Imogene had always felt herself to be a good judge of men, and she had not perceived in Verhulst this kind of rare understanding.

Then if her husband was such a gem of understanding, she asked herself bluntly, *why could she not forget the lean buccaneer who had warned her he would abduct her and then sailed blithely away?* Memories of van Ryker tormented her. She saw his smile sparkling upon the water, his sardonic face looked out at her through the trees, his voice was borne to her upon the wind. . . . Perhaps if Verhulst found her more physically desirable, she told herself angrily—for what else could it be, this neglect of his young wife when he was in such apparent radiant health? She had expected a husband, not a guardian. And not in all this time had he taken her in his arms. . . .

Of course, Verhulst's look of health could be deceptive. Did not the eyes of a consumptive sparkle brilliantly, the cheeks of a consumptive glow with color? She paused and surveyed her husband carefully, now standing beside Schroon at the tiller. His cheeks were not too flushed, but then he had a sallow complexion. Nor were his dark eyes unduly bright.

Why—she had been a fool not to think of it before now! The reason for Verhulst's neglect of his marriage bed had been a simple and kindly intentioned one: He had noticed her pregnancy before she had; aboard ship, while his ''pains'' still plagued him and kept him away from her bed, he had learned of her morning sickness, heard her retching in the next room. If that were true, then he must be mad about children, though he had certainly never shown any interest in them either in Holland or America.

But as she studied her husband across the *Danskammer*'s swaying deck, she could see that all was right in his world. The rightness was in his face when he looked at her, in the approval in his voice when he spoke to her.

Imogene frowned and began walking restlessly along the deck. She could get her exercise that way, for the *Danskammer* was a large sloop, broad of beam, heavy of planking, and some seventy-five feet long. The sloop could hold some hundred tons and although she moved upriver with her hold bulging, there was still plenty of room to walk around the bales and boxes lashed down upon the deck. The *Danskammer*'s mast was placed well forward and her large mainsail and small jib flapped overhead. There were two cabins on the quarterdeck: one occupied by Verhulst and big Schroon, the other by herself and Elise. The three-man crew, all cheerful and speaking voluble Dutch, slept on deck beneath the stars—or beneath spread canvas when the weather was foul.

They were making slow headway because the wind slanted down upon them off the Palisades, even though the flood tide was carrying them inexorably north.

Upriver they traveled and Imogene grew used to the sturdy Dutch crew who manned the *Danskammer* and to the huge blond jovial *schipper*. Schroon spoke no English but his eyes twinkled appreciatively when she passed and he would take his long clay pipe from his mouth—for Schroon was passionately fond of *tabac*—and his big moon face would split into a smile, showing a set of big tobacco-stained teeth. He would bob his shock of yellow hair at her and whistle a merry tune as she walked away. Imogene liked Schroon better than his crew, for he was always good-natured and smiling, while they were sometimes surly—particularly after the patroon had said something sharp to them.

"I wonder what the house will be like," wondered Elise uneasily when Verhulst told them they would be arriving within the hour.

"Large," said Imogene dryly. "And filled with fine things—or at least about to be. For it seems to me that Verhulst has brought back half of Europe with him—and most of it is lashed onto this deck!" She nodded at the narrow walkway between boxes and barrels that was all that was left of the deck at one point.

But Elise had voiced something that had been plaguing her

as well and Imogene was silent as the sloop slid to its mooring at the long wooden pier that reached like a tongue out into the water.

In New Amsterdam Imogene had grown accustomed to seeing the clusters of narrow Dutch rowhouses, and in its environs the squat picturesque Dutch farmhouses. She had half expected that the great array of goods piled upon the sloop would not fit into the house at all.

Now she gazed upward in astonishment, for she was unprepared for the fortress that met her eyes. No wonder Vrouw Berghem had thought it might be defended! A lofty pile of stone, the mansion of Wey Gat rose austerely atop the bluff on the river's eastern bank. Verhulst had a right to be proud of his "castle"! All that they had brought with them could fit into a corner of it, Imogene decided, and be lost. On both sides of the water's edge was considerably undergrowth but near the pier it was clean-cut and afforded a fine view of sweeping lawns that sloped up to the frowning stone mansion.

From somewhere came the sound of hammering and she could see men and horses urging along a wagonload of stone . . . so this vast edifice was not completed yet. And then from somewhere behind the house came the baying of dogs and she remembered what Vrouw Berghem had told her about the savage pack of man-hunting dogs Verhulst maintained, and shivered.

"Welcome to Wey Gat!" Pride rang in Verhulst's voice as he handed her down with a flourish onto the wooden pier.

"It's—beautiful," said Imogene inadequately, looking up at the tall Gothic windows that sloped to a point at the top. She tried to count its many chimneys, but the intervening branches of the tall spreading trees made that difficult. "It's so much larger and finer than I had expected."

Verhulst's black velvet chest expanded and the heavy gold

chain he wore around his neck swung and sparkled in the light—sparkled with a knowing twinkle, like the small panes of Wey Gat's tall windows. " 'Tis the finest on the river," he said airily.

"Come along, Elise." Imogene picked up her skirts on one side so that she could walk the faster along the wooden planking of the pier. "Leave the luggage, it can be brought in later. We must come and view our new home."

Verhulst raised his eyebrows at this familiarity with a servant but Elise stepped forward gratefully and accompanied Imogene up the broad lawns, through the heavy oaken front doors. But just as Imogene had been struck into silence before the majesty of the looming Palisades, so Elise was struck dumb by the cold, echoing rooms through which they wandered one by one. If Verhulst had intended to build himself a castle on Henry Hudson's river, he had certainly managed to do so, for Wey Gat's steep pointed roofs and tall chimneys gave it the look of a castle against the red glow of sunset, but he had created a building that seemed dead, into which no life had been breathed. As Imogene accompanied Verhulst through barren rooms and down long corridors, murmuring politely, "It's lovely," as he showed her through the house that was to be her home, Elise padded after them jerking her head from right to left with staring eyes.

"It's a terrible place," she told Imogene shakily, when they were alone at last in the big bedroom Verhulst had told her adjoined his own, and she was helping Imogene change to a fragile yellow silk dress for supper. "And that big chair in the patroon's office looked like a *throne*."

"Nonsense." Imogene shrugged the yellow silk over her shoulders and let Elise pat the dress down around her hips. "The house is just new and only partly furnished—that's what gives it that unlived-in look. And you heard Verhulst say that big chair is where he sits to transact business with his tenants—I suppose he wants to impress them.'' She frowned suddenly. She would have preferred a man who did not gain his prestige from lounging about in a thronelike chair while the men he dealt with fidgeted hat-in-hand on wooden benches. She tried to imagine van Ryker in a similar situation and failed—*he* would be striding about, shaking this one's hand, clapping that one on the shoulder, greeting another heartily. And they would follow him because they respected him, man to man—not because they were browbeaten by a throne-backed chair and a house that had brought grandeur to the wilderness, not because they were intimidated by a pack of vicious dogs!

She shook her head to clear it. She was being unfair to Verhulst. Anyway, *this* was the life she had chosen and van Ryker cared nothing for her—he had proved that by sailing away. She looked about her at the big square bedroom with its plain walls and heavy square-built oaken furniture, doubtless fashioned right here in the colony.

"This room will look different when the blue Chinese rug is laid and these barren walls covered with some of that wallpaper from France,'' she told Elise.

"Those hunting scenes? I'd think ye'd not like to wake up and see a stag's belly ripped open and bleeding!''

Imogene gave a small shudder. She had no love for blood sports. "Not the hunting scenes,'' she replied. "They are for the great hall and the dining room.'' *Where I will cover up that dying stag with a sideboard or a cupboard*, she promised herself. "But wait till these windows are draped with lawn curtains and caught back with blue ribands. Wait till the big *armoire* Verhulst bought in Holland is brought in to hold my gowns, and wait till I change the canopy on that cumbersome bed!'' She indicated the heavy hangings of moldering green that gave the big carved four-poster a gloomy look. ''Blue-figured calico should do nicely!''

'' 'Twill not be fine enough to suit his patroonship,'' sniffed Elise. ''He'll insist on heavy damask! Richer!''

Imogene laughed. ''This whole house will change its character once I start redecorating it,'' she boasted.

Elise rolled her eyes and quickly lit a candle against the deepening dusk. '' 'Tis not houselike at all,'' she complained. ''And listen to those dogs. Do they bay all night?''

''Nonsense.''

But as Imogene trailed down the echoing stairway where the candles in the brass chandelier cast long wavering shadows, she felt as Elise did, that this was not really a home at all, but a stage setting for some as yet unplayed drama. The feeling was very real and persisted through dinner and beyond.

That night the old terrifying dream of her childhood returned to her and Imogene woke panting from a mad run across the sand toward a gray glimmer on which skimmed a boat with a big square sail.

Something clutched her and she woke in terror. Elise was shaking her.

''There, there,'' Elise soothed. ''Ye cried out in your sleep. I had to wake ye before ye roused the house.''

Imogene was in a cold sweat. She clutched at Elise. ''There has always been a noise in my dream,'' she told Elise hoarsely. ''Something—some sound coming closer, closer—but I never knew what it was. Tonight I heard it clearly. It was the baying of dogs.''

''Ye heard the dogs baying in the kennels behind the house,'' said Elise sensibly, but some of Imogene's terror was communicated to her and she felt little fingers of fear play along her spine. "They're making a terrible noise. A fox must have passed by, or a rabbit. Hear them now?"

The baying and howling outside had indeed reached a crescendo.

"Of course," said Imogene uncertainly. "That must have been it." She started as Verhulst burst through the door.

"I heard you scream! Imogene, are you all right?"

"Yes." Imogene ran shaky fingers through her golden hair. She looked very fetching, sitting up in the big bed with her hair rumpled and the loosened top of her night rail spilling in soft lawn folds down over one white shoulder.

" 'Twas a nightmare," supplied Elise. "My lady has them sometimes. The dogs disturbed her."

"The dogs are unruly sometimes, but Groot has them well under control. I will speak to him tomorrow about the noise."

"No, no," sighed Imogene, pulling up her night rail to cover her bare shoulder. "It's just that the house is strange to me and that howling seemed to merge with my dream."

"Oh—well, then . . ." Verhulst stood undecided in the doorway, still holding the quill pen he had been using on his account books when the noise from upstairs had disturbed him. "I'll go back to my books, if you're all right."

Imogene nodded wanly. The nightmare always left her pale and shaken. It left a pall over her, like a premonition of doom. "I'll be fine," she promised.

Verhulst closed the door and departed. They could hear his footsteps echoing down the empty hall.

Elise gave Imogene's shoulder an encouraging pat and scurried back to the cubbyhole she occupied off Imogene's room. She closed the door in case the patroon should choose to exercise his marital rights, but she might as well have stayed.

Imogene lay awake staring out of the tall pointy windows until the dawn's pale light filtered through them. Then she fell into a heavy sleep and stayed asleep until Elise shook her and told her it was time for breakfast.

Just as in New Amsterdam and on the high seas, Verhulst van Rappard had avoided any nocturnal contact with his lady.

She faced him at breakfast and wondered—letting her blue eyes drop before his curious gaze—if this was to be the pattern of their existence together: to eat together, chat together, travel together—but to sleep alone. Of course it was decent of him to let her alone now that she was pregnant but . . . she remembered how it had been on shipboard when he had not known about that, and asked herself silently if this was the way it was going to be for the rest of their lives? In Stephen's arms she had learned what love could be like, in van Ryker's arms she had known what it was to hunger for passion, and now, facing her husband across the long shining board laden with heavy silver, she wondered if she could stand it. Could she endure a whole lifetime of never being held in a man's arms?

"Do you work late on your books many nights?" she asked abruptly.

He avoided her gaze. "Yes. Many nights."

"And the noise the dogs make does not bother you?"

"No, I am used to them."

Imogene leaned forward. "Verhulst," she asked desperately, "why do you need the dogs?"

"To hunt men," he answered brutally, his gaze shining on her suddenly fierce. "This is a raw new land, Imogene, and these are rough times. This is how I keep the peace at Wey Gat." He studied her mutinous face. "Last night there were Indians prowling about. The dogs gave us notice of their presence."

"And did you—hunt them?"

"There was no need, they backed off."

"And if they come again?"

"Then we will deal with them as need be."

Imogene forced herself to remember that Verhulst had reason for his actions—his parents had been scalped by prowling Indians.

"You will grow used to the life here," Verhulst promised in a kinder voice.

Imogene hoped he was right. But she doubted if she ever would.

The Bahamas
CHAPTER 16

Before leaving Holland, Imogene had written Bess Deveen a terse note, telling her of her impending marriage and asking her to inform Lord Elston. *It will come better from you, Bess, for he has always liked you and he is sure to disapprove of what he would call a "hasty marriage."*

Now at Wey Gat, she received an answer.

You may not have heard because they wrote to you in Amsterdam and I doubt you were there to receive the letter, Bess wrote, *but your guardian died after a short illness. The servants had presumed him better, for he had gotten up that morning and eaten a good breakfast, but later they found him face down among his books and could not revive him. I think it was the way he would have liked to go, Imogene, there among the things he treasured. He never knew you were married because he died the very day I went over to see him, and I arrived to find the whole place in disarray. At least, you need not blame yourself for having worried him—he did not know of it.*

Ah, but I worried him often enough, Imogene thought sadly. It was hard to realize Lord Elston was gone; he had been so crochety, so alive. She had clashed with him frequently, for they both had violent natures, but now her lip trembled and she fought back tears, for deep in her heart she had been truly fond of the old man. She scarcely took in Bess's words of heartfelt sympathy.

With blurred vision, she continued reading Bess's letter:

My uncle in Barbados has arranged a marriage for me. (Here Imogene started in surprise. Bess—married?) *He says my betrothed is handsome and young and wealthy and has a large plantation on Barbados that adjoins his own. I care not for his wealth, Imogene, but I am uneasy to travel so far to meet an unknown suitor. Perhaps he will not care for me, or I for him—although my uncle says he is greatly in need of a wife. My uncle is sending me a picture of him, but I doubt it will reach me before I embark, for I am packing now. My brothers are overjoyed to be rid of me, for unless I marry, I will end up a burden on them.* Imogene's lips tightened. How could gentle Bess be a burden on anyone? *So I embark on Thursday next and when you hear from me again I will doubtless be a married woman trying to adjust to life on a strange plantation. I suppose I could have said no, that I preferred to wait until some young man in the Scillies took my fancy, but now that Stephen is gone, it does not matter to me.*

Imogene stared down at the letter. *Now that Stephen is gone.* . . . It was the first inkling she had had that Bess, too, was in love with Stephen. Ah, that explained so many things— sweet, self-sacrificing Bess, who had contrived to help them meet clandestinely—and all the time her heart must have been breaking. Why, she must have been blind not to see it! Imogene dashed the tears from her lashes and hoped, fervently and with all her heart, that Bess would be happy in Barbados, and that this stranger she was to marry would value her as she should be valued.

But the letter had brought changes to her life, to her future, for Lord Elston and Bess Duveen were her only real tie to the Scillies. Even should the cloud that hung over her name be cleared, she now had no place in the Scillies to return to. Her guardian was gone and his heirs would have no use for her—they had shown scorn for her many times. And now that Bess—her only true friend—had departed England for Barbados, Imogene would hardly find herself welcomed at Ennor Castle by a family whose son she had jilted!

Imogene put the letter in her jewel chest and closed the lid with gentle fingers. It seemed to her a voice from the past. England and its Scilly Isles were already receding in her memory. Even Stephen seemed to fade in the afterglow.

Her future was here—at Wey Gat with a strange, cold husband who was remarkably gentle with her and with no one else, and with her unborn child who would, she promised herself fervently, grow up to be everything that she was not— virtuous, good.

And suddenly, for no reason, her thoughts strayed to the dark buccaneer captain, van Ryker. She stared out the window at the sparkling river flowing by. His quick smile had flashed at her like sunlight on water—and how wickedly dangerous his saturnine face had looked in the moonlight aboard the *Sea Rover* and again at the Governor's Ball when he had threatened to take her away with him! She wondered, with a treacherous leap of her heart, what her life would have been like if she had smiled instead of frowned, if she had not flung at him the lie that she loved Verhulst. . . . What would it have been like to sail away with him, a buccaneer's woman, into the sunlit seas?

She wrenched herself from the thought. Van Ryker had long forgotten her, she told herself firmly. Even now he was brawling in some dark hole of a tavern in the buccaneer stronghold of Tortuga, one sinewy arm around the waist of some captured but willing Spanish wench and the other holding aloft a glass to toast his lady's ivory bosom.

Imogene did not do van Ryker justice. He had not forgotten the golden English girl—although God knew he had tried. Time had raced by for him, and van Ryker, sweating on the *Sea Rover*'s rolling deck in the bright West Indian sunlight as his ship pursued some ill-starred galleon, or begrimed by black powder from the fight as his guns spat a broadside and the grappling irons were thrown over and his lean form swung across the railing onto a Spanish deck, told himself as firmly as Imogene did now, that he had forgotten the patroon's winsome English bride who had beguiled him.

Imogene would have been wickedly pleased, deep in her feminine heart, that van Ryker had not forgotten her. But she would have been stunned had she witnessed one of his encounters.

Once in the Bahamas, after a wild night of carousing on shore, van Ryker brought one of his hard-drinking newfound friends—a drifter new to the Caribbean that he hoped to persuade to sign on with him—back to his great cabin to show him the collection of small arms he'd captured from a Spanish caravel that had roved too close to the *Sea Rover*'s formidable guns. Having shown his newfound friend the braces of dueling pistols and other arms, he decided to take him back ashore where they could rejoin the drinking brawl they'd left at the tavern. But first a clean shirt, for some careless tavern maid had spilled rum upon his sleeve and van Ryker was always meticulous about his linens.

As he opened a chest and lifted out a clean ruffled shirt, he accidentally pulled out along with it Imogene's lost whisk. Feather-light and white as drifting snow, it fluttered to the floor.

"I see you keep souvenirs," laughed his long-legged friend as van Ryker's scooped up the whisk. He pushed back the copper hair that was forever falling into his eyes. "I, too, had a whisk once—from a girl who kept losing hers."

Van Ryker, replacing the whisk in his chest, turned to look at him sharply and then checked himself. No, of course it could not have been the same girl. Nevertheless he changed his mind about leaving the ship and poured his guest another glass of wine. "What did you say your name was?" he asked. "I did not catch it at the tavern."

"Linnington," was the careless reply, for what did his real name matter here? "Stephen Linnington. Late of York, late of Devon, late of half the world." He laughed again, and his face took on a rakish expression. "They think me dead in England, for this is the story I put out when the law was near catching up with me." He could admit that here in the *Sea Rover*'s great cabin, for this was a buccaneer captain to whom he was speaking; it might even gain him something in the esteem of those cold gray eyes that had rested on him in sudden speculation when he spoke of the whisk. "I suppose ye've more than one price on your head, Captain van Ryker?" His tone was curious.

Van Ryker's wry laugh rang out. "If ye're thinking of selling me, Linnington, the price is highest in Spain. The Spanish dons would pay a fortune in gold for me."

"Dead or alive?" wondered Stephen innocently.

Van Ryker leaned back so that his broad shoulders rested against the back of his carved oaken chair. He hooked one long leg over a chair arm, let the wide-topped boot swing negligently. His long body lounged at ease. "Either, I imagine. But—" the gray eyes shot a very level look at the smiling Englishman before him—" 'Tis not apt to become a popular sport, this taking of my body and slipping it back to Spain."

"No, I imagine not," murmured Stephen, gauging the length of sinewy arm and the look of force in the man before him. "Ye've my word on it, van Ryker. I've no intention of trying it."

"Several have." The gray eyes went murky. "But not for Spain's reward—remember, we'd all be heretics there and trussed up ready for the fires of the Inquisition."

"So there's another reward on your head as well?" laughed Stephen.

Van Ryker looked at his wine with distaste as if it had gone suddenly sour. He checked himself before that knowing green glance, for he had almost said, "England does not love her wayward sons," when all the world knew he claimed to be a Dutchman. Instead he said, "Last year I raided Maracaibo and several other towns along the Spanish Main. England seeks to appease Spain by putting a price on my head."

" 'Tis an unfair world," agreed Stephen jauntily, who'd have had a price on his head, too, in England if they had not thought him dead. "There are those of us who can never go home. But at least you have Holland."

"Yes, I'm still welcome in Holland and the Dutch colonies."

That admission did not make the captain as merry as it should have, Stephen Linnington noted. There was more to this man than met the eye, he thought. It would be interesting to know what thoughts just then were going through the captain's dark head.

For van Ryker's mind was not really on what he was saying as he toyed with his glass, staring into its gleaming golden depths. He was thinking of the girl with the whisk, and his sudden black frown came from the fact that he was at the moment cursing himself for not having seized her from the Governor's Ball in New Amsterdam, willing or not, and borne her away with him no matter how many guns spat at them from the fort!

His attention came back to his guest and he grew thoughtful. This handsome green-eyed Englishman was such a man as might attract a woman like Imogene. No, it was too great a coincidence. Van Ryker downed his wine and dismissed it, went back to sounding out the Englishman. He seemed to be a man of parts, he knew ships, and there was a serviceable look to the blade he carried. Van Ryker liked that.

Now he poured more wine and propped up his long legs and listened to Linnington's droll story of running away from two wives—and divorced from neither. It was a common enough story in England these days, van Ryker reminded himself. Men left for the colonies and found for themselves there new wives from the plentiful supply of widows the hardships and marauding Indians produced—and forgot to divorce the wives they'd left behind in England. Or, like Stephen, a man might marry a wench in Lincoln and another in York. Or Winchester or London. It was the turbulence of the times that produced these things.

He offered Linnington more wine, noting with approval that the fellow seemed able to hold his liquor and match him glass for glass, something few men could boast of. "Of the two, I preferred the sound of the first one—the highwayman's sister," he commented. "Was she a beauty?"

"Aye." Stephen's green eyes kindled as he held out his glass to be refilled. "The comeliest lass I ever knew—save one.'' He was thinking of Imogene and was lost for a moment in the memory of her loveliness. For a stabbing moment he wished he'd never left her. He shook his head to clear it. Had he stayed they'd both have hanged—he'd done her a favor by leaving!

''An English beauty. . . .'' van Ryker sighed.

Stephen shrugged. ''Kate was an English beauty all right, but she looked to have Spanish blood, perhaps gypsy blood. She had wild black hair that reached to her knees, and sparkling black eyes and red lips, and hips that swayed when she walked. She could handle a pistol as good as a man, Kate could. She'd take a chance on anything, Kate would. She always insisted she looked like her brother, Gentleman Johnnie, but I never could see it.''

''I knew a Spanish girl once who looked like that. Wore big loops of gold in her ears. Had a voice like a purring kitten and a nasty way with a knife. She gave me a scar on the arm I've got yet before she realized I meant her no harm.''

''One of your captives?''

''Aye. I returned her to Cuba.''

Stephen Linnington looked surprised. ''I'd have thought—''

''That being a buccaneer I'd keep such a lustrous captive to warm my bed? Well, a pirate might, but we buccaneers live by a code. We return all the Spanish ladies we capture to Cuba or some other Spanish shore—minus their jewels of course. Although in this case—'' the tall buccaneer smiled wryly—''the lady returned to Cuba with all of her jewels and a few more I gave her.''

''I'm surprised she wanted to return.''

''She didn't, but a great marriage awaited her there. I'd no desire to wreck her life—or marry her, either, which was what she wanted.''

"Ye're not married then?"

Van Ryker shook his dark head. " 'Tis a pleasure I've managed to miss."

"Never even came close?"

"Once." He thought regretfully of Imogene. What a wife she'd have made him! What a wife she was making van Rappard at this moment no doubt—he envied the young patroon.

Stephen, who had given little thought to buccaneer "codes," became thoughtful. "And if I should sign on to a ship such as yours?" he wondered. "What are the conditions? Not that I can sign up for *this* voyage," he added hastily, "for I've a deal that carries me to Barbados."

"Oh?"

"I've met a planter in Barbados who's in need of a factor," explained Stephen. "He's offered me the post at a handsome salary." His rakish face split into a grin. "I thought I'd try my hand at something legal for a change!"

So Linnington was not up for grabs by the buccaneer captains. . . . A pity. Ah, well, there were other likely lads, good with a sword, eager to sign on such a ship as the *Sea Rover*.

"If you signed up with me, you'd sign articles," van Ryker told him, "the same as for any other ship. Only these would be a bit different from those you're used to, I expect. We buccaneers award extra money for injury, we send a dead man's share to his wife or his relatives—in short, we care for our own."

" 'Tis a bit different from, say, His Majesty's Navy!" said Stephen in surprise.

Van Ryker nodded and his gray eyes looked past the copper-haired Englishman into some distant future. "Some day we'll own the West Indies," he said quietly. "It will be our gift to

303

England—courtesy of the buccaneers.''

Stephen looked up sharply from his drink. '' 'To England'? And you a Dutchman?''

He was returned a hard challenging glance. ''To England.'' Suddenly van Ryker lifted his glass and there was a deep resonance and pride in the way he gave the toast. ''To England.''

And Stephen Linnington, listening spellbound, knew in his heart at that moment that he was talking to a counterfeit Dutchman, that this man was an Englishman, as English as Dover's white cliffs or the broad River Thames or London Bridge. He made no comment, for that hard gray look warned him not to, but somehow he believed it all would happen, that Captain van Ryker's dream would come true, that this lean buccaneer and men like him would someday break the power of Spain and deliver these islands to the English.

''Whenever ye've a mind to sign on, we'll find a place for ye on the *Sea Rover*,'' van Ryker told him, for he liked Linnington.

''Perhaps your next voyage,'' suggested Stephen gracefully. *Although not if Barbados works out,* he was thinking.

They were silent for a while and Stephen would have been floored to know that the captain's morose thoughts had been on Imogene, but there was no more talk of a whisk or of a girl who was always losing hers.

And when next Captain van Ryker pulled out the little whisk along with a clean shirt, he took care to replace it carefully. It lay there nestled among his freshly laundered shirts—always in the way yet never discarded. Sometimes he would start to push it away impatiently and then the soft touch of it would remind him of *her,* and instead of throwing it away or tossing it into some corner, he would pick it up caressingly. It had lain in seawater, it had been washed, yet to him as he fingered it, it brought back the enchanting indefinable scent of a woman. Of one particular woman, whose smile still lingered in his heart, whose lips—soft beneath his own—had promised everything—and who had told him coldly in New Amsterdam that she loved another man, was indeed bearing his child. Van Ryker would frown, but he would pause and touch the delicate white whisk lingeringly—and then push it away from him with a rueful laugh.

Even buccaneers dream.

And so, though he laughed at himself for doing so, he kept the whisk.

Wey Gat, New Netherland, 1657

CHAPTER 17

Life at Wey Gat swiftly settled into a kind of routine. Verhulst scrupulously ate dinner with Imogene—and she did not see him again until morning when he ate breakfast with her—if she was up. His day was spent out supervising his men on the work of completing the vast unfinished wings of the house, or visiting the tenants on the *bouweries,* or farms, that made up his vast estate. Once or twice he took her with him and she warmed to the sight of curtsying Dutch vrouwen in their simple home-spun aprons and caps and their smock-clad wide-breeched spouses, solemnly offering the patroon and his lady beer or cider and little cakes. Imogene remarked to Verhulst her surprise that they were not wearing wooden shoes, of which she had seen so many in Holland.

"That is because Indian moccasins are so cheap," Verhulst told her. "My people—" he always called his tenants his "people" although Imogene, now that she knew him better, always half-humorously expected him to call them his "subjects" because here at Wey Gat he was almost a king—"My people trade surplus farm produce to the Indians for moccasins."

"I should like to have a pair. They look so comfortable."

"*You*—" his voice sharpened—"will wear *shoes*, as befits your station. Let the servants wear moccasins."

"Vrouw Berghem told me she often goes barefoot as she works about the house," said Imogene irrepressibly.

Verhulst gave her a quelling look. "Vrouw Berghem is not the wife of a patroon."

Imogene reminded herself that Verhulst had been generous, kindly, about the one *big* thing—the baby's coming. The least she could do was to please him in small ways.

She wore shoes.

Life on a great patroonship was a constant source of amazement to Imogene. There was, to her surprise, a surplus of dairy products and she was told that New Netherland was the only colony in America where butter was cheap, for the hardworking Dutch had brought over their dairy animals with remarkable care and they had not died on shipboard as was the fate of so much livestock. It seemed to her that the hard work on the outlying *bouweries* never ended. Some of the newer tenants lived in hastily constructed "cellar houses," some seven feet deep, floored with planking, lined with wood and bark and roofed over with planking and sod. Next year, Verhulst told her carelessly, they would build proper farmhouses of thick stone held together with a mortar of ground oyster shells.

Imogene's heart went out to these women of the *bouweries*, who with their men had emigrated from many other European countries besides Holland—there were Norwegian and Swiss and German, but on this patroonship no Englishmen. She was disappointed in that, for she would have enjoyed talking to her own countrymen in her native tongue. And she was indignant when she learned the terms of their tenancy—five hundred guilders a year, a tenth of their produce, repair the buildings, keep up the roads, three days' service to the patroon with horse and wagon—it went on and on. And all for the price of their passage to this New World and the use of land they could never own. Imogene thought it all vastly unfair, but when she spoke up in defense of the hard-working tenants, Verhulst curtly silenced her. "Leave these things to me," he said coldly—and in the main, Imogene did.

But there were moments. . . .

Once, she rode back beside Verhulst, silent and brooding, after one of their rare visits together to a *bouwerie*. As they dismounted, leaving their horses in the care of grooms, and entered their own broad echoing hallway, it came to her sickeningly—like a slap in the face—the difference between her elegant life in the great house and the lives of those hard-working women in the *bouweries*.

The difference was love.

That Helga, whose warm hearth she had so recently left, worked perhaps fourteen hours a day, sometimes in the fields beside her Sven—but she sang over her work as she prepared the oatcakes and the beer she had been so proud to serve the patroon and his lady. Helga was happy—and her broad, smiling face showed it.

Imogene shook out her heavy taffeta skirts and let Elise take her fur-lined velvet cloak from her—and thought wistfully of Helga's warm bare living room with its crude furniture, of the big thick-furred tabby cat stretched out purring on the rude hearth, of the two rollicking dogs who had dashed up playfully to bark at the horses of the newcomers. Verhulst did not care for pets. The barn cats were left in the barn to forage—and fed surreptitiously by the kitchen help; they justified their existence by keeping the rat and mouse population down. Of all the vast kennel of dogs Verhulst kept, not one was a pet. One lonely day Imogene had wandered out to the kennels and been met by a shocked Groot. When she had tried to pet one of the friendlier-looking dogs, the kennelmaster had seized her arm and hoarsely warned her off. From his earnestness and volubility—all in incomprehensible gutteral Dutch—she gathered that the dog might have torn her arm off. She had kept her distance from the pack ever since, although sometimes at night their howling kept her awake.

Imogene stood in her front hall and looked around her sadly at the opulence of hand-carved wainscoating and imported French wallpaper and elaborate gilt-framed paintings. She had a whole house full of elegant carpets and gleaming silver and crystal, presses and trunks and a large *armoire* filled with clothes any woman would envy.

And yet at that moment she would gladly have exchanged it all for Helga's worn moccasins and hard, unrelenting life—if only she could have matched in her heart the glow she had seen in Helga's blue eyes when her Sven came striding home from the fields.

"Are you just going to stand there? Aren't you coming upstairs?" Verhulst asked her impatiently. "It will soon be time for dinner."

"Yes, I will want to change—but not yet. You go on up."

He nodded and left her and Imogene wandered listlessly into the dining room.

Elise followed her in. Noting Imogene's pensive air and surmising that it was something the patroon had done that had caused it, she seized and began to polish violently the handsome *ooma*, a sifter used to sprinkle sugar and cinnamon over waffles and cakes. "His tenants are afraid of him," she muttered.

"Nonsense," said Imogene sturdily. "And let Gretha do that. She is giving you baleful looks, for you are intruding on her territory."

Elise sniffed but she set the *ooma* down. "The *scherprecter* was here this morning while you were putting on your riding clothes. He had a long talk with the patroon and then he rode away. I have learned what a *scherprecter* is—he is a hangman."

"That means nothing," Imogene told her, turning to go. "There are hangmen in England, too, and they ride about there as well." But her face was sober, for she too had noticed the watchfulness in the eyes of the sturdy blond men in their loose shirts and wide trousers who shuffled deferentially into the estate "office" to speak to the patroon. They doffed their hats, but their faces were solemn and they shifted their feet a bit too much. The servants too were dour—and yet, she told herself, they were well enough treated. It was coming clear to her how people felt about her husband. A titled lord in this wild new country Verhulst might be, but he was not beloved by his vassals.

"How do you feel?" asked Elise, following Imogene into the handsome long living room with its carpet that Imogene herself had selected in Holland.

"I feel wonderful." Imogene kept her voice light. Physically she did feel wonderful. "The morning sickness is all gone."

"We will rot in this lonely country," predicted Elise gloomily. She glared out at the gray sky over the river. To Elise this savage river country was a penance. Its wild beauty, the hemlock-shrouded Indian trails, the thick-growing trees, the sometimes impenetrable forest reaching from hill to hill did not appeal to her—a woman fresh from the wind-lashed, open, flower-filled Scillies. To her it was a closed world—a world shut against her, speaking even a different tongue.

Imogene forced a laugh. "Soon you will have learned the language, Elise, and you will refuse ever to leave New Netherland."

"Never."

"Besides, we had guests only yesterday—the Vandervoorts from upriver."

Elise shook her head. To her they were all foreign-talking and incomprehensible, Dutch and Indian alike. Imogene hoped Elise would soon make friends among the stolid Dutch servants in the kitchen.

For herself and Verhulst there was a social life of sorts. Neighbors from nearby patroonships—if an estate so vast could be said to have a "near" neighbor—came by sloop to pay their respects to Verhulst's new bride. Most of them spoke only Dutch, and Imogene, who knew but a smattering of Dutch, did not find the conversations very interesting.

"Where do the ten Haers live?" she asked Verhulst that night at dinner.

"Just downriver," Verhulst told her. "Rychie is on an extended stay in New Amsterdam. Her father tells me that she is coming home this week and the ten Haers will give a ball for her."

"Oh? Are we going?"

"Certainly." He gave her a reproving look. "They are our neighbors and Hendrik ten Haer is a patroon like myself. We are expected to attend."

Noblesse oblige. Imogene grimaced. "I do not like Rychie," she observed.

"Nor do I," agreed Verhulst quietly.

But you did once, thought Imogene with an inner sigh. And the thought struck her that perhaps saffron-haired Rychie would have suited Verhulst better than she did. At least he had been physically attracted to Rychie and, judging by the way he shunned her bedroom, he was not physically attracted to his wife. *I wonder why he married me*, she asked herself. Perhaps he did not really have a marriage bed in mind, perhaps he only *collected* me, like a painting. Perhaps I was just one of the decorations for Wey Gat that he bought in Amsterdam.

Her face flushed at the thought and she looked down at her plate with a mutinous expression, determined to outshine everyone at the ten Haers' ball.

But as it happened, she did not attend the ten Haers' ball—nor any ball, ever again, on the river.

For the next time she sat down to dinner with Verhulst would be an evening she would never forget.

Imogene had dressed very carefully for dinner with Verhulst, as she always did. She was so grateful to him for his understanding and kindly acception of her condition that she was considerate of him in all things. Verhulst loved her in yellow—sometimes he called her his "yellow bird"; accordingly, tonight she selected a gown of pale Chinese gold satin that complemented her golden hair. It was tight now but she could still wear it. Smiling, she clasped around her neck her husband's latest gift—a necklace of topaz and diamonds. Her bright hair—combed out and brushed every night by Elise—was cleverly caught up with gold satin ribands that matched her gown, and topaz and diamond earrings glittered from her ears. And since Verhulst approved of womanly modesty, she wore a fragile whisk of delicate yellow silk to hide her deep décolletage.

"We are very grand tonight," Verhulst approved, as she

took her seat across from him at the long glittering board, for when the master was in residence Verhulst insisted the standards of service be kept high and the weary servants served him like royalty. "Is that the dress you plan to wear to the ten Haers' ball?"

Imogene shrugged her shoulders with a rippling movement that made her satin bodice shimmer in the candlelight. She gave him a gentle smile. "I thought I would let you choose my ball gown, Verhulst. How would *you* like me to appear before your friends?"

"As you are tonight." With kindling eyes, he raised his glass to her. "I drink to the most beautiful woman in all the Americas."

"Gallant—but hardly accurate," she laughed. "You should at least confine yourself to the North River. You cannot have seen *all* the women in this huge land! There will be English beauties lately come to Virginia and—who knows? Maybe Spanish sirens with melting eyes under the palms in *La Florida!*"

"None half so lovely as you," Verhulst insisted. He took a large portion of eels from a platter held by a stolid servant and smiled at Imogene. He was a fortunate man. A beautiful wife, thriving tenants. He was in an expansive mood. "I have ordered a virginal for you from Holland."

"Another gift? Oh, Verhulst, this necklace and the cloak from Paris were more than enough!" Her eyes sparkled at the thought of the beautiful dark blue velvet cloak, sable-lined, with its row of delicately wrought golden buttons from neck to hemline and its matching blue velvet French hood. "Besides," she added honestly, "I do not play the virginal."

"You can learn. I will import a tutor to instruct you."

"My new accomplishments will astonish everyone," said Imogene lightly, gazing at her plate in some alarm and wondering how she could possibly do justice to the lavish repast before her. Verhulst would expect her to eat and her stomach revolted at the sight of so much food.

"Try the sturgeon," he recommended. "And these river eels are delicious. No? Then some turkey perhaps, or pheasant? A bit of venison?"

Imogene frowned at the big chargers of meat, the lavish array of breads and jellies. At least it would not be wasted, for the servants would have their own banquet with the vast amount that would be left. Impatiently she warded off Verhulst's suggestions and toyed with the food on her plate—far too much—and suddenly pushed it aside. She had felt a sudden overwhelming desire for—"There," she cried and her eyes lit up, "that's the one thing I crave most at this moment—a pickle! A really sour pickle! And some of that custard!"

Down the table Verhulst laughed. He lifted his glass mockingly and the heavy gold chain he wore swung against the damask tablecloth, winking in the candlelight. "Pickles and custard! Did I not know better, I'd think ye were pregnant!"

Imogene paused with the pickle poised halfway to her mouth. Was it possible that—? No, of course not. He had heard—as had all the world—her bold announcement of her pregnancy at the Governor's Ball. He had been *pleased* by it! Still, before his amused gaze her face lost some of its color and she squared her slender shoulders as if against assault. She looked straight at him. "But I *am* pregnant, Verhulst," she said quietly.

For a moment his dark eyes took on a glassy look. It was as if he had been dealt some sharp blow and was stunned by its force. "What did you say?" he mumbled.

Imogene set the pickle down carefully. "But you *knew*," she said, moistening her lips and managing to keep her voice steady. "I told everyone that night at the Governor's Ball when Rychie taunted me."

Now his face was as white as her own. "I thought it was a lie," he said hoarsely. "A magnificent lie, to silence Rychie."

CHAPTER 18

A magnificent lie! Imogene was speechless. The rest of the color drained from her face, giving her a deathly pallor. Verhulst had never dreamed she was pregnant, he had believed her to be lying—on his behalf! His sudden solicitude, all this attention—it was all because she had publicly rebuked Rychie! She had come blithely upriver borne on the wings of a lie. All this time she had been living in a fool's paradise. Elise had been right to be afraid!

A servant opened the door to the dining room. He was carrying a tray of little cakes. Verhulst waited until the tray had been placed on the table, then he said something in Dutch and the servant nodded and departed, closing the door behind him. With a slow deliberation that wore on Imogene's nerves, Verhulst picked up one of the little cakes and toyed with it. When he looked up at her, he was almost smiling.

"Then tell me, Imogene." His voice was low and deadly,

pitched so that it would not reach the servants' ears in the pantry beyond. "Tell me how I came to make you pregnant.'

Desperate blue eyes looked bravely back into his. For now Imogene realized her danger. Her recklessness had got her into this—now lies must get her out!

"You do not remember coming into my cabin aboard ship? It was the night you and the captain got so drunk. You did not speak of it the next morning but—I certainly thought you would remember." She sounded hurt.

Her cool answer gave him pause. Now he studied his young wife, sitting so pale and beautiful before him, a study in white and gold. His gaze pinned her as mercilessly as a butterfly is pinned to a parchment. "And what night was that?" he drawled. "For I do not recall it."

Outside a dog howled and in the far distance it was answered by a wolf. Fear crawled icily along Imogene's spine. "It was the first night we dined aboard the *Sea Rover*. You were very angry when we returned."

"Yes, I remember that."

"And after we returned to the *Hilletje*, the captain asked you to share a glass of wine with him."

"I remember that."

"You must have shared several, for you were reeling when you arrived in my cabin. You burst in and dragged me from my bed and took me to your cabin—," she was embroidering her lies madly now—"and there you took me in your arms. Afterward I stole away lest you wake in a cramped position and bring the pains back on you again."

"Ah, yes, the pains." His voice was ironic. "So you are telling me that I threw you on the bed and raped you?"

"Not *raped*—I was willing. I—oh, don't you remember, Verhulst?" she implored. "You must remember *something*."

"No, I do not." Grimly.

"Then you must take my word." She tried to say that with authority; it did not quite come off. "You were—you were very marsterful that night, Verhulst. And now I am pregnant."

He sat regarding her with a baffled expression on his face. He—masterful? God in heaven! *Masterful!* He had never commanded any woman, let alone this beautiful lying wench who sat before him now as cool as ice, daring him to call her lie.

"How was it," he asked silkily, "that you knew so soon in New Amsterdam that you were pregnant? Was that not a bit hasty?"

How neatly he had trapped her! But she must carry it off—somehow. In New Amsterdam she had intended to tell him the truth—the whole truth—and let him be the judge. But then in a rebellious moment she had struck back at Richie and that had changed everything. The thought passed through her mind that she might tell him now, tell him everything just as she had meant to do. But she dared not. She was warned by the controlled violence in his voice, the burning anger that flared in his eyes. Ah, she knew him better now, this man with his savage dogs and his *scherprecter* and his watchful-eyed tenants! He would not forgive her—he would never forgive her! But she must buy time—precious time that would give her a chance to escape, to flee downriver and make her way into one of the other colonies of this barbarous land. So, for now, she must carry it off.

"I was not really certain then," she said steadily. "Although I suspected. But when Rychie taunted me with her own pregnancy, I wanted to strike back at her for your sake—and I did. I took a chance, of course—I might have been wrong."

For a moment his dark intense eyes glinted with something other than anger. Yes, he had wanted to strike at Rychie, too—for his own reasons. And Imogene had done that for him. Was it possible that he——? No, of course not. Still, she was right, he could not remember that night; he had been very drunk. And there was an innate honesty in Imogene that baffled him. Of course she was lying, but . . .

Verhulst had no conception of the lengths to which a woman would go to shield her unborn child.

Abruptly he rose from the table, threw down his napkin. "I find myself no longer hungry, Imogene. Summon the servants if you wish more food. I leave at dawn to inspect the outlying *bouweries* and must work on the accounts tonight."

Had he accepted her word? Oh, no, she could not believe it!

"Will you be back in time for the ten Haers' ball?" she asked uneasily.

"No, I will not return for a fortnight. But do not fret, I will send word to the ten Haers, making our apologies."

He strode from the room, closing the door resoundingly behind him. Imogene was left alone with the long table heaped with eels and sturgeon and game and pastries and wine, a table frosty with damask and shimmering with silver. And a now unwanted pickle lay among the untasted food on her plate.

She waited until her husband's footsteps faded away and then went upstairs and shut her bedroom door, leaned against it. What a fool she had been to believe herself lightly forgiven!

"I knew this would happen—oh, I knew it," Elise wailed, when Imogene told her.

"Keep your voice down," and Imogene harhsly. She was pacing soundlessly back and forth across the "Turkey carpet" of her bedroom in her soft satin slippers. "I need time to think!"

"We should never have come here to this wild place. Now he will kill us both!"

"He will not. In any event, he is not interested in killing

you. And I will escape him—I will go downriver."

"We are leaving?" Elise looked frightened but hopeful.

"I will not involve you in this, Elise," said Imogene slowly. She twisted her hands together and the topaz ring she was wearing cut into her flesh, for the terrible thought had occurred to her that if Verhulst found them, he might take delight in making Elise suffer rather than herself—to punish his wife without spoiling her "beauty" in which he delighted.

"It is dangerous to run." Elise was calmer now. "Should you not wait until you are in New Amsterdam for some ball, perhaps visiting Vrouw Berghem? You could make your escape then. For there is always the possibility that he believes you."

Imogene shook her head. "Verhulst is no fool. He will not believe me when he has time to think about it. And even if he does, what about the baby? By my best count, it is due at the end of February. Think, Elise! *He has not known me long enough for the child to be his!* What can I say to him then?"

Elise shuddered. "Do you think you could tell him the truth?" she asked timidly.

Imogene thought about that, biting her lips. "I think he would kill me," she said at last. "For he is very proud. He would find it all unforgivable."

"Then we must leave at once!"

"No, I will leave alone." *That way, if I am caught, Verhulst cannot hold you responsible.*

"I will not let you go alone!"

Imogene's blue eyes softened as she gazed at this woman who for so many years had been like a mother to her.

"Elise, if I get through, I promise I will send for you. If I do not get through, but die on the journey, you can ask Verhulst to let you go downriver so that you may return to your people in England—and I am sure he will, for he will be very glad to be rid of you, since the sight of you will remind him of me. Here, take these gold pieces. Sew them into the hem of your petticoat. There are enough of them to pay your passage back to the Scillies and your sister.''

"But I cannot let you go alone!" protested Elise, incredulous at the very idea.

"Elise." Imogene moved closer and took her old nurse's hands in her own. "Think on this: If I go alone and Verhulst finds me and brings me back, I will still have a friend at Wey Gat—you. If we run away together, we will be but two women fleeing through wild country—and if Verhulst finds us, he may dismiss you without money and send you packing downriver to New Amsterdam, where you will have to indenture yourself to anyone who will take you. I think I would have a better chance alone."

Reluctantly, Elise accepted this. "When will you go?"

"Tomorrow, after Verhulst leaves."

"He is leaving then?"

"Yes, to tour the outlying *bouweries* and see if the farmers are living up to their contracts." There was a note of bitterness in her voice. "I do not envy their position. But—he will not be back for a fortnight, so that will give me time."

"You will go by boat?"

"No, that is what they will expect. I will follow the Indian paths downriver."

"Suppose it snows?"

Imogene frowned. "We must hope that it doesn't. I will wear warm clothes and take all the food I can carry."

"What about Groot and the dogs?"

The dogs—she had forgotten the dogs!

"Groot will not turn those vicious dogs out to hunt me,"

322

she said slowly, hoping she was right. "He will be afraid to do so without orders from the patroon. He will send someone after Verhulst and they will organize a search for me. But tomorrow I will tell the servants that I am indisposed and not to be disturbed, and I will send you away on an errand so that you will not be involved. The next morning you will come rushing downstairs and ask everyone where I can be—you will say that you tiptoed in at night not to wake me and now you have found that what looked like my sleeping body was but pillows cleverly arranged beneath the coverlet. You will wring your hands and insist that the grounds be thoroughly searched—that will give me time to follow the Indian trails down some distance and work my way back to the river, where, if I am lucky, I can steal a boat or a canoe and travel by night, concealing the boat on shore and sleeping in the daytime. Once in New Amsterdam I can secure passage on a ship to Virginia by selling my jewels—and I will send for you, Elise, you may be sure of it."

Elise looked so despondent that Imogene put her arms around her old nurse and hugged her. "Don't look so woebegone," she chided. "Remember you said you'd never like it here? Well, now you won't have to stay."

Elise tried to smile—she didn't quite make it.

"And now," said Imogene energetically, "I want you to sew my jewels into the sleeves of my heaviest green woolen dress—the one Verhulst thinks is so ugly. I will put coins in my shoes and carry a purse as well as a pouch of food."

"And a pistol, for the woods are full of wild animals." *And Indians,* her frightened tone added.

"And a pistol, but only the small one from Verhulst's desk, for I will be held back if I try to carry too much weight."

By midnight their plans were well made and Imogene fell

into a fitful sleep from which she was wakened by Elise shaking her. "Wake up, the sun is shining. The patroon left at dawn and I have ordered you up a tray."

Imogene rubbed her eyes. "You should have waked me earlier. I should have left right after Verhulst."

"Ah, but supposed he had forgotten something and come back and asked to speak to you?"

That was true, Verhulst might have come back. It would be safer this way.

Her breakfast eaten, and Elise sent away on an errand, Imogene slipped from the house with her bundle. She looked quickly about her, saw no one, and sped into the woods. Behind her the dogs howled mournfully. She cast up a little prayer that Groot would not use them to search for her.

The forest closed in around her, great trees blown bare of leaves, heavy patches of undergrowth that tore at her green wool dress, and once, with thorny fingers, snatched the dark woolen shawl from her shoulders. Imogene tore it free and hurried on, following a narrow trail worn bare by countless moccasins. The hush of autumn was in the air, a breathless pause before the long winter set in. Over her head rose majestic hemlocks, chestnuts, hickories, and oaks. Beneath her hurrying feet crunched a thick carpet of leaves. The chipmunks were all snug in their winter quarters by now, but she saw an occasional squirrel, and once a raccoon, washing its food at a little rivulet, looked up and stared at her curiously before diving behind a bush. Imogene hoped there were no bears about. It was a beautiful, clear day. About her the air was cold and crisp and invigorating. Come night, it would be chill indeed. She was reminded of that by all the plants that had been killed by the frost. Hoping night would not catch her in the forest, she hurried along the narrow Indian trail.

This was an unfamiliar path and to her alarm it seemed to

be leading her inland and upward into the land of tamarack, spruce, and beech. She determined that she would take the first fork that led back southwest in the direction of the river.

Once, she thought she heard someone behind her, but when she swung around to look there was nothing—only the sigh of the wind through the branches and a few birds whose chirping her passage had stilled.

It was with relief that she heard the sound of falling water and stumbled into a little clearing where an ancient watercourse had cut through heavy slabs of rock, now black and lichen covered. At one end of the tiny clearing was a little tinkling waterfall and beneath it a crystal trout pool where silver fish darted. Imogene fell to her knees on the rustling leaves and bent her head and drank gratefully of the clear tangy mountain water. Then she sank down beneath the spreading branches of a big sycamore and prepared to eat her lunch.

There was a crackle off to her right—some animal moving through the woods, she presumed. But she paused warily with the apple in her hand almost to her mouth, and waited. There. She gave a little sigh. It had stopped.

She bit into the apple and almost choked.

Verhulst had stepped silently out from behind a big rock. "Getting your exercise, I see," he drawled.

Imogene sprang up. The blood sang in her ears. For a moment she almost broke and ran but sanity returned to her in time. "You startled me," she said lamely.

"I've no doubt I did. You've been moving fast for a pregnant woman. I've been following you," he added carelessly, "since you entered the woods."

So he had not gone to inspect the *bouweries* as he had said he would! He had tricked her into making this desperate move! Her flesh crawled at the thought that when she left the house he must have been watching, perhaps from the forest's edge, that he had melted into the undergrowth, following her.

"You might have made your presence known," she said crossly. "You move through the woods as silently as an Indian!"

"I grew up here, remember," he told her. "And this is one of my favorite paths. I would have taken you to this waterfall myself, had you shown an interest."

Imogene cast a look about. Verhulst seemed to be alone. Perhaps she could still escape him.

"I had meant to speak to you about it," she said, as calmly as she could.

"Oh, I am sure you did!"

He was baiting her! Imogene gave him a sunny smile. "Today seemed a good time to explore this path and see where it led. As you can see, I packed my lunch."

He peered down at her heavy bag of food, made from a knotted linen square. "Enough for an army, I'd say. Were you expecting guests?"

"I thought I might be very hungry after such a long walk," she defended. "Besides, I might have gotten lost and not made it back by suppertime." She was moving toward the pistol, which lay on the ground beside the linen square.

"Yes, there was always that possibility. And you have a pistol to defend yourself, I see."

Imogene bent and picked up the pistol. It was loaded. "I am told there are bears in these woods," she said, taking a step away from him.

"Then I marvel at your bravery to walk here alone. Would it not have been more prudent to bring one of the servants along?"

"Perhaps—but then I have never been known for my

prudence." She brought the barrel of the pistol up. "I am leaving you, Verhulst."

Looking down that barrel, which loomed suddenly very large and ugly, Verhulst took an involuntary step backward and his face paled visibly. "You intend to kill me with my own pistol?" he demanded incredulously.

"Only if you try to stop me." Her eyes flashed. Actually she had no intention of firing on him, but she wanted him to believe she would.

"Groot! Voorst! Janzoon! Show yourselves!"

There was a heavy crunching of underbrush and around the clearing the men whose names he had called appeared and stood silent, staring stolidly at the patroon.

"Give me the gun, Imogene."

"No." She backed away from him. "Tell them to go away. *Tell them or I will shoot you!*"

Verhulst had courage, too. He ignored her command. "Listen to me, Imogene. Whether you shoot me or not, night will surely fall and find you in these woods. This path leads nowhere; it dwindles out far up in the tamaracks. If you think to escape, you are wrong. Whether you shoot me or not, my men will follow you. Silently. Out of sight. And when you fall asleep—and sleep you must eventually—they will take you and bring you back to Wey Gat. Those are my orders, already given."

"Then rescind them!" She cocked the gun.

"No." He stepped sideways so that his body blocked the line of stepping-stones she must use to cross the stream and catch the path on the other side. "You had best shoot, for I intend to block your way!"

Imogene stood trembling.

Abruptly, she threw away the gun.

Triumph suffused Verhulst's face. He sprang forward and pounced on her, seizing her by the shoulders in a crushing grip that ground the jewels—sewn into her big, fashionably detachable sleeves—painfully into her flesh.

"Well, what have we here?" His hot breath raked her face. "More pistols?"

"Of course not. They are my jewels. I needed money to leave you, Verhulst. I would have sold them. Later, when I was able, I would have repaid you."

He laughed scornfully. "All this from a woman who was about to shoot me because I stood in her way?"

"I would not have shot you, Verhulst," said Imogene in a weary voice. "I have done you enough harm already. You can depend upon it—I would not have added murder to my other crimes."

"Another lie, doubtless," he snarled, for the soft feel of her shoulders through the sleeves was enticing him, seducing him. He flung her away from him. "Did you think I was a fool? I knew you would leave—I anticipated your every move! Since dawn I have been waiting at the forest's edge for you to appear. You have not been out of my sight since you left the house!"

"How very clever of you." She gave him a level look.

He let go of her shoulders and seized her arm in a grip that hurt, jerked her almost off her feet. "You will not use that tone with me! And since you are so interested in exercise, we will oblige you by setting twice as fast a pace back to the house! And tonight we will continue at dinner the conversation we were having last night. Perhaps there will be more truth tonight!"

"I will not have dinner with you tonight!" cried Imogene.

"You will!" His grip tightened. "If you do not come down voluntarily I will drag you downstairs myself!" As if to illustrate that, he strode forward dragging her with him. It was an exhausted Imogene, stumbling, panting, who arrived at the stone mansion she had left so surreptitiously that morning.

"Take charge of your mistress!" Verhulst flung her at a horrified Elise, who sprang forwad to gather Imogene in her arms, help her stagger up the stairs to fall upon the bed.

"The patroon has locked up all the guns in the house," Elise reported later to Imogene.

"Good," mumbled Imogene, who still lay where she had fallen across the bed. "Perhaps, if he fears me enough, he will wish to be rid of me and let me go!" She turned over and sat up; with a little rest her flagging courage had returned. "Is it time to dress for dinner?"

Elise gave a sorrowful nod.

"Do not look so sad, Elise!" Imogene threw her legs over the side of the bed. "I must dress carefully to impress my husband!"

"A yellow dress perhaps?" suggested Elise timorously. "The patroon likes you in yellow."

"No!" Imogene laughed harshly. "I will wear something he does *not* like! Why should I cater to his whims? Bring me that crimson velvet, Elise. Verhulst has decided he hates me in red."

Elise rolled her eyes. Imogene in this mood was a danger to all about her. In silence she brought the ruby slippers Imogene demanded and dressed Imogene's hair fashionably, decorating it with crimson velvet rosettes. "Your whisk." She began to put it around Imogene's neck.

Imogene tore off the whisk. "I will go without it," she declared in a brittle voice. "Verhulst married a woman of fashion—let him take the consequences!" She strode down to dinner with her head high and the whole milky expanse of her throat and bosom and the pearly tops of her breasts down to the winking rosy crests of her nipples fashionably bare. At the entrance to the dining room she gave her neckline another violent yank downward. Her face was proud and cold. She might have been going to her execution.

CHAPTER 19

Imogene swept into the long dining room with a rustle of skirts. Verhulst was standing with his back to her, looking down at the fire. For the first time, his carefully pomaded wig irritated her. She would have preferred his own hair, scanty, mousy—whatever it was; at least it would have been his own!

Her voice rang out. "I see that you have locked up all the guns." Her mocking gesture included the muskets that normally decorated the mantel and the matched pair of dueling pistols now missing from the wall beside them.

Verhulst turned an impassive face toward her. "It seemed prudent, since you seem of a mind to use them on me."

"Are you going to lock up the table knives as well?" She taunted. "Am I to expect that we will now rend the food with our fingers or attack our roast with spoons?"

His dark eyes flashed but his voice was almost gentle. "I have no fear that you will attack me with the cutlery. For if you do, I promise you that I will break your lovely fingers—one by one.''

Imogene sniffed scornfully, but she gave Verhulst a wary look, wondering what game he was playing.

"That gown is not one of my favorites," he commented with a frown.

"That is why I wore it!" she snapped. "I desire you to wish to be rid of me."

He studied her silently for a moment, then pulled back a chair for her. Imogene sank into it impassively. She was still very tired although her short nap had refreshed her.

"Are we to make small talk?" Her voice was tart. "Or shall we have the questions and the answers now?"

Verhulst, she noted, was even more handsomely dressed than usual. He was wearing a black satin doublet shot with gold threads. Gold fringe edged his sleeves and trousers and a massive gold signet ring flashed conspicuously from the middle finger of his right hand. Now his thin face took on a cruel expression.

"I think we will dine first," he said carelessly. "Lest the truth should upset my appetite."

The truth could be guaranteed to upset his appetite, thought Imogene grimly, and began to eat the tasty pheasant he urged upon her. Indeed, her long walk and interrupted lunch had made her ravenously hungry. But she restrained her urge to shout the truth at him and let him do as he would with her and get it over with, and replied steadily to the small talk that he kept flowing in her direction.

Save for the unusual elegance that marked the table and its appointments, they could have been any patroon on the river and his wife, chatting about estate affairs.

After dinner he took her to the library, closed the door and beckoned her to be seated at the heavy oaken table where he poured over his account books night after night. "Now let us have a better story than we had last night," he mocked her. "For surely you have had time during supper to invent one."

Her blue eyes flashed in anger and she shrugged off his offer of a chair. "Thank you, I prefer to stand."

"Very well." He took a pinch of snuff from a golden snuffbox. "We will hear the truth standing and totter into our chairs afterward."

She could hardly believe the light bantering tone he was using.

"Verhulst," she said haltingly. "I did not know I was pregnant when I married you. You must believe that. *I did not know.*"

"I knew this would be interesting," he said. "And am I to believe we are to have a miracle? A virgin birth, say?"

Imogene swallowed. "I realize that I well deserve your scorn," she said in a steady voice. "For I have duped you and deceived you, although that was not my intent when I married you. I meant to be a good wife to you, Verhulst, all that a wife should be."

He was silent for a moment. Then, "Go on," he said.

"I did not realize then that you found me—personally unappealing," she said in a strangled voice. "That you would not seek my cabin, that you would not claim your—marital rights."

For a moment the dark eyes boring into her face were young, miserable. "I do not find you personally unappealing, Imogene," Verhulst said thickly. "Very much the reverse."

"As a painting perhaps," she shrugged. "Not as a woman."

He made a gesture as if to brush something away from him.

"And the father of this child you are to bear," he said harshly. "Am I to assume it is Captain van Ryker?"

She gave him a look of such pure astonishment that he believed her.

"Of course not!" she cried. "How can you think it? Verhulst, I—I had a lover. In England. Between us, we killed a man. It was an accident but we knew no one would believe us. My lover fled, and I—I was sent to Amsterdam by my guardian."

"Fascinating." A bitter smile played over his face. "And why would no one believe that this unfortunate man's death was an accident?"

"Because the dead man was my betrothed," she said bluntly.

"Better and better." His tone was contemptuous. "It seems you deal not only in deception, but in murder! I was wise to lock up the firearms, it seems."

She took a step backward before the lash in his tone, and now his voice lost its urbanity and throbbed with fury.

"And how many other lovers have you had, Imogene? In England and in Holland? Tell me their names!"

He strode toward her and seized her wrist. His face had turned into a devilish mask.

Imogene stiffened. "I have had only one lover, Verhulst. One."

"And how did you mean to explain him, Imogene? What excuse did you plan to give me to explain your lack of virginity in your marriage bed? A riding accident, perhaps?"

Color stained her white cheeks. "You are right," she said miserably. "I meant to lie to you. But only in the hope that we might—" her voice caught in a sob—"that we might be happy

334

together. But now I see that we never can be, and I ask you to let me go, Verhulst!''

He flung her away from him with a force that brought her head up sickeningly against the wall. The collision with the wall sent such a burst of pain through her head that she was for a moment blinded. His voice broke over her like a wave.

''I will never let you go,'' he told her violently. ''I have not yet decided what I will do with you, but I will never let you go, depend upon it!''

Imogene pushed away from the wall and stood before him trying not to tremble, although her knees felt like jelly. ''I am going to bed,'' she said dully. ''My head is aching.''

'' 'To bed,' '' he mocked. ''To dream of your lovers, no doubt!''

Imogene gave him a cold look and would have pushed past him but he took her shoulders in a cruel grip and gave her such a hard shake that her aching head snapped back and she gasped.

''Remember that you live here by my sufferance,'' he growled. ''And I have not yet decided what I will do with you.''

She looked him full in the face, marveling. ''And I had thought you *good*,'' she murmured. ''And *kind*, that you would accept me as I was. . . . I was wrong about you, Verhulst.''

Something wavered in his eyes. His hands fell away from her and he stood back and let her pass.

After that she was watched. There was always someone around: one of the menservants finding something to do in the hall and looking up sharply at every footstep, one of the big maidservants popping in and out, eyeing her speculatively.

''You will never get out of here,'' Elise told her with a sigh.

''Oh, yes, I will!'' flashed Imogene.

But as her body thickened and became more unwieldy, and

as the hard northern winter closed in about them, dashing ice and snow against the windowpanes, she knew that her chances were dwindling, one by one. No one came to the house anymore. All invitations were refused and visitors—in a land famous for its hospitality—were turned away. The excuse: the delicate state of health of the patroon's wife. Imogene wondered what they must think, these erstwhile friends of the young patroon, frequenters of Wey Gat. What strange tales must be circulating about them along the river!

Since the night of their confrontation, Verhulst had studiously ignored her. He ate breakfast early and she took hers in bed and had her lunch brought to her on a tray in her room, so they avoided sight of each other until supper. Supper was now a silent meal served in the cavernous dining room, where the patroon and his lady stared coldly at each other across a table set as if for a banquet.

Imogene no longer dressed to please him. Angry with him, feeling somehow betrayed that she should have thought him so noble and found out he was no better than anybody else, she deliberately wore all the dresses he disliked most, concentrating on the deep jewel tones he had often remarked were too striking for her pale loveliness. She had abandoned wearing whisks entirely, carelessly letting the servants view her deep décolletage and disregarding Verhulst's deepening frown as his gaze rested upon the pearly tops of her delicately molded breasts.

"Are your jewels still sewn in your sleeves?" he demanded ironically one night at dinner.

Imogene, who had not been wearing any jewels since their confrontation, gave him a look of distaste. "I do not know where they are."

"Well, find them. I should like to see you wearing them. If you cannot behave like the wife of a patroon, you can at least try to look like one." His tone was brutal.

Imogene leaned forward. The candlelight gleamed hotly in her blue eyes, making them dance like blue flame. "You have made it clear that I cannot live up to your standards, Verhulst. The least you could do is let me go. I will divorce you quietly—or you can divorce me. In any event, you would never see me again."

"No!" His jaws closed with a snap.

"But why not?" she wailed. "I ask nothing of you. I will go empty-handed from this house and make my way as best I can. Only send me downriver and I will leave this colony and you will be free to marry again—someone you can respect."

Down the long table he was looking at her with dull hatred. He seemed not to have heard her. "I do not like your dress. Red does not become you. Tomorrow you will wear yellow."

Imogene's fingers clenched around her crystal wine goblet so hard the delicate stem broke and the red wine spilled on the tablecloth. She leaped up, dashing the glass away from her dress. "I will not dress to please you," she said through her teeth, "unless you will promise to let me go—by the next sloop that goes by on its way downriver!"

Blood suffused Verhulst's sallow countenance. With a sudden violent gesture he threw his glass at the fireplace. It shattered against the marble with a sound like a shot. One of the servants burst into the room to see what was the matter and Verhulst leaped up and waved him out, shouting at him in Dutch. In three strides he had crossed the room and locked the dining room doors. That done, he turned his furious gaze on his wife's thickening waist that threatened to burst through the bodice of her red velvet gown, even though Elise had already let it out twice.

"You mock me!" he cried. "You *dare* to mock me!"

Imogene had jumped to her feet as Verhulst threw the glass. Now, appalled by the look on his face, she sank back into her chair, gazing up at him as he loomed above her. Before she knew what he was about he had swooped down, seized her by her long fair hair and wrenched her from her chair. Imogene suppressed a scream as he swept her to her knees and began to shake her as a terrier shakes a rat.

"I *will* have answers from you!" he shouted. "His name! Tell me your lover's name!"

White-faced and silent, in agony from his cruel grip on her hair, Imogene clawed at his arms in an effort to win her release.

"You will not tell me?" Still holding her by the hair, he struck her head back and forth brutally with his open palm.

Half fainting before this assault, Imogene closed her eyes and tried to shield her face with her arms.

"Still reluctant?" His voice was an evil whisper in her ear. "Then I will tell you this! I will kill both you and the child you carry, if you do not tell me his name!"

Her eyes snapped open in horror. "You would not?" she whispered.

"I would." His lips were twisted in a sneer and his eyes had taken on a glaze of madness. She could not know that he was imagining her naked on the *Sea Rover*'s deck in van Ryker's sinewy arms. "I swear to you that if you do not tell me, I will carry you from this room and hurl you into the ice-cold river." A nasty smile curved his lips. "Who is there to stop me?"

In fascinated horror, Imogene's wide blue eyes gazed up at him. Who was there to stop him, indeed? He was the patroon, the law of Wey Gat. He could throw her in the river if he chose. Perhaps he would be brought to justice later but it would be too late to save her—or her baby. She might survive the icy waters, might be able to swim away from him and make it to shore but she would surely die of exposure even if she managed to elude him. And her baby—her defenseless child would have no chance at all.

As if to drive home his point, he began to strike her again. Imogene gasped. She could not stand this kind of punishment—not pregnant as she was. The baby would suffer.

"Linnington." the word came out as a sob. "Stephen Linnington was my lover. What good does it do you to know his name, Verhulst?"

Verhulst's face glowed with a kind of hateful triumph. At last he had made her name her lover! And with the name—and the sudden harsh reality that name brought to him—he felt a wild surge of inner rage, murderous rage. Borne forward on that gust of passion his hand reached out for the carving knife that lay on the dining room table.

Imogene saw his hand snaking toward the knife.

"But he is dead, Verhulst!" she wailed. "He is no threat to you! Stephen Linnington is dead. He was killed in a duel in England while I was in Amsterdam!"

Slowly her words sank in. Verhulst's hand wavered, fell away from the knife. This man who had held the innocent Imogene in his arms, this man who had made her pregnant, was dead. A lover dead in England could not come back to haunt him. None on the river knew of this man, and when a child was delivered of this white-faced, half-fainting wench he held so savagely by the hair, all up and down the river that child would be considered *his*. Only he and Imogene and that maid of hers would know—and none of them was likely to tell. The Dutch servants might be listening at the door but none of them spoke English and all his conversations with his young wife were in that tongue.

And now a new and heady thought came to him. When

339

Imogene was delivered of this child, *he* would be accounted the father. How that would give the lie to all the tales told about him! How Rychie would burn!

Thoughtful now, a man bemused, he loosened his grip on Imogene's fair hair and she slumped in a velvet heap to the floor. Verhulst stood looking down at her for long minutes, his rage coming back to him in waves, rolling over him like a great incoming tide and then washing away, leaving behind the cleanswept beach of his thoughts of what he had to gain: A child, an heir to Wey Gat. Not a child of his body—that was not possible in any case—but an heir who would be believed to be a child of his body. . . .

Anger at this lovely woman who had deceived him poured over him again and he picked up a glass of wine and splashed it in her face. She came to, coughing, lifting a white hand to fend off further assault.

"Tomorrow," he told her in an expressionless voice, "you will wear a yellow gown to dinner. If you do not, I will tear off your clothes before the servants, strip you naked and make you eat your meal thus!"

He turned on his heel and left her.

From the floor, Imogene lifted a hand that shook. She held it to her throbbing head and gazed after him in dazed, speechless anger.

The next day Verhulst had her abruptly moved to a different bedroom. This one was smaller, plainer, and it did not face upon the river with its flow of traffic—and its chance of escape. Now she could not see the sloops that tied up at Wey Gat's dock. She could look out only on the far-flung forests and fields of Wey Gat, which had become her prison. Imogene protested the move, but Verhulst remained adamant. A new servant girl—one who spoke only Dutch—now occupied the room next to hers. Every hour of the day Imogene felt watched—cornered.

The first snow fell and with it the weather turned bitter cold.

Imogene caught cold and was for a time confined to her bed. It was a gloomy time for her. From her window she could look out and see tracks upon the snow—the tracks of foxes, rabbits, free wild things. She envied them. What matter that their lives were often short? At least they were not caged!

Bess Deveen wrote to her again but this time Imogene was not allowed to read the letter. Verhulst, kept at home by the weather, called her into the library and waved it at her. "A letter from your friend Bess."

Imogene brightened. "When did it come?" She reached out an eager hand for it.

Verhulst snatched it away from her, held it up beyond her reach. "It came before the first flake fell," he said deliberately. "I have been saving it."

Imogene's hand dropped to her side. " 'Saving it'? For what?" she asked tonelessly.

"Until you were well enough to come downstairs, so you could watch me do this." He tore the letter across and flung it into the fire.

Now heavy with child, Imogene stood with clenched hands and watched it burn. It would have meant so much to her to read Bess's letter. "Have you done with me?" she asked dully, turning to go.

"Not quite. There will be no more letters received or sent. And go change your gown," he added coldly. "I have told you before that red does not become you."

"Good," said Imogene defiantly, giving her dark red velvet dress a pat. "I wore it because I know you dislike me in red."

So he had not yet broken her spirit! Verhulst's face darkened. "You would do well to placate me," he warned. "For I hold your fate in my hands."

Imogene shrugged. "If I am distasteful enough, perhaps you will let me go."

His laughter rang out—discordant, rude. "Do you still believe that? Lord, what does it take to convince you? You will come down to dinner tonight—no more excuses of headaches or stomach aches—and you will wear a gown of a yellow hue. You have many such. I bought them for you in Amsterdam."

She faced him squarely. "No, I will not."

"I will remove every gown you have that is not to my liking and have them burned!"

"If you do," said Imogene in a stubborn voice, "I will refuse to come down to dinner at all!"

A light almost of madness flashed in his dark eyes. Verhulst leaned toward her, a dark and menacing figure. "You will come down and sit at dinner with me tonight, Imogene, or before God, I will lock you in your room without food or water until you do!"

The pale woman before him would have flung him her defiance but—there was now another life besides her own to think about. She could not let her unborn child suffer.

That night she came reluctantly down to supper attired in a gown of heavy Chinese gold satin—and gazed at her husband with such scorn across the glittering board that he was nettled.

"You will also make conversation," he told her as he lifted a bite of capon to his mouth.

Humiliated, raging inside, Imogene looked about her.

"Why have you not replaced the dueling pistols that used to hang beside the mantelpiece?" she taunted. "Do you really think I might seize one of them and shoot you?"

The gleam of his eyes over the capon was answer enough. He wiped his mouth on his napkin. "Why not?" he asked with elaborate sarcasm. "From your own lips I have heard that you have already struck down one betrothed. What might you not do to a husband? Indeed, I had a sample of it in the woods when you pointed my own gun at me!"

Whatever else, Imogene had never thought to murder Verhulst, but only to escape from him. Now, white with fury, she leaned forward, knocking over her glass of wine upon the white tablecloth. "You can be sure of this, mynheer! *I wish you dead!*"

His head rocked as if she had struck him and his gaze went murky. "Time will sober your spirit and end these ravings," he said carelessly. "And we have much of it. Indeed, we have all our lives to look forward to—together."

It was too much. Imogene threw down her napkin and stalked from the table. Verhulst's insolent laughter followed her.

It was but the first of many humiliating nights, and they took their toll of her. Watched and spied upon, forced to eat her meals amid derision and scorn, Imogene began to change. The color left her cheeks and she lost interest in everything.

It would have stunned Imogene to know that Verhulst looked forward to these shared evenings with morbid pleasure, that he was sometimes hard-pressed not to speak to her kindly, to reach out an arm to help her as she made her way heavily up the stairs. The truth was that he loved Imogene—a fact that he had never admitted even to himself. The wild jealousy that overcame him when he thought of her lying in another man's arms, he passed off to himself as the righteous anger of a man whose possessions are stolen by another. He was punishing her, he told himself—and she well deserved that punishment. Eventually he might decide to forgive her.

He was unaware that during that terrible winter he alienated his young wife forever.

Here at lonely Wey Gat, with a baby coming, a husband who seemed to hate her, and no one to talk to, Imogene drooped. She had lost the man she loved, she had fled across the sea and driven away a man she *might* have loved, she had tried valiantly to be wife to a man who would have no true wife.

Like a flower at eventide, Imogene wilted; her lovely petals seemed closing one by one.

She might have written of her troubles to Bess Duveen— had she been allowed to. She might have wept on Vrouw Berghem's shoulder had that stout kindly woman come upriver for a visit. But she had neither friends nor kinfolk in this harsh new land.

Driven, and without even Elise to talk to, Imogene began secretly to keep a journal. Into it she poured out her heart in passionate words. She told of her affair with Stephen Linnington and how she was bearing his child here in the far fastness of Wey Gat. She told of her life as the patroon's prisoner . . . a life that would end, she believed, when her child was born and Verhulst killed them both.

Wey Gat, New Netherland, 1658

CHAPTER 20

Shrieking February winds lashed the thick stone walls of the mansion of Wey Gat. Wind howled bansheelike down the tall chimneys and moaned against the windows of Imogene's bedroom, where bustling servants came and went at the bidding of the doctor hastily summoned upriver from New Amsterdam. For the young mistress of the house was in labor and the patroon might at any minute be blessed with a son to carry on the mighty van Rappard name.

By the bedside Elise watched anxiously. During these last weeks of Imogene's pregnancy she had been allowed to tend Imogene, replacing the Dutch girl who had been guarding her, for the patroon had no fear that a woman in the last stages of pregnancy would strike out on her own in the heavy snow. Now Elise clung to Imogene's damp palm, as frightened as if she were bearing her own child.

"Has Verhulst—asked about me?" wondered Imogene, as

a spasm of pain subsided and the doctor, frowning, went across the room to peer into his medical bag.

"No," said Elise in a low voice. She bent over and sponged Imogene's forehead gently with a damp cloth. "Not yet. But he is in the house. Downstairs in the library, I think."

Their eyes met in fear and Elise, who couldn't stand the sight of naked fear on Imogene's usually fearless countenance, rose and harshly ordered the fire to be stirred up, for icy air seeped in around the windows and it was cold in that February room on the bluff above the frozen river.

"No, wait—Elise." Imogene's faint voice called her back and the gaunt serving woman bent once more over the bed and on the pretext of arranging the covers, leaned down to hear Imogene's whisper. "Promise me, Elise, that if I should die, you will take care of my baby and save it from Verhulst." Her fingers clutched the older woman's hand with frantic strength, the strength of panic. "Promise—if I should die . . ."

"I promise." Elise's eyes filled with tears and she choked back a sob.

"Come now," said the kindly doctor in his thick Dutch accent, for he had heard Imogene's last words. "This is no time to think of dying. You are giving birth! Soon you will have not only your own life to think about but your child's!"

His gruff heartiness did not cheer the beautiful woman lying on the bed. *I will have my life to think about only if Verhulst lets me live,* she thought grimly. *For now I am truly at his mercy.* And then another wave of pain began and she was borne away on it, gasping and clenching Elise's hand and trying desperately not to scream.

For Verhulst's treatment of her in these last months of her pregnancy had swung like a pendulum. Sometimes he had been deceptively kind—but those moods never lasted. At other times he had stormed at her—always in English so the Dutch-speaking servants would not know what he was talking about. He had derided her, called her a whore and a murderess who had sought protection from her crimes under the shelter of his fine old name. Imogene had dug her fingernails into her palms until they bled in her effort not to respond violently to his charges, for as she grew great with child—and was watched every minute that she was not locked in her room—she knew that there was no escaping Verhulst; she would bear her child at Wey Gat and after that only God knew what would become of her.

Frightened, holding on, keeping her head high no matter how Verhulst baited her, in these months she had learned to hate him and to wonder if he would let her live once the child was born. Or—white-faced in the night she had looked out at a cold moon shining down on wintry Wey Gat and asked herself, *would he kill them both?*

She need not have feared for her life. Verhulst had no intention of killing his young wife whose beauty even now, late in her pregnancy, was a delight to his eyes. He meant—inflexible as any Puritan—to bring his erring lady to her knees, to make her repent and atone.

If Imogene could have understood that, she might have come to understand Verhulst and thus made some kind of peace with him. But she did not understand. She would turn and see sudden burning fury in his gaze and she mistook his frustration that he could not break her spirit, quench her flame (and in his secret heart, make her love him)—for hatred.

Even now, as Imogene lay racked with the pains of labor, Verhulst was wearing a path on the library rug. His dark eyes were wild with worry and he saw neither the expensive leather-bound volumes he had imported from Holland at such cost or the oaken library table piled with the estate account books that he kept so meticulously. His heart was thudding in his chest and he was oblivious to the evidences of wealth that were all about him. From upstairs he heard a muffled scream and with a convulsive reflex leaped for the door—and then stopped.

He must not let Imogene know he was concerned about her. Indeed, he told himself hotly, in a sudden burst of shame that he should be so exercised, he was not. It was only her lustrous beauty that held him, her damnable haunting beauty. Just seeing her move about in Amsterdam had made him dream—and he had imagined her moving sensuously from room to room at Wey Gat. And when he had first brought her here, just seeing her stand outside with the wind blowing her bright hair had been enough to make him catch his breath. She was like a drug to his senses that he could not shake off. In months past he had felt she was like an addiction—he despised her, wished to rid himself of her—and yet he could not do without her.

And then he had learned the terrible truth, that she was pregnant by another man, and every time he looked in her direction he was warmed by his newfound imagined hatred for her. He had never cared for her at all, he told himself roughly in those first evil days, she was merely another ornament he had bought in Holland for Wey Gat—bought for gold as he had bought his paintings, his furnishings, his plate.

He told himself he did not want her—but he was reduced to panic at the thought that she might run away and escape him. Haggard, he had watched her covertly when she did not know he watched and thought jagged thoughts that tore at him.

Those lovely eyes—they had looked into another man's face with love. Those soft curving lips had been tasted, enjoyed by another. That slender form he had thought so virginal, so untried—at the thought his hands clenched and a tremor went through him—that lovely "virginal" body had been known in naked carnal passion by another man. Thinking it, his teeth closed down on his lips so that he tasted blood and before the pain subsided he struck the wall with his fist and ordered out his horse and rode the poor beast till it was lathered and foaming with sweat. But nothing he did could exorcise his devils. Imogene's haunting beauty rode with him wherever he went. On the river, inspecting the *bouweries*, wherever his tormented spirit led him, he carried her picture in his heart. A haunting, tempting vision—*of a wanton! A wanton!* He would think of that and his thin face would empurple with rage. Imogene had taken all his gifts, his proud old name—and flung mud on them!

But in other, softer, moods he saw her sentimentally, as she had been in Amsterdam, greeting the morning with a song. Pure, virginal she had seemed, lovely as the dawn, a woman made for love.

She was neither extreme, of course, neither so pure nor yet so bad as his fancy made her. Imogene was a woman, with a woman's frailties and a woman's strengths. She had courage and now upstairs with the baby coming, she needed all of it.

"The contractions are coming faster now," muttered the doctor. He sounded cheered, for Imogene had been in labor many hours. And Elise, her fingers nearly crushed by Imogene's agonized grip, murmured, " 'Tis nearly over, nearly over," to comfort the woman on the bed whose head turned frantically this way and that as her body strained to be delivered of the child, and whose long blond hair, soaked with perspiration, lay in a tumbled mass upon the damp pillows.

Imogene heard neither of them. Her world had become a rending landscape of pain that crested in terrible jagged hills and careened into deep aching valleys. She was one continuous agony now and she had lost touch with reality, lost her identity, she had become one with the pain that dragged her along with it.

Valerie Sherwood

And then it was over. Imogene gave a terrible hoarse scream that wavered and lingered on the air, and the baby slipped out and she fell back quivering and exhausted upon the damp bed.

Downstairs, Verhulst heard that agonized scream and streaked for the stairs, thundered up them on wings of fear. *God, was she dying? Had that cursed doctor killed her? By heaven, he would throttle the man!* He burst through the door and Elise, who had taken the child from the doctor, froze to stillness as he plunged into the room.

But the sight of the naked baby, red and giving out a tiny cry, the sight of Imogene's fair head turning slightly on the pillow, reassured him. She was alive, she had got through it! Verhulst took in a great gulp of air and managed with an effort to control the trembling of his knees.

"So my child is born," he said lightly. His eyes now focused on the baby, which Elise had swiftly wrapped in a blanket against the drafty air. "Is it a boy or a girl?"

"A girl." Elise's voice was hoarse. *My child is born. . . .* The young patroon had decided to claim the baby as his own after all!

"A boy would have been better. Ah, well, no matter." Verhulst tried to sound jaunty. "We will doubtless have a dozen more."

"Not if you wish your wife to live," said the doctor dryly. "I have brought her through this labor, but I doubt she would survive another."

"Oh?" Could that have been relief in van Rappard's face, the doctor wondered ironically. He had of course heard the stories of the young patroon's boyhood accident. "Then we must limit the size of our family, must we not, Imogene?"

The woman on the bed, eyes closed in exhaustion, still living in that black world of pain, gave him no answer.

"It is going to be all right," Elise whispered to her, after the doctor and Verhulst had gone. "The patroon claims the child as his own!"

Imogene came up out of the dark.

"No." She shook her head wearily and the pallor of her lovely face made Elise's heart ache for her. "Nothing is all right. Pride made Verhulst claim my daughter, pride alone. Verhulst has not forgiven me, Elise—I don't think he ever will."

"There, there," said Elise helplessly. "What will you name your daughter? She is so lovely, will you name her for yourself?"

"No." Imogene cradled the tiny babe in her arms and looked down upon her lovingly, but her voice was sad. "I think my name is accursed, Elise, for what good have I ever brought to anyone? I would never name her Imogene. Indeed, I will name her Georgiana—for my mother."

Elise smiled and brought hot soup and exuded relief that Imogene had lived through her ordeal.

But that night Elise, sleeping now in the small anteroom adjoining Imogene's bedchamber, was wakened by a hoarse cry. Imogene had had the dream again, the dream that had haunted her since that long-ago day when she had seen her parents shot down in their Penzance garden.

" 'Tis all right, 'tis all right." Elise tried to comfort her, holding the shuddering woman in her arms.

"I felt—I felt as if the dream . . . was my future," whispered Imogene haltingly. "I felt I had seen death—*my* death. Elise." Her voice was hushed. "I've seen the way I'm going to die."

Elise held her and rocked her and spoke soothingly but her gaunt face was troubled. *For who was to say that Imogene had not foreseen the future?*

Imogene did not come down to dinner for two weeks. But

when she did the back of the winter had broken. The river ice had broken up. Great floes dotted rushing waters swollen by the snow melt. And eagles and crows alighted on those floes and floated past Wey Gat in stately fashion on their way downriver. Everywhere the snow was melting, running in bright dancing rivulets to swell the torrent. The promise of spring was in the air and across the long dining table, on that first night that she came downstairs to eat with him, Imogene and Verhulst declared a silent truce.

For a time Imogene was almost happy at Wey Gat. For the most part she ignored Verhulst, spending all her time with the baby, delighting in her, loving her, holding that small warm body close to her heart. Preoccupied with the child, she no longer thought of escaping. Verhulst sensed this and withdrew the spying servants. For Imogene it was a welcome change and the thoughts that she confided to her journal were happy thoughts.

Spring came suddenly, bursting out everywhere. Imogene walked out on the lawns and strolled about. Beneath azure skies she sat with her skirts spread out amid the fragrant junipers and sang soft lullabies to little Georgiana in her arms. She loved to sit beneath the great walnut and chestnut trees that dotted the yard, to stroll through the pleasant pastures carpeted with wild flowers or among the big trees that surrounded those pastures— tall pines and sycamores that rose among the sturdy oaks and hickories and hemlocks. The north side of these trees were moss- and lichen-covered. Once, walking among them, she paused to watch a long, irregular line of swans flying north—then caught her breath and marveled at a great cloud of passenger pigeons that darkened the sky as they flew over the newly spongy earth. Snowbirds were everywhere, Canada sparrows, thrushes. The air was filled with their silvery notes.

With all of this to enchant her, Imogene no longer minded

not receiving mail. Nor did she care to write any letters. She did not miss the social life of the river—she had never been part of it anyway. Her whole world was filled with the magic of spring—and baby Georgiana.

In one of his mellower moods Verhulst told her the riverbanks would soon be ablaze with luscious wild strawberries and at the base of the mountains there would be masses of northern green lilies and other wild flowers. He offered to bring her some and at this gesture of goodwill, Imogene's gaze softened. She had never been one to bear a grudge. Now she felt a sudden bittersweet yearning for a complete family—not only a baby but a husband who would truly love her—and wondered if they might not make a go of it after all.

But Imogene's body was a woman's body. She had a woman's wants and a woman's needs. As spring deepened into summer, as brilliant wild flowers painted the meadows with saffron and pink, she grew restless. When the air was redolent with honeysuckle and silvered with the flutelike call of the wood thrush and other mating birds, she looked up at the forest of hemlocks and spruce towering above her, heard the wild call of the loon and felt a stirring in her blood. The very meadows seemed to sing to her—a love song. And Imogene was weary again of her empty marriage. She looked toward the south—and dreamed.

Verhulst, who had been satisfied enough to have a wife wrapped up in the care of an infant all believed to be his, felt this change in Imogene and was nettled by it. Shut out by her all-consuming attentions to the child, he became jealous of Georgiana, feeling the baby was somehow interfering with his life. Given to brooding, he brooded over this.

And so one day in early June he confronted Imogene as she sat with her baby in her arms beside the sundial atop the bluff near the house. Her gaze was following an Indian canoe floating downriver, drifting lazily on the sparkling waters.

"Your face is always turned toward the south," he complained.

Imogene had not heard him come up. Now she looked up and laughed. "There is more excitement there."

Verhulst frowned. "Think not on New Amsterdam," he said bluntly. "You will not see it. I have no plans to take you there. It is time you left off mooning, turned the child over to a nurse, and learned to be a proper Dutch housewife and wife to a patroon."

Imogene sighed. "Perhaps Vrouw Berghem could come upriver and visit us? She was so kind to me in New Amsterdam, and I am sure she would be glad to teach me all that I should know."

Verhulst thought he perceived something devious in this. "Vrouw Berghem would decline your invitation. She is very busy closing her house. Next month she sets sail for Holland to visit her married daughters," he told her, a note of triumph in his voice. "She will be gone a long time, perhaps as much as a year." He shrugged. "I very much doubt she will ever return."

That was bad news. Imogene had hoped that the ebullient Dutch vrouw would inspire Verhulst to take them all downriver to New Amsterdam in turn to visit her. There at least they would see people—people who spoke English, people who laughed and danced. "I hope she finds her daughters well," she said gravely.

"You did not come down to dinner last night," he observed.

"I sent you word that I would not be down. Georgiana was feverish. I wanted to stay with her."

"In future you will dine with me whether the child is sick or well."

Imogene gave him a mutinous look. "It is not Georgiana's fault, Verhulst, that I do not please you."

"No, but perhaps you would make more effort if she were not with us."

Fear tickled Imogene's spine. "But she *is* with us," she rejoined warily.

"You spend too much time with her."

"That's not true! And anyway, Elise takes care of her as much as I do."

"Then let Elise do it."

"Verhulst, I am her *mother!*"

It seemed to Verhulst, looking at this indignant beauty in azure linen, that every problem in his life would be solved—if only they were rid of the ever-present Georgiana.

"I have come to a decision," he said rapidly, making the decision as he went along. "We will send the child to Holland, to my cousin. He and his wife are childless. They will take good care of her. Moreover, they will teach her Dutch—something I doubt you will be eager to do, since you have made no effort to learn it yourself."

Imogene ignored this jibe; her mind was on the main point. "Georgiana is too small to be sent to Holland, alone," she said sharply. "If she goes, Elise and I must accompany her!"

Verhulst leaned forward. A pulse throbbed in his forehead and his dark eyes seemed to bluge. He was trying to control his fractious lady and it was an effort he was really not up to. "You do not seem to hear me, Imogene," he said, spacing his words. "When the child has been weaned, when *I* decide she is old enough, I will ship her forthwith to Holland to my cousin. A servant can escort her! And you, my lady, will remain at Wey Gat and learn to be a proper wife to a patroon! You may start by learning to play the virginal that I bought you. It arrived a fortnight ago and you have not touched it.''

"I have been too busy!"

"With Georgiana."

"Yes, with Georgiana!"

"I have sent for a tutor and when he arrives you will begin your lessons on the virginal.''

Imogene held Georgiana the tighter. She could see that Verhulst, for whatever spiteful reason, had made up his mind. He was determined to send the child away. Fury welled up in her, and indignation, but she held on to her temper, although the effort made her pale. Verhulst might well decree that Georgiana be put in the care of a wet nurse and sent downriver at once—he had the power to do it!

"Time enough to think of the virginal when the tutor gets here," she said distantly, and took her leave of him, gathering up her blue linen skirts and hurrying away, for she could not stand the sight of him just now.

Now once again Imogene was determined to escape—and swiftly, before Verhulst, who now thought her cowed and quiescent, discerned her intentions.

Her chance came the next morning and—impetuous as always—without a second thought she took it.

As she was coming down the stairs to breakfast she paused at the stair landing to tie a sleeve bow that had come untied. Through the window she saw that a river sloop, a "flyboat" as the Dutch called them, was tied up at the pier.

Imogene's heart began to pound as she drank in the sight of that large mainsail and small jib and the lee boards that were the mark of these swift craft that plied the North River. This sloop was not large as riverboats went and she stood studying the stout rugged figure of the captain as he stood at the tiller. What kind of man was he? Dared she hope that he would take her and Elise and the baby with him?

Imogene drew a deep shivering breath. She had to chance it.

Moments later Elise was hurrying down the sloping lawns to inquire as best she could when the sloop would be leaving. She came back to report to Imogene—who had somehow endured breakfast with Verhulst—that the sloop would leave in two hours' time, for while the patroon had offered his hospitality, the patroon had chosen not to buy this particular trader's goods.

Ah, that was a good sign! There was obviously some coldness between Verhulst van Rappard and the captain of this particular river sloop. Encouraged that from animosity toward Verhulst the captain might agree to take them along, Imogene put on several petticoats and two overdresses—at least she would have a change of clothes!—and bade Elise to do likewise. Looking a little stouter than usual from their extra clothes, Imogene, with Elise carrying the baby, sauntered down the broad lawns toward the landing, apparently lost in the beauty of the big chestnut trees about them.

Imogene would have done well to have observed her husband more closely at breakfast. Verhulst had been unusually silent, watching his wife through narrowed eyes as he sifted cinnamon from the handsome silver *ooma* upon his pancakes. He had noted the quick anxious glance she threw toward the river and a ghost of a bitter smile had lit his dark countenance.

But Imogene, lost in her reckless plan, was unaware. . . .

In an agony of doubt, the two women crossed the green lawns. They were so near, so near the pier. Before them the captain stood at the tiller, the sloop was ready to cast off and—yes, she liked this captain's looks, a good, steady man with a sailor's distance-scanning gaze.

"Now," muttered Imogene to Elise. "We must not appear to hurry but the sloop must not leave without us. We will stroll down the pier toward the sloop and go aboard at the last minute." She cast a quick glance back at the house. "No one is watching us."

Elise ducked her head as if to make her tall, gaunt form less conspicuous and both women fought to keep from breaking into a run as they saw escape loom so tantalizingly close.

"Captain," called Imogene in a light voice.

He turned and at that instant the cabin door opened and Verhulst stood in the opening. He was resplendent as ever. The heavy gold chain he always wore glittered against his black brocade doublet and a smile of wolfish triumph spread across his dark face.

"Going somewhere?" he asked.

Imogene and Elise had frozen in their tracks and now Imogene lifted her head, determined to carry it off. "I had thought to inspect the captain's sloop before he left, for it is very different from the *Danskammer*."

"True," mocked Verhulst. "I thought you might care to see it." And Imogene knew that he had guessed her intent, *had allowed it to happen*.

He had wanted to humiliate her—*one more time!*

Still, Elise and the baby were here. She had to carry off this charade—somehow. She allowed herself to be handed aboard by her husband and introduced to the captain, who bowed low. She inspected the sloop through an anguished blur. And then, as Verhulst wandered some distance away, Imogene turned with a little gesture of appeal to the smiling captain. "Please take a message to Vrouw Berghem in New Amsterdam," she begged. "Ask her to invite me downriver to visit her. Tell her I am a prisoner here."

The captain gave her a puzzled look and muttered something in Dutch, shrugging her shoulders. Imogene's heart sank—he spoke no English.

A moment later Verhulst was at her side, mockingly handing her ashore.

Next was Elise's turn to come ashore. Imogene took the baby from her but Verhulst waved Elise back. "I believe you both meant to go downriver," he said smoothly. "Surely at least one of you should be allowed to do so."

Imogene turned to Elise, standing on the deck. "The patroon says you may go, Elise. He will pay for your passage downriver. Vrouw Berghem is kind, she will take you in."

But Elise, horrified at the thought of leaving Imogene, shook her head.

"Come, come, ladies, make up your minds," mocked Verhulst. "The captain here is in a hurry to cast off."

"Go!" cried Imogene. "It is your chance to escape!"

For a moment Elise hesitated. She cast a look downriver at the bright waters that led perhaps back to England—and then her troubled gaze fled back to Imogene, standing tense on the dock with her child in her arms. Imogene trembled as she watched the play of emotions struggle across her old nurse's countenance. If only Elise would realize that with someone to help in New Amsterdam, her own chances for escape must increase tenfold!

But Elise could not leave her. Tears of apology spilled from her pale blue eyes as she scrambled over the side to rejoin Imogene on the pier. Impulsively Imogene threw an arm around the older woman's neck and hugged her. From the deck of the river sloop, the Dutch captain watched this display, puzzled.

These English were more demonstrative than he had thought! He wondered what the patroon's wife had said to him in that choked strained voice and why two women who had been companionably together when they clambered aboard his sloop some moments before were now having what seemed to be a tearful reunion on the pier.

The captain shrugged. Foreigners, he told himself, had mysterious ways—they were not easily understandable, like the Dutch. He barked an order and left the pier of Wey Gat behind him and headed his sloop downriver toward Storm King and the Highlands and thence to New Amsterdam.

From the shore Imogene watched him go with terror in her heart.

For now Verhulst knew her intentions.

At Verhulst's command, Elise took the baby and trailed along behind them miserably as the patroon, holding Imogene's arm in a punishing grip, escorted his errant lady back to the house. In the front hall Imogene jerked away from his restraining grasp, losing her light shawl in the process, and would have confronted him then and there but that he seized her again and dragged her upstairs to the big front bedroom that was now hers again, had been ever since the child was born.

"You seem to have gained some weight," he observed, standing back to view her.

"Perhaps I am pregnant again," said Imogene crushingly, hoping to face him down.

"Ah, now I see what it is." With a swift ruthless gesture, Verhulst ripped off her gray overdress, laughed as he saw the blue overdress beneath. "So you hoped to run away and take your wardrobe with you?" he mocked.

"Only a change of clothes. Surely you would not deny me that?"

He stepped back, secretly admiring the spirit with which she faced him. "I am surprised you do not lie about it," he marveled.

"About my desire to leave you? Verhulst, you *know* I wish to leave you!"

His answer astonished her. "Why?" he asked in a puzzled voice. "Have I not bought you everything, even a virginal? Your possessions are the envy of all on the river. Why should you wish to leave?"

"Because I cannot live with your scorn, your jealousy, because you wish to take my child from me!"

"Oh, the child?" He shrugged and paced about the floor. "You may keep the child," he flung over his shoulder.

Imogene felt her knees go weak. She sagged toward a chair, grasped the carved back in time to keep from falling. She had won—something at least. Verhulst would not take Georgiana from her.

"Unless you displease me again," he added dispassionately. "Then, of course, the child must go."

Barbados, The West Indies, 1658

CHAPTER 21

It was ten o'clock and a light breeze ruffled the brilliant flowers of the bougainvillaea vines as Bess Duveen stepped out on to her wide veranda. Before her stretched the wide green fields and fruit trees of her uncle's island domain—a domain that was now hers, for her uncle had died two fortnights ago and been buried in the churchyard at Bridgetown. Bess had breakfasted in the high-ceilinged dining room, made sunny by its big fanlight windows encrusted with dainty wooden louvered shutters. Those windows were only one of the many refinements of "Idlewild," for her uncle had loved the big stone house he had built and had spent the last years of his prosperous life in making it a showplace of the island. It was indeed a fine home and much envied, for even its stones had been brought across the seas— thick blocks of the soft Bermuda stone, which could be cut with a carpenter's saw and yet when mortared and plastered over with a white lime wash were as impervious to the corroding sea air as granite. The stones had been brought as ballast in ships her uncle had owned.

Bess stood a moment before lifting her full skirts and walking down the wide front steps. She had paused to enjoy, as she always did, the view of sweeping lawns and carefully imported plants, which, in this mild climate, flowered lushly as did the native plants, which—save for the gardeners' constant efforts—would soon have overrun everything with tropical vines.

Bess knew she should hurry to her waiting green-and-gilt coach, for her liveried coachman was even now giving her an inquiring look, and a black footman, equally resplendent in green-and-gold livery, stood patiently waiting to hand her into the coach.

There was much to do this morning. Bess was going into Bridgetown to check out the unloading of a vast lot of goods her uncle had ordered before his death. Although most plantation owners would have left such matters to their factors, Bess intended to supervise the unloading personally. She'd much have preferred to ride in on horseback, but since she was in deep mourning for her uncle, it seemed more respectful to ride in the coach.

Still, hurried as she was, Bess paused and gave a quietly happy look around her.

She had come a long way from the broken-down grandeur of Ennor Castle in the Scillies—and all in such a short time. None of the Duveens had had any idea how wealthy Uncle Dicken had become in the island trade—they had thought of him as a planter of modest fortune and never realized that the major source of his wealth lay in inter-island trade, plus a sprinkling of piracy when he chanced upon a Spanish ship with fewer guns than his own. Of late years he had retired from the sea, sold his ships, and devoted his energies entirely to the development of his plantation—and it had flowered beneath his benign reign.

Bess had been astonished to find herself met at dockside by a coach and bowing footmen to take her luggage, and doubly astonished to find herself ensconced in a mansion and thrust into the busy social life of the island. Not only social but snobbish, for only last week one of her neighbors had been sending a trunk of old clothes to relatives in Boston and had laughed behind her fan to Bess as she lifted out a black lace whisk as being "too fine for Boston, they'd have no place to wear it there!"

But Bess Duveen's mind had not been on the parties and balls at which she would be guest of honor, nor on the beautiful clothes her uncle had promised to have stitched up for her the moment he had laid eyes on her sweet face and pronounced her a beauty. All her attention had been riveted on the stranger she was to marry—someone named Robert Milliken, whose plantation "Mill Oak" adjoined "Idlewild"—and almost as she greeted her uncle she implored him to tell her what Robert was like.

To her astonishment, her uncle had grown choleric. He had cursed roundly, consigning Robert Milliken to the devil in various languages—and finally admitted sheepishly to Bess that Robert Millken had discovered two days ago that his young housekeeper was pregnant and had come round last night to announce bluntly with some embarrassment that his marriage to Bess was off because he had "made an honest woman of Bonnie at last, and indeed he'd have done so before had he known she was pregnant, for his first wife, God rest her soul, had given him neither chick nor child."

Bess, far from falling into tears as her worried uncle had imagined she might, had let out a great sigh of relief and sunk laughing into a cane-backed island chair. That night she had slept well for the first time since leaving the Scillies.

Her apologetic uncle had been charmed by Bess's forthright attitude as well as by her serene acceptance of the situation. He had always valued young Robert's friendship and hated to lose it, so when Bess graciously called upon the bride, thereby guaranteeing her an entrée into island society by way of Idlewild plantation, Uncle Dicken's joy in his hitherto unknown niece overflowed into a concrete display of gratitude. He had called in his solicitor and drawn up a new will leaving everything to Bess on the condition that she stay with him throughout his life.

It was a condition easy to meet, for his doctors had long since told him he was a dying man and "living on borrowed time" and Bess met it gladly—not for what she could gain but because she had swiftly developed an affection for the old man. She liked his pleasant, gruff ways and his sly little jokes and the brave way he met his often painful heart condition. He was dying by inches—but Bess, with her sweet staunch ways and her gaiety, made those inches the best of all the long miles he had traveled in his hectic life. She brushed aside his halfhearted offer to try and find a husband for her, told him she was well enough as she was, and settled down to life on Idlewild plantation as if she'd been born there.

Now, standing on the top step, she smiled down at Lucifer, the big, handsomely furred, copper-colored cat who'd escaped over a ship's side in the harbor, swum to shore, and strolled inland until he had found a plantation to his liking. That plantation was Idlewild, which had seemed to offer the best selection of feminine feline fur in the locality—and a shortage of pussycats was why masterful Lucifer had left the sea in the first place; he had diligently roamed the ship and to his disgust had never found a single one! He had arrived at Idlewild pawsore and tired and had brightened immediately at the sight of a beautiful long-haired tabby sitting atop one of the stone gateposts with her wide fluffy tail draped over the edge. She had stretched luxuriously, displaying her charms, and Lucifer had paused to watch appreciatively. With a long green look at Lucifer, she had leaped down from the gatepost and strolled toward the house, tail waving.

Lucifer had followed, limping on a paw that had picked up a thorn.

She had led him straight to her dish and Bess had found him there, sitting expectantly beside the empty dish, when she brought out a pitcher of milk to feed the cat.

"Annabel," she'd chuckled, "You've brought a friend home to dinner!"

By nightfall Lucifer had had the thorn gently removed from his paw by Bess, he had washed the dust from his fur, and his acquaintance with Annabel had reached the yowling stage.

Now, seeing Bess come out of the house, he had hurried forward to greet her. He rubbed against her black mourning skirts, left a dusting of copper hairs, for he was shedding in the island heat, arched his back as she petted him and then curled up beside a white pillar and began to give himself his morning bath with an energetic pink tongue. Bess's affectionate gaze went from Lucifer to the box in one corner of the veranda from which a loud purring rose and now a gray tabby cat lifted her head to peer at Bess over the box's edge. She gave Bess a sleepy green-eyed look, yawned and went back to washing her kittens— she hadn't been getting enough sleep since they were born. Bess chuckled. Lucifer had not been idle since his arrival—and he and Annabel did not spend all their time mousing. The fluffy copper-toned tabby kittens were proof enough of that.

With a feeling of deep content, Bess let her long black veil fall across her forehead, went down the steps and allowed herself to be handed into her coach, and set out for Bridgetown with its splendid harbor. Bess would much rather have ridden one of the spirited horses in her stable to Bridgetown, but she had thought it more dignified for one in mourning to travel by coach. Her uncle, she knew, would have liked it that way, for he had been basically a very proper man. Bess was proper, too, but now as she felt her bones almost rattle as the coach jolted along the rutted road, she half regretted her decision.

The new factor of Mill Oak plantation had been up since before dawn. He had supervised the driving of several carts into Bridgetown—heavy carts, for Robert Milliken had ordered several stone mantels and other improvements for his plantation from England, and Stephen Linnington, who had disembarked but yesterday and seen his new quarters by candlelight only, had been roused on this, his first day as a factor, by a white bondservant who had tersely informed him that the mantels and other goods awaited unloading from the ship and hauling to Mill Oak.

Rubbing the sleep from his eyes, Stephen had stumbled from his narrow uncomfortable bed and swiftly gotten into his breeches. Hardly had he gulped a hasty breakfast before his horse was brought round and he threw a leg over an unfamiliar saddle. The horse was not much to look at, young and very skittish, for Robert Milliken had no intention of trusting his best stock to a new man, and Stephen found his work cut out for him to keep the mare from shying and bolting at every bush or bird. Once at the dock he worked grimly, supervising the reloading of this heavy yet delicate stuff that had been placed into his keeping. By midmorning the goods were all loaded onto Mill Oak wagons and Stephen was on his way back to the plantation, wearily jollying along a mare who had the bit in her teeth and was rolling her eyes wildly so that the whites showed as she pawed and neighed—just as if she had never seen this road before rather than having traversed it a few short hours before.

The creaking of the wagons, the whips cracking above the draft horses' heads, and the general shouting among the men kept Stephen from hearing the approaching coach until it was upon him, coming into sight suddenly around a blind turn beneath the thick trees whose foliage met overhead.

True to form, the mare reared up, this time unseating her surprised master, who fell to the road and was struck by a wheel of the careening coach.

Bess Duveen, thrown almost on her head as the coach came to a lurching halt, and aware that they had struck something, from the curses and bawling shouts now rising from the road, stuck her head out the window.

What she saw almost stopped her heart.

A tall man in worn russet clothing, his copper hair and angry green eyes unmistakable and seared into her memory, was trying to struggle up from the dust of the road and cursing as he did so.

Bess threw back her long black veil.

"Stephen," she called haltingly. "Stephen—can this really be you?"

Wincing from the pain in his leg and suddenly throwing his weight upon the driver who had sprung down from a wagon to support him, Stephen looked up at the sound of that familiar voice. All expression was wiped from his countenance as he found himself looking up into Bess Duveen's sweet anxious face.

"Surely I've misplaced myself," he muttered. "This isn't the Scillies!"

"Stephen, it *is* you." Bess had the coach door open and was being helped down into the road by her footman. "But we thought you dead!"

"So did many people," agreed Stephen laconically. "But I've risen." He sighed.

Bess's heart was in her gray velvet eyes. "And now to think, I've nearly killed you!" she cried. "Can you stand on that leg? Or is it broken?"

Stephen tested the leg ruefully. "Broken, I'm afraid, Bess."

She bit her lip, then turned to her coachman, taking charge not as sweet Bess Duveen but as the competent mistress of a great plantation. "Unharness the horses," she instructed. "You, Jack, ride for the doctor—the leg shall be set here in this very place. I'll not have Stephen carted about, injuring it worse. And you, Simon—" this to the footman—"ride back to the house and bring a wagon with a mattress upon it and pillows—and bring a flask of brandy." She turned to Stephen. " 'Tis not so far to Idlewild and Doctor Stapleton lives this side of Bridgetown, but a little way farther along this road. Now make him comfortable." This to the men who had clambered down from Stephen's wagons and now shuffled their feet in the road.

"Bess, ye've changed," grinned Stephen. "I've not heard that note of command in your voice before."

Bess flushed a little at the flicker of admiration in his green gaze. "At home I let my brothers bully me. But I'm a woman of property now and responsible for an entire plantation full of people. 'Tis a responsibility, I can promise you."

"I can see ye're up to it." With relief Stephen let them ease him into a sitting position and make him comfortable by the roadside.

"Yes, I'm up to it," said Bess quietly, looking down on that copper head she had thought never to see again. "What are you doing in this part of the world, Stephen?''

That brought him abruptly back to his duty. ''I'm the new factor at Mill Oak,'' he said ruefully. ''Off to a bad start, I'm afraid.'' He turned to the wagon drivers. ''Take the wagons on to Mill Oak, and tell them what's happened. They can send for me, Bess. There's no need to trouble you.''

'' 'Trouble'?'' she chided him, waving her coachman and footman on their way. ''Why, 'tis no trouble at all. I can go into Bridgetown this afternoon and check out this inventory. Or tomorrow, for that matter. I am sure the captain will wait. 'Tis you we must see to, for the leg must be properly set—I will assist the doctor with that, for my brothers were a wild lot and always breaking their bones. And then you'll need rest and a soft bed and hot food if you're not to take a chill and perhaps the fever—and we have all those things at Idlewild.''

Stephen thought of the narrow, uncomfortable bed from which he had been routed before daybreak, of the semihot tasteless gruel he had forced down before mounting the fractious mare.

''I see you're riding Haygirl,'' added Bess disapprovingly. ''I'm surprised that Robert Milliken would let his factor ride that shackling mare. She's thrown everyone at Mill Oak.''

''Add me to the list,'' sighed Stephen. ''I looked up as your coach rounded the bend and the next moment she'd reared up like a mad thing and tossed me.''

''Ah, well, you're more used to sailing than riding, I don't doubt,'' said Bess airily. She spread out a kerchief and sat down beside him now that the men and lumbering wagons had gone. ''And I remember what a sailor you were!''

''For I sailed away from the Scillies in your brother Hal's boat without his leave, didn't I?'' His face was grim.

''But you sent it back,'' pointed out Bess mildly. ''And the circumstances were unusual. I never believed you and Imogene murdered Giles—although there were some who did.''

He flashed her a grateful look. '' 'Twas an accident, Bess. And Imogene had no part in it. We were together when Giles found us. He leaped upon me unaware. I managed to dodge his blade and drag out my own—and he tripped and fell on it. 'Tis a story no one would believe.''

''I would.''

His voice softened. ''But you aren't the law, Bess. 'Twas the law I fled.''

''Why didn't you take Imogene with you?''

''She wanted to go,'' he admitted. ''But I realized it would never work, Bess, that it couldn't work, that I'd only be dragging Imogene down with me—perhaps to her death. She's all right, isn't she?'' he asked anxiously.

'Yes,'' said Bess slowly. ''She's all right. But how came we to hear you were dead, cut down in some duel in Cornwall?''

He could not meet her candid gray eyes. ''I—realize that must have been hard on her,'' he mumbled.

Hard on *her?* Bess gazed at him in wonder. She had died a little herself the night she heard it.

''When the law got too close, I got some trusted friends to put out word I was dead and my body 'committed to the deep' as was my last wish.''

''But you never let *us* know.'' She sounded wounded. ''You let us think—''

His voice roughened. ''It was better that way, better for us all, better that I go out of your lives.''

Bess shook her head and looked away where a bright-colored bird flitted through the branches of an oak. A golden bird, the color of Imogene's hair. . . . Her face clouded. Imogene's golden shadow still lay between them.

"Imogene's uncle sent her away to Amsterdam lest she be taken and questioned in Giles's death."

Stephen's shoulders gave a slight start. "But she'd naught to do with it!" he protested.

"Giles's family was very vengeful." Bess studied that loved face. She had to tell him, and already her soft heart ached for him. "Imogene is married, Stephen. She met a Dutch patroon in Amsterdam and married him and went to live in America."

Her heart hurt at the sudden tightening of his jaw muscles, at the shutters that went down over his turquoise eyes leaving his face for the moment devoid of all expression. "I hope she's happy," he said huskily.

"I believe she is," Bess told him. "She wrote me from Holland and I have not heard from her since—but the mail is so uncertain. She told me that her husband's patroonship is on the North River and that he has a very handsome home there. She said he was filling a ship with his treasures to bring home to America." She stopped, realizing it must hurt him to contrast his poverty with the patroon's wealth, a wealth they both believed had won Imogene.

"I am glad for her." The words were wrenched from Stephen. Something inside—something he thought he had forgotten—hurt far worse than his broken leg.

Gently as a feather, Bess's hand brushed his arm. He started at the touch, for he had been lost in thought—lost in memories of silken skin and shining hair that smelled faintly of perfume, lost in delft blue eyes deeper than all the oceans. He was remembering Imogene, and the thought that another man was holding her in his arms, that another man was taking her to his bed—of course he had known it would happen eventually. Still it seared him. He gave Bess a miserable look. "I think you know how I feel," he said.

"Yes. I know." She was silent for a while, letting the pain of this fresh raw wound subside.

After a moment he shook his head as if to clear it. "But how came ye here, Bess? Did ye marry?"

She shook her head and began to laugh. It was a happy, triumphant laugh, for in whatever shape and wherever his heart had flown, Stephen Linnington had been restored to her and with a broken leg he could hardly take himself off.

"My uncle arranged a marriage for me, Stephen. I came to this island to marry your employer, Robert Milliken—who wed his housekeeper the night before I arrived!"

"The devil he did!" Stephen felt honest indignation rise in him. Bess deserved no such foul trick.

"I can't tell you how delighted I was," said Bess demurely. "For Robert Milliken—pleasant neighbor that he is—takes snuff and is addicted to wormwood wine, neither of which I can tolerate. Besides, he tells interminably long stories that have no point at all—oh, I should have been miserable married to him and I wish poor Bonnie joy of him."

Stephen remembered Milliken's overdressed wife who had gazed at the new factor with more than the usual interest. "So ye married somebody else, then?" he asked, bewildered, suddenly noting her black garb, which he took to be widow's weeds.

Again she shook her head. "No. Oh, my uncle offered to trot out all the eligible men on the island but I simply refused. It had been such a long, tedious voyage and all the time I worried about this stranger to whom I should be chained for life—it was a real relief to find out he had married someone else! My uncle was in failing health and asked me to stay with him. I did and I do believe I was some comfort to him these last months. He left me everything—Idlewild, the furniture, the indentured servants, the slaves, the livestock—everything.''

Stephen's mouth formed itself into a grin. "So now ye're a grand lady, Bess, with minions to do your bidding?''

"Oh, yes,'' Bess laughed. "We are very grand at Idlewild—too grand. When I looked over the books, I found there was not enough set by for bad years, crop failures, the storms that visit these islands. I have no intention that Idlewild shall go under as so many of our neighbors have. I have lived on islands all my life and I know that their economy is uncertain. So I am setting out to improve things—not in the way my uncle did, by adding mantels and paneling and liveries and plate—but in commercial ways. I have learned that three of my bondswomen are accomplished weavers—they but need the flax, which I am importing for them. Two are lacemakers—I rescued them from our kitchen! And two others are excellent seamstresses—and how were they spending their time? Bending over laundry tubs and hanging up clothes! And I myself have a flair for fashion!''

"Indeed I noticed how modish you look, for all your black weeds,'' Stephen said gallantly.

She gave him a reproving look. "Not for myself—I do not need them to make clothes for me; I have all the clothes I can wear. But fabrics are cheap in the markets of Tortuga—''

"I know,'' he interrupted. "I met one of the buccaneer captains who supplies them!''

"—and I have commissioned a captain who was a close friend of my uncle's to bring me back from Tortuga a whole list of fabrics so these women can work, not as scullery maids or chambermaids, but at their highest skills. Do you know the price a handsome gown will command in the Carolinas or Virginia? Or for that matter, right here in Barbados? So I will have a whole new industry for my plantation to help keep us going in the lean years—for there *must* be lean years. And I am training my footmen to do useful things as well as merely running errands and the like about the house. Simon is learning to make cheese and, for Wilbur, who claims he was brought up in the trade, I have even bought a potter's wheel!''

"Bess, Bess," laughed Stephen. "I see you will soon have a thriving city at Idlewild. And at Ennor Castle you seemed so meek and self-effacing!"

"Do not mock me, Stephen," said Bess gravely.

"I'd no thought to mock you, I assure you!"

"I know I seem more optimistic than the situation warrants. I know it will take years to realize my dreams but—at least I have made a start and it will all grow day by day."

"We did not know your potential on the Scillies," he teased her.

She gave him a level look. "No, you did not. At Ennor Castle, my parents ruled—and I could do nothing with my brothers; they were all dedicated fishermen and would not listen to me. But here at Idlewild all must listen to me. And together we are going to make the plantation a great success. Did you know, I plan to give every bondswoman who marries a bridal gown stitched here on the plantation and a dowry?"

"I could hardly hear about it, Bess. I've been on the island only since yesterday."

"I thought you might have heard of it anyway," said Bess ruefully. "Robert Milliken has heard of my plans and is furious—he says I will spoil all the servants on the island, that next they will all demand beaver hats!"

"You have grown up," he said soberly. "You are not the shy little girl I knew."

"Ah, well, I suppose I *have* changed since the Scillies."

Bess's laughing gray eyes met his. "There's responsibility here, Stephen, and someone must shoulder it. I am responsible for all the people on my plantation, Stephen, and for the house and livestock and all the lovely things my uncle left me. I must not let any of them suffer."

Stephen smiled back into those candid gray eyes. He felt she never would.

"And now," she added in a tone that had in it a touch of imperiousness. "I see the doctor coming in the distance. We'll soon have you to Idlewild, where I—having downed you—will personally nurse you back to health. And as for your job as factor at Mill Oak, mine has left me because he refuses to work for a woman and you shall take his place. I will send a note over to Robert Milliken and tell him that you are leaving—and scold him as well for giving you that witless mare to ride!"

Stephen's eyes kindled. This new Bess had a spirit and tone he liked. She was not Imogene, of course, but she intrigued him. "Bess, I'd be happy to be your factor," he said, adding honestly, "but you must remember this plantation life is new to me and I won't be the assistance an experienced man would be. At Mill Oak there's Robert Milliken to train me but—"

"Not another word!" Bess touched soft fingers to his lips to silence him, and at the contact a swift quiver went through her and her cheeks grew pink. "You shall be my factor only after you have recovered—until then you shall be my honored guest. And as to learning the job, I have already learned it—at least well enough that I can impart it to you. 'Tis none so difficult, if one sets oneself to learn it."

Stephen caught her hand, pressed it to his lips. "I will do my best," he promised huskily.

She smiled on him fondly. "You always have—done your best," she said in a soft voice, and Stephen was shamed by the glowing light in those steady gray eyes. "I knew," she added, "why you left the Scillies. 'Twas to save Imogene from the consequences of her folly. No—" when he would have spoken—"we'll talk no more about it, for 'tis good to see you again and there's so much here to interest you. Oh, Stephen, you're going to love Barbados once you get to know it!"

Her soft glance promised much and for the first time there was a hint of steel in it, a sparkle of humor. For Bess had always known Stephen Linnington was a rake and a ne'er-do-well. But now, she told herself gaily, that was all over. With her to guide him, with her steady good sense and her newfound fortune, Stephen Linnington would become the man Bess had always known he could be—a man respected in the islands, a man to depend upon. A man to come home to . . .

Stephen would have been astonished had he known the wild thoughts that teemed through Bess's dark head as she smiled at him. He took her sudden show of interest to be only a reflection of her kindly nature—but it was so much more. Bess, in her busy heart, was spinning out a whole life for him—happy, proud, successful.

And so, for the second time in his life, a Duveen determinedly hauled a wounded Stephen Linnington back home to the family manor. But this Duveen had soft hands and a smiling way with her. And Stephen knew, as his leg mended and the days passed in this scented land of summer, that he was falling in love with her and that he would never leave this enchanted isle of Barbados.

Wey Gat, New Netherland, 1658

CHAPTER 22

A soft south wind was blowing, fragrant perhaps with the scent of the Carolinas, far to the south. Gently it stirred the wide rye and wheat fields of Wey Gat, making them ripple like silk. Far above, frolicking swallows swooped and skimmed against a blue dome of sky so clear it seemed to extend forever. Out in the meadows fat woodchucks waddled through heavy red clover and bumbled through great swatches of white and yellow daisies, ahum with bees. The air was rich with the scent of honey locusts and wild grapes and the promise of a rich harvest to come.

A kind of uneasy peace, somnolent as the summer, hung over Wey Gat, as the patroon and his dashing lady moved like checkers across a board of his devising. For managing not to "displease" Verhulst van Rappard was no easy task, Imogene had soon learned.

Always eager to separate her from her child, of whom he had become almost insanely jealous, Verhulst ordered Imogene to take lessons on the new virginal he had imported. But forcing his rebellious lady to take lessons was one thing—making her proficient on the virginal was something else. Imogene might have enjoyed playing such a lovely instrument, now installed in gilt and rosewood grandeur in a corner of the drawing room, but now that she had been ordered to do so, she stubbornly refused to learn. Dutifully she would run her slender hands across the scales—and then come to a full stop at the cry of a hawk or some other wild creature and pause to envy its freedom in the vast outdoors, a freedom that with Verhulst for a husband she was not likely to know. Indifferently, under her elderly Dutch teacher's careful tutelage, she even learned a piece or two. But play for Verhulst she would not. When he ordered her tersely to play for him after dinner that he might note her progress, she merely dragged her hands listlessly over the keys, striking at random as many sour notes as sweet ones.

Listening, Verhulst winced. "It would seem ye have no talent for music, Imogene," he taunted her.

"Perhaps not." Seated at the virginal, Imogene gave him a tight little wisp of a smile. "Prisoners are seldom at their best, Verhulst."

" 'Prisoners'?" He was taken aback. "But ye're my wife!"

Imogene ended the piece with a discordant chord and swung around to face him. "It amounts to the same thing."

Baffled—for Verhulst had been sure the gift of the virginal would please her—the young patroon now attempted to learn to play himself and asked Imogene to sing an accompaniment to his efforts, but she refused to do it; she told him woodenly she did not feel like singing. She looked so sad as she said it that for a moment he felt guilty—but irritation soon swept that softer emotion away.

To his regret—and he did not understand it, for he could not know the crushing weight his overbearing personality had put upon his wife—Imogene no longer sang for joy in the mornings as she had after the baby was born. How often he had paused to listen to those sweet caroling notes drifting to him softly as she rocked little Georgiana's cradle. In showy outward ways she pleased him, but her heart was not in it. Passively she wore the yellow dresses he loved, but her golden feathers drooped, he thought, and sometimes he wondered why. After all, he had not sent the child away—he had only threatened.

To make amends, he gave Imogene a pearl and ruby necklace, telling himself that would surely cheer any woman. But even its flashing splendor brought only a momentary sparkle to her sad blue eyes.

"I have enough jewelry, Verhulst," she said quietly, pushing the gems away from her. "The only jewel I would have from you is the jewel of freedom—freedom to walk about, to go where I wish, not to be spied upon, watched."

"Then I will give the necklace to someone who desires it more!" cried Verhulst. He snatched back the necklace and stomped from the room.

It was not long before he convinced himself that Imogene was conspiring with her elderly Dutch-speaking tutor to escape and sent the bewildered old gentleman back to his home in Beverwyck.

Verhulst could not understand Imogene. Alternately, he hated and adored her, but he never at any time understood her. Why did she not respond to his overtures, he asked himself petulantly. Was he not in every way a kindly husband? Indeed, was he not a *noble* husband, to overlook her bearing another man's child beneath the shelter of his name? That he had not done it with good grace, that he had bullied and frightened Imogene, he did not take into account.

She was his and she should behave as if she enjoyed being his.

He took to needling her with veiled insults in an attempt to make her betray at least some emotion toward him, but she was deadened to his anger, to his contempt. She was walking a narrow path, a desperately narrow path, in an attempt to keep her child, and while her proud nature would not let her smile at him, her iron control kept her from an open break with him. So she turned a deaf ear to his most barbed thrusts, sat woodenly at the table while he insulted her.

Verhulst found this lack of animation maddening. For in his heart he wanted much more than a golden painting come to life—a trifle he had purchased for gold in Amsterdam; he wanted a woman, warm and willing and—although he would never have admitted this to himself—a woman who loved him.

And Imogene was not that woman.

She could not see behind the mask of indifference and mockery that he wore. She could not see the man—frightened, bitter, yearning behind the protective wall of his pride. If she could have understood him, she might have averted what came to pass, but she did not. A woman like Imogene would never understand such a man as Verhulst van Rappard.

And still the golden days drifted by. . . .

One day in an excess of fury that he could not reach through the wall of her indifference, Verhulst sprang to his feet, knocked over the armchair in which he sat, and began to rail at her.

Still she was silent, distant, letting his harsh words beat over her like raven's wings.

All of Verhulst's venom toward her seemed to concentrate in one great burst. "I warned you against displeasing me!" he shouted. "And by your indifference you are indeed displeasing me!"

Imogene turned toward him as if seeing him for the first time. "What is it you want, Verhulst?" she demanded wearily. "I thought it was acquiescence and, before God, I have not crossed you."

Rage was churning within him. "Your sins are those of omission!" he shouted. "It is what you have *not* done that displeases me."

Imogene looked down at her folded hands. "And what would you have me do?"

"I would have you—by God, I *will* send the child away! Next spring, no later! Unless you mend your ways before-times!"

He stalked away leaving Imogene staring after him with dull hatred in her lovely eyes. Acquiescence was not enough—now she must feign joy at his taunts!

Once again she determined to escape him. This time she would leave Elise and take the baby. She would go downriver—and once in New Amsterdam, her jewels would buy her a hiding place! Getting aboard ship would be trickier, for Verhulst's agents would doubtless be watching New Amsterdam's docks. That was where Elise came in. She would weep over Imogene's disappearance—and beg the patroon to let her return to her people in England. She would then take passage south on the first sloop. Verhulst, who would have lost her trail by now, would follow Elise, hoping to pick it up again. Elise would take passage on a ship bound for Barbados and somehow—*somehow* she would get the baby to Elise just before the ship sailed and, after that, make her own presence known among the Dutch burghers. Word would promptly reach Verhulst and she would play hide-and-seek with him through New Amsterdam's winding streets—if necesary, she would play hide-and-seek with him through these hills. But she would lead him away from Elise and the baby, who would find a safe haven in Barbados with kindly Bess Duveen. And eventually, God willing, she would join them in Barbados. But if she did not, if Verhulst caught her, killed her—at least her baby would be safe!

Fired by the thought, she watched her chance and over Elise's protests, slipped down in the night and stole a rowboat, put little Georgiana in it and eased it into the dark waters unnoticed. Once on the river's broad breast, she clutched her baby to her and prayed that the current, which was flowing swiftly south, would carry them safely to New Amsterdam.

Wooded shores floated by in the moonlight and sometimes floating logs and once an Indian canoe. Imogene crouched down in terror lest they see her, but the canoe continued on about its own business. Perhaps the canoe's occupants had not noticed, across a forest of floating logs and branches, a woman crouched in the rowboat.

They would have been amazed at the sight of her, had the moon come out full from behind its bank of clouds. For under the dark woolen shawl that gave her the anonymity of other night things moving through the darkness was a woman of light and sun. Her usually bound-back hair streamed down long and golden and three jeweled necklaces sparkled around her slender neck. They flashed in sharp contrast to the cheap sprigged calico dress she wore, the cotton stockings—but under that dress was another dress of silk, and beneath that three silken petticoats, and beneath the cotton stockings another pair—of silk. For Imogene did not know what role she would have to play downriver—impoverished petitioner, traveling aristocrat—she was prepared for either.

And cuddled sleeping in her arms was the reason for her desperate venture: little Georgiana, trustingly asleep in her mother's arms as the broad North River swept them southward.

Imogene had been tense and wakeful all the night before as she planned this venture, tense throughout the evening as she had managed to outwit Verhulst and the servant he had set to spy on her. Now at last her stamina was exhausted and in the bottom of the boat she fell asleep with her arm curled protectively around baby Georgiana.

That nap was to cost her.

Rushing down from the Adirondacks, the current did indeed sweep her along toward the south, but this was the river the Indians had long ago christened "The River that Flows Two Ways," and as Imogene slept, the floodtide from the sea pushed mightily upriver. For the great river Henry Hudson had discovered was tidewater far north of Wey Gat, it was tidewater as far north as Beverwyck. And while she slept the flow reversed itself, the northbound tide overcame the southbound current, swept over it and carried Imogene's boat inexorably back upriver.

Imogene woke up at the sound of a shout. Stiff and bewildered as to where she was, she sat up with a jerk, one arm flung over the side of the boat. The sun was in her eyes and she blinked at the sight that met her gaze.

The rowboat that had been carrying her so confidently south the night before was now drifting northward past Wey Gat. As Imogene's startled gaze flew incredulously up the sloping bluff to the great stone house, whose windows sparkled mockingly in the morning sunlight, she saw men running down the slope toward her.

She seized an oar but it was too late. Directed by Verhulst from the shore, they set out in boats and pulled her rowboat to shore with long hooks.

It was a shaken Imogene who was escorted firmly back to the great house and breakfast.

Verhulst could hardly conceal his triumph. He would not

permit her to change her clothes but forced her to break her fast with him clad in her simple calico and her three sparkling necklaces.

"Layer on layer of clothes,' he murmured. "And those—" he indicated the necklaces with some amusement—"were to buy you safe passage away from me, I suppose?"

Conscious she was being mocked and too tired and disappointed to eat, Imogene refused to answer. She sat and gazed steadily back at her husband.

"But you must eat to keep up your strength," he pointed out blandly, "if you are to continue this folly. Here, will you not have some pancakes?" And when she shook her head and still refused to speak, he launched into a gloating explanation of the river's tides and currents, which even an experienced navigator could run afoul of. He told her how sometimes when the river seemed to be flowing south, a boat would barely make way—for beneath the southward flowing surface waters, the ocean tide was making its inexorable way north and pulling the boat in that direction below the waterline.

If Imogene understood him, she gave no sign, merely staring back at him with a blank expression. Finally this maddened Verhulst.

"Don't sit there like a statue!" he roared. "Speak! Admit I have bested you! Admit I will always win!"

Tired and defiant, Imogene's chin lifted, and even in her rumpled calico with her hair tangled and windblown, Verhulst could not help thinking that she looked a very queen. Her voice was colorless, exhausted—but it held no spirit of defeat.

"Had I not fallen asleep, I would never have let the river carry me back north—and you would not be breakfasting with me now," she said calmly.

Verhulst looked taken aback. "Then you have not yet

learned your lesson?'' he murmured in surprise.

Imogene fetched a deep sigh and looked past him out the window—to freedom. ''I will find a way to escape you yet, Verhulst. You cannot hold me forever here at Wey Gat.''

''Empty words,'' he mocked her, glad to have at least this defiant cry from her. ''Empty words, Imogene.''

She gave him back such a look of pure contempt that he was lashed again to fury.

''The next time you try to escape,'' he warned her in a voice gone low and deadly, ''I will kill you.''

Then next time I must be more careful, her proud face promised him. But Imogene kept her silence. It would not do to provoke the patroon further; he might deny her even the companionship of her child.

''I bid you think on it,'' he warned her. ''For you are becoming the talk of the river, with your wild attempts to escape me, and I will not have people laughing at me behind my back. Do you understand, Imogene?''

Imogene's throat was dry. ''You bring it only on yourself, Verhulst,'' she declared steadily. And then on a pleading note, ''Oh, *why* can you not let me go? Why is it so important to keep me here?''

''You are mine,'' he said simply. ''I have never given up anything that belonged to me.''

She stared at him for a long time, drinking that in, realizing that it was the shape of her future.

But that aborted escape attempt had made Imogene cautious. Verhulst might indeed keep his promise to kill her.

Things worsened between them after that until their hostility reached a near fever pitch. Sometimes Verhulst, goaded by her contempt, talked about next spring when he would send Georgiana away. Once Imogene leaped up, white-faced.

"If you send her away, I promise you, Verhulst, that I will kill myself!"

He was taken aback by her desperation, but it made him thoughtful. His valiant lady had said she would escape him—and she had tried, how she had tried. In an effort to kill herself, she might well succeed.

"There is no need to think on death," he said uneasily. "It is a long time till spring. Perhaps I will change my mind about sending the child away."

But now Imogene knew she could not trust him. When spring came to New Netherland and the sea-lanes to Holland were crowded with wooden ships voyaging to and from America, Verhulst might any day on a whim rob her of Georgiana.

She could not let it happen.

Wiser now, she sat down and wrote a letter to Bess Deveen in Barbados and contrived so cleverly that the letter was taken downriver by a Dutch captain who promised to see that it was delivered.

And where was Captain van Ryker tonight? she asked herself bitterly, pondering on the inconstant ways of men. For Vrouw Berghem had told her in New Amsterdam that the captain frequently sailed upriver with his captured Spanish goods to dispose of them at Beverwyck when the Dutch burghers of New Amsterdam did not offer a price high enough, but although Imogene had had Elise make casual inquiries, no one seemed to have seen or heard of him.

Was he perhaps enamored of some wench in the Caribbean? she wondered, and was surprised and ashamed to find her nails biting into the flesh of her fingers at the thought.

That the buccaneer captain was avoiding her because he did not want to spoil her perfect happiness would have shocked her—and made her choke with bitter laughter.

In point of fact, at that moment Captain van Ryker, fresh from a successful voyage and in company with his ship's master, Barnaby Swift, and his ship's doctor, Raoul de Rochemont, was just sweeping into one of Tortuga's better taverns. His entrance caused quite a stir, for van Ryker was not only a popular sea wolf, but was solemnly believed on Tortuga to be the best blade in the Caribbean—and on this night his left arm was in a sling.

"Aye, 'twas a Spanish blade that pierced me," he laughed in answer to a gust of eager questions. "But not the blade from the front—'twas the blade from the side and he'd have spitted me, too, had not Barnaby here cut the fellow down."

Young Barnaby flushed proudly and his chest expanded a bit. It was very pleasant to hear his captain give him credit for saving his life—although Barnaby was morally certain that had he not intervened van Ryker would have swung around and demolished both opponents in a series of lightning thrusts. Barnaby was very impressed by his captain's prowess—he had reason to be: he'd seen van Ryker fight five men on the slippery deck of a Spanish caravel and come out almost unscathed. There was good reason for the lean buccaneer's awesome reputation.

The three newcomers seated themselves, calling careless answers to the grinning pleasantries that were tossed their way. From the back, through a forest of arms and tankards upraised in raucous greetings, a new tavern maid picked her way. She had a thick shock of long black hair that fell loose to her hips and a pair of jingling gold earrings—gift of a buccaneer who had already drunk himself under the table. Her gray linen apron was tied on carelessly over a red satin kirtle that had seen better days, and her shoe soles were nearly worn through, but she had a saucy smile and a swaying walk that made men notice her rippling bust and slender waist and the curving outthrust line of her hips and bottom. A curtain of black lashes shadowed her dark eyes as she rested her knuckles on her hips and asked the buccaneer captain in a sultry voice what he would have.

"Faith, *I'd* have *her*," muttered Barnaby to the ship's doctor.

Raoul de Rochemont studied the girl's challenging smile and lavish bustline—hardly fettered by the thin white cotton blouse she wore. "Ye'd be right, Barnaby," he muttered, arching his head about. His eyes lit with admiration. *"Mon Dieu,* what a charming *derrière!"*

But the black-haired barmaid's attention was all riveted on the famous Captain van Ryker, who returned her scrutiny with a wary grin. He'd bedded barmaids in Tortuga before and had found them an adventurous lot. One of them—uncaring of his dangerous reputation—had even made off with his purse and watch! He'd not had the heart to pursue the wench, for it had been a splendid evening—not that he could have, for she'd promptly stowed away on a ship bound for God knew where.

"Your best Spanish wine all around," he told her. "I've acquired a liking for it from lifting so much of it from their vessels!"

A hoot of general laughter greeted the captain's remark and the dark barmaid sidled away with a sidewise glance at him. When she returned with a bottle of good Malaga, Barnaby edged down the bench and made room for her. He patted the bench. "Rest your feet a bit," he suggested.

"I don't mind if I do." Cheerfully, the black-haired girl swung a leg over the bench—being careful to display a long expanse of white leg along with a swish of chemise. Sitting down by Barnaby had placed her next to van Ryker and now she moved a little closer to him, edging her leg against his lean thigh.

"Have some wine," said the captain equably.

"There's no glass for me," She smiled up at him through her thick forest of lashes.

"Here, ye can share mine," offered Barnaby, quickly reaching around her with his glass so that she came within the circle of his arm. "What's your name, lass? For I don't remember seeing you here before."

The girl turned and gave Barnaby a faintly irritated look; it was the buccaneer captain she'd set her sights upon—not his young ship's master. "Aye, I'm new here," she agreed. "My name's Kate."

"I'm surprised to find a likely lass like yourself in this rough place." Barnaby was determined not to be outmaneuvered by his captain—who needed rest, he told himself solicitously. He was pleased to observe his captain launch into a conversation with de Rochemont, leaving him a clear field. "D'ye have no protector, then?" he wondered.

Kate, who regarded her voluptuous charms as sufficient bait to attract any number of new "protectors" at will, gave Barnaby an astonished look. "I need no protector with a brother like mine. He's laid up just now, recovering from a fever he took on shipboard after we fled England, but once he's up and around I'd match him against any man." Her voice rang out proudly. "Ye'll no doubt have heard of my brother—Gentleman Johnnie's his name."

Van Ryker heard that and his conversation with the doctor was arrested in mid-sentence. This was Stephen Linnington's first wife—the black-haired highwayman's sister! His dark head swung round in surprise to get a better look at her. The lustrous wench now had his full attention.

"I see ye've heard of my brother, Captain van Ryker." The sultry voice sounded pleased.

"Aye, and I've heard of you, too—through a friend of mine. Stephen Linnington."

The girl's red mouth dropped open in astonishment. " 'Stephen—'?"

"Linnington. A relative of yours, I believe—through marriage."

Kate's head went back and she gave a great peal of laughter. And when she had finished rocking with mirth, she leaned forward and told the captain behind her hand a story he would never forget. It was a whispered conversation filled with giggles that caused Barnaby, who could not hear, to shuffle his feet and frown. At the end of it, Captain van Ryker dropped a gold coin down the neck of her bodice and rose. Very pleasantly he excused himself and took himself off with the ship's doctor, leaving the disappointed Kate to a surprised and happy Barnaby.

It was as well that Imogene did not know who Captain van Ryker was with that night, for it would only have deepened her bitterness.

Barbados, The West Indies, 1658

CHAPTER 23

At Idlewild, Bess Duveen was happily pondering her trousseau. She had already decided that they would take a wedding trip to Jamaica, where she would have Stephen fitted with the most spectacular pair of boots to be found anywhere. She had ordered from London a ruby ring that would be her wedding token to him and had bought at a shop in Bridgetown a handsome dress sword of Toledo steel, doubtless once loot from some Spanish galleon—it would look lovely swinging against his lean thigh, she thought. What a figure he would cut at their wedding in the new suit of turquoise satin she had chosen to match his eyes!

In the weeks that he had been at Idlewild, Stephen's leg had mended and now it was well. But even lying in bed he had not been idle. Along with handsome red and green leather-bound books from her uncle's library, Bess Duveen had brought him the plantation's account books and together they had pored over them, discussing the items until Stephen felt thoroughly acquainted with the plantation's various projects. Once he could walk, Bess had given him the best horse from her stables and they had set out together, combing every inch of the estate, introducing Stephen to everyone who worked there.

The new factor had "taken hold" nicely, Bess thought. Like herself, Stephen learned fast. And in the long scented evenings, when he was not squiring her to one island social function or another (where heads always turned to admire the handsome pair), they discussed at length what should be done to improve the property and its revenues.

They spent so much time together, revelling in each other's company, that the inevitable happened. On a night when the soft wind sang gently through the bougainvillaea and the world seemed a magic place, the account books had been tossed aside, the wine glasses released from careless fingers. Flesh had met tingling flesh in a wild embrace—for it had been a long time since Stephen had held a woman in his arms and Stephen was Bess's first and only love.

In the shock of that first contact, that first burgeoning moment, Stephen might have drawn away—he might even have apologized to his gentle employer for the liberties he had taken. But Bess lost her shyness of a sudden. With luminous eyes she surged into his arms, letting him take her with wild abandon. Her trembling fingers helped his own hurried ones loosen the hooks of her flowered bodice. Over and over she murmured his name: *Stephen, Stephen . . .*

Forgetful of the consequences his rash lovemaking might have for Bess, amazed by her sudden unexpected lack of restraint, Stephen drew Bess down with him onto the soft velvet divan. The candles flickered as a soft breeze drifted through the louvered shutters—he did not even pause to blow them out.

They might have been alone in the world, so rapt was their concentration.

"Bess—are ye *sure?*" he murmured, as his hand slipped down beneath her loosened bodice, sliding along her spine, and he felt her tremble violently.

"I'm *sure.*" It was only a breath of a sound, a wisp on the evening air, but it sent his pulse pounding and his arms tightened about her.

She was giving herself to him, this lovely woman he had admired—worshipped almost! It was unreal as the night, a part of this island magic that held them both in thrall.

And because he knew this must be Bess's first experience with a man, he was gentle, playful, tender, thrusting carefully, trying not to hurt her, until at last on a burst of feeling he threw caution aside and made her wholly his, sweeping her along with him, rocketing skyward to velvet heights of emotion that overwhelmed them both.

And when it was over, after they had drifted back from that wonder world that only lovers knew, Stephen had taken her by the shoulders and gazed gravely into her clear gray eyes and asked himself in amazement how he had overlooked her.

"You were made for me, Bess," he murmured huskily, still astonished that virginal Bess could have matched him kiss for kiss, sigh for sigh.

"I always knew it." Bess pressed her hot face against his throbbing chest, hiding her blushes as his hands, loving in the afterglow, caressed her tingling body. "And now—you know it, too."

"Yes." Stephen looked down at her, smiling. "Now I know it, too."

Bess lifted her head and this time she did not flinch from his gaze. This was the lover who had come to her from the sea, tossed up by a wave. This was the lover she had nursed back to health at Castle Ennor.

Imogene was only a passing fancy, her fearless gaze told him. *But you will find a home in my heart.*

Stephen, pensive, smiling down at her in the afterglow of passion, had lost the lighthearted banter his other loves had known. In Bess Duveen he had been confronted by simple goodness—and it was that direct, openhearted goodness that had confounded him. He was humbled by it, made to look inward, to see himself as he was—and as he might have been. *As he still could be,* her steady gray eyes told him. And now abruptly he wanted to be that man. He wanted to "take hold" of the plantation, to make it thrive and prosper, he wanted to read approval in Bess's gray gaze.

Bess, whether she knew it or not, was making a man of Stephen.

Stephen had not actually asked her to marry him that night, but to Bess the agreement to wed was tacit between them. All this past week, ever since that first lovely night, she had been making plans for their life together. Giggling girls were already stitching up Bess's trousseau and the kitchen staff was bracing for an enormous wedding, for Bess meant to share her newfound happiness with everyone on the island.

As she lifted up a long length of ivory satin from a bowed leather trunk, Bess caught a glimpse of her glowing face and sparkling eyes in the mirror and hugged herself to make sure it was all real.

His! She was his at last. A smile curved her lips at the thought and her face took on a wondrous light. Every kiss, every touch, every sigh . . . she would remember it all to the day she died. All last night, while a pale moon hung like a scimitar over

Barbados, she had lain in Stephen's arms, thrilling to his touch, overwhelmed by the miracle that he should love her, want her, need her.

And morning had not dispelled the dream. She had waked luxuriantly to feel his naked hip brushing hers, his wandering fingers questing down her spine, exploring a tingling nipple, waked to find a gently teasing lover in her bed, waked to a life of new beauty and new meaning.

"Look, Stephen," she laughed, gesturing with a naked arm at the candles that had guttered out. "We forgot to blow out the candles again last night!"

Stephen was stroking her dark hair lovingly. "Let's not be in a hurry to wed, Bess," he murmured. "Life is so fine as it is."

"But 'twill be even better then," she promised him gaily, pulling away and jumping up. "Come, we're lying late abed! What will the servants think?"

"They'll think no wrong of ye, Bess—no man could." But he turned his troubled face away from her. He was cursing himself inwardly for his folly. To honest Bess there was no other course: having fallen in love, having lain in each other's arms, of course they must wed. What else?

Miserably Stephen found himself approving her trousseau gowns—each more dashing than the last. Indeed he had thrilled Bess by telling her that she needed no trousseau to please him, he would take her as God made her and they could live like Adam and Eve in the Garden, naked to love on these warm nights.

"No, we must both have new clothes," she told him energetically. "It is expected of us."

At that point he managed to protest. "I bring you nothing,

Bess. I am a landless man. My father has cut me off without a farthing. In England my family will not receive me. I can bring you nothing—''

"But yourself," supplied Bess. "It is enough, Stephen."

"Are you sure, Bess?" His turquoise eyes searched her face with a desperation she could not understand. "Are you sure you will not regret—?"

Quickly she reached up and pulled his copper head down to hers, silenced his protesting voice with a kiss. "I am very sure. And I will never regret my love for you, whatever happens. Of that you may be certain."

Whatever happens . . . She'd forgiven him his early preference for Imogene—but what if she knew he had two wives already and was divorced from neither?

The doubt she saw in his face she swept aside. "Oh, Stephen." On a sudden gust of affection, she leaned against him, fitting herself close into his arms. "We are going to be so happy!"

"Ye're too good for me, Bess," he muttered, and it was well she could not see the torment in his eyes. "I ne'er thought to find heaven on earth here in Barbados."

How she thrilled to hear him say that! Ah, it was all too perfect! With a song in her heart, Bess pushed him gently away. "We've work to do!" she laughed.

"Aye. And I want to see how the men are doing with the new shed they're building. Don't look for me till suppertime, Bess." He turned and left her.

Bess was not troubled by his abrupt departure. All her duties were a joy these days and the hours passed like minutes until she dressed in the pink sprigged calico dress that was Stephen's favorite and swept with a swish of taffeta petticoats into the long dining room of Idlewild.

Stephen was waiting for her. He was staring out the window with his hands behind his back. He turned as she entered and considered her gravely.

"You look tired," she said, concerned.

He did not answer, but walked over and closed the doors.

His haggard expression alarmed Bess. "But you're shutting out the servants," she protested. "They'll be wanting to serve us our supper."

"Bess, I have something to say to you and after I've said it, you may not wish to sit at the table with me. Indeed, you may wish to turn me off the plantation."

Bess, whose color had heightened at sight of him, had the sudden feeling that she was going to have to ward off some great blow of fate. "I would never do that, Stephen."

Stephen came forward and stood looking down at her. She was almost swept away by the virile maleness of him, the anxious regard for her she could read in his eyes, the *caring* in that handsome, abandoned face. Confidently, she smiled up at her tall lover.

"Bess." Stephen moistened his lips and found his throat was dry. This was the hardest thing he had ever said in his life. "Bess, I can't marry you."

At this abrupt pronouncement, a ripple of protest went through Bess's frail body. She frowned and studied him. "Why not?" she asked uneasily. "Are you saying that you aren't in love with me, that Imogene still—"

"No, no." He ran distracted fingers through his copper hair and it glinted in the candlelight. "All that seems long ago, forgotten now." It was not forgotten, but the memories no longer hurt and the warmth of Bess Duveen's smile would soon have dispelled them all. "I must be honest with you, Bess."

"Please do." Bess sat down stiffly as if to receive some

harsh pronouncement, some judgment.

Stephen seized her hand. It seemed cold. He caressed it. "I love you, Bess. I want you to remember that."

"I will try to remember that, Stephen." She removed her hand. The look on her face made him swallow.

"Bess, I *would* marry you—if I could."

"If you 'could'?" she repeated woodenly. "I take it someone is holding you, that you cannot? Or perhaps you do not desire to marry me, perhaps you think I am some light woman who sleeps with any man she admires?"

This harsh, contemptuous note in her voice was new to him and he shook his head as if to clear it, telling himself he deserved worse.

"Bess," he said desperately. "Listen to me. I *will* marry you, if that is your desire. But first hear me out, for I've spent this whole day wishing I *had* been killed in Cornwall as you once thought."

Truly bewildered now, Bess sat and stared at that loved face, so miserable now as it considered her. In silence she waited.

"Bess, I can't marry you for the same reason I couldn't marry Imogene. I'm already married."

Her face whitened to a deathly pallor. " 'M—married'?"

"Yes. To two women, and divorced from neither. I'm a bigamist, Bess, pursued as such in England."

" 'To two women'?" she faltered, looking at if she might fall off her chair.

He sank to his knees beside her. " 'Twas long ago, Bess. And under assumed names. They're in England, we're here, and none on Barbados would be the wiser if Stephen Linnington and Bess Duveen chose to wed."

Her dark head sank and she stared unseeing down at her

hands. After a long time she lifted her head and looked at him. *"I* would be the wiser, Stephen."

He winced. He had been afraid she would take it like this. But he had had to tell her. The old Stephen would not have, but he had changed. With Bess Duveen he could not live a lie. His past had to be out in the open—to her at least.

"I will do whatever you want," he said humbly.

"I will have to think about it." Bess rose unsteadily and he leaped up to help her. She waved him away, flinching from his touch. "I will have to think about this alone, Stephen. Perhaps—perhaps tomorrow we can talk about it."

Feeling like a murderer, hating himself for having put out the light that had burned in those clear gray eyes, Stephen watched her go. Perhaps he should not have told her—oh, yes, he should! He should have told her much sooner, before that night when she had melted into his arms like butter, and the distant singing of the slaves in their quarters had drifted up to them on the sultry night air. A white scimitar of a moon had knifed the velvet sky and Stephen had eased his lady back onto the soft divan and there plundered her of all her secrets.

That Bess had been willing, that she had fallen asleep beside him, waked dreamily and pulled him back into her arms, made no difference now. She had believed—for he knew searingly that she would never have believed until now anything dishonorable of him—that this was a betrothal and that marriage would shortly follow.

In the long dining room at Idlewild Stephen's copper head dropped between his hands and there were unaccustomed tears on his lashes. He loved Bess so fiercely and—he had brought her this.

He roused himself as a house servant came into the room, bearing the first course. What would Bess want him to do?

Stephen asked himself. Why, she would want him to keep up appearances, to act as if nothing had happened. Having announced that the lady of the house might not be down, he sat down and grimly forced himself to eat.

Bess, alone with her heart and her new knowledge of Stephen's past, was fighting it out alone. Dry-eyed she sat in her bedroom with the candles unlit. She stared out into the scented tropical night and wondered about those other women. Had they loved him? Where were they now? Did Stephen know? Or care? She must ask him, she told herself, and lit a candle with trembling fingers. She glanced up at her reflection in the mirror and was startled at her vengeful expression. Bess winced. Was this what love was making of her?

She passed a shaking hand over her face. She must think, she must consider what was best for them. That Stephen had made an appalling mess of his life, she could readily see, but how to extricate him now? She was half tempted to take the way he suggested, to forget those other women somewhere in England and marry Stephen Linnington here on Barbados.

But if they had children . . . and if one of those other women turned up? It was hard to be a bastard in a society where illegitimacy carried a social stigma. Bess shivered. There were not only herself and Stephen to think about, there were also the unborn who must not be hurt.

Stiffly, like an old woman, Bess prepared herself for bed and all that night wrestled with her conscience. Supperless, undecided, she tossed sleepless with her thoughts veering this way and that. Morning found her still unresolved, too distracted to eat.

Stephen was wise enough to stay away and let Bess breakfast alone. He knew in his heart what agonies of conscience honest Bess must be enduring and he was afraid to interrupt her silent struggle lest he precipitate a decision against him. For now Stephen had learned what Bess had known all along, that she of all the world was the right woman for him, a woman to love and cherish and look up to and spend his life with.

But in midmorning a caller arrived who was to change the course of both their destinies.

Captain Middler of the ship *Annabelle* arrived at Idlewild plantation carrying a letter that had been entrusted to him by a Dutch captain named Hooergaave, who had had the letter from a woman in an enveloping cloak and hood who had thrust it into his hand hurriedly along with a ring, just before Hooergaave's sloop pulled away from the dock at Wey Gat.

"The ring is for your lady, whoever she may be," a soft vibrant voice had told Hooergaave, "if you will only deliver this letter to my friend in Barbados."

"But I do not go to Barbados, mevrouw," protested the sloop's English-speaking captain. "I go downriver to New Amsterdam!"

"No matter," she interrupted hastily. "My husband is coming. Entrust the letter to any captain of your acquaintance who is sailing to Barbados."

Abruptly she turned and walked away from him and Hooergaave climbed aboard his sloop and cast off. From the water he watched her progress down the pier. He saw a richly clad man who had been running down the slope hurry up to her, seize her wrist—why, it was the patroon of Wey Gat with whom he had dined alone in the vast dining room last night! The woman was struggling with him and now her French hood fell back to reveal a wealth of golden hair. Could this be his hostess whom the patroon had said was "too ill to come down to dinner"? Certainly she looked fit enough as she struggled—and lovely to boot. Hooergaave had been disappointed not to meet the fabled beauty of Wey Gat, for he had heard praise of her face and form all the way upriver—and snickers that she had on several occasions tried to run away from her husband, Wey Gat's unpopular patroon. Hooergaave started as he saw the patroon's hand lash across the woman's face, saw her stagger back only to be seized again and dragged back up the hill toward the house. For a moment Hooergaave's chivalrous heart almost made him turn the sloop around and go back to try to intercede for the lady but he reminded himself quickly enough that a man who interfered between husband and wife usually turned out to be the loser himself. With a shrug he continued on downriver. But once arrived in New Amsterdam, the remembered urgency of that low vibrant voice made him promptly find a ship sailing for Barbados and entrust to its captain the letter.

And so it happened that Captain Middler of the *Annabelle* was, at the urging of his Dutch friend, riding to Idlewild plantation on Barbados this day to deliver a letter from Imogene.

Bess, who had not seen Stephen yet this morning, saw the captain riding in when she looked out an upstairs window and guessed his mission, for he had a nautical look about him. Letters were her only ties with home and family—and they arrived infrequently. Each one was an occasion!

Bess hurried downstairs to receive her mail from his hand. Disappointed to hear that the letter was not from the Scillies, Bess put the letter aside, offered the stout captain a tall cool drink and sat down to talk to him. When Stephen came by, attracted by their voices, he found Bess entertaining a strange ship captain on the long veranda. He gave her a keen look and Bess, who had mixed feelings toward her lover just now, promptly suggested that Stephen show Captain Middler about the plantation and bring him back to the house for lunch.

The captain hesitated. On his voyage to Barbados he had

stopped at the port of Philadelphia and there picked up a handsome married lady returning to Barbados after a visit with
relatives. The lady had been equally smitten and the voyage
under fair skies had been a lightsome affair. As he set out for
Idlewild this morning, Captain Middler had observed the lady's
husband supervising the unloading of stores a little way down
the dock and little doubted he would be thus occupied all day.
Faced with a choice between a pair of welcoming white arms
and a yielding white body—or lunch with this tense pair—there
was no contest at all. Captain Middler said he would enjoy a
brief ride around the plantation but he must regretfully refuse
lunch as he had pressing business in Bridgetown.

Still troubled, Bess watched her copper-haired lover ride
away with the stout captain and broke the seal on Imogene's
letter. The very first line evoked a gasp from her and she sank
down onto the nearest chair, a tall fan-backed reed chair woven
on the island, and read it through twice.

Bess, I am in deep trouble, Imogene wrote. *Georgiana was
born in February and Verhulst knows she is not his, but Stephen's.
At first he seemed to accept her, and I even thought that we might
make a life together, but now he has become wildly jealous of
Georgiana and resents any time I spend with her. He plans to
send her to Holland and keep me here. Bess, I cannot bear it.
Verhulst is alternately cruel and kind and keeps me tense and
afraid. Now he will take Georgiana from me. Three times I have
tried to escape downriver and each time he has thwarted me.
Next time I will be more careful so that my plans cannot go awry.
I believe that he will follow me, Bess, and may even kill the baby
if he finds us—he has said he will kill me if I try to escape
again—so I am writing this to ask you to receive us in Barbados—if
we can get there. I will need a place to recover and make plans,
and I promise not to be a burden on you, Bess. Tomorrow I will*

entrust this letter to a riverboat captain who has called at Wey Gat. Verhulst entertained him at dinner but I was locked in my room; he is afraid to let me speak to people lest they aid me to escape. But I saw this captain from my window and he looks to be a kindly man—and I have heard of him that he speaks English. Tomorrow morning I will find a way to slip down to the pier and somehow manage to give him this letter. Do not write to me, Bess, as Verhulst will only seize the letter and destroy it before I can read it—as he does all my letters. I hope you are happy, Bess, in your new life and only wish that I were there with you instead of here at Wey Gat with a man who hates me.

There was more but Bess could hardly read it through her tears. She dashed them away and read on, then read it all again.

When Stephen returned, he found her sitting on the veranda, perfectly composed but with her eyes wide and dark as if she saw visions of hell. She sat so still he was almost afraid to approach her.

"You have decided—about us?" He tried to sound casual but there was fear in his voice—fear that he would lose her, the best woman he had ever known.

Silently Bess handed him the letter and his face went white as he read it. A child! Imogene had borne his child! And now she was in desperate case because of it.

He stood tall above her. "You need not have shown me this, Bess," he said quietly. "I'd have been none the wiser."

She looked up at him. "I know—but then I'd have had to live with it."

Stephen looked down into those clear gray eyes and for the first time felt he really understood her. And was shamed by the extent of her goodness.

"Have ye written to tell her I'm alive after all?"

Bess shook her head. "I neglected to do that," she said,

dryly and proudly suppressed the note of heartbreak in her voice. "I thought it could do her no good now to know—but that was when I thought her to be happy with her patroon." She laid her hand gently on his; it was gossamer soft and he ached at the touch. "I know you must go to her, Stephen, for she's in dire trouble and then there's the child—your child. But—" Bess gave him a crooked smile, "if you've a mind to, after you've done what you must, you can come back to me."

"I'll be back, Bess. You can count on it."

"Don't be so—positive," she said in a soft slurred voice as he swept her up in his arms. She was remembering Imogene's bright disastrous beauty.

His arms tightened. "Oh, Bess," he sighed. "I do love you. I do."

"I know that, Stephen, but once you see her again . . ." *In all her shattering beauty*. Bess's voice trailed off forlornly. "Go now, Stephen," she said thickly, pushing him away. "Pack quickly and go to Bridgetown and make your arrangements. Captain Middler said there's a ship leaving for America in the morning. She's called the *Godspeed*."

He gave her an anxious look. "Take care, Bess."

"You know I will."

He came back after he had packed.

"Are you taking only what you can carry in your saddlebags?" she asked, startled.

"Aye," he nodded. "To convince you I'm coming back to you."

She gave him a sad, unbelieving look. "God go with you, Stephen."

Stephen gulped. He had never felt so miserable at any leave-taking—not even when he had left Imogene in the Scillies and sailed away. He could hardly believe how calm Bess was.

She bore her heartbreak well. Back straight, chin high, she stood and fluttered a handkerchief and watched him go, saw him hesitate and turn as if he would come striding back to her. Bess waved a determined good-bye and he gave her a light salute and climbed onto his horse. "I'll take a groom and send the horse back," he called.

Bess nodded. She could not speak right now.

He said he would come back, but Bess knew. This was good-bye. She could not compete with Imogene. Dark-haired Bess sank into a tall-backed reed chair and watched the spot where Stephen's tall form had disappeared. She knew in her heart that she would never see him again, for once he found Imogene he would fall under the reckless beauty's spell once again. And be lost to her forever.

As the tropical twilight settled over beautiful Barbados, Bess, the stouthearted girl from the Scilly Isles, her hopes crushed, her air castles tumbled to dust, sat alone on the dusky veranda and thought about her future—a future that stretched out bleakly before her. She decided she would stay on Barbados and grow old here at Idlewild, an old maid with her cats and her parrot. She gave a wry look at handsome Lucifer, the ship's runaway, purring at her ankles and at Annabel and her kittens, spilling out of the box at the end of the veranda, and looked up at a squawk from the beautiful green and gold parrot that had been her uncle's pride. Cats and a parrot . . . she already had both.

The days, the weeks, went by for Bess—and still no word from Stephen.

But Stephen Linnington was not the only man headed north.

In Spanish Town, Jamaica, a certain buccaneer captain, strolling through the marketplace with a likely lass on each arm,

paused to watch a flight of northern birds winging south overhead down the Great Eastern Flyway to their winter home in
South America. They made a wild sound as they passed over and
van Ryker's gray eyes followed them.

Hanging on to his right arm, with her dark brown eyes
flashing, her tumbling words clacking like castanets, was a girl
who was either French or Spanish as the mood seized her, a girl
he had met in a tavern last night and taken to bed with him. Van
Ryker's head was inclined toward her as she volubly described
all the things she wanted the gallant *capitán* to buy her.

On his left, a giggling little red-haired whore who had
come to Jamaica by way of the London streets, dangled from his
arm and entreated him drunkenly to buy her another drink.

But van Ryker forgot their babble, and the world of Spanish
Town spun away from him as a white feather from the flying
flock overhead drifted down—like a whisk . . .

His wide boots came to a sudden halt in the dusty street and
both women pouted and tugged at his strong gauntleted arms,
urging him forward. But the captain had for a breathless moment gone back in time. He was standing again on the *Sea
Rover's* swaying moonlit deck beneath the stars, looking deep
into the delft blue eyes of a woman—*his* woman, although she
did not know it, the only woman he had ever desired more than
he desired his life. And fool that he was, he had given her up.

Brought back with a thud to Spanish Town, with a diamond-
hard blue sky and a brilliant white sun burning down overhead,
Captain van Ryker disentangled his gauntleted arms from the
curving ones that held him. He smiled down into brown eyes and
hazel, pressed some coins into the hand of the London whore
and told her to buy herself a royal hangover. She staggered away,
laughing. The girl who was sometimes French and sometimes
Spanish stood with her hands on her hips, bare feet planted wide

apart, and gazed at him malevolently from beneath a thatch of dark lashes. Did this mean she was being abandoned? she demanded. And without her promised shopping spree?

Van Ryker laughed, and this time it was a boyish, light-hearted laugh, as he tossed her a velvet purse. "Buy yourself all the silks in Spanish Town!" he told her, and gave her a light spank on her handsome rump. "Wear them and think of me!" As he strode away, still laughing, her head was bent, her hair streaming down as she delved into the purse, ooohing and aaahing at how generous the tall buccaneer had been.

The bright sun beat down on van Ryker's heavy shock of dark hair, highlighting it with gleaming bronze, and flashed on his white wolfish smile as he walked with a springy step toward his ship, with his sword swinging against his lean thigh. And the spring in his step came from his just-made decision to round up his roistering buccaneers and clear Spanish Town by this evening, to be off with the tide on the *Sea Rover*. He'd go adventuring again!

He sought, as he always did, forgetfulness, for the pull of the golden-haired beauty he had left in Dutch New Amsterdam was forever drawing him north.

And he had vowed he would leave her there with her patroon—to happiness.

With all the Caribbean to choose from, the *Sea Rover* beat steadily northward. He'd go to the Carolinas, van Ryker told himself jauntily, and turn around, prowling the islands he knew so well.

But off the Carolinas the *Sea Rover* ran into a piece of luck. A storm had driven a Spanish galleass, *La Golondrina*, onto the Outer Banks and torn her masts and shrouds from her. She was floating adrift, manned by an exhausted crew, when van Ryker sighted her. A little good sailing and the exhaustion of the oarsmen even under the lash brought the *Sea Rover* in range of a broadside—and *La Golondrina*'s Spanish captain struck her colors without firing a shot. She was out of Barcelona, the boarding crew learned, laden with supplies for the Spanish colonists; she carried wine and leather goods, plate and china, brocades and fine laces and boots of Cordovan leather. Van Ryker smiled; he had captured a prize to be envied.

As part of his share he selected, somewhat to his own surprise, a big curved-top trunk full of ladies' clothes, doubtless destined for the wife of some misplaced Spanish grandee, sighing on alien soil for the civilized comforts of Spain. He had chosen the trunk, he told himself, on a whim—these silken things, so dear to feminine hearts, could be distributed to any number of transient loves—he would strew them around the Caribbean to any winsome wench who momentarily caught his fancy. As he lifted out these rich garments one by one, his sleeve caught on something. It was a sheer white whisk and for a moment as he studied it, it twisted his heart.

Gently he replaced the whisk and went back on deck. There was ransom to be arranged for the Spanish officers, who would accompany him back to his base at Tortuga and be released unhurt when that ransom was received. There was repair work to be done, for *La Golondrina* drifted like a bird with a broken wing—but van Ryker saw her as she would be, a beautiful vessel again, cutting the seas with her gilded prow, as lovely as the swallow for which she was named. And there was the captured Spanish crew to be quartered—these men would be treated more humanely than English, Dutch, or French prisoners would be if they had the bad luck to be captured by the Spanish. This Spanish crew would not be forced into the galleys or burned as heretics or maimed; they would work out a ransom on Tortuga of some three or four years—and many of them would elect to remain on Tortuga; some would even join buccaneer crews and harry the ships of Spain.

Uppermost in van Ryker's mind was the disposition of the galley slaves, those bedraggled men of many countries who had been laboring, chained to the galleass's oars. Most of them were guilty of nothing more than trespass, sailing in Spanish waters—for, to Spain, the waters of the entire Caribbean were Spanish waters. Van Ryker wondered if there were any buccaneers among them, closed the trunk with its memory-jogging whisk, and went up on deck to inquire.

The galley slaves, dirty and ragged and with tangled beards—but now freed of their chains and with hope burning in their tired eyes—crowded around him, talking excitedly in many languages. Here and there he spotted a dark Morisco—a Moor living in Spain who had accepted the Spanish faith— perhaps imprisoned for backsliding and worshiping in the old way. And here and there a tall Scandinavian with a pale matted beard and weathered face and the look of a sailor about him— those men he could use on the *Sea Rover* if they cared to sign on; if not—well, they were seamen, they could sail out of Tortuga on one of the many merchantmen who came in to trade for captured Spanish goods. Van Ryker spoke in French with several of the freed French galley slaves, assuring them they'd see Paris and Marseilles again. And then a blue-eyed, heavyset man stepped forward and asked him in good Holland Dutch:

"Captain van Ryker, I've heard ye're a Dutchman. My name is Johann Culp. I was born in Leyden but now I call New Amsterdam home. I was fishing in the sea and a storm swept me south in a small boat. I thought to perish in the rough weather but I was picked up by a Spanish vessel and chained to an oar. That was three years ago and my wife and children still don't know what has happened to me. Captain, where are ye bound?"

At that moment there was an enormous noise from the sky as a huge flight of wild geese darkened the sky overhead. Van Ryker, in the sudden din, turned his head toward the north from which they were steaming down the Great Eastern Flyway that encompassed Carolina. And suddenly he remembered the floating white feather, so like the little whisk he had just seen in the Spanish trunk, the drifting white feather that had sent him restlessly adventuring again, away from the taverns and brothels of Spanish Town.

What better place to sell his goods than a wintry New Amsterdam, where there'd be little competition and merchants would be stocking such stuff as these captured goods for holiday buyers? Faith, he'd stayed south long enough!

"Johann Culp, ye're in luck," he laughed, clapping the sturdy fellow on the back. "I'll even take ye home to New Amsterdam—for that's where I'm bound!"

La Golondrina would need extensive work before she could be sailed to Tortuga. Van Ryker towed her to the little town of Port Royal on the Carolina coast and left a crew making the needed repairs. He'd pick her up on his way back—and the *Swallow* would be added to his little fleet, which now numbered five ships.

He took on fresh water and what food he could find and set sail for New Netherland. The birds were flying south, drawn there by some ancient urge, and van Ryker—drawn by an urge even more ancient—was going to sail north. North to New Netherland! North to Imogene!

He would have been astonished to learn that Stephen Linnington was already there, seeking The Girl with the Whisk.

Wey Gat, New Netherland, 1658

CHAPTER 24

Winter was coming to the Catskills, to the Adirondacks—all along Henry Hudson's river the trees, in a luminous burst of red and gold and bronze, were enjoying their last brilliance. Indian summer had brought a last breathless hush to the land, and the field mice and chipmunks were making their last forays, storing up winter supplies of nuts in dead trees and holes in the soon-to-be-frozen earth. Save for the brilliantly tinted trout that spawned in November, the fish had all run downstream. By day the air was brisk, by nights it was chill—a cold warning of the snows to come.

In his river-bluff castle, Verhulst van Rappard, patroon of vast Wey Gat, sat alone with the moon and considered his life. He was not very happy with what he saw. For he was guiltily aware that he was neglecting his estate's affairs in an effort to subdue his young wife, to make her into the pliant female he wished her to be. By God, she was keeping him from his work!

In his ever-present terror that she might escape him, Verhulst feared to leave the house without locking Imogene in her room lest he return to find her gone. Even today had brought him humiliation when a riverboat sloop, the *Onrust*, had called at Wey Gat. The sloop's *schipper* had always been friendly with him and normally Verhulst would have invited the *schipper* to stay the night in the great house. Tonight, driven by his anxiety over Imogene's imminent escape, Verhulst had locked Imogene in her bedroom and entertained the *schipper* at dinner, making the excuse that his wife was ill.

All on the river, he was privately convinced, knew that Imogene was not ill, and he had been ruffled by the *schipper*'s steady distant gaze when he spoke volubly of his wife's frail health.

Imogene was destroying everything for him!

The riverboat *schipper*, who should have been staying in one of the guest bedrooms of Wey Gat, was sleeping aboard his sloop this night, Imogene was locked in her room, and he, Verhulst, lord of the mannor, was sitting alone glaring at the moon.

Why could he not control this frail slip of a girl he had married?

But no man, Verhulst was coming reluctantly to realize, could permanently break Imogene's rebellious spirit. For long periods he had locked her in her room, he had even denied her food until he was afraid he would damage her health—nothing worked with this desperate English beauty who held his heart in a vise. She seemed more frail of late, and her cheeks—being denied her usual outdoor diversions—had lost their bloom. But somehow her increasing fragility only made her the more appealing. Her pallor worried him, but it did nothing to diminish her enchanting loveliness.

It was her lustrous beauty that held him in thrall, he told himself, shifting his booted legs restlessly upon the hearth-rail and morosely pouring himself another glass of Madeira, her damnable ethereal beauty. Just seeing her move sensuously from room to room, or watching her stand outside on the bluff—as he had not allowed her to of late—with her bright hair blowing like the bright fall leaves in the wind, caught at his heart. She was like a drug to his senses that he could not shake off, she was like an addiction—he told himself he despised her, wished to rid himself of her—and yet he could not do without her.

By day he would watch her move about and was warmed by what he thought was his hatred for her. He had done everything for Imogene, he told himself, given her everything—a home, a name for her child, jewels, furs—what more could he have done? And yet he saw in her haunted delft blue eyes every time he looked at her a desire to run from him, to escape him!

Convulsed by sudden anger, Verhulst almost choked on his wine. He set his glass down hard on the polished arm of his chair, thinking of the woman locked above him in her bedroom. Was she in bed now, one arm flung outward on her pillow like a child's? Or was she still up, standing in some stage of undress, perhaps viewing herself in the big gilt mirror? Had she removed the silken stockings from those lustrous legs? Was one rosy nipple peeping from the top of a chemise whose neckline had fallen carelessly low? Pain twisted in his groin at the memories of her lovely flesh, glimpsed through the keyhole of his adjoining room. Well, now her room was down the hall from his, he could watch her no longer.

He twisted about in his chair, trying not to envision Imogene's naked loveliness. He had never loved her, he told himself roughly—and at that moment he honestly believed it to be the truth. Imogene was merely another lavish ornament he had bought for Wey Gat—bought with good Dutch guilders.

Involuntarily his glance roved upward above the mantel to the likeness he had had painted of her in Amsterdam. Not a very large portrait, nor by a celebrated painter, and yet the artist had managed to capture Imogene's roving spirit on canvas. The sparkling blue eyes flung a challenge, the mouth curved softly on the brink of laughter.

There was a companion portrait, one of himself, but he had rejected it, saying that the chin appeared too weak, the mouth a trifle slack, the eyes shifty. Imogene, who liked the artist and did not wish to see him deprived of payment for his work, had cajoled Verhulst by insisting that the painter had exactly captured his coloring and had made him look very distinguished indeed. Mollified, Verhulst had paid the artist, but on arrival in America he had stuck the portrait away to gather dust. The portrait of Imogene was another matter. Looking up into that reckless laughing face he again fell under her spell.

Verhulst passed a trembling hand across his line of vision and reminded himself that those lovely eyes had looked into another man's face before him—with love and surrender. Those lovely lips had been tasted, enjoyed. That fair form he had thought so virginal, so untried—his thin hands clenched and a tremor went through him—that lovely ''virginal'' body had been held in naked carnal passion by another man. He rose giddily and his fist struck the wall so hard that blood spurted. He bellowed for his groom, ordered out his horse and rode the poor beast in the cold night until it was lathered and foaming with sweat. But even so he could not exorcise his devils. Imogene rode with him wherever he went: On the river, inspecting the *bouweries*, boarding the sloops of passing traders to inspect their goods, wherever he went he carried her picture engraved on his heart. A haunting, tempting vision would rise up before him—*of a wanton!* His face would empurple with rage.

But in other, softer, moods he saw her as she had been in Holland, greeting the morning with a song. Pure, virginal, she had seemed, lovely as the dawn, a woman made for love.

She was neither extreme, of course. Imogene was a woman with a woman's frailties and a woman's strengths. And on this late autumn night, as Verhulst glowered cursing belowstairs, she listened for Elise's soft scratching at the door. Now she heard, even through the heavy panels, Verhulst's bellow for his groom from below, and minutes later she went to the window and saw him riding across the pastures and into the woods as if pursued by devils.

She heard, she saw him—but tonight she did not care. She was through with wondering how to come to terms with her jealous husband, through with giving lip service to the way of life he would force her to live.

For Imogene, something wondrous had happened.

Elise as usual had gone down to the sloop when it arrived, hoping forlornly for news of home—it was rare to hear much of England here but Elise was ever hopeful. Imogene of course had been promptly locked in by Verhulst himself and Verhulst had marched away bearing the key. She had been allowed to come down for a light lunch with her husband while the captain was rowed upriver to range among the *bouweries* with his trade goods—but told her presence would not be required at dinner.

"Because you are entertaining the captain of that sloop out there?" she had demanded indignantly. "Verhulst, you are driving me mad! Am I never to speak to anyone except you?"

"You will obey me," he told her in a sulky voice, and as soon as she had finished her dessert he escorted her upstairs. But as they left the dining room Imogene collided with Elise, who was just walking down the hall. Verhulst reprimanded the woman but Imogene interrupted impatiently. "It is of no account, Verhulst—I blundered into her and not the other way around."

Nothing could have been further from the truth. Elise had set her course for Imogene and at the moment of collision had pressed into Imogene's hand a folded letter, which Imogene had quickly concealed in the folds of her caught-up brocade overskirt. Her heart was beating rapidly as Verhulst saw her to her room and ceremoniously locked her in.

Could Bess Duveen, heedless of her penned warning, have answered her cry for help? Could the letter be from Bess?

Waiting only for Verhulst's footsteps to recede down the hall, Imogene tore the letter open and held it close to the flickering candle by her bed. It was terse and to the point:

Imogene, she read in Stephen's scrawl, *Bess has told me of your plight, and that you thought me dead. I am in New Amsterdam, ready to take you and the child away with me downriver and out of this colony. Let me know how and when. The bearer of this letter is to be trusted. I have instructed him to give the letter to Elise, who Bess tells me is with you. Ever your devoted servant. Stephen Linnington.*

Stephen! He was alive! Imogene staggered to the bed and almost knocked over the candle as she collapsed upon it. But how—? Why had he not written before? How could he be with Bess? Her confused thoughts spun round and round.

Downriver . . . he would take her downriver, down that river that flowed by the other side of the house, the river she could not see, cooped up here with her windows staring out at the wooded hills. Ah, she had tried to escape down that river before, and found its currents treacherous. They had brought her back to Wey Gat—and Stephen was a stranger here. Good sailor though he was, he knew less of the river than she did.

The river, she thought bitterly—that damnably beautiful

river would be the end of her. For, like her heart, it flowed two ways . . . toward the heartbroken violent fool she had married and—treacherously—toward a handsome buccaneer captain who had spoken of love and sailed away never to return.

Verhulst might have overcome her bright memories of the Scillies, of the *Sea Rover*, had he been less in love with her. But Imogene felt only dimly that he was in love with her. She knew for certain that she could not trust him. Still she might have settled for a safe haven for herself, a rich future for her child. But his all-consuming passion for her had made Verhulst vengeful—and cruel. And so he had lost her.

So, although for a while her questing affections had flowed back and forth, like the strange and beautiful river that flowed by Wey Gat, at the end her soul had only one guiding star—Stephen.

On long silent evenings she had wept for his loss.

And now that she had learned he was not dead, it was like a resurrection.

Stephen was alive, her copper-haired lover was coming for her!

But if it was to work, if they were to get away, she must plan carefully. Through the night she lay thinking, remembering her own mistakes, how easily she had been caught and returned to Wey Gat. This time the fox must outwit the hunters!

When dawn broke over the river, turning the rising mists to pink, Imogene had penned her message:

I know not how you have come back to me. Indeed it seems a miracle, for I would not have married—I would have waited for you, Stephen—had Bess not written that you were dead, killed in a duel in Cornwall. Indeed I would not have married even then save that she wrote that I had been implicated in

Giles's murder and could never return to my own country. I did not know where to turn and when Verhulst offered for my hand, I accepted his offer. It was a mistake . . . as I write this, I am locked in my room, watched every minute.

Stephen, Wey Gat is not a castle you can storm. Verhulst is all-powerful here. He has men and dogs and guns, and swift horses and sleds, and the fastest sloop on the river—the Danskammer. *We cannot count on the Indians to aid us, for they fight among themselves—and might as soon return us to Verhulst as they would scalp us for our clothing. We cannot escape by water or by land—but there is a way.*

Sail upriver to Beverwyck and there procure an iceboat, the fastest you can find. Verhulst had a boyhood accident with an iceboat in which he nearly lost his life. He hates them and will not allow his servants or tenants to sport with them. Be patient, for both our lives depend upon the outcome. Wait until the ice is sound and let me know when you are coming. Elise and the baby can meet you a short distance upriver by the huge blasted tree that was struck by lightning last year—it is a big sycamore, a landmark you cannot miss. But I am closer watched. Somehow I will contrive to steal the key to my room and will wait for you on the ice, crouched beneath the pier. Iceboats travel faster than anything Verhulst can muster. You can sweep me up and we will be away downriver!

Have a care for your life, for Verhulst has a vengeful nature and I think he would not hesitate to kill us both if he knew I was writing this. Elise will entrust it to your messenger.

> *Always your own,*
> *Imogene.*

In the dawn's pale light, Imogene read over what she had written, folded the parchment and melted sealing wax upon it.

Then she pressed an ardent kiss against the parchment, wishing that he who read it could feel the warm pressure of her lips.

The miracle had happened. Her lost love had been returned to her. Somehow he had found out about her plight and he had come all this way to save her.

Carefully she secreted the letters in the folds of her voluminous skirt and waited for Verhulst to unlock her bedroom door and escort her down to breakfast. She would find a way to slip the letter to Elise, who would be lurking nearby and then—!

With brooding eyes she looked out upon the mists that cloaked the meadows and were just beginning to clear away from the base of the woods.

If Verhulst intercepted that note, if he read it, he might do anything, anything.

Imogene pressed her hot forehead to the cold glass of the windowpane and consigned her fate to God.

Some days later, downriver in New Amsterdam, Stephen Linnington tore open Imogene's letter, laconically handed to him by a member of the river sloop's crew who had assumed this note entrusted to a servant concerned some minor smuggling operation and accepted his bribe almost carelessly.

But Stephen, when he scanned what Imogene had written, felt his throat constrict at her simple heartfelt declaration: *I would have waited for you, Stephen.* It reminded him how he had loved this girl for a season and thought her the loveliest of all his conquests, it reminded him how knowing her had made him reflect on his wild ways and learn what it was to regret.

And now Bess, his guiding star, the truest, most honest, most compassionate woman he had ever known was waiting for him on Barbados.

He was torn between them.

But for now he must rescue Imogene. Whatever happened

later. He thought over her plan and decided it had a good chance of success. But in case it did not, he carried besides his sword a brace of pistols.

He did not know, as he climbed aboard a river sloop headed for Beverwyck, that the crew member he had bribed had talked too much and that Jan Dermeer, one of the patroon's men, had heard him. Seeking a reward, and knowing—as all at Wey Gat knew—that the patroon kept his young wife a virtual prisoner, Dermeer went back to Wey Gat and, shuffling his feet uneasily, told Verhulst van Rappard that an Englishman named Stephen Linnington had sent a message via river sloop to his wife.

Stephen Linnington! The patroon's face had lost so much color that Dermeer feared he would have a stroke. But in a moment Verhulst had regained control of himself and rewarded Dermeer generously, telling him to speak of this to no one. With an enormous effort he managed to hide his feelings from his young wife, and set a close watch on all comings and goings from the estate.

When an Indian brought Elise a note to be delivered to Imogene, Verhulst intercepted it and read it—and then allowed it to be passed along to Elise. Stephen, ashamed of himself for near forgetting this woman who had borne his child, had written in warmer style, a style that made the blood pound in Verhulst's temples.

I will be waiting for you when the moon is high. I have done all that you asked. Come swiftly, my darling, and we will be away on the wings of the wind!

Verhulst had throttled a desire to crumple the note and shred it. He wished the Indian who had brought it had not run away before he could be questioned. Ah, well, he was from one of the downriver tribes. Linnington would be coming upriver tonight—possibly on skates, for the temperature had dropped so in the last hour that it was a good bet that the river would freeze clear across its surface tonight.

Verhulst's gaze grew vindictive. Linnington would find someone else besides Imogene awaiting for him when the moon was high!

And downriver in New Amsterdam a dock worker looked up and sighted white sails billowing out to sea. He squinted his eyes and studied her lines—he could not know she'd sailed north in near record time before a gustily strong wind—but he recognized the ship by her size and her gunports and her rakish lines.

"Look there!" he cried. " 'Tis the *Sea Rover!* I wonder what brings Captain van Ryker here so late in the season when the river's near sure to be iced up?"

The North River, New Netherland, 1658–1659

CHAPTER 25

The moon was high and Imogene was listening tensely at her bedroom door. Beneath her warm woolen dress and multiple petticoats sparkled an astonishing array of jewels and sewn in the hem of her wide skirts was all the gold she possessed. For Imogene well knew that Verhulst van Rappard was not likely to show mercy to a wife fleeing him with a lover. She shivered, sharply aware that tonight's venture was a desperate one. Jewels and money could buy safety for a fleeing pair—and Stephen Linnington was not likely to have either.

In her hand was a key. Elise had filched it from Verhulst's pocket right after supper and slipped it under Imogene's door. Neither of them dreamed that Stephen's message had been intercepted. Nor did Imogene guess that Verhulst had followed Elise and seized her and thrust her into a tiny dressing room where even now Elise was clawing free of her bonds.

As Imogene listened at the door, annoyed by a muttered

conversation outside, Elise was slipping down the corridor. She stopped at sight of the two servants the patroon had set to guard his wife's door. Desperate to warn Imogene that Verhulst knew of their plans, Elise drew back in the shadows to consider. Imogene obviously would not be allowed to leave the house but she, Elise, could slip out with the baby and keep the rendezvous as planned. Yes, that was exactly what Imogene would want her to do! Outside, the ice was freezing solid as cold crept in around the windows. The iceboat could fly past Wey Gat bearing little Georgiana to safety! And later Stephen could scheme to free Imogene—for Elise no longer believed the patroon would injure his young wife; he had refrained from doing so on too many occasions. About the baby she was not so sure, and without the child to worry about, Imogene might find her own way to escape.

Elise had made up her mind. Through the windows she had seen a thin line of men melt into the trees and shuddered. Still—in the darkness and confusion she could pass as one of those men! She tucked up her skirts so they looked like wide Dutch breeches and found a pair of men's boots and a wide-brimmed hat, wrapped the baby well, threw a heavy cloak over them both, breathed a silent prayer and slipped out the back door into the bitter cold, and made her way into the woods.

No sooner had she reached the shelter of the trees than someone hissed something at her in Dutch—probably reproof to a straggler for being late. As tall as a man, with her shoulders well padded and wearing men's boots and a long cloak, a broad-brimmed hat pulled well down over her forehead and muffled up to her eyes with a scarf, Elise passed unnoticed for one of the watchers, passed through their lines and pressed northward to the spot where the blasted sycamore made a vivid landmark. There the iceboat would be waiting.

Back in the big stone house, Verhulst had withdrawn the servants from outside Imogene's door. Tonight he would teach his young wife a lesson she would never forget! But first he would give her enough rope to hang herself!

In her bedroom Imogene waited breathlessly until the sound of the servants' footsteps died away. At last, with trembling fingers, she set the key into the lock. It turned without a sound and she was out in the dark corridor. Drawing her fur-lined velvet cloak about her, she slipped silently downstairs and out through the big front doors. There she paused a moment, tying her French hood more firmly against the biting wind. Stephen's timing had been perfect—the river would be frozen solid by now, and smooth, making a perfect surface for the iceboat—and the upcoming tide that would crack that flawless surface was not due for a long time.

She ran down the slope, unaware that she was watched by silent men from the woods—and worse, by Verhulst from an upstairs window.

Even as Imogene ran toward the pier, Elise was flinging herself into the iceboat upriver, gasping out to Stephen, "He knows! The patroon knows!"

"Then—" Stephen turned to Willem, whose iceboat this was. "Will ye take us anyway?"

"Aye," said Willem uneasily, his hands upon the tiller. "Now that we have the woman on board, we can be past Wey Gat and gone—they've no iceboats there as I know of."

So he was to leave Imogene here . . . Stephen's jaw hardened. "She may be waiting for us anyway," he muttered. "Imogene is resourceful."

"No, no, she is guarded!" wailed Elise. "But the patroon will not hurt her—it is for the child she fears. You must take us away and you can come for her later."

It went against the grain, but Stephen saw the wisdom of her argument. Moments later the big square sail was lifted and they were off downriver, gathering speed before the strong north wind.

In the white stillness sound carried well. Imogene heard the first sounds of the approaching iceboat and ran out from under the wooden pier.

From the bluff he was floundering down, the patroon of Wey Gat heard it, too.

"The dogs!" he roared. "Loose the dogs!"

Imogene heard his cry and looked back in horror. Verhulst knew! From the lower shore she heard the baying of the dogs— Verhulst's man-eating pack—and gave a silent scream as she saw them streaking toward her. And now men seemed to come from everywhere, running down the slope toward the ice.

But even as she ran, Imogene was pursued by a new dizzying horror. Just as in the dream that had haunted her for so long, she was running over a gray surface—but that surface was not sand but ice! That was not a sailboat with a copper-haired man aboard she was running toward but a gray iceboat! And those leaping forms that had pursued her in her nightmare were not sharks but men and dogs! Her old dream was coming true—she was living it out this night, and with stunning certainty she knew that she was running to her death.

The scene that greeted the hurtling iceboat's passengers was a macabre one: Verhulst and his men had reached the ice—and so had the dogs. Imogene, in her blue velvet cloak, fled before them, waving her arms at the oncoming iceboat.

"Imogene!" shouted Stephen hoarsely, for he saw the huge lead dog about to leap for her throat. He brought up his pistol, took careful aim at the lead dog—a leaping gray ghost. The dog was so close, so perilously close to Imogene. Praying that the lurching boat might not deflect his aim so that he missed the dog and hit the woman, he fired. The skittering iceboat braked with a scraping screech and Stephen saw, thankfully, the big dog drop and Imogene, waving her arms and crying, "Stephen, oh, Stephen!" come a leap nearer the iceboat.

It was the last thing he saw.

Verhulst van Rappard, here confronted with the handsome substance of the man who had seemed to him but a shadow, seeing before him almost larger than life the lithe tigerish lines of this fellow who dared to try to take Imogene from him, brought out the pistol from his belt in a single fluid gesture and fired from blind rage right at Stephen Linnington's broad chest.

As the heavy shot crashed through his doublet, Stephen's tall figure gave a great tremor. He staggered, clutched at his chest, and then toppled backward in a spatter of blood.

Imogene screamed.

"Look out!" cried Willem hoarsely, trying to brake against the wild wind.

But Imogene, frozen in horror and living out her dream, looked up at the iceboat bearing down on her and could not move.

Verhulst saw her danger and gave a shout—but even that did not move the woman who stood like a statue on the ice. As Willem swung about to avoid her, the iceboat struck her a glancing blow on the head and she would have been thrown to the ice senseless had not Elise, leaning over the side, screeching, grasped her by the wrist and dragged her aboard.

Through the dogs, past the men, the iceboat flew, straight as a plummeting hawk. Amid howling and shouts, it careened out of sight downriver going now at a horrendous speed.

The patroon's men stood by helpless among the milling, snapping dogs. There was no catching it, not without another and faster iceboat—all knew that. As one, they turned silently to the patroon for their orders.

The sight that met them made them draw back and mutter among themselves.

Verhulst was bent over, staring at the big gray lead dog Stephen had shot. It lay in a pool of blood on the ice. Its great jaws were still open showing the gleaming white fangs.

But Verhulst did not see the dog. He saw Imogene.

And in his vision he was once again alone with the cold moon that scanned him critically from above—alone with his folly, alone with what he had so nearly brought to pass and in his horrified imagination he saw what had so nearly happened.

He saw again in a hellish vision the huge lead dog leaping for the running woman's throat. He heard her agonized scream, saw the savage rending that ripped her flesh and spattered her blood over the river's hard gray shining surface. And so vividly was this vision imprinted on his distraught mind that it seemed to him *it had really happened*.

Now in his mind she lay dying in her blood on the ice, torn by the savage dog, while her lover, unconscious, sped away from her downriver aboard the skimming iceboat.

Stricken, Verhulst knelt beside her.

"Imogene!" His agonized voice choked the word but she did not seem to hear him. Her lips seemed to be trying to form words but could not. Past sight and sound she was drifting away from him—perhaps in the arms of a spectral lover.

In that awful moment, Verhulst knew she was dying but—he had seen her try to speak. She had some word for him, some message. He bent closer to her lips and a wisp of sound came from them . . . a last sweet message, meant for his ears alone.

"*I love you, Verhulst . . .*" The soft whisper, like the woman, died away.

And Verhulst, overcome with emotion, collapsed with a sob on the body of the dead dog, while about him his men shuffled their feet and looked at each other in embarrassment and horror.

It was big Schroon, *schipper* of the *Danskammer*, scandalized by this whole affair, who helped the patroon up. It was second nature to Schroon—he had been helping Verhulst since he was a boy of five.

Verhulst staggered to his feet, protesting. In a whirling world he saw his surroundings, dimly, through a kind of film. And then the vision that had seemed the veriest of truths wavered into nothingness and he was standing over the body of a dead dog, with both feet planted on solid ice looking downriver where the iceboat had disappeared, and Schroon was clutching his arm and asking hoarsely what they should do now.

Verhulst shook his head to clear it.

With a jolt his world came back to him. That was a dog that lay there—only a dog. Imogene—alive or dead—was being carried away downriver, swept along by the fierce wind that was chilling their bones to the marrow. He turned grimly to Schroon.

"You will follow them, find them," he cried hoarsely.

Schroon looked taken aback. "But the *Danskammer* cannot sail on the ice!"

"Use your iceboat. I know you have a small iceboat hidden under the willows downstream." And when Schroon would have protested, Verhulst's voice rose. "Don't argue, Schroon. *I have seen it!*"

Schroon's steadying hand left the patroon's arm and his ruddy face took on a deathly pallor. He had not dreamed the patroon knew of his precious toy, so well secreted beneath the trees downriver. That iceboat was easy-going Schroon's only protest against the patroon's harsh rule. But his whole being

433

revolted at the thought that it was *he* who must seek out the patroon's wife, that lady whose lovely face and gentle ways he had so often gazed upon—*he* who must bring her back, for who knew what summary justice!

"You will—kill her?" he faltered.

"If I please to do so!" shouted Verhulst, livid with frenzy that Schroon had not promptly snapped to attention and run to obey his orders. "Go after them, Schroon. Bring me back word of what has happened to them, of where they are."

Still Schroon hesitated. He was waiting for some word that the patroon would not harm Imogene, no matter what she had done.

It was not forthcoming.

Old habits died hard. Schroon's shoulders drooped, but he turned downstream, slipping and sliding along the ice.

Verhulst looked after him with bleak satisfaction. Big Schroon had never failed him—*he* would bring Imogene back!

"I'll go with him," offered Groot, the kennelmaster. "The dogs can follow—they might come in useful."

"No," shuddered Verhulst, still beset by his all-too-recent vision. "Not the dogs. We will follow by sled."

"The horses will make little headway," protested Groot. "The ice is too slick and the snow too deep."

"We will go on skates, then," decided Verhulst, "and the horses and sled can follow us." For his heart was beset by sudden panic. Imogene was hurt, the iceboat had sheared alongside her, striking her head. She would have fallen like a stone had not the woman Elise dragged her into the iceboat, squalling like a banshee.

Imogene was hurt, her lover was dead . . . he would find his lady and bear her back by sled to his river fastness.

So Verhulst reasoned as he put on his skates.

It was a grim skating party who made their way downriver, their steel blades ringing on the ice. Far behind them floundered a sled pulled by horses but the skaters rapidly outdistanced it and were alone on the moonlit river's glassy surface. Sheer on their right rose the Hudson Highlands, seeming endlessly tall when viewed as now from the river ice. The great rounded peaks rose snowily from the wide gray expanse of the river.

Where the river was wide and the ice in the center was thin they found Schroon.

He was lying face down on the ice with an arrow in his back.

Beyond him, at the river's center, was an ominous break in the ice, a dark glittering pool.

Groot, a magnificent skater with endless power in his heavily muscled legs, was the first to reach him.

"Schroon." Gently Groot lifted him up. "Can you hear me?"

Schroon groaned and opened his blue eyes. They were glazing in death. "Indians—from the bank," he managed to get out. "No reason—just shot at me. Missed me once and then got me. I fell out of the iceboat and it—went through—the ice—in the middle of the river." He was sinking.

"Schroon." The patroon bent over him; he had to know. "Did you see my wife, did you see the iceboat you were following?"

Schroon looked hazily up at the patroon whose orders he had long so faithfully obeyed, even to this sad pursuit of his lovely young wife on whom he had set the dogs! Schroon would never forget that, or forgive it. His eyes were glazing over and through the film he got his last view of the patroon's dark worried face.

"The Indians—were shooting at them when I got here.

Their iceboat was sinking . . . all dead . . .'' His head drooped. Schroon was past answering questions ever again.

All the color drained from Verhulst's dark face.

His golden bird had escaped her golden cage—but her flight to freedom had been short. He had lost her somewhere in that evil black water, lost her forever.

It was only then that he realized how very much he had loved her.

Like a drunken man, Verhulst staggered away from the skaters toward that dark break in the ice. Closer and closer he lurched toward it, drawn by heartbreak, until the ice cracked beneath his feet and someone, risking his life, came and dragged him back.

She was down there—Imogene was somewhere beneath this thick screen of river ice that hid the river's deep chasm as it cut between the mountains, she and her child—that child who had borne the van Rappard name—she and her lover who had come to carry her away—she and her faithful servant and some unknown stranger and his iceboat—all of them were being carried downriver by the current beneath that opaque layer of ice.

He would never see her again.

As that thought drenched him, drowning him in it, the patroon lifted his head and gave a great howling wail that rent the sky and caused the little war party of Indians who had come down from the hills to avenge a woman mauled by a trapper to pause in their tracks and listen. The sound was not repeated and they went their silent way on deerhide moccasins. They had taken a life in revenge, it was enough. . . .

Verhulst had collapsed senseless on the ice.

And so the sled on which he had thought to bring Imogene back to Wey Gat carried him home, half-crazed with grief and barely conscious, moaning and seeing visions in which he spoke to her, cajoled her, bullied her.

The doctor who was summoned and who arrived at Wey Gat two days later found him lying in his big square bed. He was staring fixedly at the ceiling and he steadfastly refused the hot soup that was being urged on him. He had had time to think during the long sleepless hours, and his tortured mind had accepted a strange reality.

With sudden energy, he pushed aside the soup, brushed off the doctor's restraining hand and sat up.

"The *aanspreecker!* He must be brought, and fine coffins constructed. Stones must be carved! There is to be a funeral."

Scandalized eyes met above his head. A funeral—with no bodies?

"Three coffins."

" 'Three'?" It was the doctor's voice, internally counting. "Ah, yes, for your wife and daughter and the servant woman."

"Four coffins—I had forgotten about Elise. A pine box will do for her. The stranger who steered the iceboat can drift unmarked for eternity as far as I am concerned, but there will be three great coffins of fine wood with silver fittings: One for a woman, one for a child and—one for a man."

For a man! Eyes bulged and there were sharply indrawn breaths. Surely this grief-crazed madman was not planning to memorialize his wife's lover?

But that was exactly what the young patroon had in mind.

In those moments when he was wrenched away from his visions to bitter reality, he had seen his position more clearly—and realized the depth and breadth of what he had done to the woman he loved. She had brought him so much beauty, so much gaiety, and he had returned only material things, not the love she had asked for, the love to which, he now admitted, she was entitled. He wanted to make it up to her and so he conceived a strange quixotic notion: Imogene had loved another man—in death he would reunite them.

Verhulst might have buried Stephen's memory deep in the dark rushing waters beneath the ice where the iceboat had gone down. But he did not. Stern-faced and grieving, in the most magnificent funeral the river had ever seen, the young patroon of Wey Gat buried the lovers. Black-clad *aanspreeckers*, their hats streaming long black crape ribbons, went scurrying from house to house inviting guests to the funeral, since by custom none dared attend unless invited. Black gloves and handkerchiefs were given to every tenant of Wey Gat, and all drank spiced wine and smoked the patroon's tobacco at the great feasts that were held to commemorate her passing. Each bearer received a new black suit of mourning clothes and the wives of his neighbors all received gifts of black gloves and scarves and fans and carved jet mourning rings.

To the scandal of all the countryside, Verhulst placed three empty coffins in the family plot at Wey Gat. The stones he raised to Imogene and Georgiana bore their names and the sad words "Lost to the River." But on the other tombstone—which everybody read with whispered comments—there was carved only, "Stephen Linnington, gentlemen of Devon" and the date and a Dutch word that meant "Tomorrow."

None along the river ever guessed the meaning of that single word, "Tomorrow." But to Verhulst van Rappard, who had slain his rival in anger, it was promise and regret. During her short tragic life he had not really known he loved Imogene, he had thought he desired her only for her beauty like some striking painted face smiling down from the wall. But now that she was gone, leaving him with an agony of grief, his proud nature regretted his rash actions. If he had it to do over, he told himself with scalding tears, he would let her go—with Stephen. And he hoped on those long cold nights when he stared sleepless out on to the North River's frozen world and he saw like fireflies in the dark bushes the gleaming golden eyes of roving foxes, he hoped that like those foxes the spirits of the lovers ran free tonight, that they had locked hands and now ran laughing across the snow. He hoped with all his heart that they had found each other and were united in some special heaven.

And at other times, when the visions claimed him, when he saw Imogene's lovely face smiling at him from the fire, when the sighing winds spoke with her voice and beckoned him across the snow, that word "Tomorrow" took on another meaning for him, and he saw himself with Imogene, saw them happy, laughing, deeply in love, treading gaily the flower-strewn fields of some wondrous tomorrow, when they would be together again.

She loved him. . . . His vision that night on the ice had been too real, more real than reality itself. It must be true. He bent his head and wept for her, this woman he had loved so dearly and treated so unkindly. In some far-off heaven he would make it up to her—if only God would let him.

The Winds of Fate do not always bring tears that fall like rain; sometimes they are kindly winds, soft winds that blow from the south. To Verhulst they had brought calamity—and yet, they had brought him a vision too, a vision of true happiness.

Imogene loved him. Now in his heart he was sure of it.

And because he had not realized he was in love with her at all, because he had thought his gut-wrenching feeling for her was only carnal passion misdirected, hurt pride, possessiveness, and any number of other things—because the full glory of his love for her had not burst upon him until the moment he knew she was lost to him, Verhulst endured a hell of his own making.

Ghosts, they say, leave no footprints. But Imogene had left her footprints indelibly etched across Verhulst van Rappard's heart.

As if attacked by some frenzy, he began brave new plans for the expansion of the manor house at Wey Gat into an even more impressive building. He let contracts and signed promissory notes and even added a codicil to his will that in the event of his death, the structure should be completed according to his plans. As the years passed, all who plied the river would be awed as they passed the multichimneyed stone fortress into which the patroon of Wey Gat had poured his vast wealth.

Like the bereaved husband who had built the *Taj Mahal*, Verhulst van Rappard intended to build a mighty memorial to his lost love.

And the river aristocrats, who considered him mad—as any man must be mad who buried his wife alongside the lover he had killed—kept away from the patroon of Wey Gat, and in time the great lonely house came to be considered a place of devils.

But Verhulst did not live to see that.

Alone and weighed down by his grief, in those early weeks Verhulst mourned Imogene. He mourned her as the wolf, who takes but one mate, mourns her loss: on the lonely trail, in silence and in grief. He took to wandering out alone in the night, for he could not sleep. Sometimes he slushed through the snow for miles, barely making it back to the house by morning.

In January a blizzard struck. It shrieked down from Canada, driving ice pellets before it like ball and shot. It blasted the trees and tore limbs away and froze livestock in their stalls and before it was over it had dumped three feet of snow along the North River Valley. The morning after the blizzard struck the patroon was nowhere to be found. A search was instituted. Men with their heads bound up in stocking caps searched, red-nosed and with ice freezing on their lashes and matting their beards, throughout the nearby grounds. They were about to organize a search party to stumble into the woods and search there when someone gave a shout that could be heard even above the shriek of the icy northern winds. They followed the sound and came to the walled family plot containing the stones that Verhulst had erected to commemorate the passing of Imogene and her lover. Only the gray tops of the stones protruded now from the snow and beside them with his hands resting on a shovel as he stared down into the disturbed white mass was Groot, the kennelmaster. Around him the dogs were leaping, keening, and the men pushed through them to see what Groot was seeing.

It was a black velvet-clad arm and a frozen stiff gauntlet-gloved hand, both powdered white from the fast-blowing snow that was piling up in great drifts.

They had found their patroon. Silently, beneath a cold gray sky, the men gathered around and removed their stocking caps, letting the blowing ice particles whiten their bent heads.

Verhulst van Rappard, patroon of vast Wey Gat, had found his heaven and his hell and now—they looked into each other's eyes before they dug him out and in several faces there was a wild surmise. Had he found Imogene at last? On some far shore were they laughing now, all their terrible clashing forgotten?

In silence the men he had dominated and bullied dug the patroon from the snow and bore him back to his manor.

When the snow stopped falling and a cold gray sky looked down on a glistening white world of crystal, the servants milled about and the tenants came in and they tried to decide what to do. They did not ask the neighbors. The neighbors, they were all aware, had not liked Wey Gat's unhappy young patroon. And his only relatives—if indeed any still existed—were far away in Holland.

So they buried him themselves—unceremoniously, in a shallow grave, for they could dig no deeper in the frozen earth. His coffin lay beside three empty ones and because they sensed some deeper meaning in the word he had chiseled into the stone that marked the passing of Imogene's lover, without comprehension they chiseled on Verhulst's stone, along with his name and the dates, the single Dutch word for "Tomorrow."

BOOK IV
The Buccaneer's Lady

A toast to the wild sweet laughter
From the Indies claimed by Spain,
From the warm sweet lips on buccaneer ships
That prowl the Spanish Main!

PART ONE
The Lost

A toast to her charms, held close in his arms.
Because he loves her so. . . .
Ah, he would be more than human
If he were to let her go!

New Amsterdam, New Netherland, 1658

CHAPTER 26

Downriver the charging iceboat carrying Imogene and Stephen had fled, downriver and out of sight. For hardly had Imogene been hauled aboard by a wailing Elise before Willem let the wind take them and they skimmed south. Past the men, past the dogs, they flew downriver as the swallow flies, driven by the wild Canadian winds.

"My God," screamed Willem, who spoke English. "That was the patroon of Wey Gat out there! Who is this woman?"

Elise, who was cradling Imogene's limp body in her arms, called over the crunching and grinding as the iceboat shot forward, "She is his wife."

" 'His *wife*!'" howled Willem. "In *my* iceboat? I am a dead man if he finds me! You damned Englishman!" He turned to glare at Stephen's inert form. "You deserve to die! You lied to me—you told me the woman we would pick up was a servant who had borne a child and whose father would not permit her to marry until she had first repaid him for bringing her up. You told me this one—" he jerked his head vengefully at Elise—"was her aunt who had a house in New Amsterdam and would take care of her. I suppose that is not true either?"

Sorrowfully, Elise shook her head. "I am her maidservant —and her friend." As she spoke she was gently sweeping back the cascade of golden hair from Imogene's closed eyes, being careful not to disturb the wound at the side of her head where a little blood trickled down—that spot where the iceboat had struck her.

Willem cast a wild look back at the little clump of men fast disappearing in the distance as the iceboat gathered speed, spurred by the driving northern winds. "Thank God the ice is smooth! His *wife!*" He looked anxiously around at Imogene. "Is the woman dead? Have we killed the patroon's wife?"

"No! Of course she is not dead!"

"Wrap her well in blankets," advised Willem. "And this one, too." He indicated Stephen with a toe of his boot. "He is bleeding like a stuck pig."

"I will try to stanch the wound." Elise finished wrapping Imogene carefully in blankets against the awesome cold, giving her only a little space to breathe. Leaving her beside the well-wrapped baby, she staggered in the rocking iceboat to Stephen's side. He lay sprawled on his back and she muttered to herself as she saw the ugly wound that stained his doublet. She tore off strips of her underpetticoat and managed to stop the flow of blood.

"Wrap him well," called Willem, "or he will freeze." He began to curse. "Damme, I can feel my whiskers freezing to my face!"

Elise nodded. Panting from the effort, she managed to wrap Stephen up warmly in the heavy blankets he and Willem had brought along for the long cold journey down the frozen river. Then she made her way back to Imogene. With cold-stiffened fingers she pulled a heavy Indian blanket over all their heads and prayed the iceboat would not be wrecked when it hit stretches of rough ice that bounced them unmercifully about and that might well break open Stephen's wound. Once or twice she checked on his condition, for now he had come to and was groaning.

"Imogene?" he asked hoarsely.

"She is all right," Elise told him in a firm voice, knowing it was not so because Imogene had not yet waked, but remained still and white as death beneath her blankets. "She tells you to be still, for you are hurt and if you move you will open your wound. Edge close against us, so that we may not all freeze."

Stephen's head sagged back in relief. Imogene was safe!

Willem, steering the iceboat, rubbed a woolen-mittened hand across his eyes in an attempt to keep his lashes from freezing to his cheeks. His breath sobbed painfully in his throat, but he kept them grimly on course, no matter how dizzying the pace. The Hudson Highlands were flying by. He wondered if the men at Wey Gat had recognized his iceboat. No, that was unlikely. The iceboat was featureless and Willem was from Beverwyck—he had never met anyone from Wey Gat. Indeed, he would not have recognized its patroon just now had not someone once pointed out that dark, slender, richly clad figure on Perel Straat in New Amsterdam and said, "Look at that strutting peacock, will you? That stripling can buy and sell us all!"

Thinking of the patroon's wealth that gave him powerful outreaching arms that could snatch a man from the ends of the colony and bring him to justice made Willem's heart beat faster—in some ways a blessing, for it kept him warm against the bitter cold. He speculated wildly about the woman in the velvet cloak who lay so still beneath the blankets in the bottom of his boat, and about the copper-haired English adventurer the patroon had shot. Fear crawled over Willem as he considered his dangerous cargo, and that fear made him reckless, running the iceboat full out, letting the wind sweep them forward in all its violence. If he reached New Amsterdam at this pace, he would doubtless have set a record for river travel—a record he would not boast of, for he little doubted the patroon of Wey Gat would shoot him down without mercy for his part in this affair. Helping the patroon's wife to escape with a lover! Willem shuddered and his mind darted around like a rat, seeking a way out. He tried to bolster his sagging courage by telling himself that any man who set dogs on his wife deserved to lose her, but that did not help his own situation—the patroon would shoot him anyway. Or have him hanged. Or perhaps tie him up and toss him in the river. Willem shook with fright at these imaginings and almost lost control of the tiller. He had expected his passengers to disembark well north of New Amsterdam, while he himself would go on to visit his sister, who lived on a small farm in the vicinity. Now he was saddled with two injured persons and a helpless maidservant and baby—what was he to do with them? They would be very conspicuous in New Amsterdam and as soon as the word got around of their escape, people would be watching for them and he would be unable to transport them anywhere! The money Stephen Linnington had offered him had looked so good at the time but now it had proved to be a trap and Willem wished fervently that he could give it back and erase all of this night's events. He glanced sourly at the shapeless humps of blankets that concealed his passengers. What to do?

Suddenly an arrow whizzed past his eyes, narrowly missing his half-frozen face. Willem gave a hoarse howl and almost lost the tiller. He cast a wild-eyed look at the western shore and saw his attackers—a band of half a dozen Indians, clad in deerskins, all of them calmly fitting arrows to their bows.

Willem bent over the tiller and sent the iceboat careening to the left just in time to miss the shower of arrows loosed from the shore. There was a muffled scream from Elise, for the iceboat had almost overturned and she had been thrown heavily to the side, bruising her arm as she bravely steadied Imogene's inert body and the baby's swaddled form. Elise's head came out of the blankets and she gave another scream as she saw the Indians, again fitting arrows to their bows.

"Quiet, woman!" bawled Willem, almost as much unnerved by Elise's shrieks as by the Indians, who were now running along the shore, loosing their arrows at will. He ran the iceboat through a violent series of convolutions that made it shudder from stem to stern but kept the arrows away from them. These maneuvers brought him into the center of the river where a new terror assailed him. Willem felt his flesh crawl as he heard beneath him a cracking of the river ice. Quickly he veered away from the main current that flowed here beneath the ice, for he knew the ice would be thinner in the center. Now he hewed to the eastern shore where the ice was strong and thick and the distance to the arrow-shooting Indians greater, skittering along at breakneck speed while the disappointed Indians ran out onto the ice loosing arrows at his departing boat.

It was into this melee that the unfortunate Schroon was catapulted as he piloted his small delicate iceboat, his frail "toy," downriver at breakneck speed in an effort to overtake Willem. Schroon saw the Indians spread out on the ice near the west bank shooting at some object that had disappeared. He tried to brake his iceboat too abruptly, overturned it, and sent it into a wild career into the very center of the river where the ice was already cracked by Willem's passing. Schroon leaped out, landing half-stunned on his hands and knees and sliding along for what seemed miles. Behind him he heard a horrendous crack as the ice split beneath the weight of his iceboat and big chunks of river ice gave way beneath it. In horror he watched it upend, a jagged form silhouetted against the snowy bank, and sink beneath the black water. But only for a moment was he paralyzed, watching. Then he picked himself up and tried to run. His breath sobbed in his throat as he dodged the arrows that flashed about him.

Schroon thought he had outrun them when the arrow brought him down. The stone arrowhead pierced deep in his back with a long lancing pain and he sprawled awkwardly on his face on the hard ice. He tried to claw his way up, to elude the Indians whose triumphant shouting seemed almost upon him. Across the long break in the river ice that lay between them and him, Schroon could see them running upriver. They would find a place where it was safe to cross and then they would come for him, to torture and scalp him. Schroon, who had always treated the Indians with kindness, knew that would not save him now. He panted with exertion, trying to drag himself along but the pain was too great and he slumped down, knowing that soon it would not matter whether he struggled on a few feet farther. Quiet descended suddenly over the river as the Indians stilled their wild yells.

Schroon did not know that the Indians, padding upriver to make sure the center ice was safe for crossing, had heard in the distance a faint ring of skates. One of them had pressed his ear to the ice and stood up, pointing to the north. All had understood: white men were coming. In silent accord, the Indians found the bank and melted into the trees. Bent over against the shrieking winds, they disappeared down one of the narrow Indian trails worn smooth by thousands of moccasined feet that would lead them back to their encampment. They were content—they had made their kill. They might have risked staying long enough to scalp the solitary stranger but after all, their leader muttered, it was only a squaw who had been hurt by the white man—and even that could have been an accident—had she not been a chief's daughter they might have chosen not to believe her. But one crumpled form on the ice was enough revenge; the incident was over.

And so it was that the patroon and his grim skating party found Schroon dying on the ice.

Schroon lied to his patroon—and by lying gave Imogene her destiny.

Willem, of course, was not to know any of this. He careened on downriver on greased iron runners, pursued and driven on less by the screaming winds than by his own bright terror of the patroon's vengeance.

Unable to think of a better course, Willem brought his iceboat to a halt as dawn was breaking before his older sister's riverside farmhouse outside New Amsterdam. She was astonished to see his battered, half-frozen crew. Imogene was easily carried in, Elise stumbled in with the baby, under her own power, to thaw her chilled bones at the blazing fire, but Stephen tried to rise and fell back. Willem slung him over his big bearlike shoulders and carried him inside and then retreated to the kitchen to have a hurried conversation in Dutch with his sister. He told her the truth and it left her speechless. When she recovered she berated him without pausing to draw breath. The gist of her comments was that Willem had really done it this time! She would offer them all *oleykoeks* and raisin wine and they were welcome to warm themselves at her hearth. But shelter a man who'd been shot running away with another man's wife? Shelter a patroon's runaway vrouw? Was Willem mad? Indeed, he must have these people out of her house this very day. He was just lucky that her husband had been gone overnight, but he would return tonight and if he found them here he would turn them all over to the *schout* and Willem would undoubtedly hang, as her husband had always said he would!

Willem winced and ducked his head as if blows were raining on it, but he knew he was hearing the unvarnished truth. His sister's straitlaced husband had never liked him, considered him a ne'er-do-well and worse. What he would do if he learned that the patroon of Wey Gat's runaway wife was secreted in his house, Willem hated to think. With fright to spur him, he hurried back to the living room where Elise was bent over picking up something that had dropped on the floor beside Imogene. Why, it was Imogene's journal—she must have brought it with her so that it would not fall into Verhulst's hands. Swiftly Elise pocketed the journal and was bending over the baby when Willem reached her.

His sister followed him in with a tray of the hot *oleykoeks* she had been making and a jug of raisin wine and offered them to all present. Stephen waved her wanly away, but Elise, cuddling the baby, gratefully munched one of the steaming doughnuts fried in lard.

"Why, it's a dear little thing!" cried Willem's sister in Dutch, for babies—she had none of her own—always enchanted her. She rushed to heat some milk for the child as well as hot cider all around. "But—is the woman dead?" she demanded harshly of Willem. "You cannot let her die in my house!"

"She is not dead," insisted Willem in Dutch. "And I will have her out, you may count on it."

"But she lies so still!"

Willem frowned. "Is there a ship leaving harbor today? Anywhere will do—the farther the better!"

"I heard Vrouw Bergstede say the *Wilhelmina* was in harbor and would set out for Jamaica today—but I think you may be too late; she has probably already sailed."

Willem turned to Elise. "There is no time to lose. I must go for a doctor and I must get rid of you separately, else the patroon of Wey Gat will be here in force and we will all hang."

Elise blanched and clutched little Georgiana tighter.

"Have you money?" Willem's face was grim.

Elise nodded.

"Enough for ship's passage? There is a ship bound for Jamaica but she leaves at once."

Elise cast a wild look at Stephen. "But we are bound for Barbados!"

Stephen, who was slipping in and out of consciousness, said weakly, "Go with him, Elise. Willem is right, we are conspicuous all together. We will send for you."

"There is no time to argue!" Willem seized Elise's arm and pulled her toward the door. "The ship is leaving! Be good enough to pull your hat down over your eyes. God in heaven, the woman is wearing men's boots!" This as Elise hiked up her skirts preparatory to stepping out into the snow.

Elise gave Stephen a last desperate look as she jammed her hat down on her head. "Take care—of my lady," she choked. "For it hurts my very heart to leave her here."

"I will," Stephen promised gallantly, "for she is also *my* lady." *For that,* he told himself, *was the way it must be now.*

But he looks unable to take care of anyone, even himself, thought Elise in panic as Willem hurried her out.

They were barely in time to procure passage for "Mistress

Eliza Smith'' and her small niece ''Anna Smith'' on board the *Wilhelmina,* for her captain was just then casting off. He told her testily he had no time to wait for her luggage, she must come aboard now or they'd miss the tide. Both Willem and Elise were grateful for that—it spared questions.

''Go quickly,'' urged Elise as she clambered aboard. She turned and gave Willem a push. ''You must find a doctor if my lady is to live!''

The *Wilhelmina's* captain thought he had seen some strange leave-takings in his time, but this departure with a shove was a new one. ''Cast off!'' he roared.

Willem, delighted to hear those words, turned his back upon the ship and scurried away. He hoped no one at dockside had noticed him with the woman. Now if he could only be rid of the other two—for he'd certainly no intention of bringing a curious doctor to his sister's house to incriminate them all! Still, they were in no shape to move—suppose they died there?

He had put on fresh socks at his sister's house. They belonged to his brother-in-law and they were too big for him. One of them had balled up around his heel and was wearing a blister. With a curse he paused to adjust it and when he looked up, hope flared in his eyes.

That ship over there, was she not the *Sea Rover?* A buccaneer's vessel would have a doctor skilled in handling wounds—and one who'd ask no questions either. A doctor who'd patch up that battered pair and send them on their way!

With a sudden real sense that he might yet live to see tomorrow's dawn, Willem limped on board the *Sea Rover* and asked a yellow-haired buccaneer at the ship's rail if he could see the ship's doctor.

''Who wants him?'' demanded a crisp voice behind him.

Willem turned and found himself looking into a dark sardonic visage he recognized as Captain van Ryker's—for the captain's face was well known along the river. He gulped. "Could I speak to ye privately, sir?" he asked with a nervous look about. "The doctor is needed but—but I dare not talk where I can be overheard."

Over Willem's head, van Ryker and his ship's master exchanged glances. Having left so many men in Carolina, the *Sea Rover* was shorthanded and could use another man. This fellow was sturdy—and wanting a buccaneer doctor instead of one from the town. He was limping, true, but even a man with a minor injury would be welcome to sign on under the circumstances.

He took Willem to his cabin. "So ye're in need of a doctor? A musket ball in the leg perhaps?" he asked pleasantly, referring to the limp.

Willem looked startled. "Socks too big—wore a blister," he mumbled.

Van Ryker stared. "And ye want a doctor for that?" he asked incredulously.

"I've two people in need of doctoring," burst out Willem. "Indeed I don't know if they'll live. But they've money," he hastened to add. "The man paid me well to bring him downriver, and the woman wears a necklace of price."

Van Ryker's curiosity was aroused. "Who are they?"

It was the question Willem had been dreading. "I asked them no questions," he said hoarsely. "I was only paid to bring them."

"I cannot ask my ship's doctor to go into a house of fever," van Ryker told him tersely. "He might bring it aboard my vessel. Get a local doctor."

" 'Tis not fever that plagues them—'tis wounds."

" 'Wounds'?"

"Aye. The woman got a bash on the head and the man's been shot in the chest."

Van Ryker's dark brows elevated. Wounds . . . and doubtless acquired outside the law. Willem was becoming more interesting all the time. "Bring them in," he said. "My ship's doctor will treat them."

"No, he'll have to go to them. They're neither of them in shape to walk here."

The dark face broke into a cold smile. "Then ye will tell me who they are and what they've done or I'll not raise a finger to help you. I may bend the law a bit, but I'll not go into anything blind."

Willem, desperate and sensing that whatever van Ryker might do, he would not forthwith turn him over to the *schout* as his brother-in-law certainly would, burst out, "The man's an Englishman name of Linnington and the woman's the wife of the patroon of Wey Gat. Now ye see why I cannot—"

But the tall fellow across from him was suddenly transformed. Willem gasped and staggered back as his collar was seized and twisted in a viselike grip and the captain's menacing face was thrust into his. "The woman is hurt, you say?"

"Aye," cried Willem, half strangled by that implacable grip on his collar. " 'Twas an accident. She struck her head against my iceboat as she boarded—'twas after the man was shot." His voice died away but the grip on his collar was already unloosed. It was replaced by a grip on his arm that threatened to cut off his circulation.

"Raoul!" roared van Ryker. "Where are ye, man?" He stormed on deck, dragging Willem with him. Raoul de Rochemont, clad in a shirt, stuck his head out on deck.

"Bring five men and your doctoring gear," van Ryker

shouted at him. "And follow me! We're bringing a lady aboard. And bring a litter," he called over his shoulder.

Willem was horrified—a company of eight and carrying a litter! Everyone they met would remark it! He could almost feel the hangman's noose tightening around his neck. But as the tall buccaneer dragged him along New Amsterdam's streets, a comforting thought occurred to Willem. It came to him abruptly that people could easily believe him to be but an innocent bystander in this affair. A buccaneer captain had stormed into town and carried off a runaway lady! Willem could later claim—if matters were such that he needed to claim it—that he had been forced into the iceboat at the point of a gun and fled Wey Gat because of the shooting! With alacrity now he led the long-striding buccaneer and his ship's doctor and the others toward his sister's small farmhouse. De Rochemont was shivering badly, having left without his doublet. Only a cloak was thrown over his light shirt in this gale. He bent his head against the wind and wondered what was happening. Van Ryker looked in no mood to be questioned.

At last they reached the farmhouse and without preamble burst through the oaken door. Willem's sister sprang up with a cry.

Van Ryker brushed by her and knelt beside Imogene. "Raoul—here." He gave only a curt nod to Stephen Linnington, whose wan face had lit up at sight of them.

The ship's doctor pulled off his hastily donned gloves and massaged his half-frozen fingers. Then delicately he examined the wound, parting with care that tangled mass of golden hair that tumbled over Imogene's still white face. "Concussion—perhaps shock," he told van Ryker, looking up. "I do not know when she will regain consciousness." He turned to examine

Stephen, cutting away Stephen's doublet and shirt, both stiff with blood. He approved Elise's rude bandaging, and muttered to himself at the look of the wound.

"How come you to be here, Linnington?" van Ryker shot at the recumbent Englishman.

"I knew Imogene in England," Stephen gasped, almost fainting, for the doctor was probing the wound.

The girl with the whisk! Van Ryker was taken aback.

"How well?" he asked steadily.

"What?" Stephen fought back a yell as the ship's doctor continued his painful work.

"How well did you know her?"

Even through the pain, Stephen's mind had not stopped working. That anguished look in van Ryker's gray eyes—and he a "Dutch" buccaneer who came often no doubt to New Amsterdam. "Ye—have a whisk, too, I remember." The words came out grimly, with another gasp of pain.

"And from the same lady, I take it?" Van Ryker was calm. Only his knuckles showed white.

"If ye had yours from this lady, then 'tis one and the same," admitted Stephen, perspiration breaking out on his brow as the doctor probed further. His shoulders moved in agony.

"Hold him down," Raoul tersely ordered the men. "I must find the bullet."

Van Ryker stood looking down at his copper-haired rival. Well, Imogene had told him she'd had a lover in England—and now they were face to face. This was a man to whom Imogene had poured out her secrets, a man who had held her in his arms and tasted the wine of her lips, a man who had caressed her, loved her, perhaps through long, scented nights. A man she'd left her husband for.... For an aching moment, van Ryker would have given anything to have traded places with Linnington.

His jaws closed with a snap. "Hurry," he growled at the ship's doctor. "I must get Imogene aboard the *Sea Rover.* She must have care, hot food."

"I can go no faster," flashed Raoul. "Unless you want this man to die."

It was on the tip of van Ryker's tongue to say bitterly that he desired nothing more than for Linnington to be dead and gone and out of his way. He held himself back with an effort. "Take what time you need," he said civilly.

"Ah!" Raoul gave a long sigh. He had the bullet now. Proudly he held it up. "Now he's a chance of recovery!"

There was no longer any need to hold his writhing patient. Stephen had lapsed into unconsciousness.

"He should not be moved," cautioned Raoul, skillfully applying bandages. "Not until the wound has time to knit. If he starts bleeding again, he will die."

Willem turned and said something sharply to his sister in Dutch.

"But," she cried in panic, "he cannot stay here! My husband will be back soon!"

Van Ryker heard her and swung around. "Load Linnington onto the litter—carefully." He pulled out some gold coins and dropped them into Willem's eagerly outstretched palm. "Share these with her." He nodded toward Willem's sister. "Mevrouw," he added soberly in Dutch, "we trust you will keep quiet about this matter?"

She fell back, relieved, and snatched three of the coins from Willem, hid them in her apron. Her house was out of sight of the neighbors, but these people could not clear her front door soon enough to suit her!

"What will ye do with the Englishman?" wondered Raoul

as he helped the men place Stephen—still mercifully unconscious—on the litter. He watched van Ryker wrap Imogene
carefully in blankets and sweep her up in his arms as if she were
a child. He followed the litter and van Ryker out. "The Englishman
needs to recover in a stationary place," he said in an argumenta-
tive voice, for he was tired and doubted not that he would catch
cold from this hike through New Amsterdam's icy streets to the
farmhouse. "A sail across choppy waters could well kill him."
It came to him suddenly that this might be just what his captain
had in mind, and he gave van Ryker a suspicious look.

Van Ryker caught that look and turned and kicked the
oaken door shut with his foot so that Willem and his sister could
no longer hear their conversation. "Then we'll leave him here in
New Amsterdam," he said calmly.

Raoul stared. "Where?"

"I think ye're forgetting a certain Dutchman named Johann
Culp that we liberated from unwilling service in a Spanish
galley. Johann has a family here and his wife told me that when I
struck off her husband's chains I had put the whole family
forever in my debt. I think they'll be glad enough to take care
of—a wounded member of my crew." He turned to the men
carrying the litter. "Take this man to the house of Johann Culp,
and tell Culp this is the only favor I will ever ask of him."

So van Ryker was going to pass Linnington off as a wounded member of his crew too badly hurt to move, and carry off the
woman. . . . Raoul thought he would not like to be there when
Linnington woke up.

"How will you explain Linnington's wound?" he asked
bluntly. "For Culp will know this man was not with us on board
the *Sea Rover*—remember Culp sailed into New Amsterdam
harbor with us!"

"He'll keep his mouth shut in gratitude that he's not now

pulling a Spanish oar with a Spanish whip striping his naked back,'' explained van Ryker with a grin. "Memories are short, but a man should remember a kindness done at least a week or two, don't you think? As for the wound, I'll say his gun exploded and caught him in the chest—no, *you'll* say it, for I intend to stay by Imogene in case she wakes up—she'd be frightened, coming to and finding herself alone.''

The ship's doctor gave him a pitying look. "It may be a long time—before she wakes up," he said gently.

"What d'ye mean 'a long time'?"

"I mean, I've no way of knowing—" Raoul swallowed, but he felt he had to say it—"whether she will *ever* regain consciousness. Her head has sustained a solid blow—"

A pair of burning eyes bored suddenly into his. "Ye're a doctor, aren't ye?" van Ryker demanded crisply. "Ye'll make my lady well!''

"If 'tis in my power,'' mumbled Raoul, with a hunted look. "I'll do all I can, ye can count on it.''

"I *do* count on it, Raoul.'' Van Ryker gave his ship's doctor a grim look.

"I'll try.''

"And give Culp a purse of gold to pay for Linnington's keep and to be discreet,'' added van Ryker carelessly.

The doctor's head jerked.

"I know you always carry money on you, Raoul. 'Tis a habit from the time when you always thought to be leaving in a hurry. Make note of how much you give Culp—I'll replace your coins for you when you get back to the ship.''

Raoul jammed his hat on his head irritably and trudged away through the snow, following the litter. He turned as van Ryker called to him, "And after you've delivered your parcel, buy all the freshest fruits and vegetables you can find—and some wild turkeys if any are to be had. We'll have a feast aboard the *Sea Rover* this night!''

Raoul, watching his captain's saturnine face gone suddenly boyish and lighthearted now that Imogene was in his arms again, shook his head in perplexity and turned away. A feast! The man was planning to celebrate—and doubtless intended for Imogene to sit beside him at the feast. The captain had not yet taken it in that it might be a very long time before his golden-haired lady would be eating anything more than broth and hot milk forced between her pale lips.

Raoul proceeded a few paces and stopped with a curse. In his fascination with van Ryker's instructions, he'd left his gloves back at the farmhouse—no wonder his hands were freezing! He hesitated but a moment and then plunged back to the farmhouse, slipping and sliding over the icy surface.

Willem's sister let him in. As the doctor picked up his gloves and eased them over his chilly fingers she said something sharp to Willem and gave him a shove toward the doctor, who didn't speak Dutch.

''My sister reminds me of something,'' Willem told the doctor reluctantly. ''The maidservant and—'' he swallowed—''her baby took passage aboard the *Wilhelmina*.'' He was inwardly cursing his sister's stupidity in insisting on this revelation—did the fool not realize that they might yet be implicated in this thing?

''So?'' said Raoul indifferently. This would not be the first time a servant had deserted her mistress in time of stress. It never occurred to him that ''her'' referred to Imogene—he assumed the baby was the maidservant's.

''So the *Wilhemina* has already departed, bound for Jamaica,'' said Willem in a strangled voice.

''No doubt the maidservant had her reasons,'' said Raoul

indifferently and hurried out to overtake the litter, hoping he could do so without breaking his neck. In the distance he could see his captain's form disappearing in the direction of their vessel.

With a song in his heart, the tall buccaneer strode along with Imogene limp in his arms. She was so bundled up that he appeared to be carrying a heap of blankets. He held her with great gentleness and so springy was his joyful step that she rode feather light—for now that he had found her he never doubted that she would soon be well again. Well again—and *his!* For he would win her from Linnington—he would win her from anyone! He walked in happy silence with his dreams of bright tomorrows, but prudence had not deserted him. He had three burly buccaneers bringing up the rear in case anyone should challenge him. For van Ryker was well aware that the woman in his arms was another man's wife and he intended to surrender her to no one—least of all her husband.

Many thoughts prowled his head. So Imogene had been desperate enough to run away—and he had thought her so happy. . . . He frowned, wondering why she had not contacted him. She must have known that he would have stormed northward and battered his way into Wey Gat and taken her downriver out of the colony though every gun of Fort Amsterdam blazed at him!

Instead she had contacted Linnington. The lean buccaneer shook his head as if to clear away cobwebs and his jaw hardened. The little yellow brick houses were going by on both sides of him now but he gave them never a glance. Instead he faced the world with a new resolution, a new purpose in life. Whether Imogene had sent for Linnington or whether the copper-haired Englishman had gone to fetch her on his own account and found her willing made no difference now. For van Ryker felt—

incredible as it seemed to him—that he had heard her calling him from far away, heard her calling all the way to Spanish Town, all the way to Carolina.

Tenderly he cradled the limp burden that was the woman he loved more than he loved his life, tenderly he carried her—checking occasionally to make sure that the light blanket flung over her head so that the cold air might not sear her lungs neither suffocated her nor pressed upon her wound—through New Amsterdam's snowy streets. Ignoring the stares of the curious and the greetings of friends alike, he strode on without stopping until he reached his vessel.

For now he was a man with but one purpose, one resolve: He was going to make his lady well!

The Sea Rover, 1658–1659

CHAPTER 27

"Her husband will come for her, you know," warned Raoul de Rochemont when at last he came aboard with two buccaneers following, loaded down with the fresh produce van Ryker had ordered. "This is no ordinary woman you have kidnapped—this is the wife of a patroon!"

"So? Let him come!" Van Ryker was busy picking out the finest of the fruits to bring to Imogene when she waked.

"He will not come as a lone gentleman to duel with you for possession of his wife," said Raoul, vexed. "He will come with all the men of Wey Gat and half the colony of New Netherland streaming behind him, all demanding the return of this woman!"

Van Ryker looked up. "D'ye think I would give her up, Raoul?" he asked softly.

"I suppose not," the doctor sighed.

"Cheer up." Van Ryker clapped him on the shoulder.

"They will find us gone on the next tide. Tell me, was Culp happy to receive Linnington?"

"Not happy—but willing." The ship's doctor massaged his chilled hands. "I gave him gold for Linnington's keep and Culp's wife informed me she had an Indian servant who was wise in 'Indian medicine,' whatever that is. Linnington looked worse when I left him—and no wonder, the bearers slipped on the ice and dropped the litter when we were halfway there! 'Twas a miracle it did not open the wound. *Mon Dieu,* but it's cold out there!" He let van Ryker lead him to the great cabin where Imogene lay enthroned in the big bunk wrapped in the finest linens and blankets the ship possessed. "I find no change," he said dryly, rising from his examination.

"Then you are wrong," van Ryker told him in a quiet voice. "For she has already opened her eyes and started to speak—and then lapsed back."

And then lapsed back into a coma. De Rochemont's face was grim. "We must hope," he said shortly. "I am now worried about the exposure she has suffered." And then pettishly, "If only we were out of this insufferable climate!"

"We will be out of this 'insufferable' climate tomorrow," van Ryker assured him. "The burghers here in New Amsterdam were eager for our goods and all will be delivered—and paid for—by tonight. Barnaby is taking care of it. We have already taken on the fresh water—"

"Ice," corrected Raoul.

"As you will." Van Ryker shrugged. "We have near stripped the town of its available fruit and vegetables. The men have been alerted to spend the night aboard ship. We sail with the morning tide."

De Rochement gave him an irritable look. There was something inflexible about these buccaneers. No sailor himself, it chafed him to be controlled by tides and sea-politics that closed one port to a man even while it opened another. Sometimes he wished he had never left his father's house in Rouen. Then the circumstances of that leave-taking came back to him and he sighed.

"Keep her warm," he advised.

Van Ryker nodded soberly and went on deck to give instructions to his men.

When he came back, Imogene's eyes were wide open and she was sitting up with the covers thrown back, staring fearfully around her.

"What is this place?" she cried. And then as van Ryker leaped forward, she shrank back. "And who are you?"

He came to a frowning halt. "I am Ruprecht van Ryker, captain of this vessel," he said gently. "And this is my cabin."

"But what am I doing here?" she cried. "Where is Elise? Where is Lord Elston? Surely he would not let me be taken aboard some strange vessel while I slept?"

Lord Elston? "Where do you think you are?" asked van Ryker, puzzled.

"Why, in the Scilly Isles, of course! If we are on a ship, you have only to look out those windows—" her accusing gaze flew to the wide bank of windows in the stern—"to establish that!"

"Imogene," he asked gently, "don't you remember anything? Don't you remember that we met, that I loved you?"

"I don't believe you!" she cried. "I never saw you before!"

"It is cold in here," he said sharply. "Let me wrap you up warmly." It hurt him that she should flinch away from him as he pulled up her covers.

Suddenly she gave a cry—something had gouged her. She

pulled it out and looked at it wildly. "Where did I get this necklace?" she demanded in bewilderment. "And—" she clutched at her throat—"I am wearing others!" She began to snatch them off and they slid glittering into the covers. "Have I lost my mind, then," she asked fearfully, "that I who am churchmouse poor am suddenly ablaze with jewels?"

"I will bring the doctor," promised van Ryker, pushing her back down into the bed. But when he found Raoul, he said, "You will tell her nothing, Raoul—only that you are the ship's doctor who tended her when I brought her on board. I do not want her frightened by the circumstances of her leave-taking."

But when they returned, Imogene had lapsed back into unconsciousness.

"The blow on the head has knocked out her recent memories," the doctor explained. "She may wake again remembering everything or—" He hesitated.

"Or?" pursued van Ryker.

"Or she may remember only a part—or perhaps nothing at all. The past may come back to her in chunks, or in bits and pieces, loosely from time to time—a tantalizing word here, a name there."

His captain's face was thoughtful, for van Ryker had seized upon a wild new thought: He could now start fresh with Imogene with no rivals at all! He could court her as a man courts an innocent maid—he could make her love him.

But that night a new problem surfaced. Van Ryker returned to his cabin to find Imogene burning up with fever.

"It is as I feared," muttered the ship's doctor when he was called. "She will throw off her covers and doubtless take a chill."

"No." Grimly. "I will watch her. I will stay in the cabin and take care of her."

De Rochemont sighed. A buccaneer ship was not a suitable hospital. "She may alternate chills with fever," he said. "And you will have to bundle her up."

"I will follow all of your instructions. Tomorrow while I catch a nap, you will relieve me."

De Rochemont nodded. In his heart he doubted if the woman would live.

Van Ryker sat beside Imogene, sponging her hot forehead. Patiently he forced liquid down her throat. Suddenly she opened her eyes and looked at him. "I am still here?" she gasped. "But I asked you to return me to Lord Elston, my guardian!"

"We could not do it," lied van Ryker smoothly. "A gale has blown us off course and you have taken a fever."

" 'A fever'?" She began to shake violently. "I am shivering with cold!"

De Rochemont had warned him of chills. Van Ryker looked about him with a frown. It *was* cold in this damned cabin, there was no keeping it as warm as it should be. The heated stones wrapped in cloth at her feet were not enough.

With sudden decision he rose and began stripping off his clothes.

"What—what are you doing?" asked the woman on the bed through chattering teeth.

"I am going to warm you—with my body," he said quietly.

"No, you are not!" Imogene tried dizzily to sit up but he strode toward her and pushed her back down. She struck at him weakly.

"Save your strength," he ordered. "I promise no impropriety but I am going to make you well."

"No im—" Imogene fought him as he swept back the covers and climbed in beside her, seizing her in a grip she could not break.

"Lie still," he commanded.

Imogene screamed.

Feet pounded to the cabin door. "Go away!" roared van Ryker, and cursed as she bit his hand. He got her back to him, circled her waist with arms that seemed to Imogene like bands of steel. Still she fought him, gasping and choking. He had pinioned her flailing arms by now, wrapped his lean bare legs around her own so that her back was against his chest and her buttocks pressed against his groin, and was holding her immobile. In spite of the chills that gripped her, Imogene began to feel warmer.

The doctor's voice came from outside the door—someone had obviously called him. "Are you all right in there?" he called.

"No!" screamed Imogene, fury giving her strength. "This man is raping me!"

"Captain," began Raoul in an injured tone. "I tried to tell you that the lady is in no condition—" He was leaning against the door as he spoke. Unlatched, it gave way beneath his weight and swung open.

Van Ryker looked up from the bed. His head rose from the pillow so quickly that his dark hair swung about and the gray eyes that bored into Raoul's astonished dark ones were wickedly angry. Van Ryker's shoulders came up out of the covers in a fluid gesture and he reached over the bunk and hurled a bottle at Raoul, which that gentleman barely managed to duck.

"Get out!" bellowed van Ryker. "Nobody's raping the lady—she's had a chill and I'm trying to keep her warm!"

"Mistress," began the doctor in fright, "I assure you this gentleman has no intention—"

"We don't need your assurances!" roared his captain. "We don't need a go-between! We can talk this out ourselves—

472

we're in bed together! Get out or I'll shoot you in the leg and they can carry you out!''

''Yes—of course. *Mon Dieu*, yes!'' The Frenchman retreated in confusion and wiped his brow. Even his mustache was trembling. The man in the bed—frenzied with worry over that woman— had seemed mad enough to carry out his threat. Carefully, he closed the door and went back to his own cabin.

Alone again with Imogene, van Ryker tried to comfort her but she had gone limp in his arms. Half-mad with worry, he massaged her hands and feet. If only he could give her his strength! As gently as he would have held a child, he cradled her against his broad chest. He breathed into her hair and when he inhaled he caught the faint scent of lemons he had noticed so long ago.

Her body was warmer now, absorbing body heat from his. Tenderly he massaged her cold fingers, flexed and rubbed her toes, her instep, her ankles. He roused the circulation in her arms and legs. He held her close, as if to protect her from harm and prayed—he who was so unused to praying—for her recovery.

God, in your mercy, let her live!

There were unaccustomed tears shining on his lashes. Even through her clothes the touch of her body was a sweet torment, reminding him how much he wanted her. Her buttocks were cradled against his groin and he felt a wave of feeling every time she stirred restlessly. With iron will he held himself in check. Imogene needed all her strength—and all the care he could give her.

Morning found him haggard and worried. The ship's doctor, eager to make amends for his mistake of yesterday, tried to distract him. ''Did you know Elise had a child?'' he asked when van Ryker came on deck. ''Willem told me he had put the maidservant and her child aboard the *Wilhelmina* bound for Jamaica.''

A child! Van Ryker remembered sharply the deep rosy tint of Imogene's nipples as he had gently unbound her tight bodice so that she might breathe more freely. And had not she announced her pregnancy that night at the Governor's Ball?

In consternation he seized Raoul's arm. ''That kindly old bag of bones has borne no child. The child is Imogene's! When she wakes and remembers, she will call for her child—and we will not be able to produce it. Damme, Raoul, why did you not tell me this before? We passed the *Wilhelmina* beating south!''

''Perhaps we can still find her,'' cried de Rochemont, alarmed at this second blunder.

They turned the ship around and tried to intercept the *Wilhelmina*, but it was useless and they turned south again. How could they know the *Wilhelmina* had fouled her rudder and been driven straight east by the strong winds?

But van Ryker had not much time to contemplate Imogene's newly discovered motherhood, for bringing her aboard had begun a long grueling time for him and for his ship's doctor. Raoul had more than enough chance to restore himself to his captain's graces as they labored. Imogene alternated between restless sleep, chills in which she shook so violently that van Ryker feared she would bruise herself against his ribcage, and wild delirium. As the ship beat steadily south, both van Ryker and the ship's doctor lost weight.

For the better part of two months Imogene was conscious only for short periods and even at those times her mind was confused: she thought herself back in the Scillies and called plaintively for Lord Elston and for Elise. During that time the *Sea Rover* had sailed to the Carolinas and her crew had finished making the *Swallow* seaworthy.

They were off the Carolina coast heading for Tortuga before Imogene's fever broke. By now she had become very gaunt and there were great hollows beneath her eyes. Her golden hair came out in handfuls when van Ryker tried awkwardly to comb it.

But to him as he watched her lying there in exhausted peaceful sleep, no longer racked with chills or burning with fever, she was the most beautiful sight in the world. His Imogene would live! Stumbling with weariness, he staggered out on deck and breathed deep of the bracing winds that swept across the Outer Banks.

The ship's doctor came up to him. "Now that the fever's broken her memory should return. D'ye wish me to be the one to tell her her husband is dead?"

For by now passing ships had given them bits of news—and that from Wey Gat had been startling indeed, for all New Netherland throbbed with gossip about the strange funeral, the empty coffins buried with such ceremony in the family plot—and then to cap it all, the patroon being found dead there in the January blizzard!

"No, I'll tell her," said van Ryker wearily. "But in my own good time."

He would tell her something else first, he thought. For it had come to him that now that the patroon was dead, Imogene was free. If Linnington had only inhabited that "empty" coffin, he would have no rival at all. . . .

So it was that after her long sleep, Imogene opened her eyes and found herself looking up into the smiling face of her "damned pirate." She tried to sit up, sank back dizzily. "What—where am I?"

"On board the *Sea Rover.*"

Her blue eyes widened as they flew over the carved black

oak table, the garnet velvet cushions, the heavy gold candle-sticks, the gilt-trimmed paneled walls—all the familiar opulence that she remembered. It was as if she had gone back in time! But the man who smiled down at her was not dressed elegantly as he had been when she had seen him last. He wore a clean white shirt with flowing sleeves, open to the waist. A pair of leathern breeches like the *boucan* hunters wore adorned his legs and he was barefoot like the deckhands, his strong calf muscles as browned as theirs.

But—she could not be aboard the *Sea Rover!* She was at Wey Gat and—!

"Why am I here?" she cried in alarm. "Where is my baby, where is Elise? And Stephen, where is he?" Her hand flew to her mouth. "I saw him shot!"

"A man named Willem brought you to New Amsterdam by iceboat and sought my aid," explained van Ryker. "You and Linnington were both badly hurt—you from a blow on the head, he from a ball in the chest."

"Yes—oh, I remember! The dog was leaping for my throat and I saw Stephen standing up in the iceboat. He fired and brought the dog down, and Verhulst—Verhulst stepped forward and shot Stephen. The iceboat was coming at me, Elise was screaming and—and after that I don't remember anything."

"The iceboat struck you."

"Where is Stephen? He is hurt—I must go to him!"

The anguish in her voice strengthened van Ryker's resolve. He frowned. "I am afraid you cannot. He was hurt badly. Raoul said there would be no chance for him at all aboard a lurching ship. We left him with a family named Culp."

"In New Amsterdam? And sailed away? But what will he think? That I deserted him?"

Van Ryker hardened his heart against this soft outburst. He

reminded himself that he wanted a clear field. For this was the woman he desired above all others—he had to have her.

"Linnington was dying, Imogene. We had no choice but to leave him there." He sighed, hating himself for this deception. "He gave his life for you, Imogene." *One could afford to be generous with a fallen foe,* he told himself grimly!

"Oh, no!" She put her hands over her face and sank back with a little cry, then started up, eyes staring. "But my baby? What of her? What of Elise?"

"Willem told Raoul they sailed on the *Wilhelmina,* bound for Jamaica."

"I must go to them!" She would have sprung up but he stayed her.

"All in good time. You are not yet well. Now that you are conscious I will carry you on deck where you can enjoy the sun.

Enjoy the sun . . . a sun Stephen would never enjoy again. A sob caught in her throat as memories wrenched her, as she remembered how gloriously the sunlight had glinted off his copper hair and sparkled in his bold eyes. She had lost him . . . *twice.* But—her chin lifted tremulously—he had come back from the dead to save her from Wey Gat and she would carry that knowledge with her to her grave. Listless now, she let van Ryker carry her to the deck. She gave no thought at all to the lean buccaneer who lifted her as lightly as a glass of wine and strode on deck with her, to deposit her, well wrapped up, in a hastily arranged hammock.

"When we reach more southern waters, we'll arrange a thatch over this hammock as a sunshade to shield out the sun's more blinding rays," he told her with a smile.

Imogene did not answer. Her thoughts were far away—he wondered if she heard him.

"I will leave you now," he said, looking down with pity

into her sorrowful eyes. She closed them and he saw tears squeezing out from under her lashes. Tears for Linnington! Van Ryker's jaw hardened and he turned around and moved away with rather more energy than was necessary. He hated himself for hurting Imogene, he hated himself for lying to her and yet—jealousy gnawed at him. It was even possible that he had told her the truth, that Linnington was dead—after all, Raoul had said he *might* die. Stonily van Ryker faced the truth—he *wanted* Linnington dead so there would be no competition for Imogene's affections.

In his jealousy, it did not occur to him that he was enthroning his rival in Imogene's affections. Van Ryker had only offered her his cabin—Stephen had given his life to save her. To an emotional woman like Imogene, the difference was clear. Lying there on deck she thought about the two men and it seemed to her that all of Stephen's actions were noble—and all of van Ryker's base.

True, Stephen had deserted her in the Scillies, but from the kindest of motives—he was trying to shield her from being implicated in Giles's murder. True, he had not written, but that too was from the kindest of motives—in hiding, he had undoubtedly heard of her marriage (and of course, he could not have known about that garbled tale of his death in a duel that had reached her!) and had no wish to intrude upon her supposed happiness. But when he learned from Bess Duveen of her real circumstances—here Imogene's heart leaped—he had rushed to save her . . . and given up his life in the doing of it.

Tears stung her eyelids and slid down her cheeks.

Van Ryker, on the other hand, had toyed with her affections. Although she was reluctantly grateful for the care he had given her, she could not but think of him with a kind of contempt. He had assailed a married woman with a shipboard romance and she—reckless fool that she was, bored and disappointed with her loveless "honeymoon"—had responded by flirting with him. She had almost driven the dangerous captain too far, for he had thought to kidnap her from the Governor's Ball and she had only driven him off by telling him she was in love with Verhulst. *His* desertion had been different! To him she had been only a plaything, a passing fancy—sweet to hold in his arms since she was there, unimportant when she was not. Resentment stirred within her, for it seemed to her that van Ryker had proved that by simply disappearing from her life. He had never sailed upriver to see what had become of her, never written to inquire of her welfare. It must have been public knowledge that she had tried to escape her husband—surely van Ryker could not have missed hearing about it when he made port in New Amsterdam. Yet he had made no move to save her—not until his aid had been actively sought! It did not occur to Imogene that van Ryker had shunned New Amsterdam in an effort not to wreck her marriage and spoil her "perfect" happiness—indeed, she would have been incredulous had that been suggested.

Yet she knew guiltily in her heart that she would indeed have gone away with the buccaneer if he had sailed the *Sea Rover* upriver and dared the guns of Wey Gat as he had threatened to dare the guns of Fort Amsterdam in her behalf. She would have become, without a second thought, a buccaneer's woman—and she was deeply ashamed of that, for now it seemed a treachery to Stephen, who had loved her so devotedly. Steady as the North Star, Stephen had never veered in that devotion, she told herself. And now *because of her* he lay dead in some foreign place. *And she was to blame*.

Van Ryker had lusted for her, but Stephen—Stephen had loved her.

Now her old resentment born of the buccaneer's "desertion'' of her led her to indifference toward him. Of course she was beholden to van Ryker for taking her away from New Amsterdam, where Verhulst's agents might have found her. She would recompense him with her jewels. She wondered with a sudden stab of bitterness how many light loves he had held in his arms since professing his love for her!

Ah, what a difference there was between them: Stephen the constant, the godlike—van Ryker of the shifting heart.

Van Ryker would have been astonished to know that he had brought this about: Unknowingly, by that single lie, he had crystallized Stephen's position in Imogene's heart. Had she known Stephen was alive she would have thought of him as mortal and having human failings. She would have looked forward to seeing him again but she would have begun to wonder why the tone of his first note had seemed so cool— something she had not questioned in her extremity at Wey Gat. She would have asked herself *why* he had stayed away so long, how the story had come to circulate that he was dead. And she would have remembered how attracted she had been to the lean buccaneer.

As matters stood, that feeling of attraction now seemed unworthy of her, base—a betrayal of Stephen.

Unwittingly, van Ryker had arranged his own undoing.

He did not leave her long on deck, but even that short time seemed to tire Imogene. Gently van Ryker carried her back to the great cabin. He ordered a tray sent in, explaining that he could not eat with her, for drifting debris from some wreck had fouled the rudder and he was needed urgently on deck. When he came back the food was still untouched and Imogene sat beside it, bent over and rocking with misery.

He was stabbed into remorse by the sight.

"Would you like to retire?" he asked gently, for she had not stirred from the chair she had requested.

"Where?" She lifted her head and looked around her without interest.

"Here," he said, indicating the bunk.

He had expected her to look startled and protest, but she said only, "Is this where I have been staying?"

"Yes."

"I have been sleeping here? In your bunk?"

"In the circle of my arms," he said steadily, and when she would have spoken, he raised his hand to silence her. "It was all quite platonic, I assure you. Raoul had given you up, but I was determined to make you live. I warmed you with the heat of my body—" his voice grew husky—"bathed you, fed you."

And all for lust! She sighed. "Poor van Ryker, too bad it was all for nothing."

"You will grow less despondent as the days go by. All things pass."

She gave him the shadow of a mocking smile and settled back into her grief.

Restless, he stood a moment in indecision. Then he began to strip off his clothes: his belt, his leathern breeches, his shirt. He was astonished that she made no move to protest. Soon he was peeled down to his smallclothes and stood before her barefoot, clad only in his underdrawers. She seemed not to see him, handsome animal that he was. He studied her with a frown. "Now that you no longer suffer from chills and fever, I will sleep there." He indicated a position across the door.

"Why?" she asked indifferently.

"Imogene, this is a buccaneer vessel," he told her patiently. "There are reckless men aboard—men who would give their lives for a chance at a woman of far lesser beauty. Knowing that you hovered between life and death gave you a certain safety but now you have appeared on deck and all have been reminded of your beauty. For your protection, it is my intention to lie with my body against the door. Any slightest effort to open it will wake me and I will defend you instantly."

Her eyes fell before that calm direct look. Van Ryker was guarding her like crown jewels—she who no longer cared what happened to her. . . . She was silent as he helped her to the bunk.

"If you need me," he told her in a low vibrant voice, "I am here. You may ask anything of me, Imogene. Anything."

She shrugged dolefully, her head still sunk upon her chest, her bright hair spilling down over her slender shoulders. She looked so young, so hurt, so defenseless, it was all van Ryker could do not to sweep her into his arms and whisper passionate words of love into her ears, to tell her that she would forget Linnington, that he, van Ryker, would care for her and her child, that her life would change, would brighten, that she need do nothing—that *he* would accomplish all this, that for her he would do anything, anything.

But he fought back that urge and having deposited her in the bunk, pulled the curtain across it. For himself he never used that curtain, but Imogene, now that she was better, would appreciate the privacy.

That night he slept rolled in a blanket on the hard floor of the cabin with a naked sword beside him. For his crew had seen her beauty on the deck this day and even fragile as she was—fo she had hardly begun to bloom into her old self—hers was a beauty to stop a man's heart. And van Ryker had pledged himself that no harm would come to Imogene—not while *he* lived!

PART TWO
The Golden Lover

A toast to the man who can never say no
To a woman's tempting smile,
To the fellow who'd fling his life away
Just to be with her ... a while ...

The Sea Rover, 1659
CHAPTER 28

The *Sea Rover*'s voyage from the Carolinas to Tortuga threatened never to end. It was a series of calamities. First a sudden gale stripped the sheeting from the *Swallow*, then she fouled her rudder and they had to stop and make repairs. Then another gale swept them back toward the Carolinas, and there they chanced upon a foundering coastwise vessel, victim of the storm. They rescued her crew, taking them aboard the short-handed *Swallow* for the run to Tortuga, after which they would be free to go their separate ways.

From a member of this crew they heard some news that caused van Ryker and Raoul to look at each other in consternation. The crew member reported what was by now general knowledge, that the *Wilhelmina* had run into a Spanish man-of-war off the Great Bahama Bank. Two good broadsides and she'd been shot out of the water. The Spaniard had raced on after another merchant ship that had dared to invade the "Spanish" waters of this western sea and left the crippled *Wilhelmina* to her fate. She had burned to the waterline, and sunk with all hands.

"Imogene is not to know of this," van Ryker cautioned Raoul.

"But you *must* tell her," insisted Raoul. "It would come better from you than from some chance stranger who might tell her an appalling tale of how fire consumed the ship!"

Saddened, van Ryker agreed. He was almost sorry now that he had told her Linnington was dead, for it would serve to magnify her tragedy. Of course, she had recovered beautifully from that—on the surface, of course; who knew what scars she carried in her heart?

For there was one bright spot in all this. Imogene had begun to eat, every day she grew stronger. She had inner strength. That first night after van Ryker had told her of Stephen's death she had stared dry-eyed at the dark ceiling above her bunk and told herself she must not cry for Stephen—she had Stephen's child to think about. Georgiana was what counted—she must grow strong so that she could take care of her. By the end of the week her color had returned and she had begun to look like her old self.

Van Ryker heartily approved this change. He welcomed her to table with his ship's officers and they rapidly became very fond of her, especially young Barnaby Swift who secretly fancied himself a poet and composed silent sonnets to her when he was on watch. These dinners were festive affairs, meant to divert Imogene—for all knew of the loss of the *Wilhelmina*, something Imogene herself did not know as yet. The ship's officers dressed for these occasions as though for some ball, they raised their glasses in gallant toasts and their voices in merry song, hoping to win a smile from her—although van Ryker cautioned them all about tiring her too much. This admonition was greeted with pity—and with envy.

"Never was a man so besotted by love," muttered Raoul.

"Never was there such a lady," sighed Barnaby, who was privately composing an ode to Imogene. "Who can blame him?"

While Imogene was fighting for her life against the fever, Stephen's wound had healed rapidly—whether from the "Indian medicine" of leaves and bark or from his own strong constitution none could tell. The Culps had scrupulously kept their word to the buccaneers and had shown their gratitude by making it clear to their prying neighbors that this was a wounded man from the ship that had brought Johann home—they owed it to Captain van Ryker to do their best for him. Since Stephen was housebound while his wound healed, and since Culp prudently gave him a new name—one that made Stephen laugh, "John Sawbones"—no one associated Culp's boarder with the copper-haired Englishman named Linnington for whom an empty coffin had been buried so ceremoniously at Wey Gat.

"And you'll oblige me by tying back your hair and putting on these leathern breeches and this apron," Johann Culp told him. "For now that ye're up from your bed, 'tis best ye look like a tradesman turned buccaneer lest somebody remember ye and all hell break loose!"

Stephen had long since told them the whole story, but the loyal Culps were sworn to silence out of gratitude to van Ryker. In turn, they had told Stephen the stories that had circulated about New Amsterdam—stories of the Governor's Ball and how Imogene had slapped Captain van Ryker's face and everybody had thought they were having an affair, stories of her attempts to escape the patroon, and how it had been whispered that the lean buccaneer would come and take her away from Wey Gat but, surprisingly, he never had.

To Stephen it was all too clear: van Ryker had fallen in love with tempestuous Imogene—as who would not? But somehow they had quarreled and he had sailed away. Perhaps she had tried to contact him and failed. A nasty suspicion now flitted through Stephen's mind. No matter how he tried to push it away, it seemed to fit the facts.

Van Ryker valued his trade with the Dutch burghers; if he kidnapped a patroon's wife, he would be denied that trade— therefore the buccaneer had needed someone to do that task for him. Van Ryker had known Stephen was going to Barbados; Bess Duveen had written to Imogene from Barbados. It was not impossible that Imogene and the buccaneer had mousetrapepd Stephen Linnington to snatch her from Wey Gat and bring her downriver where her buccaneer lover was waiting. No matter that van Ryker had seemed surprised to see Stephen or that he had questioned him—that could have been a cover-up, a sham, so that Stephen would never know he had been used. In any event, van Ryker had promptly seized Imogene and sailed away with her. Had it been prearranged? Stephen was inclined to think so. And although he recognized that he had a responsibility to Imogene and her child, he could not but feel a tug of bitterness. Imogene was a woman he had held in his arms and loved for a season—she might at least have left him a note. Granted, she'd been unconscious when he saw her last, but she could have penned something ahead of time to leave with him, or sent him some word by now. . . .

So reasoned Stephen Linnington, unwilling to accept at face value the recent happenings at Wey Gat and New Amsterdam.

He sighed. At least, van Ryker's ship's doctor had left him

in a secure place to recover—of course the buccaneer captain had owed him that, he told himself grimly, for had he not gone to Wey Gat and brought his woman to him?

As he recovered from his wound and began to walk again, he took Culp's advice and wore—although it went against his aristocratic grain—tradesman's clothes. He shunned the taverns where he might be recognized, and claimed to have been a carpenter before chance and necessity had made him a buccaneer. None doubted his claim. And because he was bored, he spent his time learning Dutch from the Culp family.

And all the while, Imogene was bitterly mourning his death and scorning van Ryker for not "measuring up" to the glorified memory she had of Stephen.

On a blustery spring day Stephen was out walking—he called it exercise but he was actually strolling out of curiosity to see the new stone house that Peter Stuyvesant had built only last year. He was passing the parsonage of Domine Bogardus and admiring its silver door knocker when a strongly built woman carrying a basket blundered into him. The impact caused her to drop her basket of tulips and when Stephen bent to pick up the basket and she looked into his face, she fell back a step and gasped in Dutch, "But it cannot be—Willem said the buccaneers took you aboard ship with the woman and sailed away!"

With a shock, Stephen realized he was looking into the broad honest face of Willem's sister, into whose house he had been carried, half-dead of his gunshot wound.

By now he was fluent enough in Dutch to understand her and even to speak to her haltingly. It was a shock to him to learn from her that Imogene had never regained consciousness in this woman's house, that she had been carried away unconscious by Captain van Ryker—whose face all in New Amsterdam knew by sight.

"I am glad to run into you like this," the woman told him earnestly. "For my brother Willem, for all his other good points, is a liar, and although I insisted that he must tell the buccaneer doctor that the maidservant and the child had sailed on the *Wilhelmina* bound for Jamaica, I am not sure that he *did* tell him. Oh, he spoke words in English and the doctor responded, but he seemed so indifferent to what Willem said. Willem had told me that the child was not the maidservant's but belonged to the unconscious lady—and now if she is not dead she must be wondering where her baby is. When you see the poor lady—" for the good Dutch vrouw never doubted that a man who had risked his life to save a woman would see her again—"would you tell her where to find her child?"

Her child . . . *his* child. All of Stephen's plans for a speedy return to Bess and Barbados went out the window. Even if van Ryker and Imogene had tricked him, he still owed a duty to his daughter—a duty to see her reunited with her mother.

"I will tell her, mevrouw," he promised soberly. "When next we meet. Can I carry that basket for you?"

She shook her head. "Willem would not wish me to be seen in your company, and although he's gone back to Beverwyck with none the wiser about the whole affair, still—I've a jealous husband to think about."

Stephen grinned broadly at her heavyset departing back as she stomped away with her heavy-footed gait. He was trying to envision this *goede* vrouw's jealous husband!

But the smile left his face as he thought of what he must do now: He must find Imogene and tell her Georgiana was safe with Elise—and where she could find her.

The first buccaneering vessel to call at New Amsterdam took Stephen Linnington away when she sailed. He was welcomed on board as a wounded member of van Ryker's crew, recovered and anxious to return to Tortuga to rejoin his captain aboard the *Sea Rover*.

Stephen could not bring himself to write to Bess because he did not know yet what demands Imogene might make on him—suppose she and van Ryker had quarreled again and she wanted to be transported to Jamaica and her child? He would feel obligated to do it. And he could not bear to disappoint Bess by a promise not to be fulfilled.

So on Barbados, Bess Duveen drooped, wondering what had become of her lover.

The days, the weeks, went by for Bess. She ran the plantation—she ran it well. She made her appearance as expected at the Governor's Ball clad in a shimmery sea green silk dress trimmed with forest green velvet ribands, the overdress caught up over a silver-shot foam green satin petticoat. That dress was to have been part of her trousseau—a typical gown for an island colonist, she had told herself, laughing, when she was having it made: For its striking Italian silk and French-made satin had been destined for the American colonies and seized as contraband in mid-ocean by a passing Spanish galleon. The galleon had been sunk off the coast of Cuba in a sea battle with buccaneers who had managed to save the cargo and sold it at the busy international marketplace on Tortuga's quays. There the lovely fabrics had struck the fancy of a planter from Barbados who had gone there to trade. He had brought them back and Bess Duveen had bought these lengths of silk and satin in the market at Bridgetown. She had enjoyed making up fanciful tales of the origin of her trousseau and telling them to Stephen.

Stephen . . . at the very thought of him her gray eyes filled with tears, as bright as the necklace of diamonds she wore, studded with dark green peridots.

Now, at the ball, she turned swiftly, fluttering her ivory fan, and spoke to the governor's lady, who asked her about her plantation.

"All is well at Idlewild," said Bess.

"I am surprised that you are not married," the governor's lady told her frankly. "You are so pretty and so well-bred and here in these islands you are a great catch."

"You are kind indeed to say so," smiled Bess, "but perhaps I was not meant to marry." Her soft voice held a touch of bitterness.

"Indeed?" Elevated eyebrows met this declaration. "I would not have thought so. "I have a cousin from Yorkshire who has arrived only yesterday from England. He is still very fatigued from the long sea journey, but I could not let him miss the ball. Come, you must meet him."

And so Bess met Francis Tourney, a younger son of a Yorkshire squire, and together they danced the night away. Francis was handsome and eligible and quite taken by Bess. And having commented in some surprise on the sumptuousness of her gown (for he had been assured in England that he would find Barbados a savage land and very out of fashion), he was astonished and delighted at her rambling tale of the fabric's history.

"Bought with blood and gold," Bess told him frankly as he whirled her around the governor's ballroom. "As are most of our goods in these islands!"

"My father has offered to buy me a piece of land here," Francis told her. "For I am a younger son and must make my own way."

"Then you have come to a good place," said Bess heartily. "And I will be glad to tell you all I know of running a plantation—for I have had to learn the hard way, by the doing of it!"

Her forthrightness and good sense intrigued him. Here was no simpering Court lady, knowledgeable only of pomades and gossip—nor was she a backward provincial as he had been led to expect the ladies of Barbados would be. Here was a woman who could discuss with enthusiasm horseflesh and trading rights and shipping and the price of rum! He determined that very night that he would offer for her hand—for he felt toward Bess a kinship that he had never felt toward any woman—he felt that it would be good to spend his life beside her. Good and refreshing and joyful.

He kept Bess laughing with his quips, his stories of English life—all of which seemed very droll to him and elicited a bittersweet homesick response from Bess. She felt drawn to him and told him eagerly that Mill Oak was for sale, for Robert Milliken had developed the gout and had decided to go back to England. It would be good, Bess told herself, to have this charming fellow for a neighbor, and she could help him get started—indeed, with no knowledge of these islands, he would need a friend!

But in spite of Francis's gallantry, she could not keep her thoughts from Stephen Linnington, and when Francis asked how she managed to run her estates, unmarried as she was, she said, "I had a factor to run them for me. Now that he is gone I—I do not know how I will manage." Her voice held a wistful note that went straight to Francis's heart.

"There, there," he murmured, touched by her quiet beauty, her sweetness, her interest in everything—and her obvious need of assistance, which appealed to his hearty masculinity. "We will find a way."

But Bess at that moment was not seeing Francis's ruddy face before her—she was seeing Stephen's. "Oh, yes," she agreed, lifting her chin defiantly. "I will find a way."

CHAPTER 29

Not until Imogene insisted on being put aboard a Jamaica-bound ship did van Ryker tell her—and then reluctantly—of Elise's and Georgiana's fate. She was stronger now and he hoped she would be able to bear it.

For a long time she was utterly silent. She sat with her head bowed, utterly still, so quiet he thought she had not taken in what he was saying. Then she lifted a white face in which the eyes were dark pools of horror.

"Oh, God," she said, looking out into a vista of hell, an imaginary landscape in which a burning ship, blasted by cannon fire, went down, down . . . a vision torn by screams and littered with dying people, some of them afire and throwing themselves overboard into waters where dark fins darted in and out to feast. . . . "And I thought Verhulst would follow them, that it would be Verhulst who might endanger them. I never thought—!"

"Verhulst is dead," he told her. His intent was to comfort

497

her, for he had had the news of the Dutch patroon's death and the monuments he had erected to Imogene and Stephen, from the captain of a passing ship who had sailed from New Amsterdam. "He can no longer pursue you. You need have no fear of him."

"Verhulst is—" She turned on him a look of pure horror. "Verhulst *too*? You mean I have killed them all? For without me, none of this would have happened. They would all be alive today if it were not for me. Oh, Georgiana, my little Georgiana—I knew you such a little time . . ." Her voice broke and she collapsed in a paroxym of weeping, her body swaying in misery.

"'Twas not your fault." Van Ryker made an awkward gesture to comfort her, but she recoiled from him.

"It was! It was!" she cried passionately. "All of it was my fault. If I had not borne Stephen's child, if I had not married Verhulst—oh, let me alone, I cannot live with it!"

If I had not borne Stephen's child . . . That caught him up sharply; somehow it had not occurred to him that the child was Linnington's. A former lover, he had thought him—but not the father of the child. He had assumed the father to be Verhulst. It put a different light on the whole thing.

Unable to watch her grief, he strode from the cabin and paced, with his head bent, up and down the moonlit deck, struggling with his own tumultous thoughts. He was captain of a great ship, master of dangerous men, and Linnington was far away. He desired this woman as passionately as a man can desire a woman; his need for her burned into his very soul. And had he not—as surely as Linnington—snatched her from the jaws of death? Raoul had believed she would never wake. But he had refused to admit defeat. During the long cold nights he had lain beside her, he had spoken words of encouragement into her ears—words he never knew if she heard—he had rubbed her wrists and exercised her frail body and sponged her perspiring forehead and forced food and drink down her throat and bathed her and held her and cared for her as tenderly as if she were a babe. In the silence of his great cabin in the pale featureless dawn, he had risen from the table where he had been morosely drinking wine and gone and knelt by her bunk and silently prayed to the God he had forsaken to grant him this one favor—to give Imogene back her life.

He had made promises to that God, promises that, in the harsh light of day had made a wry smile cross his mouth and brought back bitter memories of the days when he had cursed God for letting the Spaniards seize and destroy his father while grief ate away his mother's life. He had promised in those dark and watchful hours when he guarded Imogene that he would give up this freebooter's life—if only he could have this one woman, alive and well and in his arms, his to hold and love forever.

And now he had been forced to bring her this tragic news. . . .

Evening found him elegantly clad. He would entertain his lady at a private dinner in the great cabin, he would take her mind from sorrowful things.

She did not even look at him as he entered—or at the elegant gray and shot silver garments he had so carefully donned. She did not see the emerald ring that sparkled on his finger or the diamond of price that was thrust carelessly through the Mechlin at his throat. Her gaze never even passed over the shining dark hair he had so carefully combed or the clean-shaven jaw from which he had carved every whisker. She was not near enough to smell the faint scent of musk from the chest in which his garments had lain, or the light masculine scent of Virginia tobacco that permeated his doublet.

She did not even raise her eyes. Her head remained sunk on her chest and she studied her hands, endlessly twisting her fingers together.

At least she had stopped crying, he thought, relieved.

"Come," he said heartily. "You must eat. And here is a repast that should please the most particular." He indicated the food the cabin boy had brought and left upon the table; it looked very tempting.

"Why?" she responded with a listless shrug. "Why must I eat?"

"So that you will gain weight." He was urging her to the table as he spoke. "You are too thin for my taste."

She let him seat her in the chair he pulled out, but her lips twisted. "Does it really matter, van Ryker?"

"It does to me."

She lifted her head and gave him a haggard look. "I cannot eat. Food would choke me."

His heart went out to her. "Try," he urged.

But she only toyed silently with her food, pushed it away at last. "No, I cannot."

He waited, suffering with her, respecting her grief, and feeling jealousy gnaw at him that part of that grief was for his rival, Stephen Linnington. He drank his wine and smoked his handsome pipe and watched her, wishing he could find a way to comfort her. If only she would cry, if only she would let him hold her in his arms and sob it all out on his shoulder. . . .

But her proud white face was drawn and distant. She kept her hands clenched tightly in her lap.

Suddenly she looked up and her blue eyes were swimming with tears. "I would like to be alone now, van Ryker."

He rose at once. "I will be on deck if you need me."

Her indifference told him she would never need him. Van

Ryker left, feeling dejected. He stood alone on deck in the moonlight, wondering what he should do now. Was there no way to help her through this? It was a windless night. The sails slapped listlessly and a silvery ocean lapped against the hull of the ship. All the world seemed to be waiting . . .

After a time he heard a noise and turned. Imogene had come out on deck and was making her way toward the ship's rail. The air would do her good, he thought, moving toward her on silent feet almost without conscious volition.

When she reached the rail, he was close behind her. Wrapped up in her sorrow, oblivious to the world, she did not see or hear him. And although it hurt van Ryker's heart to see her shoulders drooping so, he hesitated to make himself known in this hour of private tragedy.

She was leaning over the rail now, far out—*too far out!* She was going over! Van Ryker leaped toward her with a hoarse cry and caught her around the waist, dragged her back. She did not resist him. She might have been a rag doll in his arms. She made no more effort than a dead woman. Even her eyes were glazed with sorrow. Haunted eyes.

For a moment he stared down at her, drenched with cold sweat and shaking at how close a call it had been, for through the silvery phosphorescence of the water he had seen dark fins moving, prowling—sharks. He had a sudden harsh vision of Imogene falling listlessly into the water and those dark fins converging in an instant. He saw a sudden silvery flash of open jaws, jagged teeth, a rending while the sea turned red. He shook his head to clear it. Imogene was here in his grasp and he was trembling, so great had been his fear for her. With a great effort he stilled that trembling, swept her unresisting form up in his arms and carried her back to the great cabin, set her down upon a chair.

"That was a daft thing to do," he said gruffly. "Leaning far out over the rail like that. You were falling in when I caught you! Couldn't you see, there was a forest of sharks out there—and 'twas on you they'd have been feeding had you slipped from my grasp." He was careful to make it sound like she'd been going over the rail by accident, not by design. And he meant to scare her, so she'd never try that again—for it is a different thing altogether to consider death by sinking quietly beneath clear silvery water or being rended by a slithering field of sharks. But his words made no impression on Imogene. Instead of being frightened, she looked up at him queerly.

"Why did you save me?" she demanded. "Couldn't you see I wanted to die? Don't you know I'll only do it again, sometime when you're not looking, sometime when you're not there, sometime when your back is turned?" She turned her head away from him.

Van Ryker had been bending over her. Now he straightened up and brushed his hand across his forehead. Droplets of water from the cold sweat that had seized him at her nearness to death flipped from it and danced against the light. "Life is all you have," he said roughly. " 'Tis all anyone has. I've given you back yours; the least you can do to reward me is to hold onto it."

She turned to him with a wild feline gesture.

"Oh, can't you understand?" she cried in a heartbroken voice. "It's because of me they all died—my baby, Stephen, Elise, even Verhulst! It is as if I were a scourge, a curse upon the world! I should die myself, I deserve to be punished!" Her hands balled into fists and her eyes closed as her voice rose almost to a wail. "Can't you see, I *want* to die! I killed them all, I'm responsible. Oh, God, van Ryker, don't stand in my way— I've nothing to live for!"

In consternation he stared at her, this woman for whom he would so willingly give up his life. In astonishment he saw her rise from her chair and try to dart past him out of the cabin—on her way to the rail again, doubtless.

He tossed back his damp dark hair with a flick like a whip and in one stride he had intercepted her. His strong fingers seized her arm in a cruel grip and swung her back to face him.

"Nothing to live for?" he roared. "I'll *give* you something to live for, Imogene!"

He dragged her back and this time flung her not into a chair but upon the bunk. He kicked the door shut with his boot, tore off his boots individually and tossed them across the room.

Imogene watched him, paralyzed.

"This night ye shall find a reason for living," he promised her through his teeth.

Even as he spoke he was ripping off his handsome clothes—his shot silver doublet, his gray trousers, his full-sleeved cambric shirt with its ruffled cuffs. Stockings, boothose, garters all vanished as if by magic. The frosty Mechlin left his neck so violently that the lace tore and the diamond so cleverly caught in it fell to the floor and rolled away like a drop of water, glimmering as it went.

Imogene flinched as he tore off his smallclothes so that he stood before her, a naked giant, lean and sinewy and purposeful. She slid back nervously in the bunk as he advanced upon her, striding across the room in the moonlight cast through the long bank of windows in the stern. Almost in one rippling gesture he flung his lithe muscular body across her on the bed, rose on one knee and seized the neck of her gown and her chemise in his powerful right hand and ripped both of them from her body in a single violent gesture.

"Van Ryker—no!" she gasped, her blue eyes wide and dark. There was a lively interest in them now, he noted with satisfaction as he insolently cupped one of her bared breasts in his hands—brushing aside her swift attempts to cover them with her hands. He gave her a sardonic look and bent to kiss it, to nuzzle its rosy crest with his tongue.

"No!" Imogene made an abortive effort to free herself from him but he dashed her hands aside and kept one arm around her in a steely grip.

He was nuzzling her other breast now and a dangerous feeling of warmth was trickling through her, warming her cold flesh. She had the sensation of the approach of an impending storm. It was moving forward inexorably, a storm from which she could not escape—that would sweep all before it.

Screaming, she knew, would do no good—this was a buccaneer's ship, and this man whose hot breath fanned her face was its captain. Imogene closed her eyes and groaned.

Van Ryker lifted his head and laughed. "You have forgotten how to be a woman," he mocked her. "I will remind you!"

He buried his head in her bosom and in response she clawed at his face. He seized her hands, held them negligently above her head and let his gaze rove meaningfully up and down her naked body. She flinched as he studied her naked breasts and he smiled down at her. "I deem it an honor to be marked by you," he said pleasantly. "My crew will see the scratches on my face and be green with envy."

Imogene hastily balled her hands into fists. "I will not mark you so that you may brag about it!" she choked.

"So there's life in you after all?" He sounded surprised. "Faith, who'd have thought it?"

"Van Ryker, release me! What good—"

Abruptly his lips closed down on hers, silencing her angry

protests. She stiffened as his mouth slid luxuriously over her own, as his tongue probed impudently, teasing, promising . . . Once again she felt that dangerous warmth rising inside her. A wayward pulse throbbed somewhere in her throat. Her head felt dizzy, swimming with strange disjointed thoughts, unbidden memories of the nights she had flirted with him aboard this very ship. She had thought she had forgotten her "damned pirate" who had deserted her the night of the Governor's Ball and sailed away. Resolutely she had put him behind her, but now, now . . .

He lifted his head, allowing her to gulp in air. "What good, you say? I do not know about *you*, Imogene, but this will do *me* a world of good. It has been a long time since I've held a woman in my arms—I've been too busy ministering to the sick!"

Even as he spoke his hands were busy, sliding along her shrinking form, causing her to gasp as he fingered a nipple here, caressed a hip there, intimately probing, teasing.

"Damn you, damn you," came her sobbing whisper. "May you burn in hell, van Ryker!"

"Undoubtedly I will!" he said with aplomb. "But not just yet!" With an abruptness that made her catch her breath, he brought her hips up against his in a gesture so abandoned and sensuous that her very senses seemed to melt before the onslaught. Laughing now, he turned her about to suit his convenience. Imogene struggled—but her struggles were weakening. The summer storm that was raging just outside her consciousness was nearly upon her—the floodgates of summer rain were about to burst through.

She fought it, but his bare leg rasped along her thigh and she trembled. His male hardness brushed that downy golden triangle at the base of her hips and in spite of herself her stomach muscles contracted violently. Van Ryker chuckled and hot shame coursed through her. In this hour of her grief, when already she had consigned herself to death, her rebellious body was betraying her by responding to the lust of this—this damned pirate!

A sudden deft thrust and he had entered her and all her feelings converged into one white-hot passion—was it rage or pent-up desire? She was swept away by longings she thought she had forgotten, langorous, sensuous feelings that had to do with this tropical sea so far from any port. About her the storm burst suddenly and Imogene let it happen. With a sob, she forgot the world, forgot all the dreadful things that had happened and clung to van Ryker. Here was a man whose lean body understood her every thought, her every desire, a man who melded his own long length to her silken softness, who probed, who tempted, who teased, who caressed—and incited her to molten unbridled joy.

All her defenses were down now, swept away in a raging tide of feeling. In sudden wild abandon she flung herself against him and van Ryker, swept along on his own storm, was touched and felt a great tenderness stealing over him.

He loved her so much. And her love affairs had been so—paltry to his way of thinking. Abandoned by Linnington, mistreated by van Rappard. *He* would show her what it was like to be loved by a man who thought the world of her, who wanted to give her pleasure even more than he desired to pleasure himself. He had waited so long, so long for this moment, and now that it was at last at hand he found himself climbing the heights with great delicacy and he handled the frail woman in his arms with compassion and artistry and aching tenderness, bringing to her sweet magic and earthly delights.

But the storm that raged round them could not be gainsaid. It would not let them pause. Onward and upward it swept them, like gods, to high peaks where jagged lightning lit their inward skies, down damp rainwashed valleys it plunged them, their bodies bound together in eternal longing, caught up in time, rising to infinite bliss—until with a last crashing crescendo of such magnitude that it shook them both, they became mortal again, a man and a woman who fell apart from sheer exhaustion.

Drowned by her desire, sated by fulfillment, washed clean at last of everything save overwhelming fatigue, Imogene slept.

After a time during which he listened while her troubled breathing become steady and even, van Ryker got up and ordered food and wine brought to the cabin. When he returned, Imogene had risen, too. She stood naked with her back to him, holding her torn chemise in her hand.

"No need for that," he said calmly, studying her lovely conformation, the perfect curve of her back and buttocks, the daintiness of her legs. "Dawn will break soon. 'Tis a warm day and ye can have breakfast in bed. 'Twill be along shortly."

She did not turn. "Van Ryker, how could you?" she whispered.

He moved toward her, frowning. She flinched as his hands closed over her shoulders. "You had no right!" she flared.

"I had every right." His voice had a rich depth that surprised her. "Someone had to save you from yourself."

She spun around in his arms and looked up at him with a tight twisted little smile. "And you think you have done that?" she asked him scornfully. "By using me thus, taking me against my will?" Her short laugh was brittle as breaking glass.

"And *was* it against you will?" that rich voice asked caressingly. One of his hands left her shoulder and roved down her arm, leaving a trail of fire that made her stiffen.

A rosy flush spread over her face and down over her white body, turning her pearly breasts pink and changing her whole delicate form from white to rose. He was speaking of her wild surrender in his arms. "How dare you remind me of that?" she asked in a low furious voice and jerked away from him.

His hands dropped to his sides and he made no move to bring her back into the circle of his arms. A lean naked giant, he stood and contemplated her for some time. *So she did not wish to remember the bliss she had known briefly as she lay beneath his heaving body* . . . Very well then, he would try some other tack. His hand snaked out and encircled her wrist.

"Come." He drew her unwilling form back to the bed. "You should know more about this monster who has ravished you." His tone was mocking but his eyes were wary. She must not know he loved her—God, what power that would give her over him! His very soul cringed at the thought.

"I know enough," she said savagely. "I know that you are lustful and violent and lost to shame."

"Doubtless I am all of those things—and more," he agreed cheerfully, inducing her by the power of his grip to join him on the bed. "But I am also a man who has suffered—as you are suffering."

Her scornful look of disbelief was answer enough.

"There should be truth between us, Imogene," he said quietly. "Van Ryker is not my real name, nor am I Dutch."

"So you are a renegade Englishman after all?" She gave a mirthless laugh. "My instinct about you was sure!"

"My real name is—"

"I do not want to know it," she interrupted. "And no matter what it is—Smith, Jones, Warburton—I shall always call you van Ryker and think of you as a damned pirate, a ravisher of women!"

Well, he had wanted to jolt her from her lethargy, her self-pity. Why should he now feel such pain at her words?

"Think of me as you will," he said lightly. "So long as you warm my bed!"

"And that will not last long either!"

"You would wager on it?"

"Even a pirate cannot always lie about!"

Idly he caressed her body, feeling her tense and pull away, seeing her nipples harden beneath his expert touch.

"Stop that!" she cried.

He gave her a dangerous smile. "Well, if you will not let me talk, I must do *something* to while away the time!"

"Talk, then," she said hastily, pushing his hands away. "I will listen."

"Good. I will tell you about myself—not my name since you do not wish to hear it, but something of my story, the events that shaped me." He smiled into her stormy eyes. "I grew up in Devon."

Devon . . . Stephen had grown up in Devon and in Imogene's fevered imagination it seemed to her that he had died twice. Stephen had almost reached sainthood in her eyes; she could not quite see his halo but it was surely there. He was all that was good and this—this pirate was all that was bad. A very devil!

"So you grew up in Devon," she muttered.

He was looking beyond her now, remembering, and his grip on her loosened a little. "My father was a merchant trader and when he made a voyage to the West Indies his ship was seized by the Spanish and he was made a prisoner. My mother sold all that we owned to raise a ransom for him. He was returning to us when he died. He had been too harshly treated in the dungeons of the Spanish dons and he died of that . . ." His face was formidable to look upon now, and in spite of her still pulsing body and her personal disaster, Imogene found herself carried along by his words. "My mother died of heartbreak and the family was left destitute. It fostered in me a deep anger against Spain. I swore a great oath that I would wreak vengeance upon the Spanish for my parents' deaths and—'' the wolfish gleam in his gray eyes held her fascinated—''I have done so. In Plymouth I found some lads of like mind and we stole a boat— since returned to its rightful owners with Spanish gold to boot. 'Twas but a small boat but we rowed her right up under the guns of a Spanish caravel and took her with small arms fire. It was a night attack.'' Imogene shivered at the temerity of that encounter, imagining the shots and the darkness and the unknown terrors that waited on a slippery Spanish deck. ''With the caravel we moved on to larger prey until at last I had the ship I wanted—*El Cruzado*. I refitted her, made her faster, renamed her the *Sea Rover*, and with her roamed the Spanish Main. Her forty guns I call the 'widowmakers,' and when they speak they resound all the way to Spain as I lift her treasure and humble her captains. Many times my sword has tasted Spanish blood.''

''Do you not tire of all this killing?'' she asked tonelessly.

He answered her dreamily. ''I am not a madman, Imogene. I do not kill for sport. And those who surrender to me are ransomed back to Spain or returned to Havana or some other Spanish port after they have worked out their ransom in labor. But when I see the Spanish colors flying I remember how my father came to die. I was told of the rats in the Spanish prison that gnawed off his toes as he lay chained, and of the hot irons they—''

''Enough.'' She flinched away from him. ''I can see you have reason to hate the Spanish. I would hate them, too. But what has that to do with me?''

He turned to her in some surprise. ''You do not understand? No, I suppose you are too wrapped up in your own troubles to give it thought. I was like you, Imogene. The night my mother died I went down to the shore and swam out into the ocean, intending to swim until fatigue overcame me and I drowned. All night I swam and when the dawn was breaking I came upon a derelict hulk floating in the water. One of her ratlines trailed down in the water and I used it to climb aboard her. Lying there, exhausted, I realized that finding this rotting abandoned hulk was a sign. I had it in my power to strike back. Once I had meant to be a scholar. I had always sailed for pleasure, but now I turned my face toward the sea as a profession and set my sails for the Spanish Main—and toward Spain for my vengeance.'' He turned to smile deep into her eyes. "I have had some success, Imogene.''

"And have you ravished their women as well?'' she asked rudely. She did not know what made her ask that.

"No,'' he said on a sardonic note. '' 'Tis their men I have slaughtered—and in battle, a far better way than my father died. Their women I leave to die of heartbreak—as my mother did.''

Imogene looked into that cold, implacable face as if hypnotized. Who was he to claim heartbreak above hers? Had not her parents been killed by a volley of shot that had echoed through their pleasant Penzance garden? Had *he* had a child and a lover and a friend who was almost a second mother all wrested from him at the same time? *No, he had not!* Her hands clenched as his fingers ran lightly down her arm, moved impudently over her smooth naked torso. At that moment she hated him.

"Come,'' he said lazily, falling back upon the bed and dragging her down toward him. "Compensate me for all those Spanish ladies I might have ravished and did not.''

Was he laughing at her? She could not tell. She tried to strike at him and found her hand caught negligently in midair, her body pulled inexorably toward his until her tingling breasts were grazing the lightly furred hairs of his deep chest.

"I do not want to hear your stories,'' she cried, her voice muffled in his thick dark hair as he buried his head in the hollow of her throat and drew her to him. "I want to die!''

"Still death-bound?'' he mocked. "Well, I'll give you yet

another reason for living!'' His lean body tensed and he felt rather than heard her sob as his male hardness thrust into her shivering body again.

Frantically she fought him—fought not only the man but life itself and all the wild ardor that coursed unbidden through her veins. Her hatred of herself for this response to him assumed wild proportions. She felt herself a murderess—she deserved to be punished, not caressed.

She would die!

And so when it was over and van Ryker tossed her a dressing gown and let the cabin boy bring in a sumptuous breakfast to set before her, she turned her face steadfastly away and refused to leave the bed.

Annoyed, van Ryker hauled her to the table and set her down firmly in a chair. Imogene closed her teeth and refused to eat or speak to him.

Hoping to induce her to hunger, he ate with gusto, smacking his lips and waving a chicken leg under her nose that she might smell its tempting aroma. She turned away as if sickened.

''There is more than one way to die,'' she told him in a flat, toneless voice.

Watching her uneasily, van Ryker finished his meal and carried her back to the bunk. For a moment he frowned down at her. Her mind might stand like a stone wall against him but her body was his pliant captive!

He made love to her again and after it was over—because he was afraid he would go to sleep and she would do herself some harm while he slept—he tied her hands to the bunk with a scarf. So exhausted was she that she hardly moved or protested.

It hurt him to do it but—his tender expression hardened. He would save his valiant lady—yes, even from herself he would save her! Imogene was a sensual woman, a woman who took deep delight in the things of the flesh. She could not escape her heritage. By God, he would make love to her every hour of every day if that was what was necessary to instill in her a will to live!

He lay down beside her on the bunk and slept—deeply, silently, dreamlessly. All that he dreamed of, forever to have and hold, lay asleep beside him in the sunlight as it streamed down over the shimmering ocean.

He waked to a vicious kick in the shins.

"Untie me!" Imogene hissed. "How dare you tie me up like this, van Ryker?"

Van Ryker came awake instantly and in full possession of his faculties. It was the way he always woke—heritage from a life spent in dangerous places. "You look better this afternoon," he said critically. "Your eyes are brighter. I'll order us a bite to eat."

Her blue eyes flashed dangerously. "Untie me! I've no desire to eat!"

"Indeed? Then you must be of a mind to make love—and so am I." He rolled over lazily and toyed with one of her ankles, caressed her shapely calf.

She kicked out at him. "Untie me this instant!'

"In a moment," he told her maddeningly. "When I am better settled upon what you women choose to call your 'female form divine.' "

As she struggled he rolled over upon her, laughing, and tickled her until she was gasping, laughing uncontrollably and choked with fury at the same time. Her fists were clenched and she was tearing so at her bonds that he was afraid she would hurt herself and with a flick of his fingers he untied her wrists. Immediately her hands came up and she tried to drive her sharp nails into his eyes, but he caught both wrists in one big hand and smiled down at her dangerously. "If you try that again, I'll tie you hand and foot."

She desisted, panting.

"I've never seen you look so angry," he observed. "It bodes well for a pleasant bout before supping, don't you think?"

He had entered her again with a single satiny thrust! And now he was laughing at her struggles, enjoying it, chuckling deep in his throat, a merry sound that resounded through her own indignant body. Little waves of sensation began to steal over her as his clever expert hands found secret places to touch and stir and set atremble, as his body moved to a silken rhythm that increased in tempo even as it stirred her.

"You cannot always keep me tied up!" she choked, trying to tear herself from his grasp, trying to steady her own tumultuous feelings. "I will escape you—I will! Yes, and I will put an end to myself, you cannot stop me!"

"If you do not repent you of these death wishes, you will spend the rest of your life tied to my bunk," he told her calmly. "Enjoying yourself."

"Oh!" Tears of rage sprang to her eyes. "That you could use me so!"

" 'Tis a delightful use I make of you," he said, sliding his body along hers in a way that left her breathless and throbbing. "Your body tells me so."

For four days he kept her tied to the bunk in his cabin—and during all of those days Imogene refused to eat.

But like some beautiful Christian slave at the mercy of her Roman master, Imogene could not escape him. Even when he slept—which was seldom and in catnaps—he pinioned her body with his own so that she could not struggle up and seize a bottle and try to dash out his brains or cut her own throat with a piece of broken glass and so escape him forever. And at last, after these tormentingly beautiful bouts of lovemaking, worn out by sorrow and despair and grief and revulsion at her own vivid response to his fierce yet tender assaults upon her senses, Imogene would sleep. She slept the worn-out sleep of a child. And then the man beside her would sigh and tie her wrists gently but firmly with silken scarves to the bunk—for he must sleep, too. At his touch she would stir but not wake and he would smile down at her limp lovely body, so temptingly outflung, so soft and infinitely desirable. He had never known a woman with so raging a desire to live—and now so raging a desire to die. *And he must turn the tide.*

On the fourth day he looked down at her lovely exhausted face, studied her tenderly as she slept. He who had held so many women in his arms, had given his heart away at last, given it to this rebellious slip of a girl.

At first as he studied her, his face had looked boyish, but now it took on a worried look. This refusal to eat was dragging her down physically and she had no reserves to call upon. He loved her but she was slipping away from him. Into her shattered dreams of all that she had lost.

Into the sea where the sharks would eat her.

His square jaw hardened. While he lived, that would not happen.

And now he saw too clearly the path that he must tread: To save her, he must forever alienate her.

And he knew with a bitter flash of insight that if she left him, his life would be ashes. He knew as he watched that lovely sleeping face that whenever the *Sea Rover*'s great sails billowed and he looked out into a wide cerulean sky, he would be seeing the blue, blue shimmer of her eyes. He would never walk through a lemon grove or plunge a knife into the golden fruit without remembering the heady sweetness of her golden hair.

He would never again clasp a woman in his arms without a rush of memories of skin like silk and lingering kisses and a torrid blur of passion and tenderness that transcended anything he had ever felt for a woman.

And now to save her life, he must make her hate him.

He turned from the bed and walked to the window, stood gazing out at the blue Caribbean that stretched away from him.

It was strange what a man would do in the name of love.

He came back to the bed, untied her, woke her with caresses.

"I hate you!" she sobbed, beating her fists impotently against the mattress. "I hate you!"

"Good," he said tonelessly. "It will give you something to think about. I had the Spanish. *You have me.*"

"I will make you pay for this!" she panted. "As God is my witness, I will make you pay for it!"

He shrugged and left her, locking the cabin door behind him. He hated leaving her at all but he had a ship to see to, so it was a chance he had to take. If she got free, there were so many ways she could end her life, if she chose to do it. The cabin was full of sharp objects—the small arms were locked up but she could always break a bottle or a goblet and slash her wrists—so many ways. He could only hope that her very fury would keep her from despair.

Now he locked the cabin door and leaned against it. *Hate me, Imogene,* he thought with a violence that rent his whole being. *Hate me and live.* His jaws clamped together and his whole hawklike face hardened with resolve. He would do it—in spite of the fact that he loved this winsome wench, he would do it. He would engender hatred in her until the spark of desire to live was rekindled and the flame burned steady and bright.

His men thought their captain looked exceedingly fierce

and grim as he strode about the deck. 'Twas their opinion that he should have looked more relaxed and sleepy for one who had just spent four whole days locked in a cabin with so lustrous a lady!

CHAPTER 30

Imogene and her buccaneer were like two gladiators locked in mortal combat. As he battled the woman he loved for the life she would throw away, theirs became an almost superhuman clash of wills. Having chosen death, Imogene would not let him reverse her decision. And next to death, she preferred the sweet oblivion of sleep—a sleep from which van Ryker rudely roused her to take her into his arms. But when she was awake and not fighting off his relentless assaults upon her body, his ruthless efforts to subordinate her will to his, she fell into wild paroxyms of grief. They were exhausting her.

There was more than one way to die. . . . Imogene was still refusing to eat. All the color had left her cheeks and the new-found strength van Ryker had so carefully nurtured was deserting her. It terrified van Ryker to see her grow physically weaker even while her indomitable spirit pressed on—toward death. And these wild nights in his arms were sapping her strength as well. He debated leaving off, but having gone this far he felt he must go further—he had to establish for all time this hatred that would give Imogene a will to live.

He taunted her, mocked her weakness, wore on her senses with passion, drove her to fury and ecstasy and guilty delight—for which she suffered a heavier burden, for she felt she must atone.

They were nearing Tortuga now and Imogene was barely able to leave her bed but her bright spirit still flashed in resentment at sight of him.

Now as he came into the cabin, she lifted her head in disdain.

He measured his bound captive with a sardonic glance. "There is no reason for you to die," he said mockingly as he unloosed the knotted scarves that held her. "You have already had your funeral, Imogene—while still alive."

She frowned, hating him for baiting her like this. "What do you mean?" she asked sulkily.

"That the patroon—your late husband—held a great funeral for you. And buried an empty coffin. All the river mourned you, Imogene—indeed, they could not help it. There were lavish gifts to the mourners—suits of clothes, scarves, gloves, mourning rings. It was such a funeral as has never been held on the North River and probably never will be held again. Rest assured you will not be forgotten there. I tell you clearly, you cannot hope to rise to such heights again. A funeral at sea is of small consequence compared to the one you have already had at Wey Gat!"

"Be silent!" she cried, driven too far by his taunts. *Poor Verhulst—whatever else, he had loved her....* "What would you know of love, of anything?" Her shoulders trembled with rage as she fought not to cry for the man who had driven her to such extremities.

"That's right," van Ryker agreed cheerfully. He reached out a long arm and stroked her shoulder. She pulled away. "What would I know of love?" He smiled into her eyes. "But I can teach you the ways of lust, Imogene, and they are many."

She jerked away from him as if hot irons had seared her. "I hate you, van Ryker! I hate your touch—I hope the Spanish drop you with their first shot the next time you try to seize one of their ships!"

"A fitting end," he said carelessly. And then with cold flippancy he added, "Have you ever wondered what would happen to you in the event such a misfortune occurred?"

The question was asked politely but there were spikes in it.

Imogene swallowed. "You mean—your crew?" she whispered.

"They would share you, share and share alike," he said flippantly, knowing it was not the truth, for buccaneer crews behaved with gallantry toward women. Even their female Spanish captives were allowed to reach Cuba or some other Spanish port, and an English woman could certainly walk safe among them. He hoped his crew never heard his calm assessment of what they would do if he were killed—there'd be general indignation! But he felt it necessary to terrorize Imogene, he had to bring her to some semblance of reality, he had to make her a woman again instead of a self-willed sacrifice to grief—else he would surely lose her. "I see you are thinking on it," he added on a cheerful note.

"I would kill myself," she breathed.

"Ah, yes, that is the answer to everything." He stretched out his long legs and tried to look bored. "Imogene will waste away, Imogene will refuse to eat, Imogene will throw herself into the sea that sharks may dine on her! My lady—" he leaned forward and grasped one of her wrists in a paralyzing grip—

"you were made to live, to love, to sing into the wind. *That* is your destiny—not to sink to the sea bottom and be eaten by the hungry prowlers of the deep."

"What would *you* know of my destiny?" she gasped, wincing.

"Because I will shape it," he said calmly, loosing his grip and letting her reel back from him. "Just as I shape you to my arms, so I will shape your future, Imogene."

She struck at him weakly and he fended her off with ease, laughing. She did not see the sudden flash of concern in his eyes that her blow was so weak. She leaned panting against the wall and closed her eyes, hating him. Her knuckles clenched white and her fingernails bit into her palms. He dared to make sport of her in her grief—oh, the beast!

"How did you know—about my funeral?" she asked him haltingly.

Her voice was sulky, reluctant, but van Ryker felt a glimmer of hope. She was showing an interest in something at last! "I had it from the captain of that Dutch ship who hailed us. He'd been pursued by a Spanish galleass and wanted to tell me her last position. He was late of New Amsterdam, which was still agog with the news of your funeral."

She digested that. "You told him of course that I am still alive?" she challenged. Perhaps, she thought forlornly, the *schout* would arrest him when next he stepped onto the dock in New Amsterdam!

"Of course I did not tell him." He watched her through narrowed eyes, following the progress of her thoughts. "For that part of your life is over, Imogene. You shall live out your days here on the *Sea Rover*—and ashore in my house on Tortuga. Wherever I will, at my pleasure—but you will always be with me."

"You deceive yourself! When I am strong again—"

"But you will never be strong again," he cut in smoothly. "For you refuse to eat, you take no proper exercise, you will not even stroll around the deck and take the air. No, Imogene, you will always be with me. I doubt me you will ever leave this cabin."

She sat up, enraged by his suggestion, and flung a leg over the bunk. But she was very weak and staggered as she rose.

Van Ryker fought back a desire to steady her, and let her waver across the room on her own, grasping at chairbacks and table corners to keep from falling. Compassion for this gallant girl rushed over him and he had to turn his face away from her lest she see the leaping love in his eyes. "It will do you good to walk about the cabin," he flung carelessly over his shoulder. "And I mind it not, for you have not the stamina to escape me."

"Have I not?" she gasped, and he could hear her white teeth grinding. *"Have I not?"*

Van Ryker hid a smile—this was the old Imogene, flinging back a challenge. He pretended to yawn.

"As you will," he said indifferently, rose and turned at the door to give her a mocking smile. "If you have in mind to drag yourself on deck and once again consign yourself to the deep, let me tell you that I have posted a guard at this door who will escort you and stay by your side and keep you safe —on pain of a thrust with this." He patted his basket-hilted sword contentedly and strode away from her, his ears alert for her gasping sob of chagrin as he left her.

"I would I had a sword of my own!" she called after him. "I would run you through!"

He paused regally, a sultan reproving an impudent but valuable slave. "You are not strong enough to lift it," he said contemptuously, and was gone.

Imogene leaned dizzily against the cabin wall and realized the truth of what he had spoken. Weak as she was, she would not be able to lift his sword, even were he to hand it to her hilt first. Indeed, she could barely stand. She tottered back to the bunk, collapsed upon it.

Van Ryker came back for something and she turned on him with tears spilling from her lashes. "Oh, damn you!" she cried hoarsely. "Do you think I want to forget? I want to remember my baby—and Elise and Stephen—all exactly as they were! And even Verhulst—I want to forget the bad and remember the good! Why can you not leave me to my grief, van Ryker? Why must you—?" She covered her face with her hands and he watched her with compassion.

She was weeping in deep gulping sobs when he left and when he reached the deck he leaned against the rail and felt sick. For he knew he was forever damning himself in the eyes of this woman who meant everything to him—everything.

When one of the buccaneers swaggered by and winked broadly at him and mouthed a bawdy jest, van Ryker ripped out an oath and seized the fellow by the throat with a murderous grip.

As swiftly as it had come over him, the madness left him and he flung the terrified fellow away from him and ran a shaking hand through his hair. To him the woman in the great cabin was no joke. If she died a part of him would die, too—the best part, he told himself grimly.

But in the cabin now Imogene was reacting to her grief more normally. Feeling abused and with half her thoughts on van Ryker and her vindictive desire to punish him, she wept for the child she had lost, for the woman who had been like a mother, for her first lover. . . .

Van Ryker knew that forever in her heart she would carry Georgiana—and all those she had loved. Save one: He was determined to replace Stephen Linnington in her affections! And yet he was certain now of what must be done. His broad shoulders sagged with the realization that by what he must do now he would forever destroy his chances with Imogene. He must destroy them forever that Imogene might live—live to love again.

He came back to the cabin to set in motion his harsh decision. Having already given her hate, now he must give her hope. Imogene was too frail, too near the verge of irreversible decline to tamper with further.

"What, still refusing to eat?" He looked significantly at the platter of food placed temptingly near the bunk and still untouched.

Imogene dashed the tears from her eyes and turned to face him with a look of enormous contempt. Her eyes were great blue lamps of accusation.

The buccaneer stood steady before that look, feeling her hatred strike him as palpably as a blow. He reached out wistfully to touch her hair and she flinched away from him.

"Well, on one count at least, you need not concern yourself," he drawled, watching her face. "I lied to you—Stephen Linnington is alive."

Indignation and astonishment and delight and horror fought for mastery in the beautiful countenance before him. "How could you do it?" she demanded. "How could you take me like that, knowing he was alive?"

"Easily." His voice had a lazy harshness, like the edge of a blade. "You are mine, not Linnington's."

"You are wrong, van Ryker. I am his—and I will go back

to him." She gave him a suspicious look through her lashes. "You are not just saying this to torment me?"

"On the contrary. Linnington was badly wounded, yes—but hardly dead. Raoul examined him and said he would recover. Would you prefer to hear it from him?"

Imogene studied his face. He kept it expressionless. She must continue to think him cold and terrible, he told himself, using her only for the gratification of his lust.

"Now perhaps you will eat? Or would you prefer to play games?" He moved a hand intimately down her pulsing throat and caressed her breasts.

"If you will leave off these hateful intimacies, I will eat," said Imogene hastily, drawing back and reaching out unsteady hands for the soup.

"All of it. The bread too."

"Yes!" Violently.

Van Ryker smiled and leaned back and watched her teeth snap into the bread. There was more fire and life in her today. She was moving away from death, although she did not know it.

For the first time he was not afraid to leave her alone and untied in the great cabin. But to taunt her he shoved a heavy chest before the door and slipped through the opening. "It will be beyond your strength to move this," he told her pleasantly.

"And if the ship sinks?" she asked in a flat tone.

"Then I will be back to rescue you. If not, you will have found the death you have so earnestly sought!" With a laugh, he pulled the chest across the door by a leathern thong, making it effectively bar the entrance. Noisily, he locked the door that she might hear and be nettled.

After he had gone, Imogene, refreshed a little by her unaccustomed meal, dragged herself from the bunk and leaned, half fainting, against the cabin's paneled wall. With her eyes tightly closed, she swore a great oath: She would grow strong enough to escape van Ryker; she would exercise when he was not looking, she would eat all her food and demand more. She would live and grow strong for Stephen—they would be together again. She would escape this damnable pirate who held her captive here! She would!

Van Ryker, had he been able to observe her, could not have been happier to see Imogene's plan put into effect.

He came back to find her exhausted from her first efforts at rejoining the world and he lay down beside her, careful not to wake her.

That night they sighted the island of Tortuga and van Ryker was on deck early. He came back to find his lady nibbling at an enormous breakfast.

"We will put into Tortuga shortly," he told her. "We are just now entering Cayona Bay. Would you like to come on deck and view the quay and the Mountain Fort? They are a pretty sight from this distance."

Imogene put down her spoon. "I care not for your pirate town or your pirate island! Stephen will take me away from both!"

"I doubt it," he said indifferently. "Remember, he deserted you before!"

"He will come for me if he can find me!"

"Linnington knows I took you aboard the *Sea Rover*," he told her sternly. "Remember, we were face to face! And all know that I reside in Tortuga when not at sea. My house is well known. Come, I will point it out to you—it overlooks the bay. And Linnington—" his mouth twisted in a wry smile—"knows his way about the Indies, for it was in the Bahamas that I first met him."

Van Ryker knew Stephen!

"Then if you know him," she said steadily, "you know that he will find me and take me away with him. No, do not shake your head and laugh. *Would you care to wager?*"

A wager? This was a show of life indeed! "And what would you have to wager that would interest me?" he asked silkily.

"My jewels," was her prompt reply.

He gave a short ruthless laugh. "You will have to do better than that, Imogene!"

"I could swear that—that if I lose, I would no longer try to escape."

He studied her thoughtfully, standing balanced on the lightly rolling floor with his legs wide apart, the very picture of male vigor. "I will make you *this* wager, Imogene, for I do not believe Linnington will ever come for you: If you will preside over my house in Tortuga as a wife should, if you will entertain my friends and grace my table with your presence—do not look so surprised, I do have friends there. True, they are gentlemen fallen upon evil times like myself—although at times I also entertain the governor and his family. If you will do all this and make no effort to escape—then if Linnington comes and you still wish to go away with him, I promise that I will not stop you."

"And you will make no further attempt to—to touch me *in that way?*" Her pale face reddened; it had a desperate look. "You will sleep in a separate room and stay away from my bed?"

"Yes, even that," he agreed sadly.

"Swear it on your honor as a gentleman!"

A ghost of a smile played about his lips. "I thought you did not consider me a gentleman?"

She brushed that aside. "For this purpose I do. Swear, van Ryker!"

"I swear—but there must be a time limit. Two months will I wait for Linnington—no more."

"And then?"

He shrugged. "And then you are free to try to escape me, and I to foil your attempts. We will be back on our old basis—daily confrontations between the sheets!"

Her eyes gleamed. "Your hand on it!"

He took her small white hand in his big bronzed one. It was delicate as a feather. He caressed it before she snatched it away.

"You have made love to me for the last time, van Ryker!" she exulted. "You will never humble me again!"

For a terrible wrenching moment, bathed in her victorious glance, he wanted to die. By an effort, he kept his face impassive. "We will see about that," he said, and turned away. "We are about to make port," he added tonelessly. "I will help you dress and carry you on deck."

"I can dress myself!"

"This time *I* will help you. When you reach my home, you will have a maidservant to assist you."

Just touching her, just sliding the light blue silk dress with its billowing skirts over her head, was balm to his aching heart. Every rustle of her skirts seemed a melody. Lightly—as if it were the last time—he carried her out and set her upon her feet.

"I will walk by myself," she said, pushing him away.

There was a little color in her pale cheeks now, he thought fondly, watching her take her first halting steps along the deck. "Raoul." He beckoned the ship's doctor. "Would you take Imogene's arm and assist her to walk around the deck? I am afraid she may fall."

Raoul, who had been itching to do exactly that but too leery of the buccaneer captain's wrath to do so, bounded forward promptly and offered the lady his arm with a gallant bow.

Imogene took his arm with a crushing look at van Ryker and a blinding smile for the ship's doctor, who looked quite dazzled. As he supported her around the deck, she engaged him in lighthearted conversation—just to make van Ryker squirm.

She was drooping with fatigue when she finished her stroll but she had the satisfaction of seeing a frown bring van Ryker's dark brows together. "I am practicing," she told him, "on how to entertain your friends. I think I shall take the air every day!"

"An excellent idea," he said shortly, and held himself back from helping her to the cabin, where he knew she would sink down from exhaustion—no, perhaps her hatred of him would carry her all the way to her bunk and she could collapse there.

He was leaning on the taffrail, gripping it so hard his knuckles whitened, when Raoul came back and joined him.

"I think she is improving," Raoul told van Ryker. "Of course she is still very weak and undernourished but her eyes are brighter today and her voice is stronger. I think she has developed what she needed—a will to live."

A will that he had given her!

"Oh, yes, her eyes are very bright, and her voice snaps with more authority," agreed his captain wearily. "But the struggle is not over yet. She could slip back." *If word reached her that Linnington is dead after all. . . .*

"You are right," agreed the doctor quickly. "She needs good food and much more exercise—and she will have them on shore. He hesitated, coughed delicately. "I could come and take her for daily walks in Tortuga, if you approve?"

"Oh, I approve—if you will not find that too great

sacrifice, Raoul," said van Ryker ironically. "I am sure that Imogene would appreciate it—she prefers any arm to mine!"

The ship's doctor watched him stride away, busy now for they would soon cast anchor. He knew for a fact that the buccaneer captain had cared for the golden-haired English beauty like a babe, that he had slept beside her, warmed her with his body as they cruised from the cold north to warmer waters. That van Ryker loved Imogene with all his heart, Raoul de Rochemont had no doubt. And yet, the woman would have none of him! Raoul shook his head in perplexity. A Frenchman, he told himself complacently, would have arranged things much better!

BOOK V
The Choice

A toast to the proud lovely woman
Who must seek her own heaven or hell—
Beyond riches or birth, she must judge a man's worth—
Who chooses—and chooses well!

Tortuga, 1659
CHAPTER 31

Two months had passed. On Tortuga, the swift, scented night of the tropics had fallen. Just back from a successful voyage, Captain van Ryker, with his basket-hilted sword swinging against his lean leg, strode impatiently through his iron-grilled front door. He had driven the *Sea Rover* hard to reach Cayona Bay by tonight. The men had grumbled at the pace he set them but the captain had his reasons. On arrival in Tortuga, he had left his loot from the recently captured *Santa Dominica* and gone striding toward his white-stuccoed house, ignoring the clamoring crowd on the quay.

For tonight his wager was up! Tonight he could claim his woman!

The captain's step was springy as he entered the iron grillwork doors of his house, for his keen eyes had sighted a golden-haired woman just retreating through the French doors

of her balcony overhead at sight of him. Imogene—aware tha
tonight she had lost her wager!

As he moved into the cool, stone-floored hall, his yellow
toothed house servant, Arne, a buccaneer who had lost a leg i
the raid on Maracaibo and had since become part of Captain va
Ryker's household, stomped forward on his wooden leg in th
torchlight.

"I hadn't locked the doors yet, Cap'n," Arne grunted
"because I seen your ship cast anchor in the bay." He peere
past his employer. "Is there men following with chests?"

"Tomorrow, Arne," was the careless answer. "We ra
into a bit of luck so there'll be several chests."

Arne's eyes gleamed. His "Cap'n" was always generou
when he returned from these ventures—there'd be pieces o
eight for him as well!

Van Ryker was unbuckling his sword as Arne locked th
heavy iron grillwork doors and followed that by closing an
locking another set of doors—this last pair constructed of thic
oak and garnished with heavy nailheads. The house was built i
the Spanish style, around a court. The stone-floored hallwa
where van Ryker stood led out onto an inner patio with a tinklin
rose-colored stone fountain in the center. The doors of all th
major downstairs rooms opened out onto this inner patio, a ston
stairway led up from it to a covered gallery that encircled th
patio and the bedroom doors opened onto it. It was a delightful
open plan and in the dusk the hallway entrance was lit by a torc
stuck into an iron bracket set into the white-stuccoed wal
Beneath that coating of stucco was a wall two feet thick of ston
While inside, the house was pleasant and open and luxuriou
outside it was like a fort, with heavy rooftiles, and sturd
wooden shutters that could be slammed shut across the iro
grillwork. For Captain van Ryker was ever aware of the Spani

presence in the Caribbean—Spanish Hispaniola to the south of him, Cuba to the west, and all the Spanish Main to contend with. The Mountain Fort that rose above him, built by the buccaneers to defend their stronghold and commanding Cayona Bay, was considered impregnable. But if it was not—if some night an avenging armada swept down and stormed Cayona Bay, destroyed the Mountain Fort and caught van Ryker on land, he meant to sell his life dear.

Now he looked around him with satisfaction at the handsome furniture that graced the patio. To his left was a chart room where he kept his maps, and on the other side a large reception room where he entertained his guests. Imogene had been startled to meet his friends, he thought with amusement, for these days Tortuga was a flourishing international community. Aside from the ever-present buccaneers who made it their headquarters, it had its more or less permanent residents: doctors—there was always need for them in this brawling place; keen-eyed traders, buying and selling captured goods; go-betweens who arranged ransoms with families in Spain and brought back news of captives in Spanish prisons. Tortuga even sported a governor, sent from France, who sold letters of marque for a price—those pieces of paper that ostensibly made the bearer a certified privateer. Most Spanish officials disregarded these commissions and hanged their bearers anyway. Van Ryker had no doubt what his own fate would be if he were captured. Although he entertained the French governor frequently, he had never purchased any letters of marque.

"How have things been, Arne?" he asked. For although Imogene was technically mistress of the house, sturdy Arne was actually in charge when van Ryker was away. If the house was attacked, it was Arne who would muster a defense; if there were money problems, Arne had the keys to a small chest of gold and silver coins which would resolve it until van Ryker's return.

Arne flashed his yellow teeth at him. "Things has been good, but we've missed ye, Cap'n."

Could that "we" mean that Imogene had mentioned missing him? The thought was pleasant and van Ryker looked sharply at Arne, but the burly buccaneer's broad face had gone impassive again. "I see ye've added more silver studdings to that leg, Arne," he remarked cheerfully.

Arne favored his wooden leg with a smug look. "All the coins I win at cards, I pound into this here leg, Cap'n. 'Tis my bank, it is!"

"If you have another winning streak, you won't be able to lift your leg to walk for the weight!" laughed van Ryker, and took a folded paper that grinning Arne handed him with a "This come just now, Cap'n."

Another invitation from the governor, no doubt, thought van Ryker with amusement. The governor's lady, who prided herself on her aristocratic upbringing, was all for formality. Even in a climate as hot as this, the poor governor was never allowed to peel down to his shirt in public, for fear the people would "look down on him." Van Ryker tossed his sword aside and tore open the note as he walked past the torch toward the stairs—and came to a sudden abrupt halt.

The note was not to him, it was to Imogene—and it was from Stephen Linnington. Arne had given it to him no doubt because he was still mystified by Imogene's status in this household—was she queen or captive? Now van Ryker shook his head irritably as he read that Elise and the baby had gone down with the *Wilhelmina*—this reminder of her loss could only sadden Imogene. But the ending brought him up short:

I am staying at the Green Lion. I should like to see you Can you meet me there tomorrow?

So Linnington was in Tortuga!

Frowning, van Ryker crumpled the note. He told Arne to have cook send him a bit of cold meat into the chart room, he'd eat it there. Arne looked surprised, but went to do his bidding. Van Ryker lit a candle from the torch and took it into the chart room, pushed aside a pile of maps from the long oaken table, and sat staring into the flame. When cook lumbered in with a tray of cold meats and brown bread and a bottle of wine, he ate—mechanically, for he had had nothing to eat since morning. A month and more he had been at sea—for he had not been able to bear being so near to Imogene and unable by his very oath to touch her.

And he had come home to find his rival already there. . . .

Now van Ryker hesitated to see Imogene. What should he tell her? Anything? It would be easy enough to have his buccaneers pounce on Linnington and carry him aboard a ship bound for somewhere else, easy enough—his hawklike face darkened—to stride into the Green Lion this very night and challenge the copper-haired Englishman to a duel. They could push back the tables and chairs in the common room and settle the matter then and there.

Van Ryker sighed. He could not do that. If he killed Linnington, Imogene would never forgive him. He shifted his boots on the stone floor, pushed aside his suddenly tasteless food and sat listening to the merry tinkling of the fountain in the patio. He had so looked forward to this homecoming. But now old jealousies were gnawing at him, things he hoped he had put aside. Wearily he passed a hand over his face, pushed back the thick dark hair that fell carelessly over his ears and grazed his shoulders. He must come up with something better than a duel. He drummed his fingers on the table.

Linnington was back—and must be dealt with.

By the time he went up the stairs he had made up his mind. His features were taut but they relaxed into a tender smile as he opened the door and saw the woman lying in her delicate white night rail upon the bed. The windows to the balcony stood open and a scented breeze blew in and ruffled a tendril of her golden hair, spread out like a lustrous shawl in the moonlight. The skirt of her night rail had ridden up, displaying a pair of long gleaming legs, and the blue ribbon that held it around the neck was untied in the heat and the whole thing fell down over one white shoulder displaying in dazzling fashion the pearly tops of her rounded breasts.

Van Ryker stood a moment and gazed at her yearningly.

She must have been wakened by the sound of the door opening, for now her blue eyes opened and she gave a start at sight of him. Quickly she pulled her night rail over herself to cover her.

"You are back!" she exclaimed. "Arne did not tell me!"

"He did not need to—you saw me enter the house."

"Oh—was that you?" she asked lamely. "I saw your ship in the bay earlier, but I thought you would spend your first night home celebrating in the taverns and dividing your loot."

"You thought no such thing," he said, studying her keenly. *That untied drawstring at the top of her chemise, the careless exposure of one breast—could that have been artfully contrived?* He abandoned the thought, strode toward her and sat down on the bed. She edged away from him nervously.

"We had a wager, Imogene."

"Yes."

"It is over today."

"I know that, van Ryker."

"You could have escaped at any time while I was gone," he said quietly. "Why didn't you?"

She lifted her chin haughtily. She looked very beautiful in the candlelight, exactly as when he had first seen her. "I am not so base! I honored my bargain."

She was close, temptingly close. Her perfume, the tangy scent of lemons from her golden hair assailed his senses.

"Besides." She tossed her head. "I was not sure whether the wager was over today or tomorrow!"

He smiled grimly. "You are looking well, Imogene. You seem to have accommodated yourself to the life here. I take it you are enjoying a pleasant social life here on Godforsaken Tortuga?"

She flushed. It was true she had been surprised at the intellectual level of his friends, surprised that she should have a staff of five servants to order about, surprised at the esteem in which her buccaneer was held by all the island.

"As much as any captive could," she said with asperity.

Well, that was a straw in the wind! So she still considered herself a captive!

He reached out and pounced suddenly upon her wrist and drew her to him, sliding her toward him across the sheets. She could feel the linen rasp across her bare bottom and the underside of her thighs and she gathered herself together to fight him. She looked wondrously beautiful and wild.

Holding her brilliant blue eyes locked with his own, van Ryker reached out and caressed her breast with his free hand. A tremor went through her and she struck at him. "I gave you no leave!"

Without answer, he hauled her into his arms—so suddenly that her breath left her. His kiss had all the impatience of a lover's first kiss, all the violence of a man who had been away at sea for more than a month, all the fierce yearning of a man who is saying good-bye. Imogene struggled fiercely.

As suddenly as he had taken her, his lips left hers.

"I've brought you a gift," he said tonelessly.

Imogene was shaking with indignation—and something else, something she refused to name. "I need nothing from you but my freedom—I've told you that."

"Ah, but wait till you see it." He went over to the big press in the corner which was crammed with her gowns—captured Spanish gowns that he had given her, gowns rummaged from the trunks of Spain, lovely things she had admired in the marketplace along the quay here in Tortuga. He pulled out a handsome garment of black velvet that could have been intended for the wife of a Spanish grandee and thrust it at her.

"What's this?" she demanded, bewildered. "Mourning? But you forbade me to wear mourning when I proposed it!"

"Not mourning—'tis a wedding gown. Yours. I thought black might be appropriate," he added ironically, "for having known *me*, you are sure to wish yourself back in my arms."

Imogene pushed back her bright hair and stared at him. "Have you been drinking, van Ryker? You're not making sense."

"I said I've brought you a gift and I have. His name is Stephen Linnington. He is here in Tortuga, and tomorrow morning we'll have a parson and a wedding. I'll stand for the wedding feast and give the bride away. You shall have your freedom, Imogene."

Stunned, Imogene stared at him. Stephen was back? In these last weeks she had given him up. Until this minute she had believed he was never coming for her. Van Ryker was right—she *had* adjusted to the life here, to social calls from the gover nor's wife, to the courtly bows of his friends when she strolled down toward the market in the company of big Arne; she had become used to taking charge of the house and Arne was becoming submissive in following her orders.

She had thought constantly about this moment when van Ryker would return—and promised herself he would never use her in *that* fashion again. She was not cut out for a life of lust! She would escape! She had friends on the quay now, she would have no trouble finding a merchant ship to transport her almost anywhere.

And if the *Sea Rover* overtook her and brought her back, why, she would escape again!

Now her mind was whirling. Stephen was back, Stephen to whom she owed everything—Stephen who had rescued her and come so near to losing his life. She turned to the impassive buccaneer. "Why are you doing this, van Ryker?" she demanded suspiciously. "It is not like you to hand me over to another without a fight."

"Well spoke," he murmured. "And I will admit that I do it with a wrench. But I will ask you to believe that I do it out of the fullness of my heart and the greatness of my love."

" 'Love'!" she scoffed. "You never loved me! You deserted me in New Amsterdam!"

He gave her a twisted smile. "Just as I warmed you with my body when you were chilled," he said lightly, "I'll now warm your cold heart by giving you the one thing you want—another man."

Imogene felt a flush rising that spread all over her body at the memories his words evoked. "Are you really—doing this?" she asked haltingly. "Is it true? Is Stephen here?"

"As real as this gown in which you'll be wed tomorrow!"

Her heart skipped a beat. "I can't be married in black," she demurred.

"No? Then red might be appropriate." With some violence he pulled from the press a gown of scarlet satin and flung it at her. "Or gold for a golden woman." He tossed her one of gold silk. "Or choose your own. You'll be leaving Tortuga in it."

It was true, then! He was letting her go!

In a burst of gratitude she leaped from the bed and flung herself at him, twined her arms around his neck. "Oh, van Ryker," she choked. "I do thank you—I do."

Dazzled by her shining face and cut to the quick by her ardent desire to leave him for another, van Ryker untwined her arms and pushed her away. "You'll not go sleepy-eyed from my arms into the arms of your bridegroom," he said bitterly. "You'll sleep alone this night, Imogene. I have decided I want a willing woman to warm my bed—and there are plenty of them here in Tortuga!"

He strode out, slamming the door behind him, and she could hear his boots clattering down the stairs. She threw a light silken shawl about her and went out on the balcony and leaned on the rail, drinking in the night air. Van Ryker had put on his sword and now she saw him swinging down the street below with the moonlight glinting on its basket hilt. He was going down into the town—to find one of those willing women, no doubt!

Van Ryker was going to let her go—she still could not believe it! He was going to let her wed Stephen! Old dreams raced through her mind, old longings. It seemed centuries ago that she had met and loved Stephen Linnington beneath the stars of the Scillies. So much had happened since then—so much. . . .

544

She had borne a daughter—and lost her. Her face saddened. And she had lost Elise. And Verhulst—tragic, misunderstood—lay buried in the family plot at Wey Gat beside a stone that bore her name. . . .

And yet as she leaned upon the balcony's iron railing, she found her mind dwelling most of all upon the tall buccaneer who had—at last she faced it—treated her on the whole so kindly. With hot cheeks she remembered his caresses and her whole body tingled to the memory. Time raced by as she recounted their long nights together. The sea air cooled her hot face. Below her the lights of Tortuga were going out one by one. Dawn would be breaking soon.

Why had van Ryker done it? she asked herself. Was his lust so strong? And why was he letting her go now that their wager was over? Remorse?

She was still standing there when van Ryker came back up the street, weaving a little as he walked. He had drunk deep, she guessed. Because he was giving her up?

On the street below he stood with both feet planted wide and looked up at her silently. She would never know how beautiful she looked to him with her creamy silk shawl and the moonlight gilding her long hair. Without speaking to her, he went unsteadily into the house.

Imogene heard his uneven footsteps coming up the stairs and realized that in all the time she had known him, she had never seen him really drunk. She winced as she heard a loud crash and a low curse. Van Ryker must have collided with his bedroom door.

She waited until all was quiet and suddenly it sank in on her that in his way he must really love her. That was why he had got

drunk tonight. For the first time there was a tenderness in he
gaze as she thought of him.

He would be sleeping down the hall—lonely without her
And something in his stance as he stood on the street below th
balcony, something bereft, had told her that he had not had
woman this night after all. He had honored their wager
Scrupulously he had kept his word and not touched her sinc
they had reached Tortuga—and now, without touching her, h
was letting her go.

On an impulse—for she was a woman given to reckles
impulses—Imogene stole down the hall and quietly opened hi
bedroom door. In the moonlight that struck through the ope
window she saw that he had flung himself, sword and all, full
dressed upon the bed. At the small sound of the door opening hi
big body tensed and his dark head swung around so that on
bloodshot eye was staring at her. She came toward him, bare
foot, graceful, her long fair hair swinging about her sli
body.

"Van Ryker," she said, and her voice was low and caressing
"I know what this must have cost you. And so—this la
night—if you want me . . ." Her voice drifted away like ros
petals on the wind, but every word had fallen on him like a blov
Imogene—offering him one last night as a consolation priz
before she went to her bridegroom's arms!

He shook off the feather-light touch of her fingers on h
cheek. "Imogene," he said thickly, "go away." And turne
his dark head away from her.

She leaned down and pressed a kiss lightly upon his ear.
was the first time she had ever offered him an endearment—
what he had had from her, he had had to take; it was never give
freely.

"You are better than I knew," she said softly. "And I will never forget you. Never."

She was gone. He heard the door close behind her.

Van Ryker, lying there stiffly with his eyes closed, was furious to find there were tears on his lashes.

CHAPTER 32

At Captain van Ryker's white-stuccoed residence, a most unusual wedding was about to take place. A crowd of hastily assembled buccaneers—most of them from the crew of the *Sea Rover*—shuffled their feet in the pleasant patio. Notably absent were the governor and his lady and van Ryker's aristocratic—though not necessarily law-abiding—friends.

Stephen Linnington, carelessly attired in russet, his copper hair uncombed—for the four buccaneers who had burst into his room at the Green Lion and brought him here at gunpoint had given him only time to get into his clothes and not to make himself truly presentable—stopped stock still at sight of the man who stood in the open grillwork doors. The lace at Stephen's throat had been hastily knotted on the way here and he was irritably aware that one of his garters was about to leave his leg.

He gazed, frowning, at the tall buccaneer—meticulously

dressed in gray, with a wide red satin baldric slung over one shoulder—who stepped aside to let him enter.

"So we meet again, van Ryker," he said as his escort pushed him inside and shoved him along the hall.

"You may leave him now—but stay by the door. This man is not to be allowed to leave without my permission," van Ryker told his men.

"This is your house, I take it?" said Stephen.

"Correct." Van Ryker turned his wintry gaze on Stephen. "I intercepted your note, Linnington."

So that was why he'd been dragged here! "I had to let Imogene know the fate of Elise and the child," defended Stephen.

"Of course." Van Ryker inclined his head in a nod of becoming gravity. "She already knew of her loss and has become reconciled to it. For that reason I did not give her your note."

"Oh—well, then I'll be on my way."

"Not quite yet, my friend."

Stephen looked uneasily around him. What was this gathering? What were all these men doing here? And why was van Ryker dressed as if for a ball? Nobody had told him anything. He was beginning to feel nettled. And alarmed, for had not van Ryker said he was not to be allowed to leave?

"What is the matter?" he demanded. "Has Imogene run away from you again?"

Van Ryker gave him a grim look. "She has not!"

"Look, I realize that she is your woman now, van Ryker," Stephen burst out.

"On the contrary," his host told him mockingly. "She pines for you constantly."

Stephen's mouth dropped open. He stared at van Ryker. "But I thought you and she—"

"Cease to think," he was advised. "Consider me as Cupid, for it is I who have brought you together again."

"I consider that you and Imogene mousetrapped me into snatching her from her husband!" Stephen was indignant. "Was your Dutch trade so valuable to you that you would send a lone man to a fortress like Wey Gat to bring your woman out?"

"So that is what you thought?"

"Yes! I still think it!"

For a moment the gray eyes went steely and there was a faint tremor of van Ryker's sword arm. "You make me wish that I had not brought you a doctor and sent you to the Culps to recover," he drawled, "but instead left you bleeding on the farmhouse floor where I found you!"

Stephen flushed. "I am grateful to you for that," he muttered. "And I will find a way to pay you back—"

Van Ryker raised a hand to silence him. "You will pay me back, never fear." He gave Stephen a cold look. "But so that we understand each other, had I known that Imogene was unhappy I would have battered down the walls of Wey Gat to reach her!"

Before the controlled violence of that tone, Stephen blinked. There could be no doubt this tall buccaneer loved Imogene!

"Then why bring me here?" he asked argumentatively. "You could have sent a message to me at the Green Lion and I'd have been on my way."

"On your way?"

"Yes—back to Barbados. There's a lady there I wish to marry."

"Ever hot to marry," van Ryker murmured. "But then, you have a prior commitment." He smiled, a cold, wolfish smile that showed his strong white teeth and turned his saturnine face demonic. "You will find that I am not one to stand in the

551

way of true love," he told Stephen with heavy irony. "Imogene wants you—and so she shall have you. Over there is a parson. This company is here to witness your wedding—and I myself shall give the bride away!"

Stephen's jaw dropped in astonishment. "Have you—tired of her, then?" he demanded.

For a moment he thought the buccaneer was going to strike him. "No man could tire of such a woman," van Ryker growled. "I am but giving Imogene her heart's desire."

"But you know that I am already—" Stephen was about to say "married" when van Ryker interrupted.

"*I* know what you are about to say, Linnington. But Imogene does not. And since in these islands it can never matter, you will forget to mention it. But I tell you this: You will either walk forth from this place a bridegroom with your bride by your side, or you will be carried from it on your way to your funeral. The choice is yours."

They were standing a little apart from the others and to the assembled company, they must have appeared to be engaged in pleasant conversation. Van Ryker was smiling at him. It was a bright, dangerous smile that made the copper hairs at the back of Stephen's neck crawl—he had had that same feeling once when an assailant was about to leap upon him with a meat cleaver. And so deadly was the low tone in which this ultimatum was delivered that Stephen little doubted this grimly smiling buccaneer would do exactly as he said. He squared his russet shoulders and stood a little straighter. He *had* loved Imogene, and she had borne his child, she had even written that she would have waited for him. . . . For a tortured moment his heart bled for Bess, waiting for him on Barbados. Best not to let her know better far to let her think that he had died trying to rescue

Imogene—and there was even a tombstone at Wey Gat to prove it. Sweet Bess need never know of this forced wedding in a buccaneer's lair on Tortuga! In time a woman as lovely, as true as Bess, would find someone else, she would marry. His throat constricted at the thought.

"I see you are hesitating," van Ryker said softly. His hand closed around the hilt of his sword.

"No." The word was wrenched from Stephen. "I stand ready to marry Imogene if that is her desire."

"It is her desire." Van Ryker gave him a mocking smile and motioned Stephen to precede him into the patio. "See that you do not falter," he warned. "For my temper is short and it is I who will give the bride away."

He paused at a general stirring in the room and looked upward. Imogene had come out of her room and down the hall. Now she stood at the head of the stone stairs and every head swung around to look at her—all stood spellbound.

She was attired in the kind of daring gown she most favored—a low-cut white silk that clung to her delightful figure and moved lissomely when she moved. Its sweeping skirt was caught up cleverly over a petticoat of pale flowing Chinese gold silk. From her fluffed out virago sleeves gleamed gold satin rosettes that caught up the spilled lace at her elbows. And—both Stephen and van Ryker drew in their breath sharply—she had thrown away her whisk—again. Her rosy nipples were barely covered and in danger of peeping out at any minute. Her bright hair was swept up into a gleaming mass with golden curls spilling down upon the snowy whiteness of her shoulders.

No innocent quivering bride was this. But as she smiled gently down upon the assembled buccaneers from the head of the stairs—a lovely and tantalizing woman—not a man in the company but felt a thrill of desire go through him.

Regally she beckoned to van Ryker, who thundered up the stairs to offer her his arm.

For a moment they smiled into each other's eyes, these two antagonists who had clashed so often. It was the friendliest smile they had ever exchanged and filled with memories. Stephen watched in perplexity from below. Then Imogene was floating downstairs light as a feather on the arm of her tall and jaunty buccaneer and the crowd parted, cutlasses clanking, to let then pass.

And then she came face to face with Stephen—but only for a moment, for van Ryker signaled to the parson, who stepped forward. Imogene's face was dreamy as she took her place beside Stephen in the sunny patio beside the tinkling fountain. She felt that an old dream was coming true. Stephen loved her, he had saved her, he had come for her and now he was going to marry her—just as she had planned so long ago. Strange—all last night she had tried to remember him, to blot out van Ryker's sardonic face that seemed to fill her thoughts. Why should she feel so sorry for van Ryker? she asked herself rebelliously. Had he not kidnapped her, kept her prisoner, used her? The fact that he was now trying to make amends changed nothing. But sorry for him she was, and her preoccupation with the buccaneer as she stepped forward to her destiny kept her from hearing the words the parson was solemnly intoning.

She must pay attention, she told herself—she was getting married! And to the man she had loved for so long! In a moment now she would be Stephen's wife!

"Does any man know cause why this man and this woman should not be joined in holy wedlock? If so, let him speak!"

"I do," caterwauled a loud voice from the back of the

room. As startled heads swung around, a woman pushed through the throng of buccaneers. "He already has a wife—me! And you wouldn't be the only wench he's married without divorcing me," she called mockingly to Imogene. "There's another one in Lincoln!"

In the stunned silence, the buccaneers stepped back to let her pass. Cutlasses clattered as Kate swaggered past them, thoroughly enjoying the sensation she was causing. Her wild black hair had been combed for this occasion but she still wore it long and loose. It swung about her flaunting red satin hips as she sidled forward barefoot—Kate had always hated shoes. She shook her head chidingly at Stephen with a mocking jingle of gold earrings. "Surprised to see me? Thought ye'd seen the last of me in England?" She turned her bold gaze on Imogene and laughed.

Stunned, Imogene stared back at this woman who was now leaning forward impishly, hands on hips, her piquant face turned up toward Stephen's. *This was Stephen's wife*, had been his wife all along while he . . . made love . . . to her. Imogene was white to the lips as, speechless, she studied her rival, her—*predecessor!*

Van Ryker's glittering eyes were on her all the while, watching her sardonically.

Now she turned to him. "So this was your wedding gift," she said in a tight voice.

"Aye," he told her steadily. "The gift of truth. Better now than later."

Imogene turned back toward the silent panorama with a little sob that caught unwittingly in her throat.

Stephen was standing with his copper head slightly bent, his russet-clad body shocked into rigidity. But the lissome wench with the thick black hair and the bold roving eyes had put her hands on her swiveling red satin hips and cocked her head at him.

"Come," she wheedled. "D'ye not remember me, Stephen? Although I do seem to remember that ye married me under the name of Kent—not Linnington. Ye thought I didn't know your real name!" Her laughter pealed. "I always thought ye'd come after me—after we heard ye'd escaped from that jail."

"I looked for you, Kate," he said thickly.

"Did ye now?" Something in her wary eyes brightened. "Well, that's something! Ah, don't look so downhearted, Stephen, lad! Ye'll have many a roll in the hay yet and live to bloody many a sword!"

"That I will do right now!" Stephen's head went up and he whirled to face the buccaneer who had had him dragged from the inn, duped him, arranged for him a mock wedding—and now planned to snatch the bride away—for he had no doubt that was van Ryker's purpose. "Draw your blade, van Ryker!" he snarled. "And we'll settle this right now."

That menacing challenge and the sudden lithe movement of the tall buccaneer to answer it brought Imogene to her senses. There was a murmur from the crowd of buccaneers, who edged back to give the contestants room to fight. In a moment the best blade in the Caribbean and the best blade south of the Humber would square off on the stone-floored patio to settle, buccaneer-style, the possession of a lady.

And to both men—whatever harm they had done her emotionally—she was beholden for saving her life.

With a sudden arrogant gesture, Imogene stepped between them.

"There can be no marriage," she said with finality, "fo

there's already a bride—has been, I can see, for some years, since the lady's ne'er so young.'' She flashed a contemptuous look at her dark-haired rival who bridled and returned her a smoldering glance. "This—this buccaneer—" (and here van Ryker winced inwardly that Imogene could not bring herself to use his name)—"who would seem to be in control of our destinies, has given us 'wedding gifts.' To me he has given the truth at last, and to you, Stephen, he has told me he is giving a part of his share of the loot from the *Santa Dominica*—with that you may get you gone and set up this lady as you no doubt feel she deserves.''

"I'll not take his gold!" roared Stephen, still trembling with wrath as he focused all his attention upon the scornful golden-haired beauty before him.

"Ah, but *I* will!" caroled Kate impudently, twitching her hips to give him an eloquent nudge. "With the captain's gold, however you came by it, you can buy me all the little things I've had to do without all this time—along with your company!" Again she was laughing, that rich, full-bodied laughter that went so well with her deep bustline and provocative swaying hips.

Stephen turned to snarl something at her and for a moment was arrested by something in Kate's laughing face—an impudent challenge, flung once again, reminding him even in the full flush of his anger that he had loved this woman once. . . .

Imogene saw it, too. And with a flash of inner clarity she saw how it had been with them, how it could be again. Easy liars, easy lovers, riding the wild highroads of life together. She had never been Stephen's woman, she had *borrowed* him—from this laughing, black-haired wench whose dark eyes mirrored the tigerish look of Stephen's own.

She had not lost him—she had never had him! It was all the illusion of a bored young girl who had seen something in a man's face and mistaken lust for love.

Well, she had suffered for it! And Stephen—grant him that—had come to save her, and done so, there on the ice.

But now he had lost his halo. . . .

Imogene turned blindly to van Ryker. "Get him out of here," she said thickly. "I don't want to look at him."

For a moment the buccaneer hesitated. Then he sheathed his sword, watched as—still trembling with fury—Stephen Linnington sheathed his and went plunging through the crowd toward the door with his red satin lady trailing behind him.

Gone together, thought Imogene bitterly, watching as they disappeared. *Like to like!*

Imogene did not do Stephen justice. Outside the white-stuccoed house he came to a halt. "We can't take the gold, Kate."

"Why ever not?"

"Because 'twas a gift to another—to the woman in there." He jerked his head at the buccaneer's house.

"I care not where gold comes from," declared Kate insolently. " 'Tis what it buys that counts!"

"Aye, that's always been your trouble, Kate," he sighed. For a moment there she had beckoned him, she with her bright predatory smile and her wild ways—as more compellingly, Imogene had beckoned him once, drawn him to the circle of her white arms. But now the moment was over, memories were but memories and there was Bess to be thought of.

"We'll leave the gold," he said sharply.

Kate's hand lashed across his face. "We will not! I'm going back and get it!"

Stephen shrugged and dragged her away, down toward the tavern where she worked. It was the best thing that could have happened to him, that slap. It showed him where Kate stood. "Was it for passage to England that ye needed the gold, Kate?" he asked when they reached the tavern—and he was breathing hard, for she had struggled with him all the way.

" 'England'?" Kate tossed her head and gave a scornful laugh. "They'd hang me there—as they would you! No—'twas for fine clothes and a coach!"

"Good luck to you, then, Kate." I hope you get your coach someday." He left her glaring at him from the tavern door and turned quickly away, hurrying along toward the quay. With every step away from them all he felt better. Somehow, some way he was going back to Bess—although just how he was going to do it he was unsure, for he was down to his last coins. But he was feeling better about his life. He'd done what he could by Imogene and been—thank God—rejected. Whatever happened now, he was going back to his sweet Bess to live all his life in her shadow. If only he could offer her marriage, just as all along he had offered her love!

Back in the white-stuccoed house he'd just left, Imogene had lifted her skirts and flown like a skimming swallow up the stairs. All the way to her bedroom she ran and slammed the door behind her with a force that shook the house. Below her the milling wedding guests left in a body, led out by van Ryker, who promised them "all the grog they could drink" in the nearest tavern.

He was gone a very long time.

Dry-eyed, Imogene sat in her wedding finery, and stared blankly at the rough plaster of her bedroom walls. She could not understand her emotions today. She felt caught up in a wild turbulence, a maelstrom that left her confused, bewildered, uncertain. Daylight faded and darkness came—and still she sat. The sudden velvet night of the tropics descended. The stars came out and moonlight drenched the red-tiled roofs of Tortuga, turned the gently waving green palm fronds to silver, gilded the magnificent bougainvillaea. And still she sat.

There was a knock on the door. It was Arne.

"Go away," she called tonelessly.

"The Cap'n asks that you come down to the chart room, m'lady. He says to tell you he's readying up for a long voyage and he wants to tell you good-bye."

"Tell him—" Imogene was about to give Arne a devastating message for van Ryker but she decided she'd rather deliver it herself. Come to think of it, she had quite a lot of things to say to the tall buccaneer!

Head high, she strode down the stairs with Arne stumping along behind her on a leg that was more silver than wood—and marveling at the strange relationship between the Cap'n and his lady.

Arne held open the chart room door for her—and jumped out of the way as Imogene slammed it behind her. She was alone now in the long room with van Ryker. The captain had not been looking at his maps. No candles had been lit, but the shutters were open and the room was bathed in moonlight. At the far end of the room, past the long table, van Ryker—who seemed not to have heard the door slam—stood impassively with his back to her, a dark and silent figure silhouetted against the moonlight streaming in through the open shutters. He had divested himself of his red satin baldric and of his silver-shot doublet. He was wearing now a loose white shirt. She could see the billow of its wide sleeves, the ruffle at the cuffs, for he was leaning on one hand on the windowsill and the moonlight played over his sun-browned fingers and picked out a sparkle of gold and green from the emerald ring he always wore for luck.

He did not turn to look at her. "Imogene." His voice was calm and tired, weary with the emotional storm that had racked him. "Sit down. I have something to say to you."

"More truths? I will take them standing!" She was amazed at how cool she sounded. She was not cool—her nerves were taut to the breaking point. "What new revelation do you have to confound me?"

"One you will like better than the last," he said quietly. "It is not true about Linnington—he is not married to that woman you saw."

"What?" Imogene sank down upon one of the high-backed chairs, feeling as if her breath had been knocked from her body. *"How do you know?"* she whispered.

"I told you Linnington and I had met before—in the Bahamas. In fact, I tried to recruit him for my ship's company, but he declined—he had an offer as a factor in Barbados."

"But the woman said—"

"Sometime after that I met the woman, Kate, here in Tortuga. She had fled England with her brother—a notorious highwayman who is still recovering from his wounds. 'Twas she who told me the story of how she, for a lark, had arranged a bogus 'marriage' while Linington was drunk. The 'preacher' was a cutpurse, the witnesses thieves. It was no legal marriage and she left him soon after."

"But—but the other one?"

"He married the tavern maid in Lincoln, but 'twas a bigamous marriage on her part, for she was already married. Kate knew all about it and considered it a great joke. Linnington was not a villain, Imogene, but he trusted women. He was twice duped."

"Then—?" Her head was whirling.

"He is free to marry you." Still van Ryker did not turn. "But—" his voice hardened into steel—"while I live, you will not go to him. Do you understand that, Imogene? *You are mine.* I gave you up once, to the Dutchman—and lived with regret. I will live with regret no longer." He made a violent gesture with his arm and his shirt sleeve billowed. "You are *my* woman, Imogene—*mine!*"

Her voice was bewildered and filled with pain. "You knew all along. . . . Why did you do it, van Ryker? *Why?*"

Against the pale moon, she could see him running a distracted hand through his heavy dark hair. "A man does many things in the name of love," he said heavily. "You were slipping away from me, Imogene, you were going to die—perhaps by your own hand. I had to give you a reason for living and so I did: hatred of me. I knew that if you could learn to hate me enough to want to escape me at any cost, even to kill me, you would live—if only to do the thing. And now, Imogene—," he sighed—"you shall have your chance. My sword lies there on the table." She glanced at the long table with its pile of charts and maps and saw that that was so; its basket hilt gleamed in the moonlight. "The blade is unsheathed. I have given Arne orders that no matter what happens you are to be allowed to leave the house and not be pursued. If it is your pleasure, you can run me through. I will do nothing to stop you, for I doubt not that I deserve it. *If you wish to leave me, you must use that sword—for while I live, I will never let you go!*"

Imogene stared at that broad back in the moonlight. What he was saying was incredible! He had lied to her, mocked her, plundered her of a woman's most sacred treasures, and in the end betrayed her trust when he had led her to the altar with Stephen Linnington. And he had done it all *in the name of love.*

Van Ryker waited for a long time. The room was very quiet. And then he heard it, his senses quickened at the delicate sound behind him—a rustle of silk. Imogene had risen from her chair. His ears alert to those tiny rustlings, he presently heard another sound, more menacing than the first—a chilling sound he knew only too well, the sound of a naked blade scraping over a table's wooden surface.

Imogene had taken up the sword!

All his muscles tensed, waiting for the moment when that deadly point would be plunged between his ribs.

Well, he had given her leave to kill him! And reason enough to want to.

"Van Ryker," he heard her say coolly. "Turn around. I would not strike you from the back."

Taut and ready, he turned slowly around to face her, expecting as he did so to see a single flash as the long blade entered his chest.

Instead a dazzling sight met his eyes.

Imogene had loosened the hooks of her bodice and chemise and allowed petticoats and all to slide to the floor. The delicate lawn and lace of her chemise foamed up around her slender ankles, rising from an island of white and gold silk, but the rest of her stood naked to his gaze in the moonlight. Her golden hair had been loosed and now it streamed down around her white shoulders and the rosy-tipped mounds of her pulsing breasts pushed temptingly through its silken curtain. Long strands of shining goldn hair cascaded along her white arms and caressed her smooth stomach and the soft curve of her hips. She stood very straight and proud, her thighs gleaming pale in the moonlight. In her hands she was holding the sword, which suddenly she turned about and offered him hilt first.

"Van Ryker," she said softly. "I believe you love me."

His throat constricted at the richness of her tone. "And if you do not—" the blue eyes were very steady—"I would ask that you take this blade and kill me now, for I am a woman who cannot live without love."

"Imogene." His own voice was husky. "How could you ever doubt it?" In a single stride he had reached her side. He took the sword from her and tossed it skittering to the stone floor.

His strong arms were about her. Exultantly he swept her up, burying his dark face in her lemon-scented hair. She could feel her naked breasts being softly crushed against the cambric folds of his shirt, could feel his belt buckle cutting into the yielding flesh of her stomach, could feel his familiar manly hardness press against her tingling thighs. "I *did* love Stephen," she admitted tremulously. "But it was a—a lesser love. Not the love I have always felt for you."

And that was true. She had felt challenged, threatened by him and—when at far Wey Gat she was sure he had deserted her—afraid to care. She had walled him out. But his love had been strong enough to batter down the walls she had so carefully built, strong enough to break through to the fiery recesses of her secret heart. Now she could admit that the love she felt for the lean adventurer was wide and strong and deep. It could run rivers of tears or rise to shattering peaks of ecstasy and desire. Like the North Star, it could guide her. It could claim her very soul.

Impatiently van Ryker reached down and picked up her silken "wedding gown." He tossed it over her naked body like a shawl and strode with her in his arms through the torch-lit patio and up the stone stairs to her bedroom. From where he sat smoking his clay pipe in the darkness, concealed behind a clump of graceful bougainvillaea, Arne watched. He saw the reckless smile that lit his captain's face as he took the stairs three at a time. He saw dangling from his captain's arms a swatch of gold silk and a gleaming white leg, dangling luxuriously. And nestled against his captain's shoulder and swirling down to his knees, a riot of golden hair.

And after this morning's aborted wedding! Arne shook his head in perplexity and wished his captain luck with the dazzling lady who had taken Tortuga by storm.

Upstairs his captain was having that luck. Van Ryker had charged into the bedroom, kicked the door shut with his boot and deposited his languorous lady on the big square bed. Moments later his clothes were tossed onto a chair, his boots discarded and flung across the room, and he had joined her—an impatient naked giant, lured into haste by her beckoning smile.

In that first moment of contact as he lowered his body onto hers, they tensed. Perhaps they were both remembering all the wild gales, the fury and clash of wills that had gone on between them. Then Imogene gave a small sob and flung herself upward against him. Van Ryker's hold on her tightened and his strong competent hands moved gently, lovingly, down her slender white arms that shivered to awareness at his touch. Now he was lightly fondling her breasts, exciting a nipple here, tingling along her spine there, caressing a twisting, turning hip that burned at his touch.

Imogene gasped and moaned beneath these sweet assaults.

Van Ryker was an experienced lover—she a woman made for love. And her new willingness brought out the best in him, so that for both of them their fiery joining was a thing of wonder, impassioned, overwhelming. And he—a man who had known so many women in his roving life—had in his touch this night the questing yearning, the tenderness of the man who has found the one love that will ever content him.

All of this was communicated silently to Imogene as the
swayed together there on the bed, rapt and lost in the ecstasy o
their joining, lost to time, aware only of each other. As thei
shivering bodies met and held and rippled, as their skin raspe
against each other's as smoothly as heavy silk, as they whispere
words unheard and made vows unspoken, as their blood race
and they were drenched in torrents of desire and swept away o
bright rivers of endless love, they became one in a way tha
neither of them had ever before experienced. It was a commi
ment more permanent than any wedding band—although bo
knew that too would follow. It was a pledge unspoken betwee
man and woman, heart to heart, forever.

And when at last the fever pitch had receded and they fe
away from each other, panting and spent, when she lay besi
him lazily, basking in the thrill of his touch as he ran his finge
lightly over her still-pulsing body in its afterglow of wonde
Imogene found herself asking on a long-drawn sigh of conter
ment, "Why did you not take me with you that night in Ne
Amsterdam at the Governor's Ball? Then all of this need n
have happened!"

"Take you?" he laughed, tormenting a nipple that quiver
at his touch. "By force?"

She gave him a lustrous look. "Yes, for I was very stu
born."

A half-smile played about his lips. "You told me you lov
another man and I believed you."

"I lied!"

"Poor Imogene." He ruffled her fair hair tenderly. "A
all I wanted was your happiness!"

She snuggled closer to him, stroked his long leg muscl
"When you did not come to Vrouw Berghem's that night I w

down to the docks to tell you I would go away with you—and found you gone."

His countenance went blank with surprise. "You did *that?*"

She nodded soberly. "I convinced myself I was doing it to protect my husband's life but—now I know that was not the real reason. It was because I loved you, although I would not let myself believe it."

His arms went round her, tightened, and a muscle in his jaw worked. "I did not know," he said huskily. "God, how I fought myself to keep from marching to that house and breaking down the door and sailing away with you. You'll never know what it cost me!"

"I think I do." Imogene sighed, a soft smouldering sigh that promised much. Tomorrow on Tortuga there would be such a wedding as befitted its leading buccaneer captain—a wedding procession beneath an arched corridor of raised cutlasses—and the bride would give herself away! Tomorrow all Tortuga would drink their health. But tonight . . . tonight a woman who had made so many mistakes in her short life would count her blessings and take to her arms the one man made for her alone.

She gave van Ryker a slanted look. "I think I was meant to be on the ice," she told him. "God gave me a second chance—he gave me you." Her voice was rich and sweet and van Ryker looked wonderingly at this new, softer Imogene. Out of the reckless girl had been born a lovely woman, the woman of all his dreams.

She turned toward him in luxurious abandon, rolled over on a soft naked hip and felt her breasts brush against his heavy chest muscles, felt a small surge of triumph as those muscles contracted at the soft sudden pressure of her body. She laid her arm gently across him and stroked his forearm. "Van Ryker, is it not a wondrous heaven that has brought us together at last?"

Van Ryker looked away and studied the wall decorations of this room hung with Spanish hangings, Spanish maps, Spanish weapons—all of them taken by the force of his arms. He thought of all his contriving, the wrongs he had done to Stephen Linnington and—yes, to this woman so dear to him who lay pliant and loving beside him. Why, he had taken her as any prowling pirate ship might encircle and seize an enemy vessel! And after all he had done to her—she had come to love him! He felt humbled by the warmth of her smile."

"I do not deserve my heaven," he said huskily. "But I am glad to have it all the same."

Suddenly she sat up, brought her hand to her mouth with a little cry. "Stephen!" she gasped. "He will go through life thinking he is tied to that woman! He does not know it was only a fake marriage."

"He knows," said van Ryker coolly. "For I told him myself when I had him flung onto a ship bound for Barbados."

There was a long pause.

"You—told him?" she asked slowly. "And he did not return to me?" Her pride was shaken.

"It would seem he has another love in Barbados. Her name is Bess Duveen."

" 'Bess'?" Her breath drew in with a gasp. And then thoughtfully, "Yes, of course it would be Bess. She always loved him, from that first moment. I did not know until she wrote me of his 'death.' And now he will return to her—they can marry!"

"He said that was what he had in mind."

Imogene looked into that smiling saturnine face, seeing all—all the contriving, all that van Ryker had done to bring her willing into his arms. Had ever man done more? she asked herself. She watched him as he lay on his back with his arms folded comfortably behind his head, his naked form long and lithe and competent and completely relaxed, his forearms and a deep V down his lightly furred chest burned bronze by the hot Caribbean sun. How many times had he lain beside her and she had hated him—even while she thrilled to his caresses?

"Van Ryker," she said, marveling. "You knew me better than I knew myself. And yet you took a long chance with me."

"I am given to long chances."

"But I might have killed you—in a burst of anger when you told me to take up the sword and told me how you had tricked me!"

" 'Twas a chance I had to take, Imogene. And if you had killed me—well, a Spanish bullet might do that any day." His gray eyes were reckless and alight. "I counted well the cost, and deemed the odds to be slightly in my favor."

"You gambled your life for me," she said gently. And then, more briskly, "Van Ryker, you have taken me as you would a Spanish prize!"

He studied her narrowly. "And do you still think heaven brought us together?"

She was looking into his face—like him, at heart a rover—a rover who had come home.

"Yes," she said softly. "I think you were sent to me—that I might love you. Always." And as she buried her face in the sinewy rippling muscles of his deep chest, she remembered long ago asking the tall standing stones they called Adam and Eve to send her a lover. And who was to say they had not sent her this bold breathless love that would be with her to her dying breath?

The lean buccaneer clutched her to him and smiled down

upon her bent golden head with a tenderness that changed and lit up his dark face. He had gambled his life for this woman—and he had won.

It was all that he would ever ask of heaven.

Epilogue

Unknown to all of them, the ship *Wilhelmina* had put in at Bermuda for water before proceeding to the Bahamas, and Elise—whose real identity had been discovered on board—had fled the ship there, taking Georgiana with her. Neither of them had gone down with the *Wilhelmina*. Imogene had shed her tears for those who still lived. She well deserved the happiness she had found at last.

But that night, on the *Sea Rover's* rolling deck, Barnaby Swift, who made the ship his home, looked landward and saw the lights of a certain house on Tortuga being extinguished. He raised his glass, and being a sometime poet and slightly drunk, he proposed a toast to the moon. For it was such a night, with the scented wind blowing across the shining deck and phosphorescence silvering the sea.

Valerie Sherwood

A toast to the wine of endeavor,
A toast to the worlds we have won.
Forever and ever and ever
May her golden hair shine in the sun!

ROMANCE...ADVENTURE...DANGER...
from Warner Books

DAUGHTERS OF THE SOUTHWIND
by Aola Vandergriff   (93-909, $2.95)

The three McCleod sisters were beautiful, virtuous and bound to a dream—the dream of finding a new life in the untamed promise of the West. Their adventures in search of that dream provide the dimensions for this action-packed romantic bestseller.

DAUGHTERS OF THE WILD COUNTRY
by Aola Vandergriff   (93-908, $2.95)

High in the North Country, three beautiful women begin new lives in a world where nature is raw, men are rough . . . and love, when it comes, shines like a gold nugget. Tamsen, Arab and Em McCleod now find themselves in Russian Alaska, where power, money and human life are the playthings of a displaced, decadent aristocracy in this lusty novel ripe with love, passion, spirit and adventure.

DAUGHTERS OF THE FAR ISLANDS
by Aola Vandergriff   (93-910, $2.95)

Hawaii seems like Paradise to Tamsen and Arab—but it is not. Beneath the beauty, like the hot lava bubbling in the volcano's crater, trouble seethes in Paradise. The daughters are destined to be caught in the turmoil between Americans who want annexation of the islands and native Hawaiians who want to keep their country. And in their own family, danger looms . . . and threatens to erupt and engulf them all.

DAUGHTERS OF THE OPAL SKIES
by Aola Vandergriff   (93-911, $2.95)

Tamsen Tallant, most beautiful of the McLeod sisters, is alone in the Australian outback. Alone with a ranch to run, two rebellious teenage nieces to care for, and Opal Station's new head stockman to reckon with—a man whose very look holds a challenge. But Tamsen is prepared for danger—for she has seen the face of the Devil and he looks like a man.

LOVE'S TENDER FURY
by Jennifer Wilde   (93-904, $2.95)

The turbulent story of an English beauty—sold at auction like a slave—who scandalized the New World by enslaving her masters. She would conquer them all—only if she could subdue the hot unruly passions of the heart! The 2 Million Copy Bestseller that brought fame to the author of DARE TO LOVE.

DARE TO LOVE
by Jennifer Wilde   (81-826, $2.50)

Who dared to love Elena Lopez? She was the Queen of desire and the slave of passion, traveling the world—London, Paris, San Francisco—and taking love where she found it! Elena Lopez—the tantalizing, beautiful moth—dancing out of the shadows, warmed, lured and consumed by the heart's devouring flame.

INTRODUCING
THE RAKEHELL DYNASTY

BOOK ONE: THE BOOK OF JONATHAN RAKEHELL
by Michael William Scott   (D95-201, $2.75)

BOOK TWO: CHINA BRIDE
by Michael William Scott   (D95-237, $2.75)

The bold, sweeping, passionate story of a great New England shipping family caught up in the winds of change—and of the one man who would dare to sail his dream ship to the frightening, beautiful land of China. He was Jonathan Rakehell, and his destiny would change the course of history.

THE RAKEHELL DYNASTY—
**THE GRAND SAGA OF THE GREAT CLIPPER SHIPS
AND OF THE MEN WHO BUILT THEM
TO CONQUER THE SEAS AND
CHALLENGE THE WORLD!**

Jonathan Rakehell—who staked his reputation and his place in the family on the clipper's amazing speed.

Lai-Tse Lu—the beautiful, independent daughter of a Chinese merchant. She could not know that Jonathan's proud clipper ship carried a cargo of love and pain, joy and tragedy for her.

Louise Graves—Jonathan's wife-to-be, who waits at home in New London keeping a secret of her own

Bradford Walker—Jonathan's scheming brother-in-law, who scoffs at the clipper and plots to replace Jonathan as heir to the Rakehell shipping line.

YOU'LL WANT TO READ THE BEST
BY FRANCES CASEY KERNS...

CANA AND WINE
by Frances Casey Kerns   (A81-951, $2.50)
A vast novel of the Magnessen family, respected and loved, until the
past's dark horror is exposed in the brilliant Idaho sun. Was Viktor
Magnessen the collaborator who had participated in savage Nazi
experiments and then changed his name, his country, his identity,
and his morals? The only possible end for the family is disaster.

THIS LAND IS MINE
by Frances Casey Kerns   (D82-704, $2.25)
In the shadow of the mountain, Blake Westfall hopes to find spiritual
peace as the adopted son of the Medicine Rock Indians, married to
the Chief's daughter, Shy Fawn. But there is no peace on the frontier.
Here is a fast-moving novel of moral choice and physical passion, set
against the grandeur of the Western landscape.

THE WINTER HEART
by Frances Casey Kerns   (D81-431, $2.50)
Two young Scotsmen stand at the ship's rail on the eve of their arrival
in America. They yearn for power and wealth—and a new land free
from the fetters of the past. They journey to Colorado and there they
part, caught up in the brutal present. Their goals change under the
realities of the harsh land. And, finally, each looks for the only suc-
cor—a woman.